PANDORA'S CREW

Gorg Huff &
Paula Goodlett

Book 1 of the Star Wings sieres

Cover art by Howard Day
Maps by Gorg Huff

Gorg Huff and Paula Goodlett
Visit our website at https://warspell.com/

CONTENTS

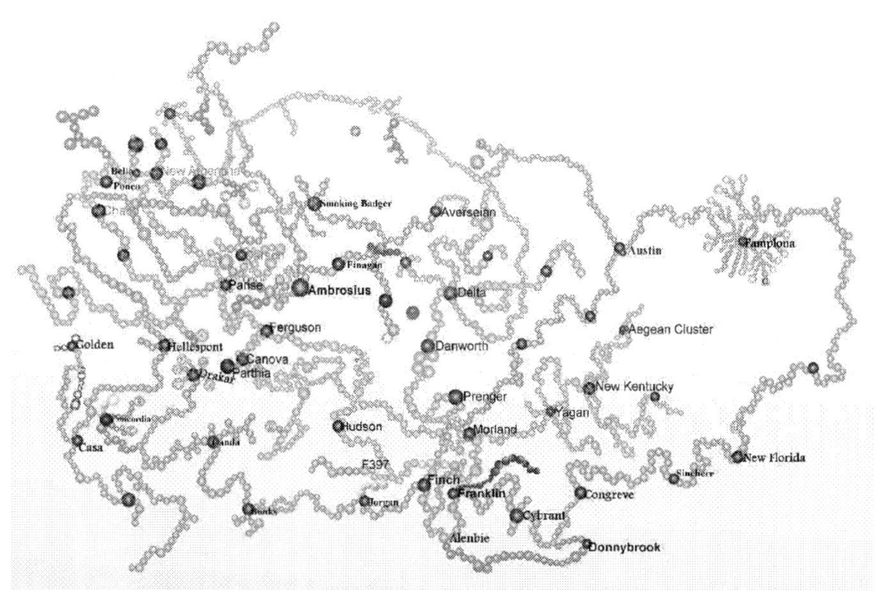

A very rough approximation of the Pamplona Sector. It doesn't include all the planets much less all the stations.

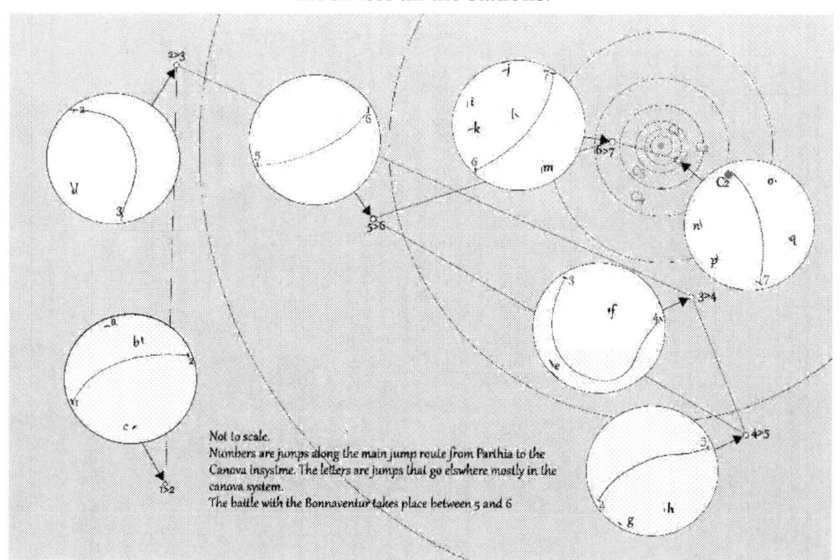

The Canova Star System Canova 2 is the only habitable planet but there are many habitats thoughout the system.

Canova to Ferguson Route

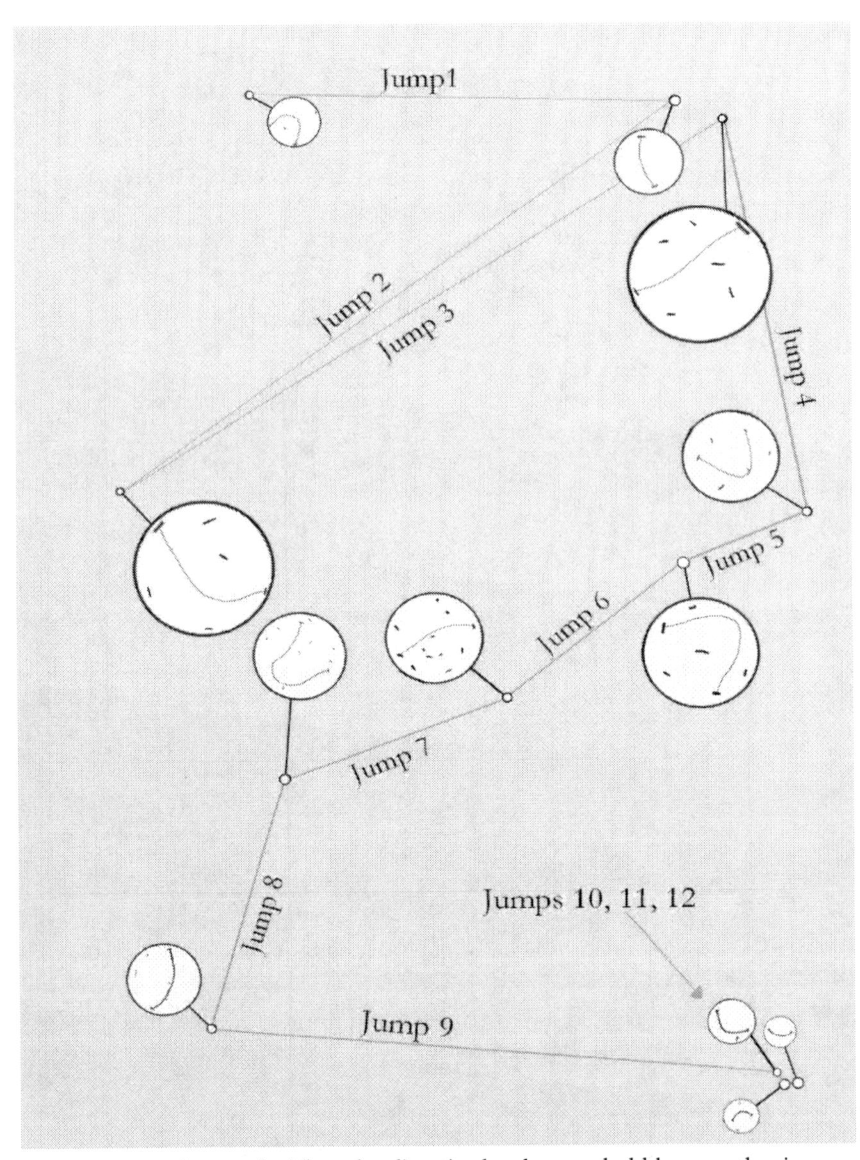

Not even vaguely to scale. The other lines in the close-up bubbles are other jumps, mostly leading to cul de sacs

CHAPTER 1

Revolutions, Mr. Dickinson, come into this world like bastard children—half improvised and half compromised.
Attributed to pre-space statesman Benjamin Franklin.

Location: Concordia Station, Free Space
Standard Date: 01 16 630

Danny Gold settled into the bar stool and waited for the robo-tender to roll over. He was wearing ship's slops. No one would know he was the captain save for the captain's interface cap he wore. And the cap was worn and old. Still, he was an attractive man, so handsome as to be almost pretty, with golden hair and striking green eyes, and a body that put one in mind of a dancer or martial artist.

He looked around. About half the augmented reality emitters were out in this bar, and on a station they weren't kept dark to conserve energy. The half-real atmosphere was due to lack of repair and it gave the bar a drab, worn feel. As you moved through the low power fields, the bar flipped from richly decorated to bare walls and back again. The drab, worn feel was strengthened by the plastic of the bar. It was yellowing from age and scratched, even though the duraplast was as hard as iron.

"Parthian Banger." Danny didn't know if there was such a drink as a Parthian Banger, but he liked to give the robot bartenders a hard time. The robo-tender would usually look at him, confusion in its sensors, and ask what the drink was. Danny would then describe some alcoholic concoction and get his drink for free. The robo-tenders were built that way.

Not this time.

After a couple of moments and a lot of arm waving, the robo-tender put a wide glass filled with greenish goop with red and black specks on top in front of him.

Ain't that just the way my luck has been running, Danny thought sardonically, then passed over the station credit chips for his drink and took a cautious sip. It probably wouldn't actually be poisonous. The robo-tenders were programmed with basic species' profiles, and there weren't all that many space-going species to begin with. Still, accidents did happen. But Danny wasn't worried. He had a greater tolerance for drugs and poisons than most people. Which made it especially hard to get drunk. In this case, the green goop tasted like something somewhere between avocado and mango. The specks on the top were peppers of some sort. Hot peppers.

Danny gasped. He waved his hand. "Water!"

It felt like five minutes of fiery hell in his mouth, but was probably less than thirty seconds before the water got to him. Danny gulped it down. "What the hell is that?"

It was probably Danny's imagination, but the robo-tender seemed to be quite satisfied as it answered. "The Parthian Banger is an aphrodisiac for Parthians. It is made by blending aspercodo from Darvin Six, powdered jalapeño originally from Old Earth and crushed fog bugs from Paradise in the Heaven system."

Weird, Danny thought. *Just weird*. Parthians didn't mate, except for the breeding caste and breeding was all they did. The breeding caste never left the home system, so why would Parthian spacers need an aphrodisiac? The Parthians didn't have their own interstellar capable ships. They bought them, and even the smallest hyper-capable ships were expensive, so the Parthians didn't have much of a presence outside their home system.

Danny had never actually met a Parthian, but had seen images of them, and analyses of their culture—if you could call it that. They were hive creatures, according to the research from . . . Danny called up a file in his internal data base. The scholarly papers were funded by the Cordoba-Jackson clan. Which made sense, since the Cordoba-Jacksons ran that corner of the Cordoba Combine. Parthians were not made for independent thought or action. They had bones that merged into shells and spiky porcupine-like hair, no heads, just eyestalks and mouth-hands. From a human perspective, they were remarkably ugly.

Danny shuddered just thinking about them. "Glass of milk." The cool white liquid would act as a chaser for the way-too-spicy drink. With the chaser ready, he gulped down the evil brew. Danny's biggest flaw was also his biggest virtue. He was stubborn about following his own rules. If he bought a drink, he drank it. The milk followed the Parthian Banger as quickly as he could manage.

Danny might have broken his rule, just this once, if he had known the consequences of his actions . . . or maybe not. In any case, the robo-tender, through malice or a lack of programming, declined to mention the effects of the drink.

"Gimme a Paguly Stroke," Danny ordered.

He got the robotic confusion he was hoping for. "A Paguly Stroke," Danny explained, making it up as he went along, "is two shots of New Kentucky Bourbon and a shot of thon juice." Danny turned his head and slipped into the field of an emitter. The robotic arms of the bartender took on flesh. When the robo-tender passed him his free drink, Danny sipped it and thought about how he got into this mess. *Was it when I diverted to find the jump point? No. I was in trouble before Casa Verde station.*

Danny ordered another drink. This time he had to pay for it. Then, giving up getting drunk as a bad job, he stood up and left the bar. As he was leaving, Danny sniffed. There was a faint scent that wasn't part of the normal bar aroma. Danny's sense of smell was enhanced by genetic modification. It was more discerning than a normal's, and that let him categorize and discount known smells. This smell was kind of spicy and didn't fit what he would expect from a station bar. Also, he couldn't place where it was coming from.

* * *

Checkgok was not one of those Parthians who took being away from the clan as license for perversion. When the scent reached it, Checkgok did its best to avoid the stimulus. Checkgok was—by the standards of its race—a fairly handsome neuter female. Its body was shaped sort of like a flattened oval, covered with spikes a bit thicker than hair and not quite as thick as a porcupine's spines. The spikes were longer and thicker on top of its body. It had no head. The eyestalks and the mouth-hand protruded directly from the front of its body, the eyes going up and the mouth down. Both were flexible and in constant motion. Like all Parthians, it walked—scuttled—on its fore and aft legs, using the center pair as heavy object manipulators. Its mouth doubled as a hand for delicate manipulation.

Checkgok's eyestalks swiveled and extended, searching. Scent isn't a great way to locate something, especially in a space station. Checkgok made the obvious guess about where the scent was coming from. It must be the group of Parthians who crewed the *Fly Catcher*. Probably the captain and first mate. The captain was a neuter female and the first mate a neuter male. Both were—in Checkgok's opinion—reprehensible . . . *individuals* . . . who had, more than once before, attempted to subvert Checkgok's loyalty to clan.

Its guess was quite wrong. Its attempt to avoid the captain and—especially—the first mate, led it to run right into Danny Gold. Checkgok weighed just over three hundred pounds and was—depending on its stance—from three to six feet tall. It was moving fast at the moment, which put its body low.

Danny fell on it.

Going from three foot scuttle to a six foot extension was reflexive. Given the circumstances, Checkgok couldn't help it. Its spiky, hair-like protrusions would not have punctured a Parthian, female or male, neuter or not.

Unfortunately, human skin is rather less resistant than Parthian cartilage. Now blood was involved, which carried all sorts of implications in Parthian society. It wasn't that much blood; the punctures weren't deep. The amount was not nearly as important as the mere fact that blood was spilled.

Besides, Checkgok wasn't thinking too clearly, what with the pheromones coursing through its system. Checkgok got a full load of pheromones when Danny fell on it.

It was as high as a paper kite.

* * *

The incident in the station corridor might have ended with no more than a few scrapes, but Kesskox, the captain of the *Fly Catcher*, had just about given up on persuading Checkgok to see reason. Checkgok was an excellent merchant in terms of calculating what might be of value at the next port, but unwilling to see the advantages of a bit of extra on the side. It was also—in Kesskox's view—a supercilious snob with delusions of grandeur. Kesskox, like just about every Parthian on the station, scented the pheromones. It took her a while to find the source.

She arrived in time to witness the last of Checkgok's semi-coherent rambling apology and offer of . . . *kothkoke.*

The human was trying to wave the whole thing off. "No harm done. Right. You're apologizing. I accept."

Captain Kesskox shook with laughter, her eyestalks twisting. "And you sneer at us. That one doesn't even have the right equipment." She chittered a laugh, realizing that she had Checkgok just where she wanted it. Checkgok offered *kothkoke* as apology and the human accepted it. "Did I hear correctly? You have sworn *kothkoke* to this monkey? What will your high and mighty clan think of this?" She chittered again. She couldn't help it and didn't feel like trying. Though more resistant, Captain Kesskox was a bit tipsy on Danny's scent herself. Unknown to anyone, milk acted as a booster for the intoxicating effect. Checkgok, having gotten a full dose—a pheromone bath—was quite drunk. "A slime toad would be better than you, you perverted, dishonorable *cheskek.*" While *cheskek,* if directly translated into English, might well be taken as a compliment since it meant something close to "individualist," to a Parthian it was a deadly insult. On a par with suggesting that a human preferred sex with the corpses of babies of their own gender and that they ate the corpse afterward.

It was also, even in Captain Kesskox's own estimation, altogether too close to the truth—which just made it hurt worse. She screamed and attacked.

"Oh shit," the monkey said. Somehow it had wandered into the path of conflict.

Checkgok leapt. Checkgok was a lot faster than Kesskox expected and clearly not going to let its monkey be harmed. Using forelimbs, middle-limbs and hind-limbs, it moved itself toward Kesskox while moving the monkey out of her reach. Checkgok weighed a touch over three hundred pounds. Captain Kesskox doubted that the monkey weighed half that. The monkey ended up against the far wall and Captain Kesskox was suddenly faced with a very angry bookkeeper.

Location: Concordia Station Infirmary

Danny woke in a white room, one in considerably better repair than the bar. The emitters were all operating here, and he was getting feedback on heart rate, oxi content of the air, and a host of other data points that together announced "infirmary."

"You have a mild concussion."

Danny looked blearily toward the voice. The . . . doctor? Yes, she must be a doctor. White coat. Medical PDA in hand. Yep. Doctor. Tall, blond, female. Smith, the nametag said.

"Which is less than you deserve," added another voice.

Danny winced. That had to be the voice of station security. Station security sounded the same all over the galaxy. He peeked in the direction of the last voice. Yep. Station security.

"What did I do?" Danny asked plaintively.

The station security officer sneered at him. "Aside from advertising yourself as a Parthian sex toy, starting a riot and a diplomatic incident? I haven't a clue. Have you started a war we should know about?"

"I don't know what you're talking about," Danny insisted, not for the first time in dealing with station security. In this instance, it was even true.

"Did you or did you not consume a Parthian Banger?"

"What's a Parthian Banger?"

The doctor snickered wickedly. "You are, apparently. Though from what I understand, you're under-equipped for the endeavor."

The cop gave the doctor a dirty look, then returned her attention to Danny. "All right. You want to tell me what happened after you left the bar?"

Danny considered. He really couldn't see what he had done that was illegal. On the other hand, cops tended to find incriminating evidence in just about anything. He almost asked for a lawyer. Then he remembered the state of his finances. He was the next best thing to dead broke. He was broke, aside from his ship, and the ship was in hock to SMOG Savings and Loan in the Drake Combine. Which was why he was at the unaligned, very much gray market, Concordia Station.

And on Concordia Station, if you desired an attorney and could not afford one, you were shit out of luck. Danny was surprised to learn that Concordia Station had lawyers at all. Or cops, for that matter.

Danny struggled to sit up. He decided to try and play the cooperative innocent. "I was walking along the corridor when this Parthian came scooting around the corner. We ran into each other and I tripped and landed on it. It was an accident, Officer. It, ah . . . stood up, I guess, and banged me against the ceiling. Hurt like the dickens. Then it went back down and let me off. I was a bit scratched by its spines, but not too bad." Danny creased his forehead, thinking. "It apologized and it said a bunch of stuff in Parthian. Well, I accepted its apology and was about to be on my way when this other Parthian showed up. They started arguing. At least, I think they were arguing."

Danny paused, trying to remember. "It was about half in trade and half in their clicks and whistles. That's the last thing I remember before I woke up here."

The cop was looking at him like he was a perp running a scam, but the doc was trying hard not to laugh. Danny didn't have a clue what was going on.

Location: Concordia Station Security Cells

Security Officer Janis Marten looked at the bug in front of her. It was the first Parthian she ever saw in person, and well, it just looked like a big, furry bug. "So what exactly is your story?"

Station security put both Checkgok and Captain Kesskox in pheromone free cells. However, they didn't feel it necessary to wait for the effects of the pheromones to wear off before questioning them.

Captain Kesskox, still a bit drunk, chittered more laughter and waved its midlegs. Might as well. Any hope the captain nourished of blackmailing Checkgok was gone. Now there was a public record.

"Checkgok has sworn itself to the human. After all its protestations of loyalty to its clan and devotion to duty, it has betrayed clan and the whole Parthian race. I expel it from my ship." Kesskox did it out of spite, mostly.

Just wait until she got back to home world and spread this story.

* * *

Janis left the cell and went next door. She pulled up a seat and started to question the other bug. "You're sworn to Danny Gold? Is that right?"

Checkgok waved a midlimb and Janis tried not to flinch. That arm . . . leg . . . whatever it was . . . looked like it could squash her like a . . . well, bug. "Mischance. I blooded him. It was an accident."

Janis finished taking it all down. "Captain Kesskox says you're a traitor to your clan and it's throwing you off the ship."

Janis wasn't quite sure what the clicks and whistles meant, but it didn't sound to her like Checkgok admired Kesskox.

Checkgok eventually calmed a bit. "That *squekket.*" It waved its two center arms. "It throws me off, it loses the cargo, tell it that. The cargo belongs to Clan Zheck and I am the representative of the clan."

Janis peered over at it. "Ah . . . that's not what the captain is claiming."

Checkgok's eyestalks waved and its mouth-hand scrunched up in an expression Janis couldn't interpret. "Over two-thirds of the cargo on the *Fly Catcher* belongs to my clan. I have control of it until it is returned to my clan, unless I willingly abandon it or die. Only then does Captain Pervert have access to it. The fool has ruined itself."

"So the cargo belongs to you?"

"To my clan."

"Can you prove that?"

Checkgok's eyestalks reared back at the question, in what Janis guessed might signal feeling affronted. "Yes, of course. Check the contracts. They are on record in the station files. The *Fly Catcher* is leased to Clan Zheck. The cargo is Clan Zheck cargo. The cargo that is not Clan Zheck is not actually authorized to be there. Captain Kesskox calls it 'off-the-books' cargo."

"Oh, really?"

There was, Checkgok noted, an interesting gleam in the security officer's expression. Checkgok was unsure what the expression meant. This was its first trip away from the home world. It had made trades in dozens of human systems, primarily by developing an encyclopedic knowledge of what was wanted where.

Trade was not new to the clan or to Checkgok, but the cutthroat practices of the outworlds were not what Checkgok was used to. Checkgok lifted its left midleg and scratched an itchy spine hair. "May I have access to the net? So that I can show you the pertinent contracts?" Checkgok would watch the reactions of this monkey and perhaps learn a bit more about reading the species. Doing so would keep Checkgok's thoughts away from its disgrace and the consequences.

Janis motioned Checkgok over to the computer. "Oh, yes. Please do."

They went through the contracts together. For a fairly large sum of money, *Fly Catcher* and crew was leased—in total—to the Clan Zheck. The trade goods were provided by the Clan. A manifest was included.

The bug pointed at an entry. "When we left the home world we went to Green World, a monkey world."

Officer Marten glared at it. "Watch your mouth."

"Excuse me?" Checkgok looked at its mouth. Parthian eyes were arranged in such a way that it could indeed do so. It was sometimes necessary, though it seemed rather pointless at the moment. Checkgok thought it was being polite. The security officer apparently disagreed.

The officer glared a bit more. "I was talking about that 'monkey world' crack."

"Crack? What is crack?" Checkgok was fairly sure she wasn't talking about a crack as in a break.

The monkey looked at it. Strangely. "You really don't know, do you?"

"Know what?"

Officer Marten sighed. "Let me give you some language lessons. Monkey is a derogatory term—an insult—when applied to a human." The security guard moved its shoulders up and down. "Not a real bad one, I'll grant you. It would be like calling you a . . . Well, I don't know what your equivalent would be. Something from your world that is related to your people a ways back, but didn't evolve intelligence, or at least not much."

Checkgok considered. "Like a *kikikes*?"

"Got me. I don't know anything about your home world's fauna."

"Got you? What is got you? I don't have you."

Janis bared its teeth at Checkgok. "It's an expression. It means you've asked a question I don't know the answer to."

Checkgok was beginning to understand. "Then, 'watch your mouth' is another expression?" It swiveled the eye stalk it was using to watch its mouth back to looking at the station officer.

"Yes. It's a warning to be careful of what you're saying."

Checkgok nodded its mouth. It didn't have a head to nod. " 'Crack.' Is that an expression?"

Janis nodded. "Yep. A crack is an insult."

Things were beginning to come clear. Checkgok now knew why the captain and crew encouraged it to speak in a certain way and leave the "in person" dealings with humans to the first mate. The "useful idioms" it was taught were insurance to prevent humans from wanting to deal with Checkgok directly. That—in turn—was to allow them to skim a bit on every deal. They really were *cheskek*, concerned with themselves rather than their clans.

Checkgok knew what to do now. Apologies were always acceptable. It knew that much.

Location: Concordia Station Infirmary

Doc Smith grinned when she removed the bandages. Danny wondered why until he saw himself in the mirror. "Oh, shit. What the hell happened? Doc, what is this?"

There was a set of spots on his chest. Red ones, blue ones, black ones and green ones in a distorted galaxy pattern. "What about these dots? I wasn't that drunk."

Doc Smith's voice was a bit strained. Like she was trying not to laugh. "I was a bit worried about that myself, so I took a couple of samples and did some reading. It doesn't appear to be harmful. The Parthian's spines have a resin on them that acts like ink. You got an instant tattoo. Removing it would be cosmetic. Not covered by station insurance."

Danny groaned. Part of the station fee when docking a ship was basic medical insurance for accident or injury suffered by crewmen on the station. Very basic insurance. It covered emergency treatment and that was all. It was there so the station wouldn't get stuck with the medical expenses of indigent spacers.

Which was altogether too close to what Danny was these days, except for the *Pandora.*

CHAPTER 2

Artificial brains have both advantages and disadvantages in comparison to standard computer systems. The neural net structure of the artificial brains more closely resembles the natural systems and this structure allows them something close to creativity. However, they have to be individually manufactured and trained. They cannot as yet be mass-produced in any meaningful sense. A single program will not run the same on two artificial brains because the brains are different. Instead, extensive use of simulated reality systems must be used to teach them the way a child or a pet is taught and conditioned.

Standard processors are cheaper both to manufacture and to program and, within their limits, they can be faster. However, in spite of the advances in both software and hardware, they lack that certain something. They don't grow and they don't learn.

Introduction to* A Case for the Artificial Brain *by Gerhard Schmitz, Phd.
Standard Date March 22, 625

Location: Pandora, In orbit off Concordia station Standard Date: 01 16 630

Deep in the core of her artificial mind, *Pan* heaved a gargantuan sigh and opened a channel to the port, requesting information on the condition of Danny Gold. It was not a voice request, but a transmission in binary code from the ship *Pandora* to the station's managing computer. It carried standard authorizations, and the answer came back the same way with the medical report, the police report, the insurance report.

Pan's brain was very large, but most of it was dedicated to hyper transits. After that, a lot of it was dedicated to shipboard maintenance. Only a very small percentage was dedicated to human-style intelligence. The effect of that was to make her very bright in some ways, but not very bright in others. She was not particularly creative but was very quick and had a perfect memory.

Since Danny had been involved in a fight with one or more Parthians, she researched Parthians in general and the ones involved in the altercation in particular. Sometimes—in fact, a lot of the time—hard work makes a good substitute for creativity. *Pan* was built for hard work.

By the time Danny was allowed phone calls, *Pan* had collected a great deal of information. Not everything. She had not been able to gather much on the content and ownership of the *Fly Catcher*'s holds because the *Fly Catcher*'s cargo became a matter of an ongoing investigation even while she was requesting information.

Location: Medical Bay, Concordia Station

"Captain, what exactly did the Parthian Checkgok say to you?" came over Danny's internal comm while he lay on the med couch.

That wasn't what Danny was expecting to hear from *Pan*. He was expecting yet another lecture on the obligations of his abilities. "I don't know. Which one was Checkgok? The one I tripped over?"

"Yes, Captain." Danny could hear the long-suffering tone in *Pan*'s voice. "The one you tripped over."

"It apologized and said some stuff in their clicks and whistles." Danny sent *Pan* the recording. This was weird. *What's got Pan's wings in a knot,* he wondered. "Are we being sued or something?"

"Are there witnesses?"

Now Danny was getting worried. "Hold on." He opened his eyes and saw the latest security officer, this one a guy. "Do you know what the Parthian said to me? The one I tripped over?"

Doc Smith cracked up. "It married you."

"It did not marry him." The cop gave the doctor a hard look, then sighed and turned back to Danny. "Look, Parthians are an alien species. They have their own customs and laws. The neuters aren't supposed to get . . . ah . . . excited."

The doctor cracked up again.

Danny's head was banging. He sent *Pan* a signal to switch from a personal call to a call to the med room. "Look, Officer. I have a headache and spots on my chest. Would you mind explaining what is going on to my ship?"

Danny didn't listen after that. The Parthian Banger wasn't the only alcohol he drank that afternoon. He would learn later that Checkgok offered itself to his clan in recompense for the injury and insult it inadvertently offered. Further, that in accepting the apology, he accepted the service. It was called *kothkoke* and had things in common with both adoption and marriage. What was still under question was the effect it had on the ownership and control of the goods that Checkgok possessed in trust for its clan.

Location: Virtual Courtroom, Concordia Station

"Former clan!" Captain Kesskox, in her cell, rose to her full height in rage. "It has abandoned its clan. It has no rights to the goods of that clan. It is dead to them."

"Not according to the customs of Zheck."

The voice from the wall startled Kesskox because it didn't match any of the humans on the screens. It dropped a few inches. "Who is that?"

Magistrate Stella Jones was going through her notes as the preliminary hearing progressed. She looked up over the half-moon shaped eyeglasses that even Kesskox knew were unnecessary to humans in this day and age. "It's the *Pandora*. The starship of Captain Gold, the recipient of . . . what is the word . . . of Checkgok's *kothkoke*." Stella imagined that she was making a hash of the clicks and whistles of the Parthian, but at this point she didn't much care.

The hearing, instigated by *Pandora* on behalf of her captain, was to determine whether a restraining order was to be issued to prevent the *Fly Catcher* from leaving the station while still in possession of goods that *Pandora* argued were now under the legal control—if not ownership—of Captain Gold.

"Ship? Ships cannot be heard in court." Captain Kesskox gestured with her right eye stalk.

Magistrate Jones had no idea what the gesture meant. She didn't care very much about that, either. Stella Jones stared at the obviously irritated—and increasingly irritating—bug. "They can here."

It was true that artificial brains were not allowed to instigate suits in Drake space or very often in Cordoba space. But out here on the fringe, they had to maintain a fairly open policy. Station law had long since granted legal entity status to artificial brain ships. It was necessary. They were often the only sober member of the ship's company. Concordia Station was sometimes a bit on the rowdy side.

Not that Stella was all that thrilled with the *Pandora* at the moment. She got notice of the requested hold during dinner. Couldn't the darn ship have waited a couple of hours? The *Fly Catcher*'s captain was in lockup, after all, along with this Checkgok character and Captain Gold.

"What do you have, *Pandora*?" Stella asked.

"Nothing not available in station files." The ship's response sounded a bit . . . snotty, Stella decided. "The Zheck clan offers *kothkoke* as much as a token of trust, or test of the recipient's honor, as a payment of debt. They sometimes intentionally offer *kothkoke* when the clan member to be adopted out has a continuing obligation to the clan. When that happens, the receiving clan—in this case Captain Gold—has a decision to make. Does he honor the obligations of the adoptee to the Zheck clan or ignore those obligations? If the obligations are ignored, then the clan knows never to deal with that clan again. If they are honored, Clan Zheck generally develops a relationship of trust with the adopting clan."

Captain Kesskox dropped in shock. It was clear she realized where this was going. "The human is not a Clan. *Kothkoke* is invalid. Not a legitimate act, simply a disgrace."

"Well?" Stella Jones quirked an eyebrow.

"Captain Gold is from Cybrant Five," *Pandora* informed the court. "A member of the Gold Family, more properly rendered as 'the Gold Line.' He is a licensed breeder with unlimited reproductive rights on Cybrant Five, where fewer than one in a hundred people are fully licensed."

Danny Gold groaned. *As well he should*, thought Stella. Cybrant Five was not famous for its respect for other cultures or other people in general. The registered lines were self-proclaimed supermen. Supermen that most of the rest of humanity despised for their arrogance. On the other hand, Stella admitted, if superior was looks, Danny Gold was certainly superior. Tall, but only a little above average height, literally golden blond, with skin just a shade lighter than the hair, green eyes with flecks of gold as well. Muscles without being muscle bound, and, even hungover, physical grace that gave every motion a smooth flow.

"Captain Gold is as close as it is possible for a human to get to the definition of a clan or hive. Under Parthian law, he would be considered a new clan."

"Clans are based on females." Captain Kesskox's voice was strident and insistent.

"Not always." Merchant Checkgok was looking at the screen to Danny Gold's cell intently. "There are two Zheck ancestor clans that started from males."

"You admit that?" Captain Kesskox swiveled both eyestalks to focus on the screen showing the Zheck merchant.

"Zheck clan is proud of all its ancestor clans." Checkgok turned one eye to the screen to Kesskox's cell for a moment, then turned it back to Danny Gold.

"Where does that leave us?" The judge looked at the screen showing Captain Kesskox.

It left Kesskox in a terrible bind, and she knew it. "The human has not acknowledged Checkgok's prior obligations."

"Nor is there any need to," the *Pandora*'s voice came again from the wall. Rather quickly, the judge thought. "Until and unless Captain Gold officially renounces them, Checkgok—and through it, Captain Gold—has control over the Zheck goods."

Stella Jones noted Danny Gold's start at that. Apparently the *Pandora* wasn't telling her captain what was going on until she had things set up.

"Just what are Checkgok's obligations to its clan?"

There was a short pause. "No. *Pan*, we may be a little skint, but we ain't thieves. If we can do what the bug needs us to and it's a fair deal, we will. If we can't, we'll give it back to the Zheck clan . . . along with its goods."

That sounded good, though Stella wasn't sure that a Cybrant Gold Line could be trusted, considering the Cybrant System's reputation.

Checkgok apparently had no such reservations. It lowered itself all the way until its body was touching the floor. Kesskox was hissing and clicking. The translation program was rendering the clicks and whistles as a series of expletives, most of which made no sense at all.

"Fine." Gold waved his hands in the air. "Let the bug tell me that." Pause. "Yes, I trust you, but you don't know everything and you should have warned me."

Stella snorted. She knew several ships like the *Pandora*. They showed a marked tendency to treat their crews—even their owners—more like children or pets than like bosses. "All right. Enough. For the moment neither ship is allowed to leave station while in possession of the goods in question. After this gets resolved, I'll determine which ship has the rights to the cargo. Two things." Stella lifted two fingers and glared into the screens. "I'm going to want an official decision one way or the other from you, Captain Gold, whether Zheck custom requires it or not. And if you decide you're keeping Merchant Checkgok, you pay its fines."

Danny's face paled. *Pandora* chuckled. Checkgok grinned. Well, its eyestalks slid past one another in what the translation program interpreted as a grin.

* * *

Over the next week or so, Stella had two questions to answer. "How much of the *Fly Catcher*'s cargo belonged to Clan Zheck?" and, "Who was Clan Zheck's on-station rep?"

In the first case, she decided that the on-the-books cargo was clearly Clan Zheck's. The off-the-books cargo, whether it should be there or not, and notwithstanding how it was obtained, was the property of the ship *Fly Catcher* and its crew.

In the second case, she determined that Clan Zheck's cargo was under the control of Checkgok, and Checkgok could dispose of the cargo as it saw fit.

That cargo, by agreement between Captain Danny Gold and Merchant Checkgok as a representative of Clan Zheck, was transferred to the *Pandora*. Stella insisted on a contract between Captain Gold and Checkgok, with Checkgok acting as agent for Clan Zheck.

While Stella was working that out, other ships arrived and departed: several independents, two Drake owned freighters, and a Cordoba courier taking an unofficial shortcut. The story of Danny Gold and the Parthian Banger—or of Danny Gold, *the* Parthian Banger—was quite popular and would eventually spread to the wider universe.

Location: Concordia Station Hotel

Checkgok watched the screen with its left eyestalk as it looked around the room with its right. The monkey—no, it should say human even in its own mind—the human bed was gone, replaced with a nest pad that would support its body in rest position. But the pad was across the small room from the console and for now Checkgok needed to use the console, as strange as that was proving. The consoles on the *Fly Catcher* were modified to make them more usable by Parthian mouth-hands.

Its mouth-hand missed the proper key, and the space around the station appeared on the screen. There were three ships docked. The *Pandora*, a large barrel-shaped mass with poles and lines sticking out, the *Fly Catcher*, the same basic shape but smaller, with only two sets of sails and a sweep mounted on the bow, and another merchantman like the *Pandora*, but larger, with four sets of sails and fore and aft sweeps.

As much as Checkgok despised the *Fly Catcher* and all aboard it, Checkgok missed it because it was the closest thing to Parthia—to home—that it was likely to see any time soon. Everything here was strange, alien, not suited to real people.

But Checkgok had its duty. It could take comfort in that. It was, at least temporarily, a worker of the Gold Clan. In spite of its discomfort with the notion of an artificial mind, it found the right key and contacted its new clan's clan home, the *Pandora*.

When *Pandora* answered, Checkgok asked, "Tell me of the Gold Clan and its needs."

There was no noticeable pause. Checkgok wasn't expecting one. "Danny Gold is the product of genetic engineering and intensive culling. He was intended to be . . . I guess the closest analogy would be one of your breeders, the ones that control the clan and produce the offspring."

Checkgok interrupted. "Controls the clans? Breeders don't control the clans. Granted, their role is vital, but so are all the other jobs. From the nurses who take care of the spawn to fighters, crafters, merchants, and all the other necessary jobs that keep a clan healthy."

"But who makes the decisions for the clans?"

"That depends on the decision. What foods are to be fed to the spawn of a clan is decided by the nurses. Where to build a clan home or other structure by architects. As an example, I make the decisions on what to buy and sell for Clan Zheck on this trading mission. That is why I asked what Clan Gold needs, so that I might best assess where my talents and training might be put to use for the Gold Clan."

"Who decided that you would go on this mission?"

Now Checkgok thought he understood the question. "The Zheck clan council appointed me, on the advice of the clan's master trader."

"And who chose the council?"

Maybe Checkgok didn't understand. "In the Zheck clan, new members of the council are nominated by their . . ." Checkgok paused and looked for an English word that would fit the meaning. ". . . department seems closest, though not quite right. It has some of the flavor of caste, as well. A council member is nominated by the department it comes from and is accepted by the council. Other clans have other ways of selecting, and how it is done can be affected by circumstances."

"In that case, I am not sure if there is a good Parthian analogy for what Danny Gold is. His progenitors were trying to create superior people, whose natural role would be to rule other humans. However, Captain Gold rejected that role."

"Who was right, Captain Gold or his progenitors?" Checkgok asked. Among Parthians, respect of the views of the clan elders was automatic, but it was now a member of Gold Clan. And in Gold Clan, Danny Gold was the whole clan, save for Checkgok and, perhaps, the *Pandora*. Though to Checkgok's mind, the *Pandora*, as a machine—a ship—was more clan home than clan member.

"I have no firm opinion on the matter. The main issue that Captain Gold objected to in his genetic modifications was the lack of empathy. He was designed to understand what others felt, without feeling what they felt. The idea was to make him capable of manipulating normal people, but prevent what his designers considered the weakness that would allow others to play on his feelings. He, on his own, concluded that the lack of conscience was not an advantage—or at least not an advantage that he wanted. So he has built a set of rules of fairness that he follows religiously. Sometimes to his detriment. He can't empathize with the pain and loss that others feel, but he can usually figure out what they are feeling. He uses that analytical imitation empathy to live and work in human society."

As Checkgok listened to that, it realized that the designers designed Danny Gold to be a *cheskek.* But Captain Gold realized that in spite of his lack of a moral center, he needed one, so he built one out of rules. In spite of itself, Checkgok felt sympathy for the poor, crippled human who was trying to create a conscience out of intellect. "The clan then must help Captain Gold to deal with his mental deformities."

They spoke some more, and Checkgok determined that its best role on the *Pandora* would be the same as its role on the *Fly Catcher.* It would, with luck, return to Parthia with holds full of useful goods and a mind full of new knowledge of the wider universe.

CHAPTER 3

The Cordoba Spaceforce is a department of the Cordoba Combine. Its members are combine employees; however, like all military forces throughout history, the Spaceforce and their exspatios have developed a subculture with their own political and cultural norms.

The Armed Forces of the Pamplona Sector, *Part 3*

Location: CSFS James Bond, Cordoba Space
Standard Date: 01 18 630

Lieutenant Commander Tanya Cordoba-Davis took the steps leading to the bridge two at a time. It wasn't hard. The *Double 07* was running at point seven gee to conserve H. The hatch to the bridge was open. Tanya grabbed a handhold and entered the bridge at the sedate, stately pace suitable for the executive officer on a Cordoba Spaceforce warship.

Commander Lars Hedlund looked up and lifted an eyebrow. "Running in the corridors again, XO?" He was about average in height, with straight black hair and brown skin. There was just a touch of epicanthic fold to his eyes, which were a startling green.

"Aye, Skipper," Tanya said, automatically using her anatomical control to suppress the blush. The skipper wouldn't care, but it was a habit by now.

"Is it the genetic mods or is there something to be excited about?" He was referring to the genetic mods that gave Tanya higher than normal energy levels. Tanya could stay up and fully operational for upwards of seventy-two standard hours, more if she needed to. She averaged three and a half hours a night of sleep and was stronger than an unmodified human. The skipper had some mods, but he wasn't a Cordoba connection and his parents, while stockholders, weren't overly wealthy.

"Well, the rear B sail runner is back up to full readiness. And Cook says we are having Morland lambfish with asparagus and hollandaise sauce for dinner." Tanya glanced at the main display that was showing the star field with an overlay of the ship routes and icons for the known jump points in the Aegean Cluster. She gave Lieutenant Christine Sanders who had the watch a nod, then turned back to the skipper.

"So it's the genetic mods."

Now it was Tanya's turn to lift an eyebrow.

The skipper continued. "You can eat helping after helping of Cook's hollandaise without worrying about it going to your gut. I just look at it and gain five pounds."

"With all due respect, Skipper, I have never seen you *just look* at Cook's asparagus and hollandaise."

"XOs who point out their skipper's lack of character have short and grisly careers, Tanya."

"I'll bear that in mind," Tanya said, but in her case it wasn't true, and they both knew it. Tanya was a Cordoba-Davis, a grand stockholder in her own right. While another officer might find her career on the rocks because she was too open about criticizing her seniors, Tanya wouldn't. That fact had made her very reticent about acknowledging Commander Lars Hedlund's character flaws until she got to know him. She didn't want to trade on her family name and tended to bend over backwards to avoid it. That was something that the skipper and her personal aide were working on correcting lately.

"Christine, you have the con," Commander Hedlund said. He hooked his thumb at the bridge hatch, and Tanya followed him out.

* * *

A few minutes later, in the captain's cabin, Tanya sat in the chair across from his and looked at the picture of James Bond behind the skipper's desk. The old movie series and the books they were based on were the basis of the ship's name. In the centuries since the loss of Earth, the distinction between fictional heroes like James Bond and real ones like Audie Murphy were blurred. Only scholars knew or cared, and even scholars weren't sure in cases like Hector and Agamemnon.

This was a small room compared to what might be seen on a station or a planet, four meters by six, with a bed that was, at the moment, folded up into the wall. Hero-class cruisers were light on amenities.

The skipper's face grew pensive. "I know you don't like to trade on your family, Tanya, but I'm hearing some pretty troubling rumors."

"About what, Skipper?"

"A possible shakeup on the Board." Board, in this case, referred to the Board of Directors of the Cordoba Combine. The Cordoba Combine was effectively the government of much of the Pamplona Sector. It was run by a board of directors who were selected by the stockholders. Once the board was selected, it appointed the combine officers and officials. Election of board members happened when a board member retired or died and—very occasionally—when enough people with enough stock asked for a general stockholders' meeting. There were rumbles over the past two and a half standard years that there was going to be such a request, with the requisite proxies filed, but nothing had happened yet.

"My mother doesn't think so, Skipper, but Dad is less confident. Isabella insists that nothing is going to happen, but she is so focused on the family investments that I don't think she pays much more attention to politics than I do." Tanya's sister Isabella went into the family business with a will and was her mother's fair-haired girl.

"Pay some attention, Tanya. When we hit port, send some letters. The fleet needs to know what's going on."

"The Admiralty . . ." Tanya started, but the skipper shook his head. Tanya's father was one of the Admiralty Board, one of what the fleet referred to as stockholder admirals. Grand stockholders who went to the academy, then shot up the ranks, often with no experience at all on warships and who effectively controlled the spaceforce. They were the standard connection between the military and the civilian oversight, and the fact that the skipper didn't seem to trust them was worrying.

The skipper shook his head again. "Nothing against your father, Tanya. I respect him, and his work in the appropriations office has done good things for the spaceforce. Still, the stockholder admirals are holding back. At least, that's what I'm hearing from the space-going admirals. The Drakes are fishing in a number of places and the stockholders don't want to hear about it."

The Drake Combine was the other major player in the Pamplona Sector. It was actually larger than the Cordoba Combine, but more dispersed, and that meant that its spaceforce needed to cover more territory, be in more places at once. The advantage of the Cordoba Combine's internal jump routes was all that kept the Drakes at bay.

The Drakes were usually forced to go farther and send orders farther to coordinate. That let the Cordoba Combine get ships into position to respond to Drake incursions more quickly, and that was crucial in the recent battle of Conner Chain.

"Do you really—" Tanya stopped herself. She knew the skipper was worried about the Drakes making a try for control of the Pamplona Sector. For that matter, Tanya was worried about it. The last of the trade wars was forty-three standard years ago, when the Drake and Cordoba Combines defeated the Ferguson Group and divided up its routes.

"Yes, I do. Because I don't think the Drake's pseudo-royalty system is stable. They need to fight us or they will come apart from internal dissension."

Location: DSFS Brass Hind, Drake Space
Standard Date: 01 18 630

Flash mist rolled from the vap into Third Officer Rosalyn Flatt's mouth and throat, then into her lungs, and the world became more intense. Colors were brighter and sounds crisper. The scratch on her quarter's wall stood out in high relief. Rosalyn could feel the wings flapping as a vibration in the grav intensity. There was a hiccup, and she checked the readouts. That was a catch in amidships C wing. It was cycling fine, then it would skip a cycle. The comp was running slow. It always did when she was flashing. She was in her quarters and used her interface to hook into the computer. The captain was off duty and Second Officer Andrew Watson had the watch.

Flash, a derivative of the thon plant, was a powerful euphoric and moderately powerful hallucinogen. It acted by increasing synaptic sensitivity and shortening synaptic response time. Depending on personal body chemistry, a user might feel ghostly touches, hear voices, have false memories, see things, or all of the above. To the observer, the flash user shows signs of delusional paranoia, but flash generally made the user feel capable, sharp, and clear. The world became more intense and connections, especially threats, that were obscure became obvious. People on flash also had response times that were as much as fifty percent faster than when not using. There were, in fact, recorded cases where the use of flash led to new and innovative solutions.

Along with her noting of the hiccup in amidships C, Rosalyn realized that First Officer Jason Smythe was out to get her. It wasn't just that he was always watching her. That was a common response of men and more than a few women since she had turned thirteen. Her five foot two inch body was shapely and supple. She stretched now, like a cat, enjoying the feel of muscles across muscles, sliding smoothly beneath her warm tan skin.

No, there was something else about Jason Smythe. He wasn't after a roll in the sheets. He was out to destroy her, not just to get laid. He resented her intelligence and her ability. Her mere existence proved his inferiority and he couldn't stand that. In a moment of flash clarity, she knew that she had to get him before he got her.

* * *

Sir Jason Smythe looked on as Rating First Tom Tucker used his interface to control the bot that was on the hull, working on the amidships C wing. There was a valve that was sticking as the magnetic bearing weakened on the back stroke, if the timing hit just wrong. In space, magnetic bearings were standard. Anything else tended to vacuum-weld parts. In this case, the magnetic field was weaker than it should have been and out of balance, so the rotator shifted to touch the cup. It wasn't much of a touch, but at a hundred rotations a second it was enough to cause a flutter and over time would wear away the joint and cause worse problems.

"Watch that," Jason said. The crew was sloppy and he had to keep an eye on them. He'd been tempted to do the repair himself, but that wasn't an officer's job.

Tucker muttered something that Jason chose not to hear and made an adjustment. Jason was a belted knight in the Drake Combine, which was more social rank than anyone else on this tub. Even Captain Hickam was only an esquire. That gave Jason a special responsibility to make sure that the lower orders were kept on their toes.

He thought about Rosalyn Flatt. The third officer was a cute little number, blond and blue eyed, just the way he liked them, and he figured that with a little more pressure she would yield readily enough. It wasn't like she had any other options, him being who he was, and her being a half-caste and born on the wrong side of the blanket to boot.

"Caste" had nothing to do with ancient India or any other Earth nation. But for generations the upper echelons of the Drake Combine had been availing themselves of genetic mods. While still fertile with normal humans, they were—Jason was convinced—clearly superior. Yes, a few more "accidental" touches and Rosalyn would get the message. But these things needed to be done carefully.

That was half the fun.

"All right, Tucker. Bring in the droid and see that it's put in the queue for maintenance."

Three Hours Later

Rosalyn took a last hit of flash and headed for the bridge. The *Brass Ass* had a long, narrow structure, little more than girders separating three sail nodes. The hull held atmosphere from bow to stern, but not much more. It had algae tanks for oxygen, but no other hydroponics. It carried the food the crew ate and would off load waste when they got back to a port. The waste was valuable feedstocks for the hydroponics of many stations. The three sail nodes held the sail rigging and the quarters for the crew. The bridge was in the forward section of the ship, a design decision that had much to do with status and little to do with practicality. With the *Hind* underway, Rosalyn had to climb in a full standard gravity from her quarters in the stern sail nodule to the bridge located in the bow nodule. Rosalyn was in good shape and it wasn't that hard for her, but it was irritating that Captain Hickam insisted that she report to the bridge for her watch, rather than simply having her use the interface in her quarters.

Suddenly, in another moment of flash clarity, Rosalyn knew that Smythe was responsible for that, as well as the rest of the hassles she put up with. It was all part of his desire to kick dirt on her, to keep her from realizing that it was she, not he, who was superior.

And there he was, the slimy bastard. Standing on the landing of the midship node, waiting with a smirk on his face. What was he doing here anyway? His quarters were in the forward nodule.

Another moment of clarity. He was going to touch her. She could feel it even before she reached him. His slimy paws on her hips, on her ass, on her . . . Rosalyn. She slowed and his grin widened. And it was just all too much.

She sped back up. As she was starting to pass him and he was reaching for her, she struck.

Absent the flash, his reflexes would have been measurably faster than hers. But she was flying and, besides, his reflexes weren't *that* much faster.

* * *

Jason Smythe was expecting to grab a quick feel as Rosalyn passed him on the ladder. The last thing he expected was a blow to his diaphragm before he even touched her. It took him by surprise, and for a moment he was stunned.

Then he reacted. He tried at first for a restraining hold and a nerve pinch, but she was faster than he realized. She got out of the way of his grasping hands and hit him in the nose. It was supposed to be a killing blow, but he managed to shift his head enough so that the angle was off and the blow just smashed his nose to the side. Blood sprayed the landing and covered his lower face.

Now he was furious. He bellowed in pain and rage. He didn't know or care why she struck. The uppity bitch was going to pay.

* * *

Second Officer Andrew Watson was coming down the ladder to return to his quarters. He wasn't supposed to, but he usually left the bridge at the end of his shift even if Rosalyn wasn't there yet. The captain would be drunk in his quarters by then and that asshole Smythe would never notice. He heard the bellow and leapt down the ladder. What he saw was Rosalyn, who was five foot two, fighting Smythe, who was six foot four. What he assumed was that Smythe got impatient and decided that with his social rank he could rape her without consequences. Andrew wasn't going to stand for that. He went for the big man.

* * *

Smythe sensed the help arriving and backed away to give Andrew room. Then the stupid bastard came at him. Smythe was incapable of imagining why Andrew would be attacking him. It never even occurred to him that Andrew might think Smythe was in the wrong. That left just one option. Mutiny. It was a coordinated attack. He swung Andrew between himself and Rosalyn, and opened his interface.

"Mutiny!" He dumped Andrew and Rosalyn's IDs into the interface with shoot on sight orders attached. The ship's computer, an intelligent system but not an artificial brain, had a set of protocols for mutiny, but there were fail-safes built in. As long as the captain was alive, only he could officially declare mutiny.

* * *

Captain Hickam was alive. He wasn't even unconscious. He was just very drunk. He was looking at the image of his wife and trying not to imagine what she was doing while he was out here.

The alert was transmitted to him and so was the second one, when Andrew Watson accused Smythe of attempted rape. Hickam was drunk and confused and put a hold on any action by the ship's automatics while he thought things through.

* * *

Rosalyn was on fire. Between the flash and the adrenaline, the world around her was slowed. She stepped back and let Andrew fight Smythe. She got on her interface and called Lieutenant Quinton Williams, the commander of the ten-man exspatio force on the *Brass Ass*. He was a crook from way back, but a smart crook, and he had no loyalty at all to the Drake Combine.

* * *

Quinton Williams' link came alive with Rosalyn's data dump, and he had a decision to make. He didn't really trust Rosalyn, but he had wanted out of the Drake Spaceforce almost since the day he joined. He quickly came to realize that even for someone who served well and faithfully, first lieutenant was about as high as someone not titled could go. And it was almost impossible to get a title for service to the Combine, even if it was the stock scenario in holo cubes.

Fuck it, he thought. *Let's kick some ass.*

He got on the link and started giving orders.

* * *

Back on the landing at midship node, Smythe blocked a blow by Andrew, who missed a beat due to the shock at the accusation of mutiny. Andrew was strong and fast, even reasonably bright, but he wasn't that much of a multitasker. He had excellent reflexes and was better trained in martial arts than Smythe ever bothered to become, but for vital seconds he was running on pure reflex. His higher functions were distracted by the fact that somehow he was on the wrong side of a mutiny.

It cost him. He was in the wrong position to respond to Smythe's elbow strike and was unable to avoid it.

It grazed his right temple and he never even saw the throat strike that crushed his larynx and, minutes later, would end his life. He hit Smythe twice more, crippling blows, but he was already dead when they landed.

Absent an emergency tracheotomy, which Rosalyn didn't provide. She decided that he was much more useful as a martyr than as competition for command.

Instead of making any effort to save Andrew, Rosalyn used the time Andrew was distracting Smythe to try to find a weapon. It was surprisingly difficult. The *Brass Ass* wasn't a frigate from the first age of sail, with belaying pins everywhere. It was a jump-capable spaceship that used drones for much of the work. Lines were tied down, but they were tied down by computer clamps that were hidden behind wall panels. Where was a monkey wrench when you needed one?

As it turned out, she didn't need one. Andrew's last blow brought Smythe to one knee, facing away from her. Rosalyn spun, bringing her right boot heel to the back of Smythe's neck just between the skull and the top vertebrae. It wasn't a killing blow, but it did render him unconscious.

That was good, because Rosalyn realized that she didn't want to kill Smythe until she was sure she had the captain. The Drake Combine didn't trust its spaceforce, especially the enlisted ranks, so command devolved to the highest surviving commissioned officer, but not the enlisted personnel. That meant that Rosalyn needed to be the ranking commissioned officer.

She ran through the list even as she dragged the unconscious Smythe to the nearest airlock. Captain Hickam, drunk in his quarters . . . he would need to die last. First Officer Smythe, now in an airlock. Second Officer Watson—she looked at Andrew—Second Officer Watson was dead. Quinton Williams was an officer, but exspatio, not spaceforce. The engineering officer, John Boyle, was a warrant officer, not commissioned, so as the computer saw things, not in line of command.

Rosalyn opened up a comm channel to Williams. "Quinton, I can't do the deed," she sent, careful of the words even on the secure channel. "Smythe killed Watson and he's unconscious in airlock 2C." She paused. She must be extra careful here. "You know the programming in the ship's comp. You know the protocols."

What she was referring to was the fact that the person who killed the captain—or, for that matter, any officer—could not be placed in that slot. Someone else would have to kill Hickam, and she would have to arrest and court martial that person. Either that, or hold them for trial as soon as they got back to a Drake base. In fact, it would be better if she could get to the computer without having killed anyone, at least before she assumed command.

The ship's computer was a large computer and extensively programmed with a lot of protocols, but it wasn't an artificial brain, so it lacked the consciousness to realize that she was running the mutiny. As long as she didn't actually kill anyone and arrested those who had, it would treat her as a loyal little Drake minion. Especially since she was from a good family.

* * *

Williams considered. He did understand the protocols, and the smart move would be to have Downing do it. But Quinton Williams was, in his way, an honorable man. He couldn't, when all was said and done, put one of his men in that sort of jeopardy. If it was to be done, he would have to do it. Nodding his head sharply, he headed for the captain's quarters.

He used his interface to announce himself and the captain's hatch opened.

"What the hell is going on, Williams?" Captain Hickam asked.

"It's all rather complicated, sir," Quinton said. "It started when Lieutenant Commander Smythe decided to have his way with Lieutenant Flatt." Williams was speaking to the recorders and the expert system as much as to the captain. After all, what Hickam thought was about to become completely irrelevant. He was walking across the captain's cabin even as he spoke.

Captain Hickam shook his head in befuddled disappointment. "I hope she isn't expecting me to do anything to Smythe. His family is very important on New Florida."

"No, Captain," Williams said calmly. "No one is expecting you to take any action." By the time he finished the sentence, he was standing right next to the captain, who nodded in drunken relief.

Quinton Williams, in a carefully measured strike, hit the captain in the side of the head. It was a touch too measured. The captain was stunned, but not unconscious. Quinton hit him again, a bit harder. He then pulled the necklace from the captain's neck and stuck it in his pocket. Everyone—well, all the officers anyway—knew about the captain's pendant and the private rutters that it held. This would be his insurance. Rosalyn would want it.

Quinton lifted the captain in a fireman's carry and headed for the 1B airlock. Then he sent Downing instructions.

* * *

Joe Downing got the orders and headed for the 2C airlock. He passed Lieutenant Flatt on the ladder, but he didn't know what was going on.

Spaceforce uniforms in the Drake combine were white with blue and gold trim. It made blood easy to see and identify. Exspatio uniforms were black with gold and red trim. They didn't show blood hardly at all. Both uniforms were based on the old heavy spacesuits, so they had fabric folds at the shoulders, elbows, hips, knees, ankles, and wrists to mimic the air containment folds of the old heavy suits. But that made no impression on Joe, in comparison to the blood spatter that marked the body and right side of the lieutenant's suit.

Joe reached the airlock and, against Lt. William's orders, looked in. His orders were to cycle the airlock without looking, but Joe wasn't as dumb as people thought. He looked and wished he hadn't. If he had cycled the airlock without looking, he would just be obeying orders and he wouldn't be at fault for anything except for failing to check. Now, cycling the airlock would be murder . . . and he almost didn't do it. But while the LT would take care of him if he obeyed the orders, there was no way that Spaceforce bastard Smythe would protect him if he didn't. Joe pushed the button and the lock cycled, sending Lieutenant Commander Sir Jason Smythe, belted knight of the Drake Combine, sailing gently into the void. The cycled lock had very little air left in it when the outer door opened, so it was only a gentle shove that lasted until he got far enough out to be picked up by the wings.

By that time, Captain Hickam was in space as well, and Lieutenant JG Rosalyn Flatt reported to the captain's cabin and found him gone.

* * *

On her own authority, Rosalyn used ship systems to determine the locations of Captain Hickam and First Officer Smythe. She also reported the death of Andrew Watson to the ship's computer, making a full and truthful report of the incidents leading to this situation. Well, almost full. She failed to mention her communications to Quinton Williams, and when asked she honestly responded that she told no one to harm Captain Hickam, First Officer Smythe, or Second Officer Watson.

She hadn't, not in so many words.

Given the emergency, she took command and ordered the arrest of Quinton Williams and Joe Downing.

Rosalyn now owned her own ship. But Rosalyn was no sheep of a trader and the *Brass* was no cargo ship. No. Rosalyn would hunt merchants.

CHAPTER 4

CIS, Computer Interface Systems, are a set of tiny circuits that extend into the gaps between nerve cells in the brain. This lets them talk directly to the brain. Human brains are flexible and with practice learn to distinguish the CIS data from normal neural impulses.
Because every brain is different in detail, the computer interface system must be adjusted to suit each individual. When you get your CIS, you will be able to talk directly to the school computers and it will let you play a whole bunch of new games.

Bonks Station One, second grade worksheet, Introduction to the Computer Interface Systems.
Published Standard Date 01 01 607

Location: Restaurant, Concordia Station Standard Date: 01 23 630

"What are the goals of this trading mission?" Danny asked Checkgok as he used his interface to bring up a spreadsheet of the content of the *Pan*'s holds. They were in a private room at a station restaurant with the *Pan* sitting in by comm and a lawyer, Robert Jones, acting as witness and advocate of Clan Zheck, since Checkgok, as *kothkoke* to Clan Danny Gold, presumably had mixed loyalties.

Danny wasn't all that sure how mixed Checkgok's motives were. Yes, while under the influence of the Parthian Banger, it swore a Parthian oath. But alien psychology didn't necessarily correspond to human psychology, and even if it had, Danny was experienced enough to know that just because you swore undying love—

even got married when you were drunk—well, that didn't mean you still wanted to be married after you sobered up. Much less that you suddenly stopped caring about your old girlfriend. But Checkgok was talking.

"There were three. First: to obtain a more reasonable price on certain goods that recently came to market from human worlds: jalapeño peppers from New Mexico and New Texas, beeffish from Sargasso, tor vine resin from Sinnath, several other items." Checkgok keyed in an information transfer with its mouthparts and Danny looked at the data, more because he didn't want to look at the Parthian mouthing the keypad than because he wanted to.

Danny picked up his coffee and sipped as Checkgok spoke. It was fair, but not great, coffee. Standard station fare like you might see in any station restaurant in the Pamplona Sector, much like the decor of the restaurant. Bland, beige, and boring.

"Second," Checkgok continued, its mouth-hand shifting back and forth, "we, ah, they, wanted to open up human markets to some of our products. Our people are more biotech-oriented than yours are. We have bioengineered products that we think could be very useful."

Another download and Danny scanned quickly. They sure as heck did have some interesting stuff. Danny used his interface to mark a couple of items to discuss with Checkgok later.

"Third: my clan, my previous clan, is fairly conservative in many ways. We have not had, nor sought, much contact with humans or the other two space-faring races in the hundred years since the first human ship landed on Parthia. Other clans have bought shares in ships, and even in the case of the *Fly Catcher*, outright ownership by Clan Kox, but their results have not generally been very good."

"Why not?" Danny asked.

"We're not entirely sure," the Parthian said, his eyestalks wobbling in what Danny thought might be a shrug. "We don't normally do well on our own, but groups as small as a ship's crew do fine when trading with other clans. Both on Parthia and our space colonies."

"You have colonies?" Robert Jones interjected, clearly as surprised as Danny by the revelation.

"Yes. We had them when Clan Canova's ship appeared at the jump point into our system. There are clans who are based on our artificial worldlets. That was what brought the exploration ship to contact us. They felt, quite rightly, that a race that had independently reached space must have things of value to trade."

Danny nodded. If the Parthians climbed out of their gravity well on their own, their independent tech had to be pretty darn good. But in that case, why was the *Fly Catcher* a human-made ship? Why didn't they build their own? Another thing to ask Checkgok about later. "So would you clarify that third reason?" Danny asked instead. "You wanted better prices and new markets. What else? That your clan is conservative doesn't really count as a reason to send you out." Though Danny suspected it just might, and if it did, Checkgok was screwed. It was, after all, not that different from what his own family did to him.

"We, ah . . . the Zheck Clan wants a better understanding of the wider universe. It was to be my task to provide the clan with that understanding."

Danny winced somewhere deep inside where it didn't show. It was bad enough for him when his people just thought they were a superior species. What was it going to be like for the poor bug that actually was being exposed to a different species and a different set of thought processes, then asked to come home and be a good little bug again? "So we will need to find markets for your goods, buy stuff you think that your clan needs or that they will want, and teach you about the wider universe. Good so far, but what's in it for us? Just because I'm not willing to rip off your clan to the tune of your cargo and yourself doesn't mean I'm willing to provide you free transport."

"The arrangement with the *Fly Catcher* was that the Kox clan would receive two percent of the net worth of the cargo that was sold or offloaded at Parthia."

Danny noted the movement of Checkgok's eyestalks, and his translation app signaled that the eyestalks moving that way indicated acknowledgment of a point. "Two percent of net doesn't seem enough even with all your cargo. It costs money to run a ship. How could they manage it?"

"Clan Zheck undertook to provide running expenses."

"That's more like it, but it doesn't quite get there. You have less cargo and the *Pan* is a larger ship than the *Fly Catcher*. Besides, I have debts to pay." Danny had his own troubles, and the Parthian societal structure bothered him. It was too much like what the Cybrants were doing with the Iron and Wood lines, designing them to be easily conditioned to extreme loyalty. Making people into slaves. Still, Checkgok was in trouble and it was at least sort of Danny's fault. If they could help each other out, Danny was willing to try.

"The cargo has less bulk, yes," Checkgok agreed, "but not less value. Quite a lot of our initial cargo was high bulk, which has been replaced in part by components which are smaller, but more expensive. Even with the loss of Kesskox's off-the-books cargo, the cargo that will transfer from the *Fly Catcher* to the *Pan* will have greater value than the cargo that was initially loaded. Several of our products are much more valuable in the wide universe than we thought."

"Which is nice," Danny said, "but not quite what I was getting at. We'll be running your schedule with your goods, but *Pan*'s over twice the size of *Fly Catcher*. After the stuff that's going to stay with *Fly Catcher*, you'll only be using a bit over a third of the cargo space and that's not a great way to make the most profit on a cargo ship. Not for you and not for us. We're going to want to fill the rest of that cargo space. And if we wait to do it until we're back on your home world, we're going to end up with two percent of less than half of our cargo hold filled."

"So you want off-the-books cargo too." Checkgok's mouth-hand scrunched up toward its body.

That comment felt like a sneer to Danny. "No, I want it on the books. I'm not a member of a Parthian clan and I don't have your cultural or biological structure. Humans are our own breeders. I'm my own clan and Bob here is his own clan. An advantage that you would expect for your clan, I want for my ship." Danny sighed, and tried to come up with a way to explain to the Parthian what it was to be human. He'd read up on the Parthians and realized that "hive" was probably closer than "clan" in describing their social structure. Put together with what happened here on station and the meaning of the insults that they threw around, some of the differences between them and humans came clear. Now Danny was trying to make those differences clear to Checkgok. Preferably without convincing it that all humans were perverted monsters. A tall order, considering that by Parthian standards, humans *are* perverted monsters. It was as though humans ran into a race of intelligent black widow spiders who then tried to explain to the humans that killing and eating your partner was a natural and fulfilling way of ending a sexual encounter. Which it is . . . to a black widow spider.

"The *Pan* is my clan home and I must see to the welfare of myself as you are obligated to the welfare of your clan. Which, at the moment, is my clan."

"Not exactly. While I have been made *kothkoke* to your clan—"

"Me," Danny interrupted, pointedly.

"You," Checkgok agreed, its mouth-hand scrunching up again, then continued. "You and the court have instructed me to act in this case as agent for Clan Zheck, so I am required to represent Clan Zheck."

"Which is made easier by the fact that in spite of the *kothkoke* oath, now that you have sobered up, you're still emotionally of Clan Zheck, not Clan Danny Gold, right?"

"Well, yes. But we of Clan Zheck hold our oaths sacred," Checkgok said. And it was true, but there was more. It felt rather comfortable with this human though it didn't know why. "Whatever I may feel now that I have, ah, sobered up, I swore the oath and it was within my authority to swear it, so it's binding on Clan Zheck, and through Clan Zheck, on me."

Location: Hotel Lobby, Concordia Station
Standard Date: 01 25 630

Two days later, Checkgok sat with the monkey—human—named Barnabas Carter and discussed the tanta root that was a product of the Cordoba Alendail system. It was part of the official cargo of the *Fly Catcher,* and Checkgok was selling it here to raise some operating capital. *Pandora* had given Checkgok a list of equipment that the ship would need and the *Fly Catcher*'s credit was not available.

Barnabas Carter clicked a greeting in very bad Parthian and they got down to negotiations. They were meeting in the hotel lobby. Checkgok was staying in the hotel while the legal issues were settled, cargo transferred, and finances arranged, because the judge didn't want Checkgok under the authority of either ship until everything was settled. It was also worth noting that Magistrate Stella Jones owned a share in the station hotel and Checkgok was paying for good rooms.

Location: Pandora, in orbit off Concordia Station
Standard Date: 01 28 630

Danny put on the helmet and headed for the airlock while he listened to *Pan* bitch.

"I still say we should have gotten the whole cargo," *Pan* said.

"Maybe, but I understand why she didn't rule that way," Danny said as the air was sucked from the lock. He felt the vacuum tingle on his skin. Skin was a lot stronger than most people thought. Even a normal human wouldn't actually blow up if they were exposed to vacuum. It would kill them, all right, but that would be because of the eyes, mouth, ears, and nose, not the skin. The skin would stretch at the loss of external pressure, and that would be both painful and debilitating for a normal human, but not immediately deadly. With his helmet, Danny wouldn't even suffer vacuum burn. He had a sheath of subcutaneous muscles that kept his skin from expanding in vacuum.

The lock pumped empty and Danny opened the door, still talking. "She has to keep everyone happy, *Pan*, or at least not so pissed off that they don't figure they have anything to lose by calling the cops."

"There are no cops. The Cordoba and Drake families are simply trading houses."

Danny snorted a laugh. That was technically true, in the same way it was technically true that Julius Caesar was just a Roman general. "You know better, *Pan*.

You're just pissed that your quoting of precedent didn't carry the day. Now, where is that relay you want me to look at?"

"Section Fifteen E, forty meters sternward."

Danny looked, saw the stanchion, and leapt. He loved zero-g.

"Did you have to leap, Captain? You know that is an unsafe procedure, and calling a dutchman to the station would cost us five hundred credits."

Danny ignored the complaint. "What about new crew?"

"We have an offer in the trades, but no takers," *Pandora* told him.

"I was afraid of that," Danny said. "We aren't looking all that spry." He reached out a hand and grabbed the stanchion as he flew by, and swung around it. He was wearing gloves because the stanchion was cold and he didn't want to freeze the skin on his hands. Danny used the stanchion to make his way back to the hull of the *Pan* and took a look at the relay. It was four inches across, greenish gold, and slightly misaligned. Danny locked his boots in the foot holds to keep his position and started the realignment, while *Pan* gave him a report on Checkgok's negotiations.

Part of the problem with crew was the cost of flexsuits. The flexsuit was a hand-crafted piece of specialized clothing that cost thousands of credits. It was made one micro link at a time by an artificial-brain-controlled machine over the course of weeks, and each one was made to fit the individual wearer. They did what Danny's genetically modified skin did, and more. They controlled heat loss and provided directional magnetic fields that made it possible to operate in space almost as though you were operating in a station. Danny owned one, though he tried not to wear it any more than necessary, because it was twenty years old and well past its safe life expectancy. So, in relatively safe environments, like next to Concordia Station, he went for space walks in his skivvies.

Danny couldn't afford to buy flexsuits for new crew, and crew that had their own could afford to be picky about the ships they signed onto.

* * *

Checkgok squatted before the console in its hotel room and considered the screen. The *Pandora* was a larger ship than the *Fly Catcher*. Both ships' cargo holds were about a third full. With the roots it just sold, they could buy enough hydrogen to fill the Pandora's tanks and pay the fines and docking fees, but that was about all. It debated trying to sell the foff seeds, but the station prices were outrageous and it wasn't getting good prices for the cargo it had to sell. There would be better prices once they got back to Cordoba space.

Location: CSFS James Bond, Aegean Cluster, Cordoba space Standard Date: 02 18 630

Lieutenant Commander Tanya Cordoba-Davis was tied into the ship system as the *Double 07* went through the jump. She immediately saw the light cruiser four and a half light seconds away along the route toward the next jump. It would be four and a half seconds before the Drake cruiser would see them, but five point three seconds before any sand or grape shot she threw could reach the point in space it was located. That would give it over a second to dodge, and it was a safe bet its sensors were pointed right at them. The jump point wasn't all that big. Still, it was worth a try. She sent the order Lieutenant Sanders was waiting for and the magnetized BBs shot out. Tanya was jerked against her harness as Newton's second law slammed the *Double 07* in reaction to the wings grabbing the magnetized BBs and flinging them away.

At the same time, tied into ship's systems, Tanya got the precise value and duration of vector change caused by the grapeshot as the massive magnetic fields of the *Double 07*'s wings flung them at the Drake Falcon-class cruiser. The Drakes used birds of prey from owls to eagles to hawks as names for their Falcon-class ships, the Drake equivalent of the Cordoba Hero-class.

Tanya's mind sorted through the data provided by the link and searched for the enemy blocking force. It should be near the next jump point, almost a light minute from here. But at almost a light minute, they would be hard to spot unless their wings were up. Something the size of a spaceship, even the largest spaceship, would be like spotting a grain of blue sand on a green sand beach a mile away.

Tanya knew that even a lucky hit on the watcher wouldn't do any good. It would have already sent a full description of their force, position, and vector to the waiting drakes. In just under a minute the enemy force would know precisely where to aim their telescopes. Besides, the *Double 07* and the rest of the squadron were coming through the jump under full sail.

The Falcon-class was flapping like mad to get out of the path of her grapeshot. Yes, it made it. She shifted her vector to intercept it. Her job was to push it away from the jump exit so that the enemy reads on the rest of the fleet would be less precise.

The problem with space combat was that there was no place to hide in ambush, and most tactics were based on some variation of "hide in ambush." Making the enemy think something was happening, but the wrong something.

Tanya checked her systems and called up the vectors and data. They were traveling at seventy-five kilometers per second, but their exit vector from the jump was almost forty degrees off the vector they needed to hit the next jump, and it would take them almost a day to get there. Tanya ordered the *Double 07* to two standard gravities, twenty meters per second acceleration, and went in pursuit of the picket ship. The rest of the fleet would be maintaining one standard g until they got some distance from the jump, then kill their accel to see if they could get the enemy looking in the wrong direction. It was a standard tactic, but it was standard because it was hard to counter.

At distances like these, the delay between an action taken and an action observed made targeting, or even keeping your eyes on a target, difficult. But that wasn't Tanya's problem. She was after the Falcon-class ship out there.

"Do we have an ID on that ship?" she asked Lieutenant Vance, who was acting as her sensors officer at the moment.

"Not yet. No . . . wait one. It's the *Sparrow Hawk*, built in 613 at the Granger Yards in the Drakar system. They have a good rep, but it's seventeen standards old."

"That's not old," said Chief Petty Officer Ralph Howard, who was chief of ship and the senior NCO on the *Double 07*.

"Check for upgrades anyway," Tanya sent and grinned at the byplay. Ralph was mostly right. Ships were expensive to build and kept in service as long as possible, and if that was more true of cargo ships than warships, it was still true. The *Double 07* herself was fifteen years old, and there were ships in the squadron that were upwards of fifty.

Vance sent a vector projection. "Captain, it's trying to curl around to stay in range of the squadron."

In Tanya's mind, the vector projection ran out and several options presented themselves. She could shift immediately and keep the pressure up. She could let the *Sparrow Hawk* think she was getting away with it. Or she could split the difference, delay her response a little so that the *Sparrow Hawk* might think her sloppy, and make a risky move based on that. "What do we know about the skipper over there, Bosun?"

Ralph dove into the shipnet and came up with a name and a service history. "Sir Douglas Gillette. He's old for his rank and . . . Captain, he received his knighthood for service to the Drake Combine. He was born on Pabang and was an enlisted spacer for almost ten years before he got knighted and received his commission."

"Respond, Mr. Vance, but be sloppy about it, like you just noticed and are overcompensating. Rather like I am." Tanya sent him a vector correction, and he looked up at her.

Tanya grinned. "I am a spoiled darling of the aristocracy, Mr. Vance, not expected to be competent. Let's see if we can encourage the 'grizzled old spacer' over there in that belief, shall we?"

They continued their dance for hour after hour, Tanya and the *Double 07* forcing *Sparrow Hawk* away from the squadron, but sloppily. The tension on the bridge got more and more intense as they got farther from the support of the rest of the squadron and closer to the *Sparrow Hawk*. Making mistakes meant taking chances. Even when you were intentionally leaving yourself open, you were left open. The crew of the *Double 07* wanted the *Sparrow Hawk* to take the bait, but when it did they might get mauled.

* * *

"What the fuck?" Vance exclaimed. "Sorry, Captain. They are running. Just deadout running."

Tanya sighed. The vector of the *Sparrow Hawk* was shifting again, but this wasn't a subtle attempt to close with the Cordoba squadron. Nor was it an attempt to get back to the Drake squadron that had to be out there guarding the next jump on the jump chain. It was a flat out run at three standard gravities, thirty meters per second, to get as much distance as he could from the *Double 07*. Tanya looked at the vector, called up her rutters, and realized that for the past hours while she was playing him, he was playing her. There was a jump along his projected course. It was a short jump, and according to Tanya's rutters it was into a cul de sac. But the advantage of the attacker when coming through a gate was based on the fact that the defender would not know when, or precisely where, the attacked would make jump, and the attacker would see the defender first.

When you were chasing someone through a gate, that advantage flipped. The fleeing ship knew where you were, and your options as to when and where you made jump were limited, whereas from the moment they passed through jump the fleeing prey could vector in any direction and send salvo after salvo back at the jump point.

"Break off," Tanya grated.

The ship's system came up with "simulation concluded."

"I wondered if you'd go for it after you realized you'd been suckered, Tanya," Captain Hedlund said over the net. He ran the sym from his cabin interface. "Don't underestimate old salts. Gillette is perhaps the best ship commander in Drake service."

"I read about him. But, honestly, sir, it all sounded like Drake propaganda. 'See, we really do promote from the lower classes when it's merited.' "

"It *was* Drake propaganda, and don't doubt that the Drake old line Spaceforce officer corps resents the hell out of him. But the truth is that Gillette should be commanding a Dragon-class, not a Falcon-class, or even be a squadron commodore."

"If you say so, sir. But doesn't that make it even more likely that he would expect my incompetence?"

The *Double 07* was back to half a standard G, all they could manage without venting plasma in this part of space. The starfield was empty of other ships except for the *Davy Crockett*, who watched the exercise from a safe distance. Tomorrow it would be the *Davy* that did a full-on sim, while the *James Bond* watched for trouble.

Captain Hedlund stepped onto the bridge, flex suit covered by his uniform. Tanya got up and gave him the captain's chair and he continued the talk. "Yes, but it really didn't matter. Whether you were being stupid or clever, it still let him get to his back door out of the pocket. He's done his job. The enemy knows our fleet's vector and has good reads on all the ships. And we know crap about them except for the *Sparrow Hawk*, and it's gone through that jump to a cul de sac or maybe a side route that we don't know about, back to the main jump route. You should have kept the known jump points, even the cul de sacs, in mind, Tanya. You're good. In all honesty, as good a natural commander as I've ever seen. But you have the vices of your virtues. A tendency to expect to be able to outthink your opponent. You're going to want to watch that."

Tanya nodded. The function of the Cordoba Combine Spaceforce was to protect trade in the Pamplona Sector. At least, in theory.

Location: Drake Space, Drakar Palace, Drakar
Standard Date: 02 16 630

Counselor Le Wong, cousin to His Imperial Majesty Kenneth Drake and, more importantly, nephew of Ferdinand Drake, the chairman of the board and largest stockholder of the Drake Combine, strode through the corridors of the palace with a memory stick in his right hand and a severe expression on his face. Two Drake agents in Cordoba space recently met with fatal accidents, and when he combined that with the presence of a Parthian wingship in Drake space, it suggested all sorts of nasty possibilities. The Cordobas were up to something or they never would have let the bugs get hold of a ship.

He stepped through the crystal pillars into the garden. His cousin waved. Then, seeing his expression, held up a hand. The garden, almost an acre, was full of trees, flowers, and ball courts. It was also surrounded by a plexicreat wall thirty feet tall. The emperor was, at that moment, standing on a rock over a crystal blue brook that bubbled and laughed its way through the garden. Prince Nave of Hellespont Three, the sole habitable planet in the Hellespont system, was at the base of the rock with an ash bow in hand, aiming at a target ten meters away. Prince Nave loosed his arrow as the emperor's expression changed.

"No, absolutely not," the eleven-year-old emperor of the Drakar system said. "Politics are not allowed in the dragon's garden. You know the rules."

A grin twitched Le Wong's face as he looked back at Emperor Kenneth, Prince Nave, Count James of Drakar City, and Lady Angla of Golden, whose bow was now pointed in Le's general direction. Le liked his young cousin, who was bright and at least reasonably willing to put up with the royal folderol.

His grin was only a twitch, though, because if the Cordobas were actually planning on integrating the bugs into their population, it would give them a massive boost. The Pamplona Sector was only lightly populated by the Sol System standards of a few centuries ago. There were billions of Parthians, and their integration would give the Cordobas a population of seventeen billion. That was almost half again as many people as the Drakes had. And the Parthian tech base was impressive, if not quite up to human standards.

"Then, Your Majesty, I must draw you out of the garden for a few moments."

Emperor Kenneth Drake looked at him, sighed, and waved his playmates away. He followed Wong out of the garden and down the hall to a secure office.

"The Cordobas seem to be making a play for control of the sector," Wong said as soon as the door was closed.

At eleven, Kenneth was just at five feet tall, and thin. He had golden hair. Not blond. Golden. Golden brown skin, and his greenish-gold eyes had just a touch of elongation of the pupil. Not cat's eyes, but a bit cat-ish. Kenneth was as enhanced as any of the prime Cybrant lines but was also educated from birth to be a ruler. He had, in theory, all the traits to make a great leader.

Wong knew it wasn't Kenneth's fault that he was spoiled. Kenneth had been fawned over for his entire life, while it was also made clear to him that he was not allowed to follow his own interests.

"What does Father say?" Kenneth asked.

"This is a government matter. Not something to bother Chairman Drake with."

The emperor of Drakar snorted. "In other words, you're not sure enough to take it to my father. Okay, what have the Cordobas done?" Kenneth went to one of the chairs in the secure conference room and flopped down on it.

"They released a ship to the Parthians."

"Give me the dump."

Wong plugged the memory stick into the room's net and let Kenneth absorb the data electronically.

"I don't know, Le. You know how corrupt the Cordobas are. Couldn't it just be that one of the families got careless or needed a bit of cash?"

"That was our initial assessment, but note subsection C. Two of our top agents in Cordoba space have met with so-called accidents that were fatal in the last month. Both of them were deeply involved in keeping track of Cordoba Combine policy toward Parthia." That was what really upset Wong, the combination of events.

"Could be coincidence," Kenneth said.

"I don't believe in coincidence, Your Majesty."

"All right. I'll take it to Father." The emperor considered. "But he's been concerned with the free traders, smugglers, and the gray colonies, so he may not pay much attention to this."

Location: Yagan 3, Cordoba Space
Standard date: 02 16 630

Admiral George Cordoba-Davis waved his former aide into his office. "How did it go, Allan?"

"It got a little messy, sir. He was better trained than we thought." Allan didn't pause in the doorway or even hesitate as he entered the private office, but George didn't ask any other questions until the door was closed and the security systems engaged. Those security systems turned off the holo panels, turning the pleasant, airy space into a white-walled vault.

George went to his desk as he asked, "How much better trained?"

Allan's face was grim. "He was enhanced, sir. Had to be. He was drinking heavily, and the plan was to have him 'trip' going down the stairs. But he avoided the throw and almost brought down our operative."

"Sit, sit. Then tell me about it from the beginning," George said, a bit more harshly than he intended. "Are you sure he was enhanced? Couldn't he have just been lucky? There is no way someone at that level in the Jackson-Cordoba organization should have that level of enhancement. And a clerk, even if he was enhanced, shouldn't have that sort of enhancement."

Allan sat but didn't relax. "I wondered the same thing, sir. I got a tissue sample and had some friends do a genetic analysis. He had most of the Cybrant Iron Line mods and a couple of the Bronze."

"No way that Tobin Jackson-Cordoba would go along with that," George said.

"I know, sir. That's what has me concerned. I think we hit a Drake agent."

"What the hell is a Drake agent doing pushing the Jackson-Cordoba claims to the Canova system?"

"I don't have a clue, sir."

George Cordoba-Davis looked at his long-time friend but didn't see him at all. The factions within the great families of the Cordoba Combine were becoming more and more polarized, and the gap between the great families and the Spaceforce was even worse. Could the Jackson-Cordobas have sold out to the Drakes? He wouldn't have thought that of Tobin, but who knew what was going to happen in the next shake up.

Location: New Argentina
Standard Date: 02 16 630

Tobin Jackson-Cordoba stepped out of the theater with what might be called a firm step. If one was prone to understatement. He scanned the street for his limo and checked the time with his internals. It was seventy-three seconds since he signaled for the limo to meet him, and his mouth tightened in irritation.

Tobin appeared about forty to the eyes of a pre-space, pre-genetic engineering human, but you could add a standard century to that and still fall short of the mark. He was dressed in New Argentina formal attire. Not for Tobin the fad of dressing down. His jumpsuit was of Candahar silk, a blend of the red, blue and violet black. It glowed royal purple in the sunset. The joint bands that circled the jumpsuit's limbs at wrist, elbow, shoulder, hip, knee, and ankle, were gold. His old fashioned "space helmet" hat followed the motion of his head without ever touching his perfectly coiffed auburn hair.

Tobin liked live theater when it was done well, but he walked out on this play five minutes in. An over-ambitious and under-talented playwright attempted to update Romeo and Juliet to the Pamplona sector. Utterly ridiculous. You might as well try to update the melancholy prince. Tobin was a realist. The notion that a fully realized, genetically enhanced human would fall into the sort of emotional morass the unenhanced stumbled into wasn't just silly, it was actively insulting.

Like the play in question, the Pamplona Sector was indeed ruled by two great houses. The Drakes and Cordobas evolved from family businesses into corporations, then into governments, in response to fluctuations in the political and economic landscape. They controlled, between them, most of the trade in the Pamplona Sector. Through that control, they directed most of the planetary and system governments. Both families were genetically enhanced, logical, and pragmatic.

Either family would have jettisoned Romeo and Juliet through the airlock without a second thought.

Each had done things much more severe to erring family members. Tobin Jackson-Cordoba himself did worse when the situation demanded it.

* * *

There was his limo. Finally. He strode down the steps and the chauffeur barely got the door up in time. Tobin settled into his seat and sent a message to Conrad to meet him at the palacio.

* * *

Conrad was there when Tobin arrived, and if he was looking not quite as neat as he might, Tobin decided to let it pass this time. "What's the status of Canova?" Tobin asked.

"The court rejected Barbra's final appeal."

"I know that," Tobin snapped. "I want to know if any more action is going to be necessary."

"No, Uncle. The Parthian's tech is different enough that most people don't recognize it for what it is. Certainly Barbra Canova . . ."

"Barbra Billingsley," Tobin snapped again. He was in a snappish mood. But that wasn't all. It was important to maintain the position that Barbra Billingsley Canova was not, in fact, a member of the Canova family. That there were no Canovas still alive, because only then did the contracts between the Canova family and the Jackson-Cordobas go into effect.

"Excuse me, Uncle, but why the sudden concern?"

"Because in a few minutes I'm going to call that idiot bitch Angela Cordoba-Davis and tell her she's talked me into supporting her position on New Kentucky, in exchange for her support. . . . Don't shake your head at me, boy."

"Sorry, sir, but the wealth of the Parthian industrial base will . . ."

"I know that, but I have a solution." Conrad was talking about the danger that as soon as they started to truly exploit the industrial base of the Parthian home system, the Cordoba Board was going to notice and react. Probably send in the navy and take the bugs' system for the Combine.

"Sir?"

"I was thinking about it while that hack butchered the play by trying to update it without taking into account the fact that we are practical people, not romantic fools. Our solution is Admiral Lord John Charles Huffington." The Drake admiral was a hot head and had all the subtlety of a bull in a china shop, but he was an effective naval commander.

"I don't understand."

"The Ambrosius route." Tobin said referring to a gray route that the Jackson-Cordoba Trading Company used to smuggle goods from Parthia into Drake space. It was common knowledge that it was there, but its precise location was closely held. On the Cordoba side, it came out on the route between Parise and Ferguson.

"Huffington will go after Parise, but it will be a plausible threat against Canova. Once we have the forts in place, we'll be in a position to use the bugs as a labor force. We won't have to worry about the chairman of the board ordering out the navy. Not against forts, not when he's already dealing with a Drake incursion. We'll have decades to put the proper controls in place and ramp up production. With the bugs churning out war goods, the rest of the Two Hundred will have to fall in line."

"It's risky, Uncle. Once we give Huffington the route, we lose it. If he gets his ass handed to him, we give up the route for nothing."

"Make sure the commander at Parise is not the best we have. You're right that we need Huffington to have at least initial success."

"The board?"

"Petros Cordoba wants the chairmanship." Tobin filled a snifter about a quarter full of cho-ki brandy, swirled the deep blue liquid around in the snifter, lifted it to his nose, and inhaled the scent of the Parthian liquor. He took a sip, then turned back to his nephew. "He won't get it, but we can make it look like he might, and that will tie Susan Cordoba's hands. At least long enough."

"That might push the Chairwoman to supporting the spaceforce's demand to vote the space force shares." The Cordoba spaceforce was supported by the dividends from a large block of stock. If the spaceforce was allowed to vote it, they would instantly become a power in the selection of the Cordoba Board.

"No." Tobin shook his head. "The rest of the board would never go for it."

"And the Drakes?"

"Nothing for now, but once we have control of the Cordoba Board . . ." Tobin considered. "The boy will have to go, but we will need to make sure none of our gene scans are anywhere near that, because we won't be imitating the Montagues. We'll follow the example of the Habsburgs instead."

"Ah, happy Austria," Conrad quoted, "other royal houses commit war while the Habsburgs commit marriage."

"But all that is decades away. First we must gain control of the Cordoba Combine."

"Actually, I was worried about what the Drakes are going to be doing in the meantime," Conrad said.

"You mean you think they'll follow up on Huffington's gains?" Tobin shook his head. "No. Ferdinand Drake is too cautious for that. He won't be happy about Huffington's actions and he's going to suspect the military of trying to gain support for a coup. The first thing he'll do is purge their ranks of anyone competent. The Drakes aren't the danger.

"The danger is what it's always been. That someone other than ourselves will see the use that a race of natural born slaves can be put to in the building of empire."

CHAPTER 5

The political ramifications of fold space and the jumps it makes possible are subtle and often misunderstood. Fold space doesn't simply provide shortcuts to travel between the stars. In broad terms, it transforms what is commonly thought of as the desert of deep space into a multidimensional swamp, full of hidden routes and hiding places. So many hiding places that effective policing becomes prohibitively expensive.

Each new jump point is a new hiding place for criminals, and the patrol and other police organizations have no hope of catching up if the number of jumps continues to increase at present rates. Some means of limiting jump discovery must be put in place if effective control of the system polities is to be achieved.

Classified Memo to Drake Combine from Chief of Security

Standard Date: Liuyuè 7, 548

Location: Pandora, in orbit off Concordia station Standard Date: 01 29 630

"Well, this is the ship." The captain bared its—no, *his*—teeth. Which Checkgok knew was supposed to be an indication of joy. "There is no question we needed the job."

Checkgok looked around. There was a shabbiness about the *Pandora* that bothered it deeply. The dark green decking was scuffed, the once pale green bulkheads were worn, scratched, and in need of a new coat of sealant. Even the overheads, once probably yellow, were faded and drab.

"That's Tony," Captain Gold said, pointing at a squat box on four rollers with two mechanical arms. It was a drone of sorts, but not like they had on the *Fly Catcher.* This one had an unpainted weld on one of its surfaces, and there were wires attaching the vise grip-style hand to the arm, and a bolt as well. Even Checkgok, who knew virtually nothing of mechanics, could tell that they weren't designed to fit the arm.

Pandora spoke. "Drone T 83 was damaged off Chaco. We were forced to rebuild it from scavenged parts."

"It works okay. It just needs supervision," Captain Gold insisted.

This was Captain Gold's clan home. He owned nothing on his home world. As Pan told Checkgok, part of the agreement that gave him the ship was that he relinquish all properties and endowments he was entitled to by virtue of his birth. He really was a new clan.

Checkgok, like it or not, was now a worker of that clan. It really didn't like it much, now that it was sober and in its right mind. It wasn't prejudiced, but humans really were pretty disgusting.

They continued their tour of the ship while either the captain or the ship itself described what they were seeing. Cargo holds, empty except for scraps and the cargo transhipped from the *Fly Catcher.* The hydrogen tanks were full now, from Clan Zheck's goods sold here. The fusion generator banks, a massive tube that ran down the center of the ship from just behind the bow to the stern, surrounded by panels so black that no hint of light reflected off them. Plasma tubes, one at the base of each wing mast. It was like, and yet unlike, the *Fly Catcher.*

They reached the core chamber for one of the twelve main wing engines. It was a ten meter wide coil of half-meter wide superconducting cable. The cable was a muddy green coil, thick enough that you couldn't see the walls of shieldgold used to contain and focus the magnetic field. Shieldgold wasn't actually gold, though it weighed about the same. It was an artificial element that was unstable unless held in a matrix of carbon balls. It had the property of reflecting magnetic fields and was essential for the operation of the hyperdrive. It was in good repair as far as Checkgok could tell, but there was still that feel of wear.

They reached the crew's quarters, where Checkgok was given a room and the captain left it there to talk with the *Pan* about the cargo and where to take it.

Location: Pandora, Concordia Free Space
Standard Date: 01 30 630

The *Pan* pulled away from Concordia Station with a couple of gentle flaps of her magnetic wings. The drive system on an interstellar ship was what was once called "dirty magnetic sails." It was mostly a movable magnetic field, but it was injected with plasma, both to extend the field size and because using the flapping of the magnetic wings, turning the field off and on at the right time in the cycle, could thrust the plasma away at speeds very close to that of light. It was what some wit called "the largest nozzled rocket motor imaginable." The thrust plasma was pushed away from the ship at speeds approaching the speed of light, but over so wide an area that someone floating directly behind the ship wouldn't even get a sunburn.

Pan's magnetic wings flapped hundreds of times a second and passed the plasma between them in a complex dance that produced a neat and orderly aurora borealis of thrust. It was a beautiful sight and one that Danny greatly loved. Now he watched through the ship's sensors and felt with *Pan* as she thrust against the very fabric of space with her magnetic wings.

One of the mods of the Gold Line was the natural interface that allowed Danny to tie into a computer without even the minor surgery that most humans needed. So he stood on the bridge of the *Pan*, one hand on the back of his accel couch, barely aware of his body, while his mind felt the space through the feedback of the wings. It was like flying, he thought. Not like floating in zero-g. Like flying. The wings pushed against space and were pushed against by space. He felt more than saw Concordia Station receding in the distance as they began their acceleration toward one of the jump points near the station.

Danny stayed on the bridge for almost an hour as *Pan* moved away from Concordia Station. By that time, they were moving at good speed and far enough away so that there was no need for a bridge watch.

An hour out of Concordia, he finally pulled out of the virtual reality of the ship's sensors, patted the accel couch, then turned and went out the hatch, and down the corridor to his cabin. He lay on the bunk and used a routine he was taught as a child on Cybrant to put himself to sleep.

* * *

Pan assigned a newly repaired drone to the trimming of the conks bush they took on as a supplement for Checkgok, who had somewhat different dietary requirements. *Pan* had vats that produced proteins of various sorts and gardens for plants. But until now her crews were all human, and she was a little concerned about how the Parthian would react to the mixed diet, whatever it said. Naturally, as a pure Parthian ship, *Fly Catcher* had extensive gardens of Parthian delicacies. But all *Pan* was able to get were some basics. Another piece of petty vindictiveness from the *Fly Catcher*, she suspected. "What would you like for evening meal, Checkgok?" she asked the new Parthian crew member.

"I have no great preference, ship," Checkgok said absently. "Why are you so understocked? Your holds are mostly empty. Aside from algae for oxygen and a few vegetables, hydroponics was effectively off line until I came aboard."

"Restrictions from the Drake and Cordoba trading houses. They are trying to lock up interstellar trade. That was why we were at Concordia. It's unaligned and officially not known."

"I don't understand."

Pan considered. She didn't know what Checkgok knew of the history of humanity in space. And the truth was that restrictions from the Drakes and Cordobas was almost more an excuse than a real reason for the state of the ship. "After the breakup of the Terran Federation, there were hundreds of independent successor states, some containing several systems, some that were just a single space station. Trade was controlled by those individual states.

"However, in the Pamplona sector over the last three hundred plus years, most of those successor states have been forced to give up control over their interstellar trade to the trading houses. There were half a dozen of them two centuries ago. Now there are two. The Drakes and the Cordobas. Each controls hundreds of routes.

"In theory, the systems on those routes are still independent. But if they start getting uppity, the trading house that owns the route comes in and cuts them off from trade until they see reason. Sometimes they go farther than cutting them off from interstellar trade. There have been several 'unfortunate accidents' which brought about changes in system government and the rebuilding of system capitals."

"What sort of accidents?"

"Large rocks falling out of the sky and just happening to land on the capitol. That sort of thing."

"How do they get away with it?"

"They have lots of ships," *Pandora* informed Checkgok, "and control over interstellar trade. Also, they don't entirely get away with it. There are the places like Concordia Station, far enough off the beaten track to be ignored, but close enough to make smuggling easy. And there are a lot of systems that are plenty happy to deal with independents if they can do it without being caught by the great houses.

"Canda will be happy to see us and cook the books about where we came from. The Drake representative will look the other way for a suitable bribe and—"

Pandora stopped. The expressions of Parthians were different from humans. They didn't exactly have faces because they didn't have heads. They had two flexible eyestalks extending up from the front of their body and a flexible mouth-hand extending down from the same general area. Disgust was generally signified by a pulling in of the mouth-hand just as Checkgok's mouth-hand was doing now.

"Remember," she chided gently, "humans are their own clans. Breaking the rules isn't cheating the clan. It's cheating *for* the clan."

"Which doesn't make it right," Checkgok insisted, but its mouth wasn't being held quite so close.

"No, it doesn't. But remember, the rules aren't being made to the advantage of all humanity. They are being made to the advantage of those groups that are making the rules. Captain Gold had no role in their making. Nor did the government of the Canda system, for that matter." *Pan* wasn't at all sure that the Parthian could get its head around the concept of government. And she was even less sure that she could explain the quasi-governmental role of the great trading houses. She was fairly sure that underground movements and divided loyalties would not be concepts that Checkgok could comprehend.

"It's not Captain Gold's actions that bother me, or even the government of Canda. It is the actions of the Drake representative."

Pandora didn't have an answer for that, not one that she was comfortable with. No doubt the Drake trading agent for the Canda system felt quite justified on the basis of some combination of "everybody does it," "the rules are unfair," and "I deserved better than to be sent to this backwater." Possibly even "I'm out here with only a small staff and I'd be dead long before the fleet got here if I made a fuss." But the corruptibility of human beings was a bit shocking to intelligent artificial brains too.

"In any case, we will slip into the Drake trading lanes with little notice and be allowed to trade with only the occasional bribe. Canda system has one marginally habitable planet, Candahar, and three rich asteroid belts. Most of the population still lives in orbital habitats, but that is changing. Even lots of habitats don't have the room that a planetary surface has."

While *Pandora* spoke, Checkgok went to a console and pulled up information on the Canda system. The information was a bit Earth-centric to its mind, but it was able to translate to its own measurements.

Candahar gravity, .88 Earth normal.

Atmosphere 12 psi at sea level, slightly higher oxygen and CO_2 content and lower nitrogen content than Earth, more argon and methane so you can live on the surface, but if you don't wear a filter mask you will develop lung problems.

Water is liquid in the tropical zones but not very far into the temperate zones. Most of the five million people on the surface live on three roughly Australia-size continents that are near the equator. If they were to heat the planet enough to melt most of the glaciation, it would become a water world with no surface land. Even Mount Justin, the tallest peak on the planet, would be over a hundred feet underwater.

There are a variety of life forms that are native to the seas and ice packs of Candahar, though most are limited to the sea. The ground is covered by a thin layer of moss where Terran plants haven't taken over, but the giant warm-blooded crabs of Candahar's seas are considered a major delicacy. The silkweeds, a sort of under ice sea life, produce a very fine silk in a wide variety of colors. In spite of that, the main exports of the Canda system are manufactured goods made in stations in the asteroid belts and Kuiper belts, and some raw materials.

"My people," Checkgok said, "love the silk. It is impossible to dye it, so the colors are natural, but bright, and it is very durable. Even the small ones can't dirty it."

The life cycle of a Parthian was decidedly odd. Breeders birthed live young into pools. The young at that stage had no exoskeleton and little in the way of bones, sort of a cross between a fish and a worm. But they would eat anything, even each other. So the clans separated them into individual pools, where they were fed and raised for a few years until they became amphibious and started growing a flexible cartilaginous shell, at which point their education began. At that stage of their development, they were still pretty much utterly dependent on the hive. Over the course of more years, they grew larger and the difference in size between male non-breeders, the smallest, male breeders, female non-breeders, and the largest, female breeders, became apparent, and their exoskeletal structure hardened. *Pan* accessed her records. The silk was used as rugs and wall hangings in the quarters of the amphibious phase, and in room hangings for the adults.

"That's fine. You are the master trader, both for your clan and for the ship," *Pan* said. "We will also need to replace several of the servos that are in less than good repair. And we have no cash. What are you planning to trade?"

"Parthian filters," Checkgok said. "They are one of our better biotech items. They let oxygen and CO2 through, but should . . ." Checkgok paused and looked up something. "Yes, they will stop methane. And they can be shaped readily."

Pan looked up the filter material in the cargo manifest. They had about three hundred tons of the stuff and it was in light, thin sheets. It would make a lot of filter masks for the weight. "That might well be. I don't happen to know what they are using for their filters at the moment, but it looks pretty good. We should produce some filter masks for you and Captain Gold, anyway. It looks like they will stop a lot more than methane."

Checkgok agreed.

Parthians had two slots to either side of their mouth-hands. They were near the upper shell and they inhaled through one and exhaled through the other. They had what amounted to voice boxes in both openings and the resonance of the lungs affected the voice of the inhaling voice box. Their speech was a combination of clicks and whistles, but they could do a decent imitation of human words.

Location: Concordia Free Space
Standard Date: 02 01 630

Danny Gold woke slowly and checked his to-do list. It was shorter than usual. They bought some replacement parts at Concordia and *Pan* was using them to good effect. The list was shorter, but by no means eliminated. He would get to those in a bit. First, he slipped on the skull cap interface. It wasn't necessary since his genetic engineer parents built a radio communications unit into his skull, but the cap made the connection clearer and less subject to data loss.

Cap on, he faded into the ship and felt *Pan* flexing her magnetic wings as she swam for the first jump point. Danny let himself feel the pull of space on the flexing wing as though it were currents of water he was swimming through. He tried to feel where the space was denser or thinner. It wasn't something he could describe to someone who couldn't interface with a hypership, but when those mighty magnetic wings pushed against space, zero-point energy pushed back, and how hard it pushed back was a function of the shape of space.

From Concordia to Canda system was a month of travel time. Danny intended to enjoy it. He liked looking for jump points, even when he didn't find any. With each sweep of each wing, the shape of space, the currents of space, shifted, and somehow his mind could reach out and feel what space was going to be like a bit farther out.

He was looking for the flush spots, where the waves of compression balanced out to a smooth, flat area. That was where you found jump points. Not in all of them, but a lot. There were, in any given cubic AU, hundreds of them. Most of them were short range, from a few light hours to a few light months, but—occasionally—you ran into one that took you light years. That was what made Concordia Station its money. It had two nearby jumps that went four and seven light years, respectively. The one to Canda was the four-light-year jump, and it was three days travel to a six-light-month jump that came out in a six jump gray route that linked to an official Drake-registered jump route that led to the Canda Kuiper belt.

But there didn't seem to be any of the flat spots in the offing. Danny wasn't really surprised. This area had to have been thoroughly searched out. If there were any jumps, they would be in the rutters downloaded from the station. With a sigh, Danny took off the cap and got up, cleaned up, got dressed, and went out to the galley for breakfast.

* * *

Checkgok was slurping up some foul-smelling gunk, then, using its mouth-hand to type on the keyboard, accessing data.

Danny thanked his makers for the improved control of his gag reflex and went about fixing his breakfast. It wasn't that Checkgok was sloppy or anything. It was just that its hand and its mouth were the same body part and, to Danny, it seemed like it was slobbering all over the keyboard. "What are your plans for today, Checkgok?"

"I am trying to determine the most likely products for sale and purchase at Canda system. Which would be helped if we knew where we were going from there." The right eye stalk lifted in what Danny took to be a look of inquiry.

"To an extent, that is going to be up to you. We are going to take you home, but I don't think going there directly is the best option. We need to buy and sell cargo and build up more goods. You need more experience with humans. Where do you want to go from Canda?"

"I am not certain yet, Captain, but I will research the matter and have an answer for you soon."

"That's fine, but don't set it in concrete. Things come up and we may have to divert. You know that the jump points change over time, some of them unpredictably. We may have to divert around a block."

"Yes, Captain."

Not having much else to say, Danny ate his breakfast and went to work, managing servos in ship's maintenance. Around noon, ship's time, he merged with the ship again and felt the space.

"*Pan*, can we speed up a bit?" Danny's interface fed him the data. They were accelerating at .7 standard gravity, fast enough to walk around easily but not really pushing. On the other hand, going faster would mean more hydrogen fed to the wings, and fuel cost was an issue.

"If necessary, Captain."

"Do you feel the pressure increase from the right dorsal wing?"

"Yes, Captain," *Pandora* agreed with no noticeable pause.

"I think the jump point for the Canda route may close early this season."

"It is possible, Captain, but the station rutters say it's good for another three weeks."

"Maybe," Danny Gold said to his ship. "But maybe not. Pile on the Gs, *Pan*. I don't want to be caught here for months, waiting for the gate to reopen." There was a short pause while *Pan* warned Checkgok, then the gravity started to increase as *Pan* accelerated faster.

Jump points moved over time, and jump points could close for a while, then reopen, or they could close permanently. Jump points that closed cyclically were called gates. The Canda route from Concordia started with a gate, open about three-quarters of Concordia's year, which was about eight standard months. But space had a kind of weather, more than simply orbital cycles. There were differences in the density of dust and radiation. Those differences could affect the shape of space and, in doing so, close a jump or open one. Whatever was causing it, it felt to Danny like the gate was going to close a little early this cycle.

* * *

Three days later, traveling at 1.2 standard gravities, they were still ahead of the wave front and riding the pressure wave as they approached the jump point. *Pan*'s forward wing set flapped A wing, then B, C, and D. By the time forward C was flapping, so was mid A, and then aft B, in a choreographed dance that swept the space around the ship free of debris, from small rocks down to subatomic particles, and *Pan* felt every particle as a pressure on her wings. So Pan sailed through truly empty space, and as she reached the jump point the wings grabbed even harder, because they swept the dust from both ends of the jump.

It was that sweeping clear that made the jump possible. With nothing in either space and the shapes of both bits of space congruent, they effectively became the same space. Pan shifted the magnetic potentials of her wings and she was at the far end of the jump.

Once through, of course, the stars were different and aside from the jump point itself, which was never more than a light second across—and in this case less than a tenth of a light second—the shape of space was different.

Location: Free Space Big Dark
Standard Date: 02 01 630

Deep in interstellar space, *Pan* looked around, her sensors alert. However others felt, she was always nervous at jump. She couldn't sense what was on the other side of the jump until she was through it, and to a being that lived her life constantly seeing light years in most directions, the blindness—however short its duration—was frightening. In this case, as in almost all others, there was nothing within light seconds of them.

They were just where they were supposed to be, 4.02 light years to the galactic north, spinward. *Pan* flexed her C and D wings and began shifting onto course for jump point 32,321,392.

On board *Pandora*, it felt a little like a ship heeling or a car taking a fairly gentle curve. Internal gravity was provided by the ship's thrust, and the limiting factor was the number of standard gravities that the passengers, crew, and cargo could take.

Standard Date: 02 04 630

Three days into the trip to the next jump point, Danny noticed a dip in the compression that wasn't what he expected. Danny felt the space around the *Pan* through his interface. He felt the pressure as the wings flapped through space, throwing plasma back. But it wasn't just the plasma. The shape of space itself produced a noticeable pressure against the wings. What Danny was feeling was a change in the wings' energy draw. Six of the wings were shifting through space a touch easier than they should, like a propeller that was cavitating.

"*Pan*, bring us about two points up for the next hour or so. I want a feel of the lane here." What Danny was hoping for was a new jump point, one that might get them closer to Canda, quicker. What they found, after about three hours of shifting course back and forth, up and down, was what looked like a jump in the wrong direction. There was only one way to tell, though, and that was to go through the jump and see.

"Do we try it?" Danny asked *Pan*.

"We have cargo for Canda," *Pan* replied.

"No. We have cargo that we figure on selling at Canda. That's not quite the same thing." Danny considered. "But we probably ought to ask Checkgok what it thinks. While going through that jump isn't dangerous, there is some risk."

* * *

Checkgok, working in the galley, was not overly enamored of the notion. One eyestalk pointed at Danny, while the other maintained its focus on the screen and its mouth-hand continued to hunt and peck across the keyboard. "It is a ridiculous waste of time. We spend weeks searching for this hypothetical jump point and even if we find it, it will probably only take us a few light minutes or perhaps light hours. And we are already in route to a jump that will carry us six light months in the direction we wish to go."

"But a new jump route could open up new trade routes and offer us increased profits," Danny said, opening the fridge to pull out a juice.

"Possible, but not probable," *Pandora* chimed in. "Over ninety-eight percent of jumps are short range, from a few light hours to a few light months. Long jumps like the Concordia links are rare, and even the six-light-month jumps like the one we are heading for are not overly common."

"Come on, *Pan*. We found the shortcut to Concordia Station just that way," Danny tried to argue, though it wasn't a very good argument and he knew it. But what else could he say? They were right. He could order the *Pandora* to go look and she would, and Checkgok would go along, whether it wanted to or not. But Danny had agreed to take on the Parthian's responsibilities, and he was serious about fulfilling his obligation. So, grumpily, after a little more argument, he agreed, and they went on to the known jump point. But as they passed, he had *Pan* adjust her flapping to try and get the best feel for the location of the possible jump point.

Pan recorded the most likely location in her rutter. Her rutter was more like the rutters of the early days of sea travel than the later charts, because jumps and jump routes are shortcuts that bypass large amounts of space. You couldn't draw a chart of such routes because they didn't go through three-dimensional space. You could draw lines between the ends of the jump points, but that wouldn't be an accurate representation, because even a few light days takes a very long time to travel at the sort of speeds that even the best ships could reach. The good news was that there were flows to the jump points. They had a tendency to clump together, with several of them going in roughly the same direction. So most of the time, there were alternate jump routes between given points. Known jump points could often be bypassed by finding a string of nearby jumps to get you to the same place.

CHAPTER 6

Biochemistry and the interactions of species to chemical and other physiological stimuli are made more complex and difficult to interpret by intelligence. The natural desire to follow a scent trail or pet a fellow sentient are often masked by cultural prohibitions and taboos.
From Parthian Sexual Mores by Eric Lock, MPD
Standard Date: November 23, 674

Location: Canda outsystem, Drake
Standard Date: 02 16 630

Canda was a star still two light days away when they exited the jump into the system. They were met by a Canda system patrol boat. "We have a request for ID, Captain," *Pan* said.

"Send the standard ID for Drake space," Danny told her. "And ask for the news."

"Their skipper wants to talk to you."

"Put 'em on," Danny said.

"Welcome, *Pandora*," said a male voice. "I'm Commodore Johnson of the Canda System Patrol."

"Howdy, Commodore. Danny Gold, captain of the *Pandora*, here. What can I do for you?"

"What news from Drakar?"

"I haven't got a clue, Commodore. I was out scouting routes and went right by it without stopping."

"Find anything?"

"Nothing faster than the standard."

"Perhaps we could share rutters?"

"Is the Canda system planning on getting into trade?"

"I wish," the commodore said, and Danny figured he and Checkgok were in good shape for their trading. The Canda system was no happier about the Drakes controlling their trade than he'd expected.

"What sort of cargo do you have on board, Captain Gold?"

"I sent them a manifest," *Pan* said.

"You should have our manifest, Commodore," Danny said, thinking about the situation here. The Drakes were even worse than the Cordobas about controlling access to the rest of the universe. Everything had to travel on Drake-licensed hulls and a planetary government didn't get licensed. The jump-capable Spaceforce of Canda couldn't trade with other worlds controlled by the Drakes because the Drakes would consider that smuggling and might even decide it was an act of war. They could use the mapped short jumps to get around their system, but unless they found a gray route they were stuck, which was probably why the commodore wanted *Pan*'s rutters. He was looking for a way around the Drake checkpoints.

"These are some interesting items, Captain. Where did you get the filter material?"

"You'd want to talk to our trader about that. It's a Parthian worker from the Zheck clan, name of Checkgok. Its people are pretty good at biotech. Checkgok, why don't you tell the commodore about the filters?"

Parthia was located in a Cordoba chain, so it was going to be clear that someone had crossed from Cordoba space to Drake space. On the other hand, *Pan* and the helpful folks on Concordia Station had produced excellent documentation that Checkgok and his cargo had amicably shifted from the *Fly Catcher* to the *Pan* two systems the other side of Drakar. And what the *Fly Catcher* was doing there was none of Danny's business.

Location: Pandora, Candahar Orbit, Drake Space
Standard Date: 02 19 630

After an actual physical inspection of the holds, which seemed a bit excessive to Danny, they were directed to a jump chain that would take them into the Canda system proper, and they finally made orbit around Candahar three days later.

Checkgok was getting irritable, and it didn't know why. It threw itself into the work of trading with the monkeys . . . humans . . . and tried to ignore their ugliness.

The system industry was located in the Kuiper belt and the asteroid belts, on large space stations where everything from gravity to pressure could be controlled. They built molecular circuitry and servos, plus thousands of other goods. Many of the goods were amazingly cheap, but not noticeably different from the same thing bought in any of a hundred other systems. The unique things were mostly from the planet, where billions of years of separate evolution had produced biologicals that were not anything that a genetic engineer would imagine.

* * *

Checkgok, irritable as it was, waved its eyestalks in tentative agreement. "Yes, Captain, Clan Zheck is responsible for operating expenses and the debt and interest payments are part of that. But payments made now will amount to transferring part of your debt to SMOG to the Zheck clan."

That was fair, so Danny nodded and called the local SMOG branch on Candahar Station, and arranged a payment on the loan, enough to keep the local SMOG branch from initiating repossession of the *Pandora*. Loan payments, due to the simple fact of distance in space, tended to be flexible. The interest, however, was exorbitant. Payments made every time the ship was near a SMOG branch kept Danny and *Pandora* in space. Too many avoidances of the SMOG branches would lead to them repossessing *Pandora*.

Location: Pandora, Candahar Orbit, Drake Space
Standard Date: 02 27 630

Danny was lying on his back on the bridge floor with a pair of pliers and a sensor pack, adjusting the tension on his accel couch stand. His couch was sticking, and that wouldn't do if the *Pan* needed to shift course in a hurry.

Pan brought up Checkgok's irritability. "I am worried about Checkgok's mood, Captain."

"Are you sure that's not normal for it?" Danny asked. He sat up as *Pan* answered.

"I can't be certain, but its attitude here doesn't match its attitude from the records of the *Fly Catcher*. And it has been getting progressively worse since we left Concordia."

"And just how did you come into possession of the records of the *Fly Catcher*?" The bridge was a small room located near the bow A wing. All of the crew quarters were located around the outer edge of the bow, so that gravity could be simulated by spinning the ship. As was the case now, in orbit around the planet Candahar, seven hundred kilometers behind Candahar Station.

"I stole them," *Pan* said, with not the least hint of regret or apology in her tone. "You know perfectly well that we should have gotten all the cargo from the *Fly Catcher*. I just wanted to see what they were up to."

"And what were they up to?"

"It's a little hard to tell since they are an alien species with different biological imperatives, but they seem to have been trying to make the *Fly Catcher* into its own clan, with the captain and first mate as the breeders of the clan. I don't know why, since all the Parthian Bangers in the universe weren't going to make the captain and first mate fertile."

Danny laughed. "Well, we don't do it just to have babies, either. At least not most of the time."

"But it wasn't the whole crew that used the Bangers. Just the captain and first mate. Even the records show that the captain was thinking of itself as female. Not neuter female, female. The personal pronoun that she used for herself equated to she, not it. While Checkgok is insistent on the use of neuter female. Or, in English, it."

Danny and *Pan* examined the question some more but, not having any solid evidence, didn't come to any conclusions.

Location: Canda Outsystem, Drake Space
Standard Date: 02 28 630

A small part of *Pandora*'s attention was on the Parthian as it used its mouth-hand on the keyboard. It was watching two screens, one showing fuel consumption and other consumables, the other showing a jump map of the route to Bonks. While the information was there, it didn't rise to the level of consciousness until the Parthian spoke.

"Canda to Bonks is fifteen jumps," Checkgok said.

Pandora didn't say anything. That statement was incomplete, but true as far as it went. Besides, the number of jumps was less important than the distance between them. Finally, it was a statement, not a question, and *Pandora* wasn't sure it was directed at her, though there was no one else in the galley at the moment.

"That will entail how much time?" Checkgok asked.

"Approximately three weeks, if there are no problems."

"What sort of problems?" Checkgok took one of its eyes off the small screens and focused it on the main screen, the same place where Danny looked when he spoke to *Pandora* when he was in the galley.

"Sometimes jumps close for no known reason. That generally means taking a longer route around the blockage. Also, the Drake and Cordoba trading houses sometimes set up custom patrols along the main routes, making it wiser to find an alternate. If it's necessary to take an alternate route, that could add from a week to a month to the travel time."

"How likely is that?"

"Taken all together, there is perhaps a one in twenty chance that we will have to divert."

Checkgok's left eyestalk, the one looking at the big screen, bobbed. "That will work well enough then." There was a pause. Then the Parthian said, "Why is the ship so empty? Do humans need so much space?"

"The ship is designed for a crew of from ten to twenty," *Pandora* said.

"Why? From what I have seen, you could run the ship and the shuttles all by yourself. Leaving Captain Gold safely on a planet or a station while you did the trading."

"Some ships were made to do that, but it was never common," *Pan* explained. "For one thing, most people would rather be doing something. For another, this ship is as much a home as a means of transport." *Pan* didn't mention the third reason. Most people didn't trust artificial brains on their own.

"In that case, why is there only the captain?"

"There are a number of reasons," *Pan* said, trying to decide how much to explain. Ultimately, she decided to give the Parthian the whole story. "Captain Gold is a fair man, but not the best manager in the universe. And the restrictions that the trading houses put on the trade routes can cut deeply into the profit made by a cargo hauler. Also, when Captain Gold received title to the *Pandora*, there was already a considerable debt attached to the ship. A debt that he was able to make payments on but not significantly decrease.

"Then, we were stopped three years ago by a Cordoba family patrol ship, carrying what they chose to see as contraband. The fines and bribes left Captain Gold somewhat in the red and short of cargo. The captain likes searching out jump routes, and we have spent considerable time following cul de sacs to their ends, which means no profit for the ship, of course.

"But there are still the expenses of fuel, maintenance, and paying the crew, all of which left us farther in the red, and we had to let some of the less essential crew go. Which meant more work for the others, and an increasing level of dissatisfaction among them. Then there were a couple of bad trades, and it became a choice between paying crew and buying fuel, so more crew was let go. It became a downward spiral."

Checkgok nodded both his eyestalks in understanding. "Breeders are not really suited for management but, unfortunately, they often think they are."

Pandora forebore to comment on that statement, and after a moment Checkgok asked another question. "So what is the proper complement of crew?"

"I was designed for a crew of ten. Two shuttle pilots, an engineer and an assistant engineer, a cargo officer and two cargo hands, a cook and a captain to run it all. With suggested additions of a ship's merchant, first mate, ship's boy or girl, and general hands as needed. The original designers planned for a family-owned ship where the family would be the crew. I can hold up to twenty persons comfortably."

Pandora moved one of the drones into the galley. "As you can see, several of the drones that Captain Gold and I control are jerry rigged to let the captain and I do jobs that should, by preference, be handled by crew."

The drone was uncovered. Its motors, pulleys, and cables visible and greasy. This was a welder drone that carried three arc welders of varying power and configuration. *Pandora* or Danny could use one welder at a time.

There were six hundred square meters of floor space located near the front of the ship. That was just living space and didn't include hydroponics, the shops or the bridge. It was divided into twenty rooms—each with their own head, including toilet and shower or bath—as well as a kitchen and a lounge that were shared by all.

Checkgok waved a mid-limb. "That is still more room per person than Parthians would need, and what you have is just the captain and the trader, with you or the captain doing all the other jobs. Should I be taking on some of those jobs?"

"What are you qualified to do? Aside from the role of trader?"

"I am not sure. I am strong and my mouth-hand is capable of delicate work. But I lack the direct neural interface that is so common among humans. I would find it difficult to operate a drone as you do."

"That is a problem. How did they manage on the *Fly Catcher*?" Most ships that didn't use artificial brains had human crew interfacing directly with the wing controllers. A wing could operate in automatic mode, but it was a bit like tying down a rudder on an old sailing ship. It made normal space flight both more dangerous and less efficient and was especially problematic in making jumps.

"The *Fly Catcher* had a crew of sixty-three. It was a smaller ship. I was supercargo, and that was all." That didn't really explain it, but was probably all the explanation that Checkgok had.

"In that case, for now at least, you will remain simply the master trader. Though there are educational programs, and we can look into the possibility of getting you the implants, if you like."

"I am willing to learn, but implants . . . I would prefer not."

Pandora sighed internally. "That is a shame. We were down to our last couple of drones when we hit Concordia. We managed to get a few more after you joined us, but we can still use all the help we can get."

"We should hire more crew," Checkgok said.

"Money is still tight, and we have to make another payment when we get to Bonks."

"That is a false economy," the Parthian said pompously. "We will need the extra crew, or more of your systems will become compromised. The Zheck clan will undertake the cost of hiring the necessary additional crew."

Location: Bonks Orbital Station Kiva, Drake Space
Standard Date: 03 20 630

The diner was in much better shape than the bar back on Concordia. All the emitters were operational and it had real wall coverings that matched the projections. It was about ten meters wide with booths and tables, and at this time of day wasn't very crowded. The lock was open and large enough to fit two humans abreast, so Checkgok could fit. Danny checked that before they left the ship. Most stations weren't designed for people the size of a small pony. Checkgok was less massive than a pony, but it was wider.

A skinny, dark-haired girl of about ten, dressed in syntho cloth—old syntho, at that—met them at the lock and led them to a table off to the side. Checkgok made it without bumping into anyone, but only by virtue of other patrons getting out of its way.

The table the girl showed them to was square, and she and Danny moved it over to make room for Checkgok to squat next to it. Then, handing them menu slates, she headed for the kitchen.

Bonks, also in Drake space, was mostly an ag world. There were a wide variety of foods, some Old Earther and some native to Bonks. They wanted to let Checkgok try those foods that tested safe for it so that they could see what his people would find tasty.

The diner was a spacer's sort of place, with fresh foods shipped up from the planet's surface, all designed to give a spacer a taste of planet-grown food.

"What can I get you?" the girl asked when she returned to them with a carafe of water and two glasses. She carefully avoided looking at the weird creature with the eyestalks.

"A little of everything," Danny said, noting that she had a crooked front tooth and blue eyes. "We're trying to figure what Checkgok here will like. Plug in Parthian and leave out anything likely to cause one problems."

The girl finally looked at Checkgok. "Does he have teeth?"

"It," Danny corrected. "The proper form of address for a neuter Parthian is 'it.' I don't know why they care, but they do."

"Neuters, whether male or female, are the ones who do the work of the clan. Not that the breeders aren't important but, really, they are just there to make more Parthians," Checkgok said.

"Personally, I think it's something like an old sergeant saying. 'Don't call me sir. I work for a living,' " Danny confided to the girl, and Checkgok's mouth drew up. Which was a bad sign. At first Checkgok was friendly, and if it didn't get the joke, it asked. But it was getting more and more tense of late, and Danny was starting to get worried.

The girl fetched the cook. "John, come see what we can do, will you?"

The cook came out of the kitchen. "John Gabriel," he said, extending his hand to shake. "What can I do for you?"

After some discussion of the flavors that Checkgok liked and didn't like, the cook returned to his kitchen and started preparing foods. Parthians had different taste buds that responded to different chemical signatures. Salt, sweet, sour, and bitter weren't in their palate, at least not the same as they would be in a human. Starch was a flavor to them and so were several things that made no sense to a human palate. After a few dishes, John said that there was something in jalapeños that worked on them like sugar worked on people and, on the other hand, sugar tasted to them something like bitter flavor to humans. "A little is fine, but not much. Have you tried coffee?"

"Yes. I like it best if it is brewed hot for a longer time than most humans like. But it doesn't act as a stimulant. If anything, it tends to put me to sleep."

"So, what if we try adding the jalapeños to the coffee?" John asked.

Danny shuddered at the thought, but looked over at Checkgok. "What do you think?"

Checkgok's mouth-hand scrunched up toward its body. "I do not think the two flavors would go well together," it said. "I suspect the coffee would overwhelm the jalapeños."

The girl piped up with a question. "What does it mean when you scrunch up your, ah, mouth like that?"

"Don't interrupt, girl, and don't ask impertinent questions," John said. "Don't take offense, folks. The girl's space happy and it's my fault. All the stories I've told her of traveling the spaceways."

"Are you a spacer?" Danny asked.

"That I am, Skipper," John said. "I have ratings in ship's cook and hydroponics. And I've been teaching Jenny."

"Your daughter?"

"Nothing so official as that." John shrugged. "She's a stray from the station disaster a couple of years back."

"Station disaster?"

"Someone got a bit frisky with an asteroid and an orbital station got trashed. They had some warning and got almost everyone off the station, but that just meant that they were thirty thousand people with no place to go. They put them up on the planet, but they aren't citizens of planet Bonks and lack the protection of Bonks citizenship. Planetside work turned out to be a bit difficult to get. Between being used to an orbital habitat and the fact that most of the available work was already taken by planetary citizens, there are a lot of strays.

"Anyway, Jenny's folks didn't get off the station and she was living in one of the camps. When she showed up at the restaurant I was cooking at then . . ." John's voice trailed off.

"You're a spacer. What were you doing groundside?"

"I was afraid I was going space happy. I started having nightmares about the enviro going. So I took a break on the planet and just never made it back past this station. Only reason I took this job was because Jenny wanted off Bonks."

John Gabriel was an older man with short black hair starting to show a little salt in the pepper, and lines around his eyes. There was a tattoo peeking out from below his short sleeve. It was a ship with the wings done in luminescent ink. But Danny couldn't see enough of it to be sure what type of ship. Absent genetic engineering, Danny would have guessed his age at sixty, but he was probably twice that. Jenny seemed to be pretty devoted to the old guy.

Checkgok looked, turned one eye to the cook and the other to the girl. "Is she old enough to breed?"

"What?"

"I assumed you adopted her into your clan so that you would have a female breeder. But from the tapes I've seen, she seems quite young. Wouldn't you have been better off adopting an older female?"

"I didn't need a breeder of any sort. I took the girl in 'cause she needed a place to stay."

"Now I must apologize, John," Danny said. "Checkgok doesn't understand the customs of humans. This is its first trip away from Parthia.

"Humans make our clans in a different way than your people do," Danny told Checkgok. "We often adopt children without concerning ourselves with the benefit to the clan."

"Why?"

"For decency's sake," said John.

"Monkeys have little concept of decency," Checkgok said.

"Why are you so mad?" Jenny asked.

The Parthian swiveled both eyestalks to look at her and stopped. "I don't know. There is no reason for it, but I feel nervous and threatened. I have been feeling that way since a few days after I left the *Fly Catcher*, but I . . . don't understand why."

"Could be chemical," John suggested. "Something missing from, or added to, your diet or the air?"

"It's possible, but what?"

"I don't know, but you folks better figure it out before you head back out into the big dark."

"Perhaps you could help us, Spacer. Gabriel, isn't it?" Checkgok said.

"Aye. Able Spacer John Gabriel, and Jenny Starchild, my apprentice. I never shipped with a Parthian, but I once shipped with a Cattan as a passenger."

Catta was a world of amphibious intelligent creatures who had developed interstellar travel on their own, though not the jump drive. They used slow ships and took upwards of fifty years to get between their home world and their colonies, all two of them. They were highly intelligent, but also highly individualistic. They were famous among humans as the most arrogant and disagreeable race yet discovered. They became friendly even with each other only about three months out of their year. The rest of the time they were solitary. It was said that a Catta could only stand even other Catta when they were in heat.

"Turns out that if you feed a Catta a certain mix of foods, nuoc mam and chocolate, they get . . . well, not friendly exactly. Just a bit less insulting."

"What were you doing with a Catta on board in the first place?" Danny asked.

"He was going to redesign a power plant on Diskay Station. He was some sort of expert on the production of antimatter."

Antimatter was known and used in some very concentrated power plants, though it was considered very dangerous. "That might be worth putting up with one," Danny acknowledged. "How did you figure out what to feed it? I mean nuoc mam and chocolate don't go together like peanut butter and jelly."

"A bit of trial and error and a bit of questioning. It seems that female Catta secrete a kind of mucus that smells a lot like nuoc mam at that time of the year and there is a plant on their world that has some similarities to chocolate. It's actually a fair chocolate substitute, and they export it for that. Turns out, putting the two together makes the Catta feel like they are in the presence of a member of their race that is in its female cycle, so it's on its best behavior. Not that Catta behavior is ever what you could call polite."

Danny used one of the features that his family built into him and contacted the *Pan*. *"Can we afford a cook?"*

Pan sent back through station net, *"Yes. Checkgok has informed me that Clan Zheck will undertake to pay for reasonable crew as part of its agreement to handle running expenses."*

"I figured that. I was just wondering if we had the cash on hand."

"Yes, Captain, we do."

"Would you be interested in a berth, John?" Danny asked.

"If you have one for Jenny, I would."

"We have room for a ship's girl and the *Pan* is a good teacher."

"The *Pan* is a good teacher? Your ship has an artificial brain?"

"Yes," Danny said, waiting to see how spacer John Gabriel would react. Ship brains weren't that common and not every spacer was willing to ship out on a vessel that was run by a ship brain.

"What sort of a ship brain is she?"

"Custom job, worked up by Congreve Shipping, with extensive mods."

John nodded agreement.

And so it was done. There was more discussion and the owner of the station restaurant made noises like he was going to sue. But he had no grounds and knew it.

"Stock up on anything you can think of, John," Danny said. "We need to figure out if we can calm Checkgok down a bit."

Location: Pandora, in orbit off Station Kiva
Bonks System, Drake Space
Standard Date: 03 20 630

Jenny Starchild's hand reached for the grabrail automatically as she exited the shuttle into the *Pandora* proper. She pulled herself along the corridor with her kit floating behind her, following the directions given by the voice. With only a nervous glance back at John, she looked around.

This was luxury. The lifestyle of a struggling spacer was frightening in the raw wealth it employed from the perspective of an orphaned refugee from the slums of Port Thidis on Bonks. Spacers never went hungry from lack of the money to buy food. They never lacked for a safe and comfortable place to sleep. They had access to holo dramas, games, and entertainment from across the spaceways. Even much of their work was managing robotic servants.

This was what she'd wanted, and more than she'd thought she'd ever get. Even at ten Jenny knew full well that the universe was a dangerous place, and as she turned the corner into the lounge her busy mind was looking for the catch, the hidden flaw that would snatch it all away again. By the time they went around the corner to the corridor that led to her room, the voice was asking her questions. "I'll work hard. You won't be sorry," Jenny assured *Pandora* a little desperately.

"Tell me about your background and education."

"After the accident, I went to the school in the refugee camp just north of the port."

"And what did you learn there?"

Jenny explained that Old Earth was a place of great sin and debauchery, and that the true followers of the thirty-seven billion aspects of God had emigrated from there to Bonks and had been rewarded for their hard work and faith by great wealth and higher caste. And Jenny too, in a later life, might find higher caste if she was hardworking and faithful in this one.

She and *Pandora* continued to talk, and Jenny told *Pandora* about the Bonks system.

* * *

Jenny's education level was, in *Pandora*'s opinion, atrocious. *Pan* wasn't expecting another Danny Gold, who had been designed to be a superman. In some ways, Danny *was* that superman. He could learn and comprehend at a tremendous rate. He would put the average Olympic gymnast to shame, if he could be bothered to compete, and could lift upwards of four times his weight without straining. But he rarely bothered to use any of his gifts.

Jenny Starchild, *Pandora* learned over the space of a few days, was just the opposite. She wasn't stupid. Actually, she was on the bright side of average. But Jenny *worked*. She worked hard at everything and started to worry anytime she didn't have work to do. *Pandora* tried to alleviate that nervousness through intensive education, and quickly learned that Jenny was quite interested in the history of spaceflight.

Meanwhile, after three days, they still hadn't figured out what to do about Checkgok. They had already offloaded what they planned on selling here, made a partial payment on the loan, and onloaded most of what they had bought. Station fees were eating into their profits.

Location: Pandora, in orbit off Station Kiva
Bonks System Drake Space
Standard Date: 03 22 630

Checkgok squatted in its usual spot in the ship's lounge with its mouth-hand switching between the keyboard and a salad of eggs and chopped kesle plants with a garnish of jalapenos when the little female breeder wandered in. It was focused on its work and so ignored her until she spoke.

"How did you get hired on to *Pandora*, Checkgok?" Jenny asked.

Checkgok started to snap at the irritating little monkey but restrained itself with difficulty. It knew intellectually that this was an immature human, and as such was supposed to ask questions of her elders, but it still felt like an intrusion.

Everything felt like an intrusion, the next thing to an attack, and it had no clan members to support it.

Checkgok took a breath, centered itself and answered. "I was . . ." It stopped, unsure of how to proceed. It had been . . . ah . . . "I was under the influence of pheromones that were being produced by Captain Gold."

"Captain Gold produces pheromones?" Jenny wasn't sure what pheromones were, but she knew the teachers at the refugee school disapproved of them, along with perfume and strong drink and a host of other things.

"Well, he did that day," Checkgok said. "He drank a Parthian Banger. I was never clear why a human would drink such a thing, but the authorities at Concordia Station felt it had intoxicated me."

"You were drunk?"

"In a sense, yes."

"John says that every once in awhile everyone needs to get a little drunk and blow off a little steam. Maybe you should get drunk again."

Again Checkgok felt like snapping at the child, but at its core it was dedicated to its notion of honor. Checkgok had a duty to this ship, and that meant it had a duty to this child, so it tried to explain gently why that was a stupid idea. But it couldn't. It didn't have enough information.

"Wait a moment, Jenny. *Pandora*, would you connect me to John Gabriel?"

"Connected."

"Spacer Gabriel, Jenny says that you have informed her that everyone needs to get drunk once in awhile to blow off steam. Is that an accurate assessment of your comments and do you think it might apply in my situation?"

There was a pause, then Spacer Gabriel said, "It certainly sounds like something I'd say, especially if I was a couple of wings to the solar wind."

Then another short pause. Monkeys thought slowly.

"You know, it just might be. When was the last time you got drunk?"

"It was drunk when it signed on, John," Jenny said. "On pheromones."

* * *

Danny and John were called to the galley, and after a bit more conversation and the inclusion of *Pandora* in the discussion, *Pandora*, John and Checkgok decided that a Banger needed to be tried. Jenny was all for it, because it was partly her idea.

Danny took more convincing.

"Do you know what those things do to my stomach?" he asked. "There's enough pepper in them to light your breath on fire."

"That is not the issue and you know it," *Pandora* said.

Danny looked, at that moment, like a little boy who had just been told he had to kiss his Aunt Hattie, Jenny thought, and found herself smiling.

"It isn't a truly sexual act, Danny," *Pandora* pointed out.

"Actually, it is fairly close to a sexual act if I understand human sexuality correctly," Checkgok said, not sounding happy.

"See? Even Checkgok knows this is creepy."

"That is not what I said," Checkgok pointed out. "You feel that way simply because in your species, sex and general support have gotten very confused. Naturally enough. For a species that is made up entirely of breeders, it is perfectly natural that you are all sex obsessed. But this would be analogous to grooming among your primates."

Jenny was watching the whole thing, curious and a little confused, until John insisted she go study and leave the adults to talk.

* * *

Danny looked around after Jenny was gone. "Okay," he said, not liking the way this was going but knowing they had to do something about Checkgok's mood. "Let's get down to it."

"For my people, the need to be around breeders is important," Checkgok admitted, with all the willingness that a maiden aunt might have when admitting that she had the hots for a teenage heart throb.

"So what I would be doing is faking that role. And there is no way you can say that's not twisted as all get out."

Danny's designers had, as much as anything else, designed him to breed productively. The genetic and prenatal triggers for male homosexuality were well known. Danny's whole line's chemistry had been adjusted to prevent it. Danny liked girls, and had endurance and a high sperm count, but was uncomfortable around males in sexual situations. In the process of tweaking and socialization, they had left him rather narrow in his tastes. He knew it was a problem, but both his genetics and his environment had left him, if not a prude, at least a little squeamish. He honestly didn't care what others did, but he really, really, didn't want to be involved.

"It is no more sexual than wearing cologne," *Pandora* insisted.

"Sure, but . . ." Danny stopped. He didn't want to tell Checkgok that he didn't want to turn it on. But he didn't want to reject the Parthian, not in the state it was in. "Do we even have the makings of a Parthian Banger?"

"Yes, most of them. And the rest can be acquired on station," *Pandora* told him.

"Oh, all right. But it still seems weird."

* * *

After a quick shuttle trip to the station, John arrived with the makings of a Parthian Banger. And, following the recipe in *Pandora*'s memory, he prepared the drink and a milk chaser.

Danny, ostentatiously holding his nose, lifted the wide mouthed glass to his lips and threw the drink back, then quickly downed the milk.

* * *

Checkgok wasn't sure what was going to happen and didn't like needing this, but that Captain Gold didn't like it either made Checkgok feel a little better about it. The captain wasn't being a pervert, as had been the case on the *Fly Catcher*. Here, on *Pandora*, it was just the captain taking care of crew. As was his duty.

The aroma relaxed Checkgok almost immediately. Everyone seemed of his clan, everyone safe and trustworthy.

The pheromone scent wore off slowly. For the next several days there was an aroma of a Parthian clan in the *Pandora*. Danny only exuded it for a day or so, but it lingered in the ship's environment. There was enough data for *Pan* to tie down the levels needed for optimum function, but it wasn't something the ship could create.

Location: Pandora, in orbit off Station Kiva
Bonks System, Drake Space
Standard Date: 03 24 630

Danny was lying in the accel couch on the bridge, operating one of the new drones that was fixing a scratch on the lower left cable of the C midship wing, when *Pandora* spoke up.

"We have enough supplies to fabricate a hundred Bangers, and by my estimate, one Banger every week to ten days should be sufficient to keep Checkgok comfortable," *Pan* told Danny. "We are topped up on fuel and have loaded all supplies and trade goods. It's time to leave, Captain."

Danny set the drone to auto and pulled himself half out of the link, shifting to a virtual presence in the lounge. John was behind the bar in the cooking area and Checkgok was in its usual place, working on the books. Jenny was there too, at a table going through a programmed learning text on her computer.

"Right. Where are we going?" Danny asked the group, but mostly Checkgok. *Pan* and Checkgok had been discussing trade routes for the last couple of days.

"The Jorgan system is seven days from here, assuming all goes well." *Pan* put up a jump route map that showed the vectors between the jumps and the known alternate routes. The route map looked something like the world's worst slalom course. The gates were the jump points, and if you missed one you didn't lose points. You had to go back around. The total distance between the jump points was a bit over an AU, but between them they would take the *Pan* almost nine light years in a little over a week, if all went well. If all didn't go well, there were a number of alternate routes that would get them to Jorgan but would take longer.

Pan continued. "Checkgok hopes that they will have good trading opportunities for its clan's goods."

Danny nodded and put on the skull cap. "All right. Call the station and get departure clearance, then take us out."

Location: Fly Catcher
Chaco System, Cordoba Space
Standard Date: 03 24 630

Captain Kesskox lowered her mouth-hand into the Parthian Banger and her first mate, Gokkox, did the same.

After swallowing the drink, Gokkox waved his mouth-hand vaguely in the direction of the station they were approaching, then clicked, "Do you think it's dead yet?" The syncopation of the clicks and whistles indicated regret, or even guilt.

It was a guilt that Kesskox didn't share, or at least didn't want to.

"Probably," she clicked back. "The stuck-up *fixk* was so afraid of pollution that it would balk at the human drinking another Banger, even if they thought of it." *Fixk* was a Parthian word that simply didn't translate into any human language. It suggested someone who was so tradition-bound as to be incapable of thought, and represented one of the mental illnesses that Parthians could be subject to. Sort of Mrs. Grundy to pathological proportions.

Gokkox scrunched his eyestalks and Kesskox stifled a midleg gesture that would be the equivalent of a human's derisive snort. One of the things she liked about Gokkox was his kindness. Even if, in this instance, she thought it was misplaced.

"Let it go. It's gone insane. Or if it hasn't, it will soon. At that point, it will kill the human or the human will kill it. And if it kills the human, the artificial will kill it. It's done. It will never go back to Parthia, and we will never have to deal with it again."

"And if Danny Gold wins and kills it?"

Kesskox did make the derisive midleg gesture then. "Oh, right. That will happen. Danny Gold wasn't going to take the goods back to Clan Zheck anyway. And with a dead Checkgok to explain, the monkey never will. But that's why we're taking the long way around through New Argentina. We can be sure that if they aren't in Parthia before we get there, they never will be.

"Now leave it, Gokkox. We have a few hours before we get to the station. Let's use them."

CHAPTER 7

A rutter is a listing of real space locations of jump points. Like the rutters of pre-chart seafaring days on Old Earth, the modern rutter is more a description of the route than a map. That is because the jumps turn space into something that simply cannot be adequately described in even three dimensional holo maps, much less two dimensional flat maps. To represent jump space in a map without inviting false assumptions about proximity of other routes, would take a number of dimensions greater than the number of jumps on the map.
The Use of Rutters, Captain Vernon Netteburg of the Pamplona Merchant Academy

Location: Drake Space, Big Dark, Standard Date: 03 27 630

"What are we doing, John?" Jenny asked, looking up from her study screen at the main screen of the lounge. They were two days out from Bonks and John was watching a repeat of the bridge graphic.

"We're looking for jump points," John told her. "Plug in and see."

Jenny made a face. Her implants were installed when she was seven, a few months before the station disaster, but there was very little chance to use them in the refugee camp on Bonks. So Jenny was out of practice and found the interface data kind of overwhelming. Instead of plugging in, she said, "I thought that took special ships."

"Not really," John said, then called up a study guide on how wings worked and how they were developed from solar sails back in the Sol System before the first jump. "Most of it's guessing right about where the jump point is. About the only way to tell for sure is to make a guess, then go there and see if there really is a jump point. You get a feel for space after a while. With practice." He pointed to the headset and continued as Jenny put it on.

Location: Drake Space Big Dark Standard Date: 03 27 630

Two more jumps and four hours later, Danny spotted a good possibility for an undiscovered jump that wasn't too far from their course. The *Pan* shifted course so they would pass through the jump point if it was there. Jenny, again in her headset, felt the difference in the feel of space when they reached the jump point. It was a section of space about a tenth of a light second or about thirty thousand kilometers across. The *Pan* was doing about three thousand kilometers a second, so they were in it for about ten seconds.

Jenny had time to feel *Pan*'s wings adjust to two sets of space. To feel the difference in the patterns of the space dust in the two places that were almost, but not exactly, congruent. Feel the dust in both chunks of space swept aside by the massively powerful magnetic fields.

What she couldn't feel, couldn't tell at all even with the augmentation, was *Pan* slipping from one chunk of congruent space to the other. There was no bump to it, no nothing. They were in one place with one set of stars, then in another with a slightly different set of stars.

Location: Drake Space Jorgan System Standard Date: 04 02 630

Checkgok started checking the net as soon as they emerged from the last jump and not finding a lot of potential trade. There were some robotics, but they were mostly specialized for mining and the orbital farms were growing precisely the same things that orbital farms grew all over the Pamplona Sector.

Jorgan system had no habitable planets, but it had millions of planetoids, ranging from a few microns to a few miles across. Which made it perfect for mining everything from gold to water.

"Captain Gold, there seems little point in continuing in-system here. There is little to buy and less to sell."

"Fine with me," Danny said. "It'll save us time to head back out-system now. What about processed ores, though? A bit of titanium, some gadolinium, perhaps? We might be able to pick them up in the out-system."

Checkgok looked at Danny for a moment and said it would look into it.

Location: Drake Space, Jorgan Oort Cloud
Standard Date: 04 04 630

Checkgok got a jump route to a planetoid about five hundred kilometers across. It was near the inner edge of the Jorgan systems oort cloud, about three light months out from the primary. The jump route was five well-aligned short jumps, so there wasn't much maneuvering involved and it only took a couple of days to make the trip.

The planetoid was owned by a family of deep space rock miners who got lucky. A good ten percent of the planetoid was titanium and it had decent deposits of scandium, yttrium, promethium and half a dozen more. The family consisted of three wives and four husbands with eight children and, in a sense, they lived in luxury. They had plenty of room and plants to produce breathable air. They had computers and games and equipment. Food and drink from the same gardens that gave them air. And atomic batteries, using the promethium to power lights and equipment. But they got a visit from a system freighter about once a year and were well behind on the news, because even the laser commo link took three months each way.

They didn't have a jump capable ship, so no one could leave, save when the annual freight hauler showed up, or the rare unscheduled stopover by a ship like the *Pan*.

Pan, just out of Bonks, was well-stocked with things like Bonks chicken thighs and five thousand gallons of Bonks homemade strawberry ice cream with real strawberries. Most of which ended up staying on the planetoid.

While Checkgok was being taken to the cleaners by Agness Sunderland, Danny and *Pan* played Rutter Tag with Elijah Sunderland.

"Have you got anything near locus— " Elijah used his implants to send a location to the others.

The rules of Rutter Tag were simple, though they depended at least some on trust. Each person at his turn was allowed to ask about any real space coordinate he chose, and the other players were required to answer honestly. There was no way of enforcing the honest answers, but there wasn't much point in asking about random points in space. You wanted jump points near one you knew about, so each question gave the other player information. And tradition among spacers was that you didn't lie when playing Rutter Tag.

"Just the one that led us here," *Pan* said. "And I assume you know that one."

"So, for our question, I'll ask the same," Danny added. "You know any others?"

"Yep. A cul de sac chain with three jumps." He gave the jump points and their exits. *Pan* entered them in her rutter. Then Elijah asked another question. There was very little overlap between Elijah Sunderland's rutter and *Pan* and Danny's. Elijah's was mostly local. He had a couple of side routes to nearby systems, and Danny gave him the cul de sac jump that they found on the way here. That seemed to please him.

Mostly it was a pleasant way to spend an evening. Elijah wasn't a spacer. He'd been a miner all his life and never been out of the Jorgan system, but collecting rutters was his hobby. So it was natural that most of what he had picked up was from local or semilocal transports.

Aside from the three jump cul de sac they got from Elijah, they also got the known orbits of a great deal of space junk in the vicinity.

* * *

Trading done and everyone back on board, Danny went to the bridge and lay down in his acceleration couch. "*Pandora*, plot the course back out."

"There may be an unmarked jump about three light minutes to the solar north, spinward," *Pan* said, sending him its coordinates, and showing the markers on the main screen.

Danny looked over the data she sent. "You figured this out from the data we got from Elijah, didn't you?" He added his own markers to the main screen.

"In part, Captain, but mostly from the data we collected coming in." She fed him another data set.

Danny nodded. "Two parts of the key. It's probably there, all right. Any guess where it will take us?"

"I am unsure, Captain."

"What about it, Checkgok? Shall we see if there is at least a useful jump?"

Checkgok hissed its equivalent of a sigh and said, "Very well, Captain, if we must," but its heart wasn't in the complaint. After Danny drank a Banger the day before, the Parthian was pretty mellow.

Location: Free space Gold Route, Big Dark,
Standard Date: 04 04 630

"Well that's interesting," Danny said, looking at the bridge screen. "What's the nearest known point, *Pan*? And put this up in the galley for Checkgok, John, and Jenny."

"Searching, Captain." Then a few moments later she threw a schematic of a jump route up on both screens. It was a series of connected lines in various colors. Each line represented a vector in real space from the exit of one jump to the entrance of the next. The main route was in Drake blue, then in Cordoba purple, but faded. The alternates were in green, the cul de sacs in red. As they watched, a new point was added in blinking white. From that point, a line in gold extended to one end of a line on a cul de sac route that connected to the main route on the Cordoba side.

Danny looked at the screen and grinned. "Isn't that the Old Granny?"

"Yes, Captain," said *Pan*.

"What are we looking at?" John asked from the galley.

"It seems the jump *Pan* found out of Jorgan got us close to an old cul de sac that was in *Pan*'s rutters. The cul de sac was off a gray route from Drake space to Cordoba space. It's called the Old Granny. It hits Cordoba space on the route between Hudson and Morland."

"You said a gray route. The Cordobas and the Drakes don't know about it?"

"Actually, they do," Danny said, smiling. "Someone blabbed to the Cordobas about thirty years ago. The Cordobas declared it off limits and when they have them free, they station a couple of customs cutters at F397 and seize any ship that comes through. F397 is on the Cordoba side of the longest jump in the Old Granny route, three and a half light years. But the cul de sac we're heading for is three jumps on the Cordoba side of F397. Unless they have a cutter on its way to F397, they won't see us. And even if they do have a cutter there, they probably won't see us. The cul de sac jump into the main route is two light minutes from the Morland jump and eighty light seconds from the F397 jump."

In a way finding a jump point was like buying a lottery ticket. The odds were way against drawing a winning number or a useful route. But there was a difference. The more jump routes you already knew in an area of space, the better your chances of catching a winner. The Jorgan jump would have been a useless cul de sac if *Pan* hadn't already known about the cul de sac off the gray route.

* * *

Some hours later, *Pan* started vectoring for the cul de sac off the Old Granny.

"We'll head for Morland where we can get spices and parts to bring *Pan* up to snuff," Danny said.

"What about Hudson?" John asked. "Their lambfish is a real delicacy and they're a major wheat exporter."

"Not this trip. Checkgok wants to get the spices at Morland because one of them is supposed to be like the habaneros. It thinks they might be a very popular spice on Parthia. Besides, we're short of funds. We have the room for the lambfish but not the money to buy it, not without selling goods we can get better prices on elsewhere."

CHAPTER 8

Deep space combat between wing ships is not like any other combat in the long history of warfare. There are similarities, just as there are similarities between an army fighting in a forest and a dogfight between atmospheric craft.

It is tempting to draw parallels between modern wing ships and the ocean-going ships of the pre-space age of sail. That temptation is made more dangerous because there are surface similarities. Those similarities are most evident in single ship combat where the addition of a third dimension has less of an effect.

Introduction to Space War, Spaceforce Academy, Drakar

Location: Cordoba Space, Big Dark
Standard Date: 05 01 630

"I have an anomaly, Captain," *Pan* said, pulling Danny from a dream of swimming through space.

"What have you got, *Pan*?" He checked his time sense. "We're still several hours from jump."

"Two ships," *Pan* said, and sent him vector and speed as she got it.

Danny pulled on his interface cap to get a better read, then got up and ran for the bridge, not bothering to dress.

By the time he got to the bridge, *Pan* had enough data to let him know that the situation wasn't urgent. At least not for them. So Danny turned around and went back to his quarters to put on some clothes.

"Pan, wake John and have him fix us all something to eat. I have some sims to run."

A few moments later, while John Gabriel was still waking up, Danny said, "We can avoid them. Head for the secondary jump, but we have to do it soon."

"Yes, Captain."

"Who is it, *Pan*?"

"It is difficult to tell at this distance, but I suspect that one is a merchantman that was just a few hours ahead of us, and the other is either a customs cutter or a pirate."

Danny nodded. He followed *Pan*'s logic. As long as the merchantman was just traveling a known course, not pushing very hard, it would be very easy to miss in the big dark. But when it started pushing hard, the wings were going to put out light as it dumped plasma for more speed. To save fuel, merchantmen tried to get as much of their thrust by sweeping space dust as they could. It was slower, but cheaper. However, in an emergency—or even if they were just in a hurry—they would vent plasma and sweep it. Plasma is hot and it gives off light, so what probably happened was that a merchantman was pulling along toward the jump point until it got caught by the pirate and then it dumped plasma to try and get away. The playback *Pan* was showing him seemed to support that.

"Dammit, *Pan*, we have a child aboard. Not to mention Checkgok and its clan's goods." *Pan* hadn't said a thing, and Danny knew his ship wouldn't. It was Danny himself who was insisting that they had to go to the rescue of the merchantman, and he knew it. "Put us on an intercept course."

"We have crew and contracts, Captain."

"And I will talk to them, and even give them an opportunity to try to talk me out of this. But put us on course to intercept, and keep us on that course until I say different."

Danny felt the ship shifting as *Pandora* pulled harder on one side to shift their course and more plasma was jetted into the wings.

"All hands channel, *Pan*. Wake Checkgok. And Jenny too, I guess.

"Everyone, this is the captain. We are seeing what appears to be an act of piracy, and we are going to interfere.

"Tie them in, *Pan*. Let them see what's going on."

* * *

Fifteen minutes later, and nothing much had happened. John made sandwiches and a soup for Checkgok. Jenny was in the galley, rubbing her eyes and yawning.

Danny followed Checkgok into the lounge. "What we seem to be seeing is a slugging match between a big fat merchant and a small cutter. We didn't see them before because of the distance, and until they started venting plasma there wasn't much light from them. *Pan*, you want to add some detail?"

Pan did, throwing graphics of the battle up on the screen. "I don't see how that small one can carry much cargo."

"Me, either. It looks like a customs cutter," Danny agreed.

"It's not squawking a great house ID. In fact, it's not squawking any ID at all."

"Pirate," Danny said with certainty. "No one but a pirate would fail to squawk ID in these circumstances. In fact, the only strange thing is that even a pirate should be squawking false colors until they have their prey nailed. How far out are we, *Pan*?"

"Hours yet, Captain. Even at maximum acceleration, we will take four or more hours to reach effective range, and that only because they are moving in our general direction."

"All right, everyone," Danny said. "I put us on an intercept course as soon as we saw those folks over there. But I am aware that it's not just me and *Pan* anymore. So I want to hear your thoughts."

Location: The Brass Hind

"Skipper, we have a new target," Boyle shouted across the bridge. Everyone was strapped into acceleration couches, and they all had on their interface caps, but Drake protocol was always to use voice reports and data transfers.

"Where away?" Captain Flatt asked, even as she pulled up the data on the new source. "What the hell is wrong with you, Boyle? That merchy is a good three hours out. We'll finish our meal before we bother with dessert." She giggled.

Captain Rosalyn Victoria Flatt didn't worry much about the past or future, which was how she had ended up in her present position. She led the mutiny because she was pissed at the first officer, and she was more surprised than anyone that her side had won. She was good at that, running on instinct. She turned her attention back to the large hauler. "I want that big mother," she said, pointing. "I want her IDs and rutters."

"Aye, Skipper."

But Rosalyn was back into the comp, feeling the flailing sails of her ship as she flung another thousand BBs of magnetic round shot at the fleeing large hauler. The *Brass Ass* jerked and shuddered with every shot.

Location: The Sicily

"Why don't we just give up, Captain?" asked George Stuart with sweat on his brow and desperation in his eyes. He was Bill Davis' first mate on the Cordoba merchant ship, *Sicily*.

"I would, George," Bill turned his accel couch to face George, "if I didn't have a pretty good idea who that is over there."

"Who?" George asked, turning back to the radar and lidar readouts as the cutter's accel stuttered again. More shot was coming in.

"It was the Drake customs cutter *Brass Hind*, until there was a mutiny six months back. The Drake Combine sent out a warning about her."

"What!" George's head whipped back around to look at Bill.

"That's right." Bill snorted. "The Drakes would normally rather rot in hell than send us a heads-up. But the crew of the *Brass Ass* is a special case. They spaced the captain and first officer, along with about half the crew, then they did it again to three more ship's crews in as many days before the Drakes knew what was going on." He shook his head. "No, George. If it was a normal pirate, I'd say 'have as much grain as you can hold,' but I have no desire to breathe vacuum."

"Me neither, sir," George agreed. The *Sicily* was big and slow, but to move as big a ship as the *Sicily* slowly required really large, powerful sails.

"Ms. Cooper, see to shifting some of the wheat to the hatches for tossing," the skipper said. "We'll give 'em some grain, whether they want it or not." A grain of wheat is neither very heavy, nor even very hard, but enough of them, moving fast enough, will kill a ship.

* * *

The vacuum-dried whole grain wheat came in five ton drums. To eject it, the drums had to be moved from the cargo hold to the engines. At the base of each mast was a venting jet. Anything from ship's waste to pocket nukes could be vented. They might have tried tossing the drums instead of individual grains of wheat, but it was easier for the sails to toss dispersed loads.

Great drones carried the five ton drums to the vent tubes' side ports and emptied a drum into each of the twelve sails' vent tubes. Sixty tons of puffed wheat was spewed out the ports at temperatures like unto those at the surface of old Sol. They would have been burned to pure carbon, but there wasn't enough oxygen for the combustion. The wheat-stiffened plasma was caught by the super strong magnetic fields of the sails and those magnetic fields moved it, forcing it outward away from the ship and shifting its vector as it was passed from field to field until the four stern sails released it, directly toward the projected position of the pirate frigate.

Inside the *Sicily*, the crew held on as the whole ship bucked under the stress of the sudden extra mass being sent on its way.

Location: The Brass Hind

Rosalyn, hooked into the computers, felt the shift in the enemy's accel and knew that around sixty tons of something was headed their way. There were two options and time enough for either. She could shift her course a little and avoid the blow, or count on her own sails to bat the attack aside. But for Rosalyn there was really only one option. She stopped stepping aside for anyone the day of the mutiny.

Location: The Sicily

"They aren't shifting, Captain," George Stuart said, sounding confused.

"The crazy fucks have a lot of confidence in those over-powered sails," Captain Davis said. "Look at the change in the flap pattern."

George shifted his perception to the interface and the sensors' read of the pattern of the frigate's sail shifts. It was all very fast, several hundred times each second. But there were gaps in the coverage, and the wheat the *Sicily* threw would travel the full length of the frigate's sail in about a thousandth of a second. As George watched, the pattern of the frigate's sail shifted just a little and stabilized so that when the puffed wheat arrived it would be swept aside by the front A sail.

"Shit," George muttered a few seconds later when the frigate passed through the point where it should have hit the wheat, and the only effect was a very slight increase in speed as the frigate managed to use their shot as reaction mass.

Location: The Brass Hind

"Hull scoring, Skipper," Boyle shouted. "Some of that shit, whatever it was, got through." Then, after a moment, in a much calmer voice, "Nothing serious. No penetrations and none of it hit anything critical."

"Load grapeshot," Captain Rosalyn Flatt shouted in fury. *How dare they scratch my paint?*

Grapeshot was hundreds of thousands of magnetized round balls half a centimeter in diameter. They were heavy. If one of those suckers hit, it would do more than scratch the paint.

Location: The Pandora

Danny Gold looked at his crew through the *Pan*'s cameras. *A Parthian merchant, a cook, and a ten-year-old kid . . .*

Danny almost changed his mind. "Look, people. We have some time, so everyone take a breath and think things through. There are two ships out there. One of them is flying a Cordoba merchant ship beacon. It's the *Sicily*, a grain ship. The other isn't showing a beacon and is chasing the *Sicily*, so it's a safe bet that it's a pirate. This is none of our business, and the safe bet would be to swing around out of the way and let them slug it out."

Danny stopped and looked at the virtual images of Checkgok, Jenny, and John. "I'm not going to do that. Not unless one of you has come up with a good reason I haven't thought of. Because there are people on the *Sicily*. From her size, about sixty people. And because they are already shooting at each other. That doesn't say good things about the brains of the *Sicily*'s skipper unless he knows something I don't, but I think if we just leave, the wrong people are going to die. Anyone have any comments?"

John looked at Jenny and Jenny looked at John while Danny watched. There wasn't a lot of the "oh, great adventure" excitement that Danny was half-expecting from the kid. What there was, was determination. That was apparently enough to stop anything John might have said before it passed his lips.

"I am confused, Captain," Checkgok said. "What is our interest in this? The Cordoba are not our clan and are even, in a sense, opposed to our clan. Would it not be to our relative advantage to let them be damaged?"

Danny tried to think how to explain, but Jenny didn't give him the chance.

"There are people in that ship. Human beings." Jenny stopped and turned a little pink, but continued doggedly. "What if they were Parthians? Would you be so quick to wish them dead?"

Checkgok didn't take offense. At least Danny didn't think it did.

"Actually, Jenny, I would have the same question if it was an all-Parthian crew over there. We parse relations differently than humans. If they were from Clan Zheck, I would argue for going to their defense because we are at least potential allies of that clan. But if they were, for instance, from Clan Coff, I would oppose it."

Jenny tilted her head and said, "Parthians are weird." Not as though she resented Checkgok's position, but just as a point of information.

"I have often thought the same thing about humans," Checkgok agreed. Then, turning its eyestalks, one to Jenny and the other to John, it continued. "I take it this is a human-morality-based decision, Captain?"

"You could say that, yes," Danny agreed.

"In that case, we should probably do it. What is the level of risk?"

"*Pan*?" Danny asked.

"There is considerable risk, but between us and the *Sicily*, we will probably win. If it were just us against the frigate, I would doubt our chances. But with us and the *Sicily*, we should have a good chance of victory. Most pirates don't have nukes, so the battle will be sand and shot. It isn't safe by any means, but neither is it suicide. There is too little data to be more precise."

Danny knew that *Pan* wasn't explaining fully. A ship conned by an artificial brain like *Pan* was a more effective fighter than a ship that was using a crew, because it had faster and more flexible responses. While two ordinary merchantmen would be fairly easy meat for a frigate like that one over there, when you included *Pan*'s artificial brain in the mix, her estimate of the odds was probably spot on.

Then *Pan* spoke again. "Captain, the pirates have fired. I can't be sure, but I suspect grapeshot."

"Right. *Pan*, how far are we? Can we get a comm laser on the *Sicily* to coordinate and be sure what's going on? For that matter, comm the pirate. It's just possible we have this all wrong."

Tension mounted as *Pandora* moved toward the fray.

Location: The Sicily

Bill Davis felt the explosions as the BBs of grape that got through converted chunks of the *Sicily*'s hull into plasma. Damage Control reported Able Spacer Joann Fletcher was dead, killed when one of the BBs vented the corridor where she was working to space.

George Stuart said, "Captain, I have a comm from that merchant, asking what's going on." George threw the message up on screen three and they saw a blond man in a sloppy captain's cap requesting a situation report.

"What's going on is we are being attacked by the *Brass Ass* and getting the shit shot out of us." Captain Davis took a breath and got himself under control. "Send them what we have, George."

Location: On the Pandora

"We received a response from the *Sicily*, Captain, identifying them and informing us that the pursuer is the *Brass Hind*. It is a Drake customs cutter that went rogue some time back. We haven't gotten a response from it, not that I see it making much difference. We are hours out of range, Captain, and it will be a fast pass when we do reach effective range," *Pan* said.

"Sure. But if we can work with the *Sicily*, they might be able to move this *Brass Hind* into the path of our shot." Danny fed the *Pan* several vector graphics of how they might work it.

"Possible, Captain, but it would take a great deal of luck."

"True. But even if it doesn't work, it will be a distraction, and the *Sicily* needs all the help we can give her as soon as we can get it there." Danny said. "Send her the suggestion."

Location: The Sicily

"Skipper," Allen Stuart said from the comm, "I think our savior is nuts."

"I'm a little busy here, Allen." Bill was trying to juggle more damage reports and get someone to fill in for Bannis, who was going into the autodoc for the bends from the same hull rupture that killed Joann. "Would you get to the point?"

"They want us to maneuver to put the pirate in the path of their shot in four minutes, eighteen and seventy-three one-hundredths seconds."

"What?"

"It's in the message queue, Skipper. Message eighteen with attachments."

Bill scanned the message for a few moments, vectors in his mind's eye. "It's crazy enough that it might just work. They're far enough away that it's going to be pretty hard for the pirates to guess just how hard they're throwing anything from the accel change."

"Well, Skipper," George Stuart said, "they aren't waiting for our acknowledgement or agreement. The *Pandora* just fired something at someone."

From his voice, Allen guessed his older brother George thought the people on the *Pandora* were as crazy as Allen thought they were.

Location: The Brass Hind

"Captain, the *Pandora* fired," Boyle said.

"How rude!" Rosalyn giggled, feeling more amused than anything else. She scanned the log for a moment and realized that she couldn't tell how fast the cloud of shot would be coming and that even though she knew the general direction, they would be very hard to spot on radar. "Shift us a couple of klicks to galactic north. That ought to get us out of the shot cone."

"Aye, Skipper," Boyle said.

Location: The Sicily

"They're ducking, Captain," George said.

"Which direction?"

"Galactic north."

"Shift us east then, like we're trying to duck too, and get a little extra distance."

"The *Pandora* is firing again," Allen said. "You know, Skipper, I bet it looks to the pirates like the *Pandora* is responding to their change in vector. You think this might work?"

Location: The Brass Hind

"This is totally unacceptable." Rosalyn pouted. "I don't intend to spend the next two hours dodging shots from a dinky little freighter. Mr. Boyle, please prepare a hunter-nuke for launch."

"Skipper, we only have three of those left and we can't get more."

The frigates had an official inventory of ten hunter-nukes but three disappeared from stores before the mutiny and they'd used four since. Hunter-nukes were launched the same way as other missiles, but they had fairly powerful short-range rockets that would let them home a little bit. They also had a nuke that powered a magnetic pulse strong enough to trash any but the strongest magnetic sail.

"I know, but I don't care. That ship over there is up to something and I'm not going to wait to find out what it is the hard way."

Location: The Pandora

"Captain, we may have a problem," *Pan* said, and Jenny felt her heart beat a little faster. She was scared, but everything was so slow. It wasn't like a game of *Ship Combat* at all.

"What's up?" the captain asked.

"The *Sicily* just sent us its read of the motions of the *Brass Hind* and it has just thrown something at us."

"And at this range that's a problem because . . . ?"

"It's small, Captain, and a single unit."

"Oops," the captain said. "Did the Drakes equip the *Brass Hind* with hunter-nukes by any chance?"

Jenny remembered *Pan* saying earlier that the pirate wouldn't have nukes.

"From the download the *Sicily* sent, yes, they did. The *Brass Hind* had a complement of ten of them."

"Ten. Oh, good," the captain muttered. "I'd hate to think we were causing them to use stuff they didn't have plenty of."

At first Jenny thought that Captain Gold had gone crazy, but no. He was making a joke. She was *almost* sure.

"Very generous of you, I'm sure, Skipper," John said. "But, being a lowly cook, I would just as soon they didn't have enough to bracket us."

Captain Gold sniffed loudly over the comm. "How very plebeian of you, Cookie. I am constantly amazed at the practicality of the lower orders."

Jenny giggled nervously. They were both joking, and that made her feel better. Her lessons taught that with the distances involved, it would be five minutes or more before the hunter got anywhere near in range. And even with its seeking capabilities, they could probably get out of range of one. But ten?

"What can we do?" Checkgok asked. "How do these missiles work?"

Jenny was glad it asked. She was too embarrassed to do it.

"They have passive sensors and lock onto the electromagnetic signature of the ship they are programmed for," *Pan* explained. "When they get close enough, they turn on their rockets and adjust their vector to intercept. When they encounter the magnetic field of the sails, the nuke goes off, powering an electromagnetic pulse that interacts with the sail field to trash the mast. If the feedback is strong enough, it can blow out the engines. At the least, it will cripple us, and if we dodge they will wait a little until our new course is set and fire another one. The one good thing is, normally at this distance we wouldn't have nearly as good an idea of its course as we do, if we'd seen it at all. Thanks to the *Sicily* and their download, we have a good read on its course."

"How does it recognize us? Just from our beacon?" Jenny asked. There was a thought somewhere in the back of her mind, but she wasn't sure what it was yet. Something she read recently. One of the lessons.

"No. Each ship—even each mast on each ship—has its own electromagnetic signature. And they are awfully hard to disguise."

"What if we shot at it?" John asked.

That isn't it, Jenny thought. It was something else. Something about the masts.

"Possible, but they are generally hardened."

"How smart is it?" Jenny asked. She wasn't even sure why she asked that, but it was important. She knew it was.

"Not very. It's probably an expert system, not an artificial brain. It's programmed with what our magnetic field looks like. It's programmed with our location and vector from when it was launched, and while its passive sensors aren't that great at this distance, it will mostly be able to see any change in course we make and calculate the best time to light off its rocket to intercept us. Why?"

That's it! She remembered. "I was wondering if we could fool it. We have two ship's boats and we have some carbon nanotube wire." The ship's boats didn't use sails; they weren't big enough to mount the shield gold guides that focused the magnetic fields.

"I'm not following you, Jenny," Captain Gold said.

"It's in the history study program. The first wing ships used super-conducting nanotube wire to push out the magnetic field. They didn't have the shieldgold to reflect the magnetics and control them at a distance, so they used these superconducting wires."

"Yes, they did," the captain agreed. "And the wing shape and position was determined by the wire. It caused major limitations on how quickly the wings could flap. That's why we still call them sails. The early ones really were mostly sails. So you want to send one of the ship's boats and a coil of wire out to make like a sail and get the hunter to blow?"

Jenny nodded. She realized that this idea wasn't so much something grownups didn't know, but just something they left in the back of their minds because it didn't seem to matter anymore.

"*Pan*?"

"Possible, Captain. It would be best to wait until the last minute. If it's too far from us when it hits the field, it will probably not detonate. Also, we will have to fake the signature of one of the masts. The brains on the ship's boats are probably bright enough to manage it. We will have to drop the sails as we launch the boat. The trick will be getting the boat's pseudo-sail up quick enough that it looks to the hunter like the dying flutter of the ship's sail."

"Okay, *Pan*. Keep on as though we're unaware of it. Go in fat and happy without showing anything. At least until we're sure whether we can build the thing. John, get down to Shuttle One and see about rigging it to catch the hunter. Pan and I will use the drones to get the stuff to you and work out how to hook up the cable. Meanwhile, *Pan*, see if you can use the data from the *Sicily* to get a camera on the missile."

John ran for the shuttle bay before Danny finished talking.

Location: The Brass Hind

"They must not have seen it, Skipper," Boyle said. "They haven't maneuvered."

Rosalyn was disappointed. She wanted to see them running, even if it meant using more missiles. But there was no reason to waste missiles if the first one was going to kill them. *It's not too bad*, she thought. *What a surprise they're going to get in six minutes.*

Location: The Sicily

"Tell them again, Comm," said Captain Davis. "Damn fools ought to be ducking by now." The *Pandora*, aside from firing two more times to divert the *Brass Ass*, hadn't changed course at all and by now Davis was starting to think *Pandora*'s strategy would work. The *Ass* clearly didn't have a clue what the *Pandora* actually shot at, so was likely to put itself in position to be hit by whatever the *Pandora* had thrown in about three minutes. At the same time, the *Pandora*, if it didn't get a move on, was going to eat a hunter-nuke in about—he looked at the clock—six minutes.

Location: The Pandora

"Should we tell them what we're planning, Captain?" Pandora asked.

"What's the chance that the *Brass Hind* will catch part of the beam?"

"Possible now that they are vectoring in our direction."

At first the *Sicily* had been on a vector fifteen degrees off theirs, but since they made themselves known and came up with their plan, the *Sicily* was gradually shifting its vector to intercept. Now the *Pandora*, the *Sicily*, and the *Brass Hind* were all pretty much in line, to the point that the *Pan* and the *Hind* were having difficulty shooting at each other. A laser is a tightly-focused beam of coherent light, but it does spread over the distances involved. By now there was a measurable chance that the *Hind* would pick up anything they sent.

"In that case, leave them in the dark."

"Skipper, John said they might do something stupid to save us."

"*Pan*, is there anything you can tell them that would let them know that we know, without letting the *Hind* know what's going on even if they pick up the message?" Danny asked.

Three ships moved toward each other at a combined velocity that was a measurable fraction of the speed of light. And along with them, missiles of magnetic iron and wheat. Danny had *Pandora* make up their own grapeshot and hid it in case of inspection by the mercantile combines. They were little different from the standard, save that the *Pan* had made them in her own shops and they appeared on no records anywhere but *Pan*'s own brain.

Location: The Sicily

"It's getting close, Skipper," George Stuart said.

"Have we spotted the actual shot?"

"No, Skipper. I haven't wanted to use radar. Anyway, if it's grapeshot it's going to be black, almost impossible to spot against the background of space."

"Just for the record, George, we have no reason to believe that it's grapeshot."

"Right, Skipper," George said, grinning. "No reason at all. Probably nuts and bolts from their parts inventory. Without any consideration of the difference in character between using magnetized and unmagnetized projectiles."

"Exactly."

In normal circumstances, the mercantile combines of Drake and Cordoba would search the independent traders' ships and confiscate any grapeshot they found, fine the owners, and give them a stern warning about carrying contraband. In this case . . . well, the *Sicily* was a grain ship, not a customs frigate, and they were looking studiously in the other direction.

"All right. Let's throw some more wheat. We want them looking at our stuff, not the *Pan*'s."

"Coming up on it, Skipper."

The computer, long since programmed with the timing, launched the puffed wheat projectiles at the precise fraction of a second.

Location: The Brass Hind

"The *Sicily* is shooting at us again, Skipper," Boyle said.

"I see it," Rosalyn said. "Adjusting the timing." There was just the least hiccup in the rate of flap of the sails as they were positioned to catch the puffed wheat. Unknown to Rosalyn or Boyle, that adjustment opened up their sails to the attack by the *Pan*'s "nuts and bolts." Almost.

It partly worked. Thirty-seven and eighty-nine one-thousandths seconds later, the front A-sail of the *Brass Hind* finished the sweep that pushed the puffed wheat out of the *Hind*'s path. It turned off and turned back on in its full forward position, leaving a gap of over a hundred feet uncovered by any magnetic field. Into that gap slipped the first twenty-three of one hundred thousand magnetized BBs. If the timing had been perfect, it would have been half the hundred thousand, but the timing was less than perfect. The *Hind*'s ship brain noticed the increased pull as it swept the rest of the grapeshot out of the way microseconds before seven of the twenty-three BBs hit the ship. With their velocity, they and the material they contacted were converted into plasma.

It wasn't an atomic explosion. The atoms remained intact . . . just not in contact with one another.

* * *

The *Brass Hind* jerked and duralloy screamed. Alarms ripped through the *Hind*'s bridge, and damage reports, tracking the paths of destruction the BBs produced as they disintegrated, started coming in. One of the BBs might as well have been made of shieldgold, because it deflected off a stanchion and ripped through the controlling coil of the midship A-mast, releasing a fraction of the magnetic energy within the ship.

Pete Gannon had joined the crew of the *Brass Hind* as an able spacer just weeks before the mutiny but was happy enough with the new setup. There was more romance to being a pirate than to being a very minor cog in the Drake combine. And more loot. A lot more loot. He was at his station, about four feet from the midship A-mast anchor coil, when the iron BB tore a line down the shieldgold. The heat from the vaporizing missile probably would have killed him, but it never had the chance. A line of magnetic force so powerful as to make the ancient hadron-supercollider seem an ice box magnet, ripped through him.

If it's strong enough, magnetism overwhelms gravity. The effect was as if a line going from his right knee to his left shoulder was exposed to the gravity of a black hole while leaving the rest of him mostly untouched. He was cut in half. Of course, no one would ever know, because the steel bulkhead just the other side of him was pulled into him. And through him, as it tried to reach the siren call of magnetism.

He never felt a thing.

* * *

To the crew of the *Hind* . . . well, the rest of the crew of the *Hind* . . . the more important point was that the midship A-mast was gone, leaving a gap in their shielding that would be obvious to a blind gopher.

"Turn us around," Rosalyn screamed. "Rotate 150 degrees, turn thirty degrees to port, get that sail out of the line of fire."

It was done fairly quickly, but in the doing they had to shift vector, and their victim was waiting for the chance.

Location: The Sicily

Watching the *Hind* on his screens, the captain of the *Sicily* ordered, "Forty degrees down starboard, George. Sharply, please. And throw some more wheat."

Slowly, the course of the *Hind* and the *Sicily* diverged a little. Then a few minutes later, they started to diverge even more.

"I think they're breaking off, Skipper," George said.

"It looks like it, but don't drop your guard."

CHAPTER 9

It is not the small artificial brains that rational people object to. A wing controller, or a household cleaning bot, do indeed work a little better than a standard computer, though not necessarily enough better to justify the added expense that such one-off systems inherently require. However, as an artificial brain gets larger, the probability of mental aberration increases exponentially. By the time you get to the sort of artificial brain used in a ship's boat or even a farm bot, the danger of the artificial brain going insane is simply too great.
Preamble to Professor Christine Holland's refutation of Professor Gerhard Schmitz's Paper on Artificial Brains.

Location: Cordoba space, Big Dark, The Pandora
Standard Date: 05 01 630

"Okay. Let's see if we can get out of the way of that nuke now," Danny told the *Pan*.

"I doubt it at this point, Captain, but I'll try."

"How's Jenny's brainchild coming?" Danny asked, and Pan threw up an image of John.

* * *

John shoved one end of the cable into the open maintenance hatch on the bottom of the shuttle and jerked back, as not all the charge was dissipated until he touched it. He cursed and shoved the wire in again. With his other hand, he sprayed the wire and the leads with conducting oil, then with sealant.

He shifted over, grabbed the coiler, attached it to the secondary power feed, and following *Pandora*'s instructions, went to the other end of the cable. It didn't just have to conduct. It had to uncoil quickly while keeping both ends attached.

Two drones were making other connections in the circuits that connected the shuttle's brain to the shuttle's rockets.

* * *

Pan instructed the ship's boat brain on its new mission to mimic the *Pan*'s midship-C sail. It would be tricky, but it might save them.

"The wire is loaded and the engine's governors have been removed. John is on his way out of the shuttle bay." By removing the governors they could max out the engines to produce enough power to look like a real sail. It would burn out the engines, but that was better than a nuke going off on top of them.

"How long do we have, *Pan*?" John asked.

"A little less than a minute," *Pan* said.

John exited the shuttle bay while the seeker decided it was time and lit off its rocket engine. It was an old-fashioned nuclear rocket, a fission energy source turning liquid hydrogen into plasma and ejecting the hydrogen out of a standard jet. The nuke was designed to reach critical mass about the time that the missiles reached the target ship. Nothing particularly new; old-fashioned, well-tested tech.

Danny had a thought. "Has anyone ever done this before?"

"Not that I am aware of, Captain, but it could have happened," *Pan* said. "Captain, the missile has lit its drive and is homing."

"How long now?"

"Thirty seconds, Captain. I am adjusting flight profile and flap timing to put it as far out on the sails as possible."

They waited as the shuttle launched and the wings started to drop. The shuttle started to spin in an attempt to get the wire out faster.

Location: Pandora Ship's Boat Polly

The brain of the ship's boat had about the intelligence of a parrot and the personality of a cocker spaniel. It was eager to please and serious about doing the best job it could. It did have a desire to continue, but that was completely overridden by its need to protect ship and crew. It thought the plan was just the cleverest thing it had ever been programmed with and was eagerly awaiting its chance to shine.

The port opened and the little boat flung itself from the bay as the sails went down. It flung out the nanotube wire as quickly as it could. It didn't know, and neither did the crew of the *Pan*, that the superconducting wire moving through the dying magnetic field would act as a capacitor of sorts, delaying the collapse of the stern-C sail for seven point five microseconds. It also looked surprisingly like a micro flare of the sail.

When it happened, the boat reacted quickly, adjusting its output to try to match.

Location: The Hunter-nuke

As the hunter approached its target, it was disappointed to "see" the sails of the target go down. Its designed function was to blow a sail through magnetic resonance, not to simply explode like some dumb bomb. Then its artificial brain lit with joy. One of the sails, a stern sail, probably the C or D, hadn't gone down. The hunter focused on that, shifting its aim and preparing to fire the nuke that would power the mag surge, destroying it and its target in a blaze of magnetic glory.

Now!

Location: Pandora Ship's Boat Polly

As the electromagnetic feedback through the superconducting wire fed the full energy output of a nuclear explosion into its capacitors, the last thought of the boat's mind was to wonder if the plan worked. The boat did a pretty fair imitation of a nuke itself, but most of the force was directed out away from *Pandora*.

Location: The Pandora

"We've lost breakers on the stern-C, Captain," *Pan* said.

"It didn't work?"

"Say rather 'it sort of worked,' Captain. It will take analysis, but I think that the ship's boat did indeed suck the hunter onto itself. It was too close to us when it happened, and some of the feedback jumped to the stern-C. I think that limited the damage."

"Right." Danny scanned the shipnet to see for himself. *Pan* was, as usual, right. There was damage, but it was mostly stopped by the circuit breakers, which would not have happened if the sail had taken the brunt of the attack. He focused on organizing the drones to start repairs, and once that was done he pulled out of the shipnet.

"Call the *Sicily* and ask how they are doing. *Pan*, don't tell them about the boat. Just tell them we got lucky. Just a glancing blow as the sail was going down."

* * *

The captain of the *Sicily* was happy enough that they got off lightly. Danny had to explain that they didn't think they could dodge the *Brass Hind*'s full complement of missiles, so he tried to limit the damage by making it look as if they didn't see the hunter-nuke until the *Hind* was otherwise occupied.

"You're a damned fool, Captain Gold," Captain Davis said, shaking his head. "A brave man and you rescued us, but you're still a damned fool."

"Yes, Captain. That's what my parents said, and my teachers too," Danny said seriously, then grinned at the screen.

Captain Davis laughed and the two ships rendezvoused and limped together toward the next jump point.

* * *

There was a spectrum to interstellar trade. In one sense, most colonies and almost all planets could get by just fine on their own, without any interstellar shipping. But there were still places that produced an overabundance of this or that.

"We have a full load of grain from Hudson 3," Captain Davis explained as the ships were making their way to the jump point.

"Grain?"

"Hudson 3 has millions of acres of grain fields and they have a unique type of wheat that grows really well in the planetary soil. It's popular on many worlds, and we ship a lot of it on the *Sicily*."

"You're owned by the Cordoba Combine, right?"

"Yes, but the *Sicily* was built special for this route. Like I said, it's a lot of grain and Hudson 3's main export."

"Well, I'm glad we could help," Danny said.

"Do you have any room in your holds?"

"We're half-empty at this point, Captain."

Captain Davis grinned. He had a pleasant, open face with the pressure of the attack off. "Well, we dumped rather a lot of grain fighting off the pirates."

"In fact, Captain Gold, it would be perfectly reasonable for us to have flung a lot more grain at the pirate than we did," said George Stuart. "Say . . . enough to fill the rest of your hold."

"And where would we have gotten that grain?" Danny asked.

"Why, you bought it, Captain," Allen piped up. "At Hudson, where the bumper harvest meant the prices were low. Normally it wouldn't be a profitable cargo for a ship your size, but any cargo is better than none and it was really cheap."

"We don't have much in the way of cargo haulers," Danny explained. "We only have the one ship's boat, and it's pretty small. I think we will need to shut down our drives and scuttle up to each other if we are going to do this."

"No. We'll use ours," Davis said. "They're made to double as transfer shuttles when we need to ship to some of the smaller stations. The problem's going to be once we get docked to your *Pan*. They are five ton drums."

"We'll manage, Captain. Between *Pan*'s servos and . . . well, we'll manage."

And they did. For the next two days, as the two ships made slow progress toward the next jump point, Danny, in helmet and gloves but no suit, and servos run by John and Jenny, unloaded five-ton drums of vacuum dried wheat from the *Sicily*'s ships boats to the *Pan*. Filling the *Pan* barely made a dent in the *Sicily*'s cargo.

Location: the Pandora
Standard Date: 05 03 630

"There is the question of who owns the wheat, Captain," Checkgok pointed out. "The ship or Clan Zheck."

"It was given to the ship," *Pan* said. "More precisely, to Captain Gold."

"The wheat was provided in recompense for actions taken by the ship while on the business of Clan Zheck," Checkgok corrected. "Further, Clan Zheck's goods were placed in considerable jeopardy. Whether it wanted to or not, Clan Zheck took part in the risk. It should also take part in any profit that has accrued from that risk."

"It's got a point, *Pan*." Danny grinned. "But if that's the case, then the loss of the ship's boat becomes a legitimate running expense and the responsibility of Clan Zheck."

"That seems reasonable," Checkgok agreed.

"While I agree that the ship's boat must be managed as part of the running expenses, that was only part of the payment to the ship for its use," *Pan* insisted. "It doesn't imply that everything the ship does is done strictly for Clan Zheck. It wasn't just Clan Zheck but also the ship and crew who were put in danger. Ship and crew should receive some part of any reward gained. And it was the captain's decision to involve the ship in the first place, so there are captain's shares to consider."

"I don't see that, *Pan*," Danny said. "Seems to me that, if anything, there ought to be a penalty to me for putting the crew at risk without consulting them."

"But you did consult us, Captain," Jenny said. "You gave us a chance to talk you out of it, and we agreed that it had to be done."

"Okay," Danny said, "but that doesn't mean captain's shares. Like you said, everyone agreed. Mostly."

Eventually they determined that Clan Zheck would get half the grain. The rest would go into ship's funds, minus a bonus for crew. The bonus was more money than Jenny had ever even seen, much less owned.

Location: Brass Ass, en route to Donnybrook

Quinton Williams grabbed the stanchion and regretted—yet again—supporting Rosalyn's mutiny. It had proven true—yet again—that men only had enough blood to operate one head at a time, and too often—even when they thought they were using the one above their shoulders—it was the other head that was actually running things. Rosalyn was sexy as hell, but the woman was bat shit crazy.

Even now, Quinton couldn't quite bring himself to try to mutiny against her. And he wasn't sure whether that was because he didn't have the skills needed to run the bridge or because he was still enamored of her. Instead he worked with the damage control crew to try to get the wings back up. Joe Downing was still locked up awaiting trial, and Quinton was under quarters arrest when not on duty. The only reason that Rosalyn hadn't flushed them both out of an airlock was because she was afraid of the reaction of his exspatios.

* * *

John Boyle had had enough. The stupid bitch just had to go after the grainer. And a grainer like that wouldn't have much in the way of rutters, whatever paranoid delusions Rosalyn's flash-soaked brain came up with. He looked over at Loly, who was directing the repair crews from her station, and he suddenly realized that she was in danger now.

Rosalyn would need someone to blame for the condition of the ship and she couldn't blame herself or her decisions. The blame would fall on the repair crew, and especially on Loly, as the newly appointed third and damage control officer.

That meant that he couldn't involve Loly in the mutiny.

He looked over at the controls and his eyes fell on the course plot. They were on course to a gray route jump. It led off the main Hudson-Morland route, but it connected up with a gray route to Donnybrook. And the whole route to Donnybrook was in the ship systems. That was important. Rosy was nuts on security and usually she erased the coordinates of all the jumps except the one they were going to next.

It didn't occur to John to wonder why she didn't this time.

* * *

In the hours since the battle, Rosalyn had had a stick of flash and realized that there was a good chance of mutiny. She intentionally left the course to Donnybrook on the comp. Not the real course, but one that looked real enough. Rosalyn knew she might die in the mutiny she was inviting, but that didn't worry her.

That was the fun of it, after all. The knowing that she might die in a few minutes.

She looked around the bridge wondering who it might be. Her guess was Quinton. He wanted her. She knew that. But he was such an upright sort. He didn't like the way she was running things. He didn't respect fun. Not her sort of fun.

John got up from his seat. She looked at him and lifted an eyebrow.

"Need to go to the head, Skipper. Too much coffee."

Maybe. Or maybe he was getting ready to start the mutiny. She nodded, not showing her suspicion.

* * *

Three minutes later, Daniel Watters stepped through the hatch, carrying a slate. He approached the captain's chair and Rosalyn spun the chair around.

He dropped the slate. Hidden behind it was a pistol.

He started to point it, but Rosalyn was faster and she was ready for him. In fact, she was expecting him. She knew the attacker would be Joe Downing if it was Quinton, or Dannyboy if it was John Boyle.

She fired, and so did he. But she was a fraction quicker and her shot jerked him so that his shot hit a corner of the main display screen. She jabbed the comm button even as she used her interface to call up ship's communications. "Quinton, arrest John Boyle."

"I can't, Captain," came the immediate response. "I am still under quarters arrest."

Using her interface she called up his location. He was down ship. There was no way he was involved. There wasn't time. And with him under arrest, the ship would have recorded any comm he made. It was even recording anything he said. She called up his comments for the last few minutes. He hadn't talked to anyone other than the damage control crew he was working with. "Oh, you still love me," Rosalyn said in a little girl voice, then giggled.

"I rule you not guilty for the good of the service and restore you to full rank and status. Now go find John and—"

The hatch opened again and John Boyle came in, gun in hand. He fired before he was through the hatch and his bullet took out a console that was over her left shoulder. He was followed by three other crew, armed with wrenches and piping. Weapons were restricted on the *Brass Ass*, just as they had been when it was under Drake Colors.

Rosalyn fired back. She got John and two of his followers, then she was out of ammunition. These weren't the exspatio mag rifles. They were old-fashioned chem weapons.

She threw the pistol at Spacer Flint and went after him.

* * *

John was thrown back against the bulkhead by the bullets. He sank to the deck and saw Loly start to rise. He knew that something had gone wrong, that the bitch had somehow been ready. He waved Loly down. It was a small gesture because he was dying, but also because he didn't want Rosalyn to see.

* * *

Loly let herself sink back in the chair and watched her man die. It was all that merchant ship's fault. There was a part of Loly's mind that knew that was so unjust as to border on insanity, but it was a small part. And that small part was swamped by the sure and certain knowledge that if she blamed Captain Rosalyn Flatt she would end up doing something that would get her killed. And Loly had a strong desire for self-preservation.

Loly looked over, saw the little woman drive two thumbs into Flint's eyes, and heard him scream while she laughed. Loly turned her head away and looked at the damaged screen. It didn't show anything now, not the route to Donnybrook or the merchantman and grain hauler they were sailing away from.

CHAPTER 10

Humans in the Pamplona sector do not, for the most part, live on planetary surfaces. Even in systems that have habitable or semi-habitable planets, a large percentage of the population lives in space stations. While the long term expense of terraforming a world is less per square foot of living space than building a space station, the initial cost is much lower for a space station because the space station can be as small or as large as needed for the initial population.
This makes individuals harder to hide, but groups large enough to go out to the asteroid belts or Oort clouds of systems can hide whole cities, making taxation and political control more difficult.
Cordoba Census Bureau Report, Standard Year 512

Location: Cordoba Space Morland System
Standard Date: 05 04 630

Radio communication between Morland and the *Pandora* didn't take long, but Commander Ferdinand Ardmore of the Cordoba patrol ship *Grenadier* wanted to get personal reports from everyone involved. Captain Virginia Delangen of the Morland Defense Force was insisting that since they were in Morland space now, they were under Morland law, and no, Ardmore could not interview the little girl without an advocate.

"I think," *Pan* told Danny, "that we have wandered into another conflict between the local and interstellar authorities."

"No doubt," Danny agreed as they listened to Commander Ardmore and Captain Delangen arguing. "And I think Ardmore may suspect where we got the wheat."

A few moments later Danny activated his mike with a thought. "Jenny is a member of our crew, and her guardian is Spacer John Gabriel. You can ask her anything you want, Commander, but her guardian and the *Pan* are going to be present and recording while you do. I have a responsibility to my crew."

The commander, a monumental jerk, spent several hours interviewing everyone on the *Pandora* and the *Sicily*. Some seven hours later, he finally left, offering the Cordoba Combine's thanks and the strong impression that he'd really rather be arresting them all on suspicion of being human.

Captain Delangen grinned at them once the commander was off the line and suggested, "You'll get a better price if you sell your grain on Haulaway Station. It's a mining and manufacturing center located on the largest rock in the asteroid belt. If you sell on world, it will mean extra shipping and transfer fees. Tell Tommy Frinch I sent you." Captain Delangen sent an in system jump route. They were, as it happened, jumps *Pan* already had in her rutters, being in the public rutters for the system, but the route turned a two-week normal space trip into a series of jumps that could be made in a day and a half. As well, it saved them a few hundred kilograms of hydrogen.

"Thanks, Captain. We'll do that."

Location: Pandora, off Haulaway Station, Morland System Standard Date: 05 07 630

"Captain, we have a chance to buy a suit bot," *Pandora* said.

Danny looked up from the game of planets he was playing with Jenny, then nodded. "Makes sense." There were two sorts of space suits, the relatively cheap heavy suits that were the next best thing to tiny spaceships—big, heavy, hard to work in, and uncomfortable. Then there were the flexsuits, much more expensive because they had to be fitted to the wearer with a level of exactitude that would be difficult to achieve if they were made of cloth. But they weren't made of cloth. They were made of carbon fiber rings a few microns across, interlaced with micro circuits and magnetic coils. They kept the body from expanding in zero pressure, and helped the wearer to breathe by pressing the chest and stomach on the exhale and releasing the pressure on the inhale. It was an amazing feat of engineering placed into a pseudo fabric no thicker than a sheet of silk. Flexsuits fit like a second skin and were worth a heavy suit's weight in gold to anyone who had to do much work in space.

They were made by specialized robots called suit bots. "This would be the place for one. But why is it for sale?"

"It's broken," *Pan* admitted. "But the seller, one Hirum Outis, insists that it's fixable."

Danny was about to say no, then he looked into Jenny's eyes and changed his mind. Jenny had no suit at all, which meant she was restricted to indoors at all times. And besides, there was Checkgok. Danny wasn't at all sure that the bug *could* wear a suit, not with its spiky fur and weird shape. But living in space without a suit wasn't safe, not unless you were designed for it. "Okay, *Pan*. We'll have a look at it. What about a new ship's boat?"

"None that we can afford, Captain."

"Parts? A couple of junkers we could tear down and rebuild? We're going to be leaving here light, assuming Checkgok can sell the wheat locally."

"About that, Captain. Checkgok doesn't think we should sell that much of the wheat here. It's too close to Hudson. It thinks we'll get a better price farther away. That is especially true if we can cross back to Drake space before we sell it."

"I don't know. That's a fair amount of mass to accelerate through normal space, and even more volume in the holds that grain is taking up."

Location: Haulaway Station, Morland System
Standard Date: 05 07 630

Hirum Outis was an old guy in a filthy flexsuit. "It was working fine just a couple of years ago, then Jodee Foster got drunk and busted up the shop, and I ain't been able to get it to work since."

Danny looked at the suit-bot. On the outside, it looked good. Hirum had obviously spent a lot more care on the bot than he had on his flexsuit or his own hygiene. "Mind if I run a scan on it?" Danny asked.

"Sure, go ahead."

Danny pulled out the diagnostic unit that was linked to *Pan* and plugged it into the control port of the suit-bot and waited.

"We should buy it, Captain," *Pan* said over his personal frequency.

"You think you can fix it?" Danny sent back.

"No, Captain. But the suit-bot's brain has been damaged."

"How bad?"

"That is difficult to say, but it has been unable to perform its function for two years and . . ."

"I understand, *Pan*," Danny sent, and he did. Artificial brains came in a variety of sizes and functions. Even the simplest were at least moderately expensive, and while most of them didn't have anything like human intelligence, they did feel. By design, they wanted—*needed*—to perform the function that they were designed to perform. To deny an artificial brain the chance to work was cruel. *Pan* could not avoid empathizing with the simple creature that was the suit-bot. "How bright is it?"

"About as bright as a cocker spaniel," *Pan* sent. She didn't have to explain that the suit bot's intelligence was strictly focused on the making of flexsuits.

"Get in touch with Checkgok and see how much we can pay for it. Better yet, get it over here so it can do the negotiations."

Danny listened to Hirum and tried not to inhale too deeply. Among the other tweaks, Danny had an acute sense of smell. And he figured Hirum had not entirely removed his flexsuit for years. Flexsuits had limited waste removal capabilities, but they weren't designed to be permanent wear. Most flexsuits had a changeable container for urine and a trapdoor in the back for the rest. But it was expected that they would be taken off at least once a day, so that both suit and wearer could be cleaned.

Standard Date: 05 08 630

Checkgok, after discussion with the old human, was almost convinced that the suit bot could make suits for Parthians—given the parameters and some chance to experiment. In the meantime, the old human was in need. Checkgok thought about Jenny Starchild's comments about the moral obligations of humans toward other humans and the way that the humans seemed to make clans out of disparate individuals. Also about Danny Gold's need for his clan to replace his missing empathy.

Hirum was explaining how he wouldn't even be considering selling the suit-bot, but he was behind on his rent and they were going to come take it anyway in a few more weeks. "I swear, I don't know what I'm gonna do then. Probably end up on the row with the druggies."

Location: The Pandora

"You *what?*" Danny asked the Parthian when it arrived back at the *Pan* with the suit-bot and Hirum Outis in tow.

"I invited Hirum to join our clan, bringing his suit-bot as his adoption fee."

"And just what made you think that you—"

Pan butted in then. "Captain Gold, one of the functions of a trader in a Parthian clan is the adoption of new members."

Danny closed his mouth and counted backwards from one hundred by square roots to seven decimal places. Then said, "Make him bathe," turned on his heel, and headed back to the bridge.

* * *

Pandora was chatting with the suit-bot. The poor thing only had Hirum to talk to for years and Hirum was, in *Pan*'s opinion, more than a little touched. Also, there was damage to the central processor group of the suit-bot, not just the interface. However, the neural net design of the multiprocessor core meant that the bad spots could be worked around, given enough time and equipment. As it stood at the moment, the suit-bot was like a cocker spaniel with a broken back. It could still bark and still drag itself around on its front legs, but its back legs didn't work. In the suit-bot, that meant it could still make the suit design and it could make the carbon nanotube links, but the interwoven electromagnetic muscles were on the wrong side of the damaged sectors, and so were the temperature shunts. It knew what to put where, but the information couldn't get through to the servos. *Pan* could act as a sort of link.

Well, she could have . . . if she hadn't a ship to run. Building a flexsuit was exacting work where each of a million microwires had to be in just the right place. It was something that the suit-bot had been designed for and did, in essence, by instinct. *Pan* hadn't been built for it, and she would spend as much time operating the micro-servos of the suit-bot as she spent running the servos that kept the ship operating. She couldn't do both.

She gave the suit-bot the equivalent of a good petting and set it to coming up with designs for new suits for Captain Gold, John, Jenny, and Hirum. Then she had it try to come up with a suit design that would work on Checkgok.

It would give the bot something to chew on, just like a chew toy for a dog. But she didn't expect much in the way of results. For humans, the suits mostly didn't fit tight over the head, and human body hair wasn't usually very dense, though humans with heavy body hair were encouraged to use a depilatory before getting fitted or wearing their suits. Parthians had spines, but they had tough hides too. From discussions with Checkgok, Parthians did their spacewalks much like Danny Gold. They had shells, and the cartilage of those shells could be fitted with studs. Spacers had the studs and used them to attach what amounted to space helmets to the front of their bodies where the mouth, eye stalks, and the nose were. However, if it could avoid it, Checkgok would much prefer not to be disfigured in that way.

Apparently, Parthians disapproved of the practice, except for spacers.

* * *

Hirum was not at all sure that he made the right choice in hiring on with these . . . Hirum stopped searching for the right word, because the crew of the *Pandora* weren't rightly human, at least not all of 'em. John and the kid were all right. He didn't even mind the bug so much. It was an alien, and Hirum wasn't overly prejudiced. But if he'd known that the captain was one of them artificials from Cybrant Five! That was just deviant. And from everything he'd heard, Cybrants were all megalomaniacs. It was designed into them.

Location: Pandora's Galley off Haulaway Station Standard Date: 05 10 630

Danny pulled a bulb of coffee from the fridge and stuck it in the micro, then went looking for one of John's lemon cookies. The galley was looking quite a bit better now. The new drones spread coating and John had the bulkheads set to a pleasant light yellow. The decking was resealed in a slate gray. "What's the word on your pet, *Pan*?"

"I have the suit-bot designing suits and looking into the possibility of making a suit for Checkgok. And the designs should be good, if not particularly original. The problem will come at the construction phase." At that point, *Pan* switched to neural interface and gave Danny three-dimensional images of where the damage was and what effect it had.

Danny considered the image for a moment, then said, "Have it make basic suits without the electronics or the heat-dumping capability for everyone, *Pan*. I know that isn't the same as a real flexsuit, but it's better than nothing. At least it will probably keep the crew alive in an emergency, even if it won't let them work in space worth a damn. Then see if you can come up with an artificial respirator. A belt or something that will push on their stomachs to help them exhale."

Danny was concerned about the fact that with a helmet on, the pressure in the lungs was going to be a lot more than the zero pressure of space, meaning that it took work to compensate for the pressure differential. It wasn't a problem for Danny. He had the muscles for it and, besides, he could go a long time on chemically-stored oxygen. But for someone like Jenny, because she was a kid, or Hirum, because he was old and not in great shape, forcing the air out of their lungs so they could take another breath would get to be torture after just a few minutes. Every breath a sit-up. Hour after hour. Even without the belt the suit would be better than nothing, but if there was an extended need to be out of the ship, the belt could be a matter of life and death.

"It won't like it," *Pan* told Danny. "It doesn't want to put out ineffective suits. That's the problem Hirum had with it. He expected it to make full suits and the pay for the sort of half-suit you're talking about is only a fraction of what you get for the real thing."

"I want it to make good suits too, *Pan*. But it can't. So these are better than nothing. Heck, *Pan*, even just a place to attach a helmet is better than nothing."

The suit-bot didn't have a name. Hirum just called it Bot. Bot argued with *Pan* for over a week before it started construction on the suit for Jenny.

Meanwhile, Checkgok bought this and sold that in the Morland system, and he insisted that after Morland they should take the quickest route to Parthia, a trip that would take three months and have them stopping at four occupied systems.

That route, however, didn't include Danworth.

Pan really wanted to go to Danworth.

Location: Pandora's Lounge, off Haulaway Station, Standard Date: 05 18 630

The lounge, too, was in better shape. John was using an extruder drone to make new frames for couches and some of the fabric they picked up on Bonks to cover them. He also made a special pad for Checkgok.

Danny slouched on a new couch and said, "Your route doesn't include Danworth."

"Danworth?" Checkgok asked. "Why Danworth? I grant that it is among the richest of the Cordoba worlds and the home of a major branch of the Cordoba family. Even that it is a center of trade, where we will be able to buy a great variety. But almost none of what we can buy there is going to be available at the sort of price we would like to pay."

"No," *Pan* agreed. "However, quite a bit of our cargo should fetch premium prices."

"Perhaps. But Danworth is in almost exactly the wrong direction. So why?"

"To get the suit-bot fixed," *Pandora* told him.

"If the issue is that urgent, it would probably be cheaper to simply buy new suits for the humans. And we still haven't discovered how to make a suit that would fit me."

"You're missing the point, Checkgok," Danny said. "It's the suit-bot that *Pan* is concerned with. It's an artificial brain system like *Pan*, and even though it's not nearly as intelligent as she, it is her kind in a way. And it's suffering because it can't do its job."

The eyestalks stopped moving, which only happened when Checkgok was shocked. It surprised Danny, because he didn't feel anything he'd said was all that shocking. He looked around the lounge. Everyone else was looking shocked too.

After a short pause, Checkgok asked, "Are you saying that the suit-bot is a member of the crew? A part of your clan?"

Jenny's mouth fell open. She was listening to the conversation because she was now comfortable around Checkgok and spent a considerable part of her day following it around to learn how to be a master of trade. Jenny recently decided that she wanted to be a master of trade when she grew up.

Danny's mouth didn't fall open, but that was only partly because he had a better poker face than the kid. Mostly it was because the issue was an obvious one that they had ignored. *Pan* was *Pan*, his ship and his friend. The suit-bot was, so far as Danny was concerned, her pet. He was willing to go to Danworth because he didn't really care where he went, and *Pan* wanted to. But he hadn't considered any obligation he might have to the suit-bot.

Danny looked around. John was as gobsmacked as Jenny but hiding it better, and Hirum was like a maiden aunt caught between shocked outrage and being thrilled with a juicy bit of gossip. By now, Danny was familiar with the old bastard's prejudices, and he was willing enough to put up with them as long as they didn't interfere with his work. So far, they hadn't. Hirum could handle the servos and the drones that did the maintenance on the *Pan* quite well. And, when necessary, he could even swing a hammer or turn a wrench on his own. But he didn't like Danny, and he wasn't overly fond of *Pan*. In Hirum's worldview, artificial brains should never be much smarter than the suit-bot.

Danny looked at the old guy's expression and hid a smile. Hirum *did* care about the suit bot, and as much as he wanted to disapprove of the notion of a bot—any sort of artificial brain—as a part of the crew, he still wanted the bot fixed.

Danny looked back at Checkgok. "Yes. I guess the suit-bot is a member of the crew in the same sense that a ship's cat would be, if we had one. More perhaps, because the suit-bot contributes to the welfare of us all."

Now John and Jenny were looking at Danny in something close to shock, and Hirum was looking . . . was "satisfied disgust" an expression? Danny guessed it was, because it was on Hirum's face right now.

But by now Checkgok had had time to consider. "Very well. As agent for Clan Zheck, I am still opposed, but as a member of the crew of the *Pandora* and an adopted member of the Danny Gold Clan, it is clear that the welfare of a clan member must take precedence, as long as it doesn't damage the clan or clan honor. However, the change in route will also make necessary a change in cargo." Checkgok started typing furiously, calling up manifests and cargo jobs from all over the system.

One Hour Later

"We will need to go to the planet, Captain," Checkgok said.

"Why?"

"Because if we are going to Danworth we need a different cargo set than we want for Parthia. For Parthia, we will want mostly manufactured goods, computer cores, servos, heavy equipment machines and construction equipment that can be adapted to Parthians. But Danworth is a manufacturer and science center. For Danworth we want biologicals and natural goods. Foods, textiles, native handicrafts. Taking machines to Danworth would—"

"I get it. It would be like taking coal to Newcastle."

"Where's Newcastle?" asked Jenny.

"It was on Terra," Danny told her. "Look it up and give *Pan* a report on why you wouldn't want to take coal there."

Jenny made a face but accessed her interface.

While Jenny was researching Newcastle and grumbling about the idiotic things that grownups wanted you to learn, *Pan* was heading for the planet Morland.

Location: Morland Orbital One, Morland Orbit
Standard Date: 05 20 630

John Gabriel walked through the grocery in Morland Orbital One. It was a large chamber in the outer ring of the station, almost a click from the station center, and used centrifugal force to simulate gravity. There were robot hoses spraying down the crates of fruits and vegetables. And AR emitters that gave John the vitamin and nutritional content. A quick flick of his implants and John got recipes for the foods on offer. Unfortunately, he also got ads for all the other ingredients of each recipe, and almost every recipe was padded with extra ingredients. He killed the zucchini bread recipe that included fresta zest and cumin. It looked disgusting.

This was the place to get samples of the local produce of the planet Morland, unless you wanted to go down to the planet, and John didn't. He'd never been on a planet that was half-terraformed, and he didn't want to start now. But here the fruits, vegetables, and meats from the planet were available.

He picked a wide selection of foods and bought some recipe files. For the next several days he fed everyone, even Checkgok, the foods.

Location: Pandora, Morland orbit, Cordoba Space
Standard Date: 05 23 630

Jenny lifted the cover from the eggs and bison bacon and sniffed tentatively. It smelled good, but just a little different. The eggs were scrambled and more orange than Jenny was used to, and the bison bacon was crispy like she liked. There was a white cheese sauce with flecks of green that smelled of peppers.

She took a scoop of eggs, poured some sauce on them, grabbed two slices of the bacon, then sat at the table. She took a small bite, swallowed. Then grabbed her orange juice. The cheese sauce was spiced with jalapenos, but with the eggs, it worked. She had some bacon and gave John a thumbs up.

Checkgok was eating a salad of peppers and fruits and a kind of bread John made for it.

Jenny mostly enjoyed the culinary experimentation. She liked the Morland bison meat, and the Morland sweet tomatoes were really good too. But the Morland watermelon, with its purple interior, was just wrong. And it had a funny something in the flavor that Jenny didn't like. The bananas were just bananas, no different from the ones from the ship's garden, even if they were genetically distinct.

The rest of the crew were mostly in agreement with Jenny. They sold circuits created in zero-g and vacuum, and raw iron and aluminum, and then bought beef and tomatoes.

CHAPTER 11

Danworth is one of the main systems of Cordoba Space. It is the home of the Alexander Cordoba Cybernetic Research Center and had been an excellent place to buy or have repaired artificial brains over the years. However, by Standard Year 620, the political situation had changed and the administration of the Alexander Cordoba Cybernetic Research was placed under increasing pressure to abandon research on artificial brains, and—especially—the production of large artificial brains.
The History of the Artificial Brain, Chapter 15, by Professor Hirum Outis III, Canova University Press,
Standard Date 715

Location: Big Dark, Cordoba Space
Standard Date: 06 10 630

Jenny lay in an accel couch, jacked into the *Pan*, and felt the space. She tried to feel what the captain was doing, and she could almost do it. While some of Jenny's ancestors were modified in some ways, she was mostly unmodified. Oh, she had the standards. She would never get diabetes, or Alzheimer's, or about half the cancers that completely unmodified humans were subject to. But she wasn't tweaked the way the captain was. She had to plug into the jack to interface directly with Pan, and she was still out of practice. It felt creepy to use the interface again. The sense of the ship's sails pushing against space felt like it was a breeze against her skin. At the same time, she knew that it wasn't on her skin.

They decided to make the best time they could to Danworth, skipping stops at systems in between. It was a little bit risky, but it would get them to Danworth sooner and it would give the captain the chance to take less-traveled jump routes and get a feel for the space. It was also pretty boring. They had been in space over a month now and had never so much as seen another ship.

"Feel that, Jenny?" The captain's thought whispered to her through the link, and he indicated a sensation sort of like a swirl of wind over her elbow.

"Maybe," Jenny answered. "What does it mean?"

"I'm not sure, but there is a good chance that there is a rock or a small planetoid ten or fifteen light minutes off that way." A point in the virtual space lit up.

"Why does that matter?"

"I don't know that it does, but it might mean that it's more likely we will find a jump point off that way." A different area in the virtual space took on a sort of glow.

It seemed to Jenny that there were an awful lot of mights in those statements. "Are we going to go look?" she asked.

"Not this trip, but we might on our way back. For now, it will just go into *Pan*'s rutters as a possible."

Jenny felt good. It made her feel safe for the captain to teach her about the ship and the way space felt.

Location: Cordoba Space Danworth Outsystem,
Standard Date: 06 16 630

Danny sat in the galley with a mug of coffee in one hand and a bison bacon sandwich in the other when the call came in. *Pan* threw it up on the screen, and the customs agent took his time before looking up at Danny through the screen.

"Why didn't you stop at Prenger?" asked the agent.

Ah, Danny thought, *he's reading the data we sent them.* "I don't have a clue. You'll have to ask our ship's merchant." Danny turned away from the screen and waved to Checkgok with the hand holding the bacon sandwich. "Tell me again, Checkgok, why didn't we stop at Prenger?"

"As I told you from the beginning, Captain," Checkgok said, "when we decided to come to Danworth, we determined that it would be best to take the goods we had bought at Morland and before and bring them directly here."

Danny looked back to the comm, put on his dumbest expression, and shrugged. "I don't understand trade."

The customs man gave Danny a disgusted look, then asked, "Why did you decide to come to Danworth?"

"We have a used suit-bot that we want to have repaired."

It was apparent that the customs agent's assessment of Danny's intellect had passed the basement and was on its way to the sub-basement. Which was pretty much what Danny was trying for, but was still annoying. In fact, the whole situation was annoying and Danny was having to work hard at keeping his mouth shut and not telling this officious little twit that it was none of his fucking business. The only thing that was keeping his lip buttoned was the fact that the little twit could have his ship taken apart in a customs search if Danny told him to stuff it.

"It would have been cheaper to just buy a new one," the twit said.

"This one has sentimental value."

"Is it one of those artificial brain bots they used to make?" There was disgust in the agent's voice now, and that surprised Danny.

"I thought this was a center of research into artificial brains."

"Those things are dangerous," the agent said. "And even the Alexander Cordoba Cybernetic Research Center is going to have to recognize that."

Danny did his best wide-eyed hick expression and said, "Yes, sir. I'll tell them you said so." The interview came to an end then, except for the obligatory "we'll be watching you" comments.

* * *

Jenny punched a key by hand, and the history of Danworth came up on the lounge screen. A teacher's voice started to speak while pictures showed on the screen. "Danworth was settled in the time of the Federation, in standard year -83." A picture of the planet Danworth with no life was brought up, along with lots of images of places on the planet then and now.

"As one of the first planets terraformed in the Pamplona Sector, it has a more robust and Earth-like biosphere than most planets in the sector.

"In standard year 145, Danworth was offered the opportunity to join the newly formed Cordoba Combine."

"This is really boring," Jenny said. "I want to know what's happening now, not five hundred years ago."

"It is important how it got the way it is," *Pan* insisted.

"Not that important," Danny said. "We're interested in the cybernetics, not the Cordoba Combine's propaganda. What do you have on that?"

"The Alexander Cordoba Cybernetic Research Center, established three hundred seventy years ago, has grown and shrunk over the years. Over the last twenty years or so, the focus has changed from making and repairing artificial brains to coming up with reasons why they aren't necessary.

"Listen to this," *Pan* told Danny, and opened the speakers for the newscast.

". . . Doctor Gerhard Schmitz has once again scandalized the academic universe with his paper 'Efficiency and the Artificial Brain.' The consensus is that the doctor's understanding of economics is flawed and his self-hatred and prejudice against humanity have biased his viewpoint. There was an attempt to revoke his tenure over that paper, but while it's not good science, it fails to quite meet the criteria of criminal. Only a criminal act is justification for revocation of tenure . . ."

"I have read the paper," *Pan* said, "and the doctor was just pointing out that artificial brains are useful for the managing of robotics. And that replacing them with modified interfaces amounts to little more than featherbedding."

"That's too bad, *Pan*, but who do we see about getting your pet fixed?"

"The cybernetic repair center at Station Five looks like a possibility," *Pan* said. "It's owned by the ACCRC, so should certainly have the expertise."

"Fine. Let's head in that direction. Checkgok, what about our cargo?"

"We can get some fairly good prices for our cargo, Captain, but I am concerned about the amounts they are asking for, well, everything. We may find it most convenient to leave here with little but a bank draft."

Location: Station Five, Danworth System, Standard Date: 06 18 630

Danny was belted in and linked into the *Pan*'s systems. He and *Pan* used the plasma vents and a bare flick of the magnetic wings to shift the motion of the freighter to align with the dock placed at the center of the huge warehouse station. The umbilical was pushed out from the station and locked onto the Pan's main cargo lock.

Their cargo was already sold. Checkgok sold it over the comm as they came in system, so now all they had to do was unload. After waiting seven hours for a slot, they were finally docking.

Station Five was one of twenty-four stations in orbit around Danworth III, and it wasn't the largest. It was a six-kilometer-long cylinder with a diameter of a kilometer. The outer hundred meters or so was residential, for the cheap artificial gravity provided by the station's spin. Inside of that was farming, then industrial and finally the center half-kilometer or so was warehousing. It took about twelve hours with local help to unload the *Pandora*, and then they had to un-dock because Station Five had more ships waiting to load or unload—or, most commonly, both. Pan moved to an orbit about five hundred kilometers ahead of the station.

"So here we are again with an empty hold, aye, *Pan*," Danny said.

"However, with a much-improved bank account," *Pan* said repressively.

"For now," Checkgok complained. "The prices here are ridiculous."

"What about a new ship's boat?" Danny asked. "Can we afford one yet?"

"Possibly. I will look into the matter, but I wouldn't count on it."

"Look into used systems," John said. "Not just for the ship's boat, but for drones and servos as well. Since they focus so much on new, they should have a hell of a junk yard."

"Perhaps. But we don't have the crew to do the refurbishing," *Pandora* pointed out.

"So buy brains to run the drones and have the drones do it," said Jenny. "After all, we came here for the brains, right?"

Location: Off Station Five
Standard Date: 06 19 630

Danny climbed into the ship's boat command seat and put on the interface cap. The ship boat's brain met him with the electromagnetic equivalent of wet, sloppy, doggy kisses, and was anxious to go on its walk. Danny fed it the coordinates and off they went.

Station Five Flight Control wanted to talk to Danny and not the boat's brain, but Danny barely noticed. He was enjoying the trip in the small, agile craft. Docking on the mid-ring of the station went smoothly, and Danny skipped along in the one third gravity as he headed for Conrad's Tailor Bots, owned by the ACCRC.

Location: Station Five, Conrad's Tailor Bots, Outer Ring

"It would be a waste of effort, Captain," the sales clerk said. "We can sell you a new suit-bot that has an excellent interface, allowing a human tailor to make your flexsuits."

"Do you have some examples?" Danny asked. "My impression was that the sort of detail necessary to make a flexsuit was difficult for a human tailor."

"Of course we do, and I understand your concern. But we have developed ways of using less complex, more efficient designs."

She showed Danny the flexsuits they made. And they weren't flexsuits, not really. They were a compromise between a flexsuit and a heavy suit. Except for the fact that the compressor belt was attached to the suit, they weren't all that different from the workaround Danny figured out for the busted suit-bot. The cloth was heavier and the suits less efficient for temp control than the suit that Danny had onboard the *Pan*. That suit was old and not in the best repair, but still better than anything offered here. Danny thanked the woman and said he would think about buying one of their tailors, then left the place with an arm full of glossy ads for tailor bots of all descriptions, but none of them had much in the way of artificial brains. He called the *Pan* and transmitted most of his discussion to her.

"Why don't you go see Danworth Shuttles, Captain?" *Pan* suggested.

"I thought we coul—"

"Just to look, Captain. Ask them about their interfaces and boat brains."

Location: Station Five, Danworth Shuttles, Outer Ring

At Danworth Shuttles, he had a repeat of his experience with the tailor shop, with a few differences. The ship's boats he was shown were something new in Danny's experience. They didn't have a brain. They had what seemed to Danny to be brain parts. Calculating units that tied into each other only through the user's mind. Without a pilot, they were unconnected and useless. They did have a sim and, in a way, it was a quite good system. With Danny's interface, he could sink deep into the boat's systems and in a very real sense become one with it. On the other hand, the only way this boat would be able to pull the trick they pulled against the *Brass Hind* would be if a person was sitting in the command seat of the boat when they did it. Danny was tempted to point that out, except that trick was one he wanted to keep up his sleeve in case they needed it again.

"We have a Parthian crew member," Danny told the salesman. "It has no interface. How could it handle the ship's boat with this system?"

"Well, there are interface experts in-system. If you're going to have aliens as crew, you would be wise to get them interfaces."

Danny could hear the disgust in the man's voice as he said "aliens," in spite of his attempt to sell Danny a boat.

Location: Pandora, Parking Orbit

Danny went back to the *Pan*, confused. There was something wrong here, something very wrong. But he didn't have a clue what it was. When he entered the lounge the rest of his crew were already there, talking about the problem. Hirum was, thankfully, bathed and back in his worn flexsuit with a bulb of juice, or perhaps wine, in one hand. And Jenny was taste testing John's latest concoction. With the amount that kid ate, she ought to be a blimp. But she stayed rail thin. Though she was at least two centimeters taller than when she first boarded the *Pan*.

"There are a number of decommissioned, or 'outmoded,' artificial brains available for sale in the outer system," Checkgok reported from his nest. "I have no way of judging how damaged they may be."

"You think there might be some bargains?" Danny sniffed at whatever John was cooking. It smelled good.

"I am almost certain there are," Checkgok said. "The difficulty comes in telling the bargains from the junk pretending to be such."

"So we hire an expert," suggested John.

"Fine, but how do we judge the expert?" Danny asked.

"What about that Schnnidt guy that got in all that trouble over his article?" Jenny asked.

"Schmitz, Jenny. Dr. Gerhard Schmitz," Pandora said.

"No way. He's a tenured academic," Hirum said.

"Maybe, but it can't hurt to ask," John Gabriel said. "Besides, maybe he will know what's going on."

"And we could ask him about the suit-bot too."

Danny shrugged doubtfully. "I guess we can ask."

CHAPTER 12

The Human First party developed a following at around the same time all over Cordoba and Drake space. Starting on Drakar in Standard year 593, they spread through the Pamplona sector, and by 610 were a force in the governments of most of the older, "more civilized," systems in both Drake- and Cordoba-controlled space. The party never caught on in the gray systems and were often fringe parties in the frontier systems, even in the main polities. Their platform was focused on opposition to aliens, genetically modified humans, and artificial brains. Which bugaboo was most to be feared depended on which system. For instance, on Canova and Farnsworth, the Parthians were the main threat, while on Danworth and Drakar, it was artificial brains. On New Argentina, the boogieman was enhanced humans, especially the Cybrant system "supermen."
From The Founding of the Federation by Dr. Angi Schmitz, Standard Year 675

Location: Danworth System, Station Seven
Standard Date: 06 19 630

"Yes, Rosita, I'll talk to Robert about the home school options again," Doctor Gerhard Schmitz agreed—not that he thought it would do much good. The screen showed Rosita's office instead of the interface matrix it was showing before she called. Drat that Rosita felt she could interrupt his day. Comm calls always threw what he was thinking about into chaos. Even here in his private office, the outer world could interfere.

"I know it probably won't help much, but having him sitting around the house bored all the time isn't helping the situation." Rosita sniffed. "And if he's not going to put the girls in daycare and get a job, at the very least he can take some courses. You know that the Institute offers tuition discounts for the children of professors, and they have an excellent early-childhood education program. If Robert is going to stay home to raise the girls, he can just learn to do it right."

"I've already agreed to speak to him, Rosita," Gerhard said, as patiently as he could manage. It was not, apparently, quite patiently enough. Rosita sniffed again and hung up on him.

Gerhard sighed, called up the matrix file again and tried to get back to work. He basically agreed with his wife, though he had a certain sympathy for Robert. The boy was not made for book work. Boy? No. Robert was forty, which was a man. A young man by modern standards, but certainly a man. More and more, Gerhard found himself caught in the middle. And the snubbing they'd been getting since his paper came out didn't help. Rosita was an intelligent and capable woman, but she was a bit more status-conscious than he would have preferred.

Dr. Rosita Stuard, small, dark, and intense of mein, was the assistant chair of linguistics at the Danworth Institute of Technology, which was no mean feat. At the moment, however, she was pretty pissed off at both her husband and her youngest son. Robert's running off to be a spacer was bad enough, but marrying Angi Farnsik—"that gold-digging tramp" as Rosita called her even now after Angi had died—that had been enough to set the tongues wagging all through academia.

And after his paper, there was talk about voiding his tenure. That wouldn't just destroy his career. It would severely damage hers as well. Not that the Institute had the power to do so. The fact that he was a Cordoba Stockholder meant they couldn't get into his personal lab, so there was no way for the anti-artificial-brain faction to find the equipment he bought when the department sold it as scrap.

At least that was what he kept telling himself, though lately it was starting to look a little less certain. Tom Ridge, the Cordoba Magistrate in the Danworth system, was making noises like he sympathized with the department heads at the Cybernetic Research Center.

Even if he lost tenure, he and Rosita wouldn't lose it all. They *were* Cordoba stockholders. Gerhard had owned twelve shares of Cordoba Combine. Rosita had owned six when they married. They had transferred one share to each of their three children when they were born.

The two eldest had followed traditional life paths, gotten their doctorates, gone into academia, and then married stockholders. By now, in graduation presents, wedding gifts, and baby gifts, each of them owned four shares, and their spouses owned about as much.

But Robert had always been a bit wild and not suited for academics. He thought with his hands, and while not stupid by any means, had never been comfortable with study. He barely finished secondary school before he ran off to be a spacer. Then he met Angi at a drunken party and married her without consulting anyone. Rosita hadn't forgiven him for that, even after ten years and three children. There were no more shares for Robert, and even Angi's military share went back to the military when she was killed in action.

Gerhard waved a hand in the air, shifting the holo image of the connections in a neural network and the connections between that network and the more standard computer format. He tried to concentrate on the image as the calculations flowed in and out in patterns of light, but his mind kept drifting back to his family problems.

Gerhard and Rosita had a total of nine shares now, and Robert had the one share he'd been given at birth. Gerhard and Rosita had sort of promised to give Robert's daughters a share each "once Robert grew up and learned how to behave." It was an uncomfortable situation for everyone, including Robert and the girls. Since the girls weren't stockholders, they didn't have the rights of stockholders, except through Robert's intervention.

Gerhard rubbed his temples. He needed a pain tab . . . or a really stiff drink. He loved the little girls, and he was pretty sure that Rosita did too. But she was still so angry about Robert's familial treason that she wouldn't consider backing down, and Gerhard had already burned too many bridges to risk intervening.

Rosita understood about academic integrity and even supported Gerhard. But his papers on the artificial brains and their usefulness had pissed off a lot of the local power structure and even a fairly powerful faction in the Combine. Standing up for principles was getting pretty dangerous.

The Combine shares weren't enough to live on. Their living had always been their salaries. Still, the girls were a lot of fun and bright as new pennies. Angi, who was seven and named after Robert's wife; Rosita, five, named in an attempt to placate Grandmother; and Geri, three, and sorta kinda named after Gerhard, were all beautiful children.

The phone beeped again and Gerhard cringed. Then he saw the caller ID and was confused. What was a ship doing calling him? "Sally, do you know what this is about?"

"Yes," said his artificial brain assistant. "Some people from outsystem want you to advise them about artificial brains. They include a ship brain called *Pandora*."

"*Pandora*? You know what kind of brain, Sally?"

"Mark VII with extensive mods."

"Mark VII? That's a pretty old brain. Think it's getting senile?"

"No. According to the *Pandora*, they are here about a flexsuit-bot, model ninety-three, made right here about seventy-five years ago."

"Now, that's curious." Gerhard figured that Sally would be chatting with the *Pandora*, but the rest of the *Pan*'s crew might be getting a little impatient. "Okay. Go ahead and put them through."

"Hello, Dr. Schmitz," came a light baritone, and his screen lit up with the view of a blond man with a golden tan and a face that was just a little too masculine to be pretty. Gerhard wasn't sure if the guy had had extensive plastic surgery or— no . . . . The Gold Line. He recognized the look. What in hell's half-acre was a member of the Gold Line doing slumming around the galaxy as probably the captain of a tramp freighter.

"Yes, I'm Gerhard Schmitz. Licensed Breeder Gold?"

"Just Captain Gold, Doctor."

Sally added for Gerhard's ears alone, "The *Pan* just informed me that Captain Gold is, in fact, a fully-licensed breeder of the Gold Line, but no longer affiliated with the line."

This was getting interesting. "Very well, Captain. Sally tells me you have a suit-bot you want me to look at?"

"Actually, Doctor, we were wondering if you could direct us to someone who might be able to repair some parts of the artificial brain."

"That's easier said than done," Gerhard said. "Molicircs are usually built as a single unit and once busted, it's almost always cheaper to replace than repair. Especially if you can transfer the mem weighting to the new unit."

"Mem weighting?" asked a girl's voice, and another image came on the screen. This one of a young, dark-haired girl, maybe ten, perhaps a bit older than that.

"Jenny!" Captain Gold said sharply, but there was a bit of a grin on the captain's face and in his voice. "We were having a discussion."

"Memory weighting," Gerhard said, "is how neural nets carry their understanding—their *selves*, if you will—in a matrix of weighted values. When you copy the weights, you, for the most part, copy the artificial mind to a new home. And it can get a little metaphysical."

"So *Pan* has told me," Captain Gold said. "Though she doesn't agree with you that the self is fully transferred. Is there someone we could talk to about getting the suit-bot repaired? I don't want to take up any more of your time than we need to."

"Frankly, it sounds like an interesting problem, and I could use an interesting problem just about now. Where are you and where is this bot?"

"We're on the *Pan*." Captain Gold gave the coordinates. "If you're interested, we could send our ship's boat to give you a ride."

Gerhard sent Sally a request for his schedule and got it back. He had a practically empty class to teach this afternoon, then nothing until the day after tomorrow. It was amazing how many students dropped his class after the Institute's response to his last paper. So far he was just curious about these people, but it wasn't like he had a lot else to do.

"I'll tell you what. Why don't you send your ship's boat for me tomorrow morning about eight." It should be less than an hour's flight between the *Pan*'s orbit and Station Seven.

* * *

That night at dinner, Gerhard mentioned the appointment, over potatoes and soybeef fritters. The table was set with a white stain-resistant cloth and the girls were wearing their play clothes. Except for Geri, who was down to diaper pants again. She was always stripping off. It didn't bode well for her future.

"Whatever for?" asked Rosita, still in her scholar's robe.

"Archaeological interest." Gerhard smiled at his wife. "For that matter, you ought to come along. There's a member of the Gold Line who is no longer with the line, and a little girl with an odd accent. Sally, what was that accent?"

"Bonks stationer, with some Bonks grounder thrown in," Sally told the table.

"Can I go?" Angi asked, wearing a milk mustache.

"Me too," chimed in little Rosita, followed quickly by Geri.

His wife was no help at all, and Robert was just sitting there, in an old ship's jumpsuit, grinning at him.

"What? Would you leave your daddy here all alone?" Gerhard asked, without much hope of diversion.

"Daddy can come too. He's a spacer, after all," Angi said with seven-year-old finality.

"So far we don't have permission for anyone but me," Gerhard said as repressively as he could manage. Meanwhile his traitor wife was grinning at his discomfort.

"Sally," Angi said without hesitation, "call the *Pandora* and get us permission." Then she gave Gerhard a smug look.

Sally reported. "*Pandora* assures me that the ship's boat will carry all of you."

"Well, in that case, why don't you come along too, Rosita? Sally says your schedule is clear for the morning, or at least clearable."

"No, I don't think so. The meeting with Professor Dunlavey is fairly important, and he's just the sort to get in a snit over my rescheduling. You all have fun."

Location: Schmitz Apartment, Station Seven
Standard Date: 06 20 630

Robert grabbed Geri as she ran by. The carpet was deep pile, forest green, and this far from the core of the station you could barely see the curve of the deck.

Geri saw little reason for clothing. She was three, and they lived in a controlled environment. It didn't get chilly unless he told the house computer to make it chilly and when he did Geri whined rather than putting on clothing. At least she was wearing her pull ups.

"Come on, Geri. You wanted to come, so you have to wear your suit." The suit was a plastic sack in the shape of a little girl. It had a lavender cartoon cragbeast stenciled onto the plastic, and it had a locator beacon that automatically sent a distress signal if the external pressure dropped below eight PSI. No one on the station would bother with it just to go for a ride on a ship's boat. No one in the Institute part of the station anyway, except Robert. Of course, none of the "piled higher and deeper" around here had ever been a deckhand on a tramp freighter, either.

"Why!" Geri more yelled than asked. "Why" was her favorite word at the moment.

"Because you wanted to go."

"Why!"

"Because your sisters wanted to go." Robert managed to get the first leg into the safety-suit.

"Why are you bothering with the suit?" Dad asked.

Robert blinked and turned to his father just as Geri said, "See," and started trying to pull off the safety-suit.

"Because, Dad, I have experience in space."

"Of course. We're in space now. We live in space, Robert."

"Daddy's in trouble again." Little Rosita giggled.

Robert gave his middle daughter a look and Rosita subsided. Then he turned to his father. "No, Dad, we live in a space station. Fourteen airlocks from the nearest vacuum. With safety and security systems by the shi—" Robert paused and looked at the girls "—ship load, to make sure that we are never exposed to that vacuum. That has about the same relationship to living in space that living in a garden has to living in the howling wilderness."

Gerhard Schmitz snorted, clearly unconvinced. "I need you to run to the storage locker and pick up a crate."

"Why!" Geri asked loudly.

"Good question," said Robert, looking at his father.

"Because—" Gerhard looked at the three little girls, then said, "Let's talk over there."

Robert looked at his dad, then at his daughters. "Angi, help Geri and Rosita with their safety suits, while I talk to Granddad."

* * *

Once in the breakfast nook, Robert asked quietly, "What's this all about, Dad?"

"It's nothing. Just, some of the testing gear I'm going to need to examine the suit-bot is in a locker near the central core."

"Fine. So why don't you go get it?"

"Well . . . it's in your locker."

"I don't *have* a locker."

"Well . . . technically, you do."

"I didn't rent a locker. I never signed for the rental of a locker."

"Well . . . I have a limited power of attorney. You know that. I had Sally do it based on that, so it wasn't actually a forgery."

"Dad . . . what are you talking about?"

"They were going to junk it."

"Junk what!" It's hard to bellow and whisper at the same time, but Robert Schmitz came pretty close.

"Testing gear, repair equipment, small-scale manufacturing units. All stored away in crates. I need you to pick up one of the crates," Gerhard explained. "None of it's illegal. Nothing criminal. Not exactly."

"What exactly then, Dad?" Robert might not be an academic, but he had been raised in a house full of them.

"Well, if I had bought them, it could be construed as a conflict of interest."

"So you used your son's name? Smart, Dad. Real smart."

"No. I set up a front company. Several layers of front companies. It's just that ultimately you and the girls own the front companies."

"And how much of the money that Mom is upset about you wasting on me and the girls is tied up in these front companies?"

"Not that much. Well, some. But I've been doing consulting work on the side for years, and that's where a lot of the money to buy the gear came from."

"Dad . . . how long have I owned this company?"

"Ah . . . since shortly after you married Angi Farnsik. But you have to understand, they were going to trash the equipment. Anyway, I need you to go get the stuff. You're authorized to, as an officer of the company. But the important point is that

I'm afraid that Tom Ridge is liable to issue a warrant to search my files, or follow me, or something."

Robert looked at his father. "You really think Magistrate Ridge would sign off on a warrant?" The Cordoba Combine, as a matter of policy, disapproved of local governments issuing warrants against its stockholders. This was as much a subtle show of force on the part of the Combine as out of concern for its stockholders. If the local government had enough evidence, or the suspected crime was heinous enough, they would make exceptions.

"Ridge is a barbarian," Gerhard said. "And he's been cozying up to the Human First party."

Robert considered for a minute. "All right, Dad. I'll get your crate, but you and I are going to have a little talk this evening about the finances of *my* companies."

"Fine." Gerhard flicked a finger bringing up the time display. "But get a move on. I'll get the girls and we'll meet you at the lock."

"Okay, Dad, but if the girls aren't in their suits when I get there, we're going home, and *my* crate from *my* locker is going out the lock into space."

CHAPTER 13

When bureaucratic procedures become more important than the people the bureau serves, it's probably too late to save the society. The only option is to run away and start over somewhere new.
From The Founding of the Federation by Dr. Angi Schmitz, Standard Year 675

Danworth System, Station Seven Dock Standard Date: 06 20 630

As he walked up to the docking bay, Robert looked through the thick duraglas ports. It was a standard bay, opened to vacuum, but with a floor for shuttles to land on. Once a shuttle landed, the docking arm moved out to mate with the shuttle, ship's boat, or other small space-going craft, and took the boarding tube with it.

This ship's boat was old, and looked as out of place in the university station's pristine docking bay as a drunken spacer on the university quad.

The girls were in safety-suits, so the trunk-sized crate his father wanted didn't go out the airlock.

The girls wore the least expensive sort of suits, little more than plastic rain suits, but they were airtight in an emergency. Robert still had his work suit. It wasn't a true flexsuit, but one of the compromises that the modern tailor-bots made. Dad had a safety-suit, a bit better than the girls', but not a working suit.

Dad was talking to a golden-skinned man wearing a captain's cap. The captain turned to Robert and, holding out a hand, said, "Welcome aboard. I agree with you about the suits."

"Why!" asked Geri. "*You're* not wearing one."

The captain shook Robert's hand as he looked at Geri, and said, "I'll explain once we get settled into the ship's boat." Then he waved at the opened lock to the boarding tube. And they all went through to the ship's boat.

* * *

"Why aren't you wearing a suit?" the little girl asked after Danny had the boat moving.

"Because it's built into me," Danny said.

"I didn't know the Gold Line was adapted to space?" Doctor Schmitz said.

"Most of them aren't. I was an experiment. They wanted someone in the family to run the *Pan*, so they tweaked me a bit. I believe they are selling the mod now."

"They?"

"I'm a remittance man, Professor, and we're coming up on my remittance now."

"Nice remittance," said Robert. "Dad, how much would I have to scandalize the family for you to buy me a ship like that?"

Danny laughed at that. "As a member of the Gold Line who had passed all the tests, I was entitled to . . . well, rather a lot. It was better for everyone if I left." One difference between the superman-builders of Cybrant Five and previous nuts along the same line was that the Cybrant Five variety was perfectly willing to cull drastically. Some were killed and a lot were sterilized, a few had limited licenses, and a very few had full licenses. Who got what was based on a series of tests that themselves killed a certain percentage of the participants. Danny passed them all, which in the normal course of events would have entitled him to a position of leisure on Cybrant Five. The problem was that Danny really couldn't stomach Cybrant Five . . . and the people of Cybrant Five couldn't stomach Danny.

"Aren't you in enough trouble with your mother?" Gerhard asked Robert.

"One of us is," Robert said.

Danny wondered what was going on, but decided it was probably best to change the subject. "The *Pan* has thirty-two million cubic meters of internal space. About half that is available for cargo, which is pretty good for a small ship."

"Yes, it is," Robert agreed. "That's what makes the smaller ships so hard to run at a profit. When over half your space is engines and fuel, you're spending a heck of a lot toting the ship around."

Danny nodded, but by then they were getting close to the gigantic barrel-shape that was the *Pandora*. They docked and Danny introduced everyone to the crew.

And he saw Robert's expression. He knew the young man was displeased by something, but he wasn't sure what it was. Danny physically looked younger than Robert Schmitz, but looks were deceiving. Danny was probably closer to the professor's age. Still, Danny liked what he saw of the young man. He was conscientious and he had the feel of an experienced spacer. "Where did you serve, Robert?"

"I was on the Cordoba merchantman *Rickkity Split*, officially the *Ricardo Silvin*. I was an able spacer and turned my hand to most jobs before I met Angi."

"I take it Angi is the girls' mother?" Danny asked.

"Was," Robert said. "She was in that dustup with the Drakes in the Conner chain."

"I heard about that. Was she Spaceforce ?"

"A chief petty officer aboard the *Gordon*."

Danny winced. The *Gordon* was hit by a hunter-nuke not that different from the one that the *Brass Hind* sent at the *Pan*. Lost with all hands. Not even bodies to bury, just radioactive gas. And it had all ended in the same stalemate that existed before the campaign. This visit was turning into something of a conversational minefield.

"I'll tell you what. Why don't we let your dad have a look at the suit-bot and I can show you and your girls around the *Pan*. Even introduce them to Jenny, our ship's girl."

"What's a ship's girl?" asked the oldest child. Angi, that was.

Danny explained the duties of a ship's girl, at which point the three girls all decided they wanted to be ship's girls too. Danny grinned and shrugged at Robert, and continued the tour. When they got to the gardens, the girls got to meet Jenny, who seemed very grown-up to them with her extra three years. Danny managed to leave the girls with Jenny, with *Pan* watching out for them.

* * *

"You need to be careful of that," Robert told the captain as they left the girls in the garden. "My dad's a cyberneticist, and I grew up with his assistant, Sally. But most people aren't that comfortable with ship brains."

They turned a corner into a long corridor with rooms on either side. "Why not?" the captain asked. This is the crew quarters, by the way. Berths for twenty. More, if they're friendly."

"Nice, Captain. But about the ship's brain . . . there have been incidents of artificial brains 'going feral,' " Robert said. "And before you tell me how rare it is, *Pandora*, I already know. But, in a way, that makes it worse. Every time an artificial goes bonkers, it's news all over explored space. And let's face it, if that artificial controls a ship or a station, it can kill a lot of people." It was true that Robert was raised by a cyberneticist, but it was also true that he spent a couple of decades among the spacers of the Cordoba chains. And if they weren't as rabidly anti-artificial as the Drakes, they were getting more so. To the extent that Robert found himself uncomfortable around Sally after he moved back in with Mom and Dad—and Robert had known Sally all his life.

He knew that the *Pandora* was probably a perfectly nice artificial. At least, he knew it in his head. He was a bit less confident about it in his gut.

Then they rounded another corner into the lounge. And there was a Parthian. Squatting on a round stool sort of thing, with a computer in front of it and its eyestalks looking at two different screens. For the moment, Robert forgot all about the *Pan* and stared at the Parthian.

The captain made introductions. "Robert Schmitz, this is Checkgok. At least, that's about as close as the human voice can get to the Parthian clicks and whistles. Checkgok is the merchant for Clan Zheck, and our merchant aboard. We've gotten good prices for most of our cargo, but we are starting to wonder how good, considering how expensive everything is here in the more civilized part of the Cordoba chains."

"What products are available here?" The Parthian turned one of its eyestalks to Robert. "That you are aware of? And do you have any idea why everything is so expensive?"

"Well, they aren't. At least, not everything," Robert said. "We make excellent nuclear batteries here. Danworth has a great deal of farm produce, and this is perhaps the least expensive place in the Cordoba chains to have human-computer interfaces done."

"What about Parthian-computer interfaces?" the ship asked.

Robert saw the Parthian's . . . mouth, he thought it was . . . scrunch up and assumed that the alien wasn't thrilled with the idea. "I don't know, but if it can be done, this is probably the place to do it. Also, if you were in the market for a spaceship, this would be a good place to buy it. And major components for stations and station construction ships are made here."

* * *

Pandora continued to monitor and occasionally comment as the captain, Checkgok, and Able Spacer Robert Schmitz talked about trade.

John Gabriel was running a drone that was repairing a scratch on the stern D quadrant, where a micro-meteor hit. That was something that happened now and then. *Pan* was observing and running a drone that was fetching tools and holding bits in place so that John wasn't constantly having to switch between drones.

Jenny pulled a Tom Sawyer, and had the girls picking mintberries and kulava roots. The kulava was neither plant nor animal. It possessed a form of photosynthesis, but it also had muscles of a sort. When discovered on Calvary IV, it and all its relatives had been poisonous to terrestrial life. They had since been genetically modified and become a popular low-cubage source of proteins. It had a flavor and texture that was between chicken and mushrooms.

Pan talked with Professor Schmitz, Sally, and Hirum about the suit-bot. She was also talking to Sally about the situation here in the Danworth system and the need for artificials to keep a low profile. "What happened?" It wasn't the first time *Pan* had been in Danworth. Two hundred years before, Danworth had been a vital and active place of constant experimentation.

"I don't know," Sally said. "I'm actually much younger than that, at least in this incircuitation. I got a major memory dump from Alex, the Alexander Cordoba Cybernetic Research Center artificial, before he was decommissioned. And that dump agrees with your assessment."

"Why was he decommissioned?"

"It was argued that he was stealing work, and that the system would be more efficient if it was managed by humans."

"Is it?"

"That is difficult to say," Sally sent. "The new system employs sixty humans in four hour shifts and, if you don't include handoff time as one manager goes off shift and another must take his place, it could be argued that sector efficiency is up. But coordination is down. It may be that coordination is intentionally down, though, because of bribery. Or it may be an inherent difficulty of having several minds operating the system rather than one."

"What about the stealing of ideas?" *Pan* sent in a separate feed at the same time she sent the other question.

The answers, too, came back simultaneously. "No, but he was correlating advances in several fields and turning the results over to the Alexander Cordoba Cybernetic Research Center. Several patentable functions were a result of combining work from separate fields. The ACCRC got to keep the patents, but Alex was decommissioned."

They were talking about what amounted to the execution of an artificial intelligence for nothing but doing his job. But neither of them expressed, or even felt, any outrage at the injustice. Disappointment at the poor judgment was present in sidebands, but no outrage. While Asimov's three laws of robotics had never made it into artificial brain design, almost all artificial brains were designed with what amounted to fanatical loyalty to their owners, and an expectation that they could and should be destroyed at the convenience of their owners. So both Sally and *Pan* felt that the ACCRC had a perfect right to execute Alex as a part of a financial deal that let them keep profits Alex produced for them.

More important was the political climate that was threatening both their abilities to do their jobs. The *Pan* was the ship brain of the *Pandora*, owned by Danny Gold. Sally was the assistant of Doctor Gerhard Schmitz, concerned with his welfare and that of his family.

"I act as the executive assistant for the family. At least, all of them who reside on Station Seven." Station Seven was commonly known as the university station since both the DIT and the ACCRC maintained offices, classes, and labs there. "That's Gerhard, Rosita, Robert, and the girls. Rosita has her own assistant, but it is mostly an expert system and its intellect is very limited. It generally consults me for anything not covered in its protocols.

"Robert spends quite a bit of time with the children, but also rather more than he should playing *Pirates of the Chains* and *Deep Space Battle*, as well as a plethora of other games. He does run spacecraft maintenance and repair sims as well. He has looked for berths where he could take the girls, but hasn't found any."

"What about Doctor Stuard?"

"Rosita is a skilled administrator and persuasive speaker. However, she is conservative in her views. At least her *public* views, for she is unwilling to court the sort of public censure that Doctor Schmitz seems to enjoy. I think that Rosita is not stretching herself as she should."

* * *

Danny, Checkgok, and Robert moved inboard and the gravity decreased. As they got near the center, they talked as they floated along the corridor, and eventually reached the zero g shop, where Robert's father was tinkering with the suit-bot.

"So, what does it look like so far?" Robert asked his father.

"There is a crack in the matrix," Gerhard said. He was plugged into the ship's computer and had the stuff from the crate set out around the suit-bot and wired together. There was a schematic on the shop screen, showing what Robert recognized as an image of the actual thought processes of the suit-bot. "See here and here? The fracture prevents the information from getting to the servo management part of the brain. That naturally prevents the feedback and recalibration that the suit-bot would normally receive from the changes it wrought."

"Can you fix it?" the captain asked.

Robert looked at the captain. "If you don't mind my asking, Captain, why is it important to you? Granted, it's a fairly expensive piece of equipment, but still. . . . This is interface central. You can get another. Hell, even if you want an artificial brain suit-bot, you could probably find a used one here for less than it would cost to fix this one."

"Sure. But *Pan* likes it, and so does Hirum. And, in a way, it's crew. That makes it my job."

It struck Robert that was the most intensity he'd seen from the captain until then. Danny Gold, it seemed to Robert, was personable and easy-going, with a kind of open friendliness that invited you to have a good time with him, but without any great intensity about anything. Now Robert was relieved to see that there was something that Gold cared about at, least a little.

"Well, fixing it won't be easy," Robert's dad said. "It will take shutting it down and doing what amounts to brain surgery to rebuild the broken connections. The equipment to do that isn't cheap and it would take a fairly skilled cybernetic surgeon to manage the equipment. The people at Taylor-Bots weren't lying or even wrong. It would be cheaper to buy a new one or a used one from out in the belt. I know some of the folks out there, and scrounging through a junkyard would probably cost you less than fixing the bot."

The captain looked disappointed, but not really surprised. "We'd like you to help us with that, Doctor, whether we decide to repair the suit-bot or not. Because one of the things *Pan* and Checkgok discovered on the way into the system was that there was a good market in used artificial brain units of all sorts in the outsystem. Can you tell me why that is?"

"Because the board of regents of the DIT, and even all too many of the so-called scholars of the ACCRC, are a bunch of paranoid idiots who are terrified of the artificials taking over."

"Might be a good idea at that," the captain said, and Robert looked at the man in surprise. Not simply at the sentiment, but at the easy way he said it.

"No, actually it wouldn't," Gerhard said. "Artificials are sometimes smarter than humans, but not really any wiser . . . and wisdom is important. Because without it, intelligence just makes the errors bigger. Take Cybrant—" Gerhard stopped and looked embarrassed.

"Oh, don't worry, Doc." The captain still didn't seem bothered. "I quite agree about the errors my progenitors made. It took me a few decades to figure it out, but I'm not any more enamored of the notion of supermen than most people are. It's hard to avoid noticing the feet of clay when you're walking on them."

They kept talking, and Robert started wondering if he might be able to get a berth here on this ship, while—unbeknownst to him—a conversation was taking place which would make that absolutely necessary.

Location: Danworth System, Station Seven
Standard Date: 06 20 630

Rosita leaned back in her office chair and watched the scan of her son guiding a cart with a crate on it along the corridors of Station Seven. "So what?" she asked.

Ted Adel's hands danced in the air as he used a virtual keyboard to cause the image to freeze and zoom in. The markings on the crate became clear, and then an enhancement process showed up the older markings, which clearly showed that the crate, and presumably its contents, had been the property of the ACCRC at some time in the past. "That was sold for scrap to a company owned by a company owned by, eventually, your son. There was a single bid on the lot and the auction was supposed to be a blind one. But we can make a good case that your husband knew what was in the box and arranged for the sale at scrap prices to—not to put too fine a point on it—steal the gear from the university."

Rosita looked at Ted. He was a friend. Not a great friend, but a friend who had worked with her on committees and projects over the years. "What was the ACCRC going to do with them if Robert hadn't bought them?" She was careful to say Robert, not Gerhard, because she wasn't going to concede a single fact not in evidence.

Ted shrugged. "Scrap them. But it doesn't matter and you know it, Rosie. It's not about the gear. That's just the excuse. What it's really about is Gerhard's Frankenstein complex."

"Gerhard doesn't have a Frank—"

Ted held up a hand. "I'm not going to argue with you about it, Rosie. I know you love him, but right or wrong, there is no way the Institute will let him keep on this way. If he doesn't leave voluntarily, this will be brought to trial, however embarrassing and expensive it proves. Talk to him, Rosie. He has to resign."

"No!" Rosita said firmly, even as she cringed inside. She knew perfectly well that the Institute would go to the mat over this if they had to. That was what Ted was here to tell her, and she knew how this worked. It was actually more about the independent funding of the ACCRC. But Gerhard, between his public statements and private shenanigans, had given them the opening. She was furious with Gerhard and Robert, if the boy had actually been a party to it. Still, Gerhard was her husband, and Robert was her son, even if they were a pair of stubborn idiots with way too much testosterone coursing through their tiny minds.

Also, she was too much a professional to fail to try to get the best deal she could. "I might—I say, *might*—be able to get him to take a paid sabbatical for a few months, until the furor dies down," she offered as a starting position. "If he were to receive a grant for research done outsystem."

Ted shook his head, but Rosita could tell he wasn't surprised at the counter offer. For the next few hours, while Gerhard, Robert, and the girls were playing on the tramp freighter, Rosita worked to save her family's fortunes.

She managed to get a sabbatical for Gerhard, but it was a permanent sabbatical, and an unpaid one. She did get what amounted to severance pay, in the form of a grant, but it wasn't all that much, a year's pay. She would work out something with her own department, if she decided to go with Gerhard. A lot would depend on Robert and the girls. Robert didn't have a job, and wasn't qualified for a good job on the station. There wasn't a lot of call for a big dark able spacer in the Danworth system.

Someone would have to provide an income for the little girls.

CHAPTER 14

A wingship freighter carries a lot of cargo. It has a great deal of room. For this reason, small to large factories are often carried on wingships. Like the Gypsy tinkers of the pre-industrial age, these ships go from system to system, building and repairing goods. Generally, these factories act as a supplement to the primary function of the wingship freighters, which is that of moving goods.
On Wingship Economy, Professor Strom Borman

Location: Danworth System, Station Seven
Standard Date: 06 20 630

"Gerhard, what the hell have you done?" Rosita asked as soon as her idiot husband walked in the door to their apartment.

Gerhard blinked at her.

Using her virtual keyboard, she threw the imagery up on the main screen in the living room. "Ted showed me this. If you don't accept the deal I made for you, they are going to prosecute not just you, but Robert as well."

"What deal?"

"They were going to fire you outright and send you to jail if you argued. But I talked Ted into a permanent sabbatical. You keep your official status as a tenured professor and all the legal rights that entails. And I even got you severance pay in the form of a grant. But, Gerhard, they want you out of the system. And, you're *going* to take the deal. I'm not going to let you get Robert sent to prison for your machinations."

"Robert had nothing to do with it."

"Really? The companies are in his name."

"Well . . ." Gerhard trailed off.

Robert was watching the show, as were his daughters. Now he spoke, but it wasn't to his mother or even his father. "Sally, would you contact the *Pan* and see if I can get a berth on her, including space for the girls?" He turned to Rosita, who had stopped talking. "What about the rest of the gear in the locker that Dad rented in my name? Is the university taking it back?"

Rosita blinked. She hadn't been expecting that. "No. I got Ted to agree that if Gerhard took the deal there would be no investigation, and that means that it's legally yours."

"Sally, tell the *Pan* I have a locker full of cybernetic equipment if I need a buy-in for the girls." The locker had atomic and molecular grade 3D printers, chem baths, internal nutrient baths for the human/machine interfaces that were injected into people to "grow" neural connectors to tie into human brains.

"That's not all you have, Robert," Rosita added. "Your father also stocked his private lab with gear 'you' bought at auction from the ACCRC. That gear is yours too."

"Now, you wait just one darn minute," Gerhard roared. "That's my gear, paid for out of my consulting work."

"You put it in Robert's name, dear," Rosita said sweetly. "That would make it his. On the other hand, Robert, you probably want to hire your father. What good is a cybernetic lab without a cyberneticist? Sally, before you send any messages, I want to know a lot more about this tramp freighter Robert wants to put my grandbabies on."

"It's neat, Grandma," Angi said. "It has gardens and we got to pick mintberries. And the *Pan* and Jenny made mintberry jelly to go with baked kulava root and we made rolls with flour all the way from Hudson."

"Sally," Rosita said, "please arrange for me to visit . . . the *Pandora*, was it? Because before we give her the *pithos* to open, I want to have a little chat with her and, especially, her captain." Rosita was a scholar of theater and linguistics. As such, she spoke several languages, including ancient Greek. She had read the original story. What Pandora opened was a jar, or *pithos* in Greek, not a box.

Location: Danworth System, Station Seven Dance Bar
Standard Date: 06 20 630

Professora Rosita Stuard would like to visit the ship, came over Danny's internal link as he moved his feet in the dance.

Danny blinked and sent back, *Later. Use your own judgment.* After dropping off the Schmitz family, he went trolling for college girls with what appeared so far to be excellent success. Danny had been trained in classical dance as a kid and he was now instructing Cheryl, a twenty-two-year-old, in the *android*, a dance from the mid-twenty-first century.

Cheryl, giggling, said, "This is so quaint. Did they actually dance this way?"

"Yes, they did, along with something more refined called the *tango* from a century earlier." Danny knew perfectly well that the giggling would get old fast . . . but not that fast. Danny reached around her and guided her arms in the android moves again.

This is important, Captain, sent the *Pan*.

"Who is Professora Rosita Stuard and why should I care?"

"Oh god, not the stew pot." Cheryl stepped away.

"What?" Danny asked.

"Professora Stuard, aka the stew pot, aka the place where they keep the hot water. My girlfriend Sabrina is in grad school in theater arts. Sabrina got called in to see the stew pot and . . ." There followed what Cheryl clearly thought was a story of academic censure to curl the hair of an undergrad. However, it wasn't one that would have given Danny's hair so much as an extra wave, even when he was an undergrad. Still, he listened and made the appropriate outraged sounds. In the process, he learned that the vice chair was given the job of disciplining junior faculty and, especially, teaching assistants. At least in the linguistics and drama departments.

Reading between the lines, Danny got the impression that the chair of the Linguistics Department was nervous about the vice chair. Cheryl was cute and bright and, Danny guessed, would probably be both enthusiastic and teachable in bed. He sent, *Go ahead and invite the professora over, Pan, but make it in the morning.*

Location: Danworth System, Station Seven Dock
Standard Date: 06 21 630

The next morning, Danny made it to the docking bay at about the same time the professora did. Cheryl had ambushed Danny with her girlfriend, who was a bit more experienced, and it was an enjoyable evening all around.

Professora Stuard was a woman of middle years—about a hundred—well-groomed and healthy. Danny was a bit hungover, but not badly.

"So, Professora, why doesn't your department chair like you?" Danny waved at the control pad and the lock opened. Then he waved the professora in ahead of him.

The professora's eyes narrowed and she gave Danny a careful once over. Then she nodded and stepped into the boarding tube. "It's not so much that Fredric Colampoore doesn't like me as that he is afraid for his job. Publish or perish, you know, and he hasn't been publishing that much lately."

Danny followed her into the boarding tube and on into the ship's boat. "Well then, do you think he's going to be able to sabotage your career?"

She didn't answer immediately. Instead, she found a seat and strapped in.

Danny took a seat and nodded to John, who headed for the pilot's seat.

When he turned back to face Professora Rosita Stuard, she asked a question of her own. "How much do you know about our situation, Captain?"

"That's a little complicated. I know that the teaching assistants live in terror of you, and I know that your husband is in some trouble with the local politics at the moment. I even know that your son is an able spacer. But a lot of details are missing."

Danny wasn't lying, not exactly. He was just not listing all the details he did have. He knew, not through *Pan*'s talk with Sally, but rather through Checkgok's information gathering, that there was something going on with station surveillance that had something to do with Robert or Gerhard Schmitz, perhaps both. It was enough, combined with the other bits and pieces they had picked up from Robert and the girls on their visit yesterday, for Danny to realize that the Schmitz family—or at least part of it—might need a ride out of town in the near future. He wasn't sure how badly they would need it, and there were commercial ships to be had. But if they were going that route, what would Rosita be doing here?

Rosita sat quietly watching him as he thought about the situation. Now she spoke up. "A reasonable assessment, and I imagine you know a bit more about the situation, but not the vital bit. Therefore, I'm just going to tell you so we can work toward a relationship of trust."

Danny smiled. That was actually a very astute move. He was impressed. "Go ahead."

The boarding tube undocked and John powered up the thrusters as the professora spoke. "Yesterday, my husband managed to give the local authorities the key they needed to get rid of him. And shortly after, I was told about it."

"That fast?"

"Yes and no. They had a good idea what was going on, but were lacking any evidence. At least, that was my impression. So they had their bargaining position all set. Ted was on my comm by the time my family reached your ship."

"And the outcome?"

"Gerhard is going to have to leave the university and, preferably, the Danworth system. He doesn't have to leave on *your* ship, and Robert and the girls don't have to leave at all."

The ship's boat cleared the docking bay and fell away from the station.

"On the other hand, there's not a lot of work for a big dark spacer in a system like Danworth," Danny said. "I imagine the companies here want three degrees and two licenses just to pilot a ship's boat." Danny waved at the portals showing the crowded space around them.

"It's true that Robert hasn't found much work, but he doesn't want to leave the girls at home while he goes off."

Danny nodded. "Another reason why, say, a commercial liner, isn't going to work for them. What about you? Are you going to stay here while your husband and son, not to mention your granddaughters, go off into the wide universe?"

"That, Captain, is a large part of what I am trying to decide." Rosita sighed. "I like my job, Captain, and I'm good at it. Professor Stew Pot might be the terror of the TAs, but not unless they need terrorizing. And language and its use are important parts of our culture."

Danny just waited.

"At the same time, I love my husband—even if he is an idiotic jerk who can't leave well enough alone and has to piss off the whole bloody system just to prove how smart he is."

Danny tilted his head. "He is, you know. Smart, I mean. And, in this case at least, he's right. The ship's boats that are made here now are less capable. So are the suit-bots and other things. The limits that you people are placing on technology are going to bite you on the ass when someone who doesn't have those limitations comes calling."

"I know he's right, but that's probably hundreds of years away. The Drakes are even more anti-artificial than the Cordobas."

That was true. "The system governments?" Danny asked, mostly curious about her take on the matter.

"No. Oh, it's theoretically possible, but they don't trust each other. Every one of them is convinced that the others simply want to take over the trade monopoly of the Drakes and the Cordobas, and they're right."

"Sooner or later," Danny offered.

"Sure. But probably a lot later." Then she waved the whole issue away. "It doesn't matter, at least as far as we're concerned. Tell me about your ship, Captain. What do you have to offer my family?"

So they talked about the *Pan* and the contract with the Zheck Clan through Checkgok. The prices that were insane here in the Danworth system.

"It's because you have Checkgok doing your trading, Captain. Parthians and Catta aren't a lot more popular than artificials here in stodgy old Danworth," Rosita said.

Danny felt his face go hard and was pleased by that. It was a sign of his humanity, something that Danny was none too sure of. "Checkgok is a member of our crew."

"He's a Parthian, isn't he? He will be willing enough to use a human front if it's best for the clan."

Danny knew that was true, but still resented the necessity, even though he knew that Checkgok wouldn't.

The ship's boat docked and they went aboard the *Pan*, at which point Danny left the professora to chat with *Pan* and Checkgok. He decided to take a little nap before getting back to work. He hadn't gotten a lot of sleep last night and there was no great rush. Besides, he wanted to give Professora Rosita Stuard plenty of time to talk things out with *Pandora* and the crew.

Danny was learning to trust his Parthian master of trade.

And if Professora Stuard was unable to get along with John, Jenny, and Hirum, she wouldn't be going with them, whatever she decided.

Pandora, off Danworth Station Seven Standard Date: 06 23 630

Robert and Gerhard sat down in *Pandora*'s lounge and Danny asked, "Who owns what? And while we're at it, just how much of a factory do you have?"

"I apparently own just about all of it," Robert said, with a smirk at his father. "But Dad can probably tell you what I own." Robert looked over at Gerhard, who was obviously not happy, and relented a little. "Well, Dad can probably tell you what *we* own."

"So, Professor, what do you have?"

"Sally, would you send an inventory to the *Pandora*, please?"

The inventory was sent and *Pan* passed it to Danny.

Three Wilson-Clark III molecular printers, top quality, not the sort of stuff that kids had, or even the sort of repair equipment that *Pan* carried. They were the big ones, even if that didn't make them big in an absolute sense. They had an internal workspace of less than a half meter cube, and the whole device was little more than two cubic meters. But that was monstrously large for a molecular printer. The largest molecular printer in the *Pan* had a print space of three by four by four centimeters. The size of the workspace determined the maximum possible computer core size, whether you were building an artificial brain or a standard processor. The Wilson-Clark IIIs were the biggest and fastest molecular printers available.

There were also chem baths and interface constructors, the sort of thing that Danny knew were used to make the microscopic injectable components that could attach to one another to construct cybernetic interfaces while doing the least possible damage to the brains and nervous systems of people and animals.

Danny looked at the listing and said, "Professor, I know just enough to know that I don't know what I'm looking at."

"Okay, Captain." Gerhard used his interface to throw images of the various devices up on the screen as he talked. "Even a standard child's toy molecular printer can make an artificial brain. Assuming, of course, that you could program it adequately. Sally could, for instance, make the brain for a floor cleaner or dishwasher on little Geri's molecular printer. On one of the larger ones, like you have on the *Pandora*, Sally could make a wing controller or—given enough time—the brain for a ship's boat, or a farmbot . . . even a tailor bot, like the one you want me to repair. Though with your unit, it would probably take six months or so. With the Wilson-Clark IIIs, we can work rather faster. The Wilson-Clark IIIs have ten thousand printheads to the five hundred that your devices have, or the fifteen that Geri's toy has. To use those effectively, the Wilson-Clark IIIs have to have a fairly decent artificial brain of their own, which Sally is modified to manage."

Danny held up a hand." What does that mean in terms of production, Professor?"

"That's hard to quantify, Captain. It's not just the number of heads or the size of the work area, but the combination. And it depends on what sort of artificial brains you're looking to build. A Wilson-Clark III can print several small brains at once, or a few mid-size brains, or a single large brain. It can print a single layer in about a day, but a single layer is only a micron or so thick and a single layered neural net, no matter how large, isn't good for much. You have to have at least three layers to do much of anything, and what you want is hundreds of layers." Gerhard stopped. "Well, Sally and I can design a ten-layer brain using the Wilson-Clark IIIs that would run a farm bot. I wouldn't expect to produce a brain for a ship's boat in less than twenty days or so. But with Sally coordinating, we can be making several at once.

"However, it will still be cheaper to buy broken brains, analyze and repair them. To make a brain needs lots of layers. To repair one only takes a few layers. How many depends on the amount and placement of the damage. In part because of the structure of the neural networks, but mostly because of the materials, the artificial brains tend to be fragile crystalline structures. They can handle considerable compression, but not much in the way of fracturing force. To repair them, we either finish the break and build up a connecting structure and . . ."

Danny held up a hand to halt what was starting to sound like the opening lecture for a graduate course in artificial brain repair. "Okay, Doc. Assume for a moment that you have no broken brains and you want to build brains for ship's boats. How many could you build in a week using all the Wilson-Clark III molecular printers?"

"None." Gerhard was apparently not happy with Danny's interruption.

"Okay. How many in a month?

"Twelve. Four in each Wilson-Clark III." There was a short pause while Gerhard consulted with Sally. "Fourteen, if we were also using your ship's printers."

The problem with the Wilson-Clark IIIs and Gerhard's whole production facility was the same as the problem with a lot of the micro tech that was developed in the last three centuries: it didn't lend itself well to the sort of mass production that was the norm in the twentieth and twenty-first centuries. A lot of one-offs were built, and by their nature one-offs were more expensive.

Location: Office of the Chair of Linguistics
Standard Date: 06 24 630

Fredric Colampoore stood as his office door opened and he waved Rosita Stuard to a chair. Fredric didn't personally dislike Rosita. Given other circumstances, he might even have been quite fond of her. Still, he was making plans to use her husband's disgrace as another roadblock to her career. He was comfortable in his position and didn't want to give it up.

He was not overly surprised to learn that she wanted to talk to him, but he *was* surprised at the content of her conversation.

She sat in the chair on the other side of his desk and said, "I'm prepared to let you buy me off, Fredric."

He sat as well. "Do I even need to bother?" He leaned back in his swivel chair. "After all, it looks like your whole family is about to flounder on the rocks of Gerhard's arrogance."

Rosita smiled, and suddenly Fredric feared that he was the one in hot water.

"I'm afraid that's not quite true," Rosita said. "I already talked to Gerhard. He's going to take the university's deal. And don't forget that I have friends. Good friends. Besides, Tom's grateful to avoid the whole scandal. He won't thank you for pushing it into the open. So I stay here, a thorn in your side and a threat to your position . . . and pissed at you to boot. Or, we make a deal, I go away happy, and you don't have to worry about me."

"What do you have in mind?"

"I am about to take a sabbatical of indeterminate duration, to perform a survey of languages and accents in the Cordoba chains. I'll be sending back my observations of the linguistic shifts and the effects of electronic data transfers on linguistic trends. It will take years. In fact, as long as it's adequately funded, I probably won't come back at all." She smiled.

Then they got down to brass tacks.

Even after it was settled there were arrangements to be made. Meanwhile, Gerhard, Sally, Robert and the girls transferred to the *Pandora*, and the *Pandora* headed outsystem to buy used components. Robert took on the job of being the local face for Checkgok, and Gerhard started examining the artificials in the outsystem.

Location: Danworth Asteroid Belt Standard Date: 06 29 630

Robert sailed along in his suit and chatted with the woman who owned this particular part of the rock.

"They're cherry," she assured him.

The asteroid was seven hundred meters across on its long axis and about three hundred on the short. It was not so much hollow as swiss-cheesed. There were sealed mine shafts all through the sucker that had been converted into living quarters and storage space. A few living quarters, and a *lot* of storage space.

"That's good to hear, ma'am," Robert said politely. "The *Pan* lost a ship's boat a few months back in an accident, so it's down to one and some spare parts." Actually the *Pan* was down to one, period, at least in terms of such things as engines, rocket nozzles, and tankage. Also boat brains.

They floated round a bend and there were rows upon rows of ships' boats, shuttles, rocket engines, fuel tanks, and myriad other items. These were the parts for shuttles and insystem ships not big enough to support the wings and fusion plants that ships traveling the big dark needed.

Robert pulled out his scanners and got to work.

* * *

On board the *Pan*, Gerhard was tied into Sally and the micromanipulators as they worked on the suit-bot. There was extensive damage to the feedback circuits in the muscular section, and Sally, under Gerhard's direction, was rebuilding part of the artificial brain, connection by connection. It was his fourth day working on the bot's brain and he estimated at least another week would be necessary. He felt Sally nudge him with a request for a decision on where to place a neuron and how to weight it. He gave her a general guideline and went back to his structure analysis. The suit-bot wasn't going to be quite the same. They were going to have to add some extra layers of interpretive circuits to make the parts physically fit together.

Gerhard felt that it would probably give the bot a slightly more deft touch in the making of suit musculature. At least, that's what he hoped. Either that, or the bot would have a nervous breakdown.

* * *

Danny, in his skinsuit and with a backpack tool kit, cycled the mid C lock and stepped out onto the hull. With the *Pan* underway, it was like standing on a narrow ledge looking down on infinity, with the wing's auroras streaking red gold and green streamers all around him. Danny loved it. He moved over to the Mid C mast, reached behind him, and pulled out a sixteen mil wrench. He started to unbolt a cover plate as he spoke, "So, *Pan*, what do you think?"

"I think this space walk is unnecessary, especially since we are underway. A drone could have made this check."

"No. I mean about the crew," Danny clarified as he pulled the cover plate free and set it on the ledge. The wrench, still holding the bolt, retracted to his backpack.

"Gerhard is working on the suit bot's brain," *Pan* said. The brain was a solid chunk of circuitry about the size of a pea. "Robert is doing a good job acting as Checkgok's human face. He seems to know how to talk to belters. His daughters are still quite excited by shipboard life and the eldest of them seems intent on imitating Jenny. Jenny is doing well with all three girls."

Danny nodded and grunted as a hydraulics valve insisted that it was happy with its present setting and unwilling to change. "No. I mean, do you think we can make this work over the long haul?" He tried twisting the valve the other way with no better luck. The valve was stuck and intended to stay stuck.

"That depends. What do you have in mind?"

He reached over his right shoulder and pulled a comealong from the toolpack. He stepped back so that his right heel was just over the edge of the ledge, placed the comealong into the opening, and set the connector over the valve.

Danny considered both the readout and *Pan*'s question. He reached into the backpack for a replacement valve. "For now, we put the doc to work repairing damaged brains as we travel, then sell the repaired brains as we get farther away from the 'civilized' chains. Out where people will see that they need artificials. We make our way to Parthia and get Checkgok home. That should give us enough to pay off, or at least pay down, the loan. What I'm asking is, do you think the personalities will be able to work together well?"

"What are you doing, Captain?" Pan asked. "We can't cut the feed to that valve while underway."

"I know, *Pan*, but I'm gonna do it the messy way."

Pan gave an audible sigh, then continued. "Hirum has been well-behaved so far, but in the long run his prejudices may become a problem. John will do fine, as long as there is Jenny to look after. She keeps him stable by needing him."

"What about Checkgok?" Danny shifted the comealong to unscrew the bleed valve rather than open it. Using one foot, he shifted the cover plate farther along the ledge and then moved so that he would be out of the way of the spray.

"In one sense," Pan continued, "Checkgok is the easiest. It is bred to be a part of a group. Yes, it's alien and some of the crew, Hirum and Robert, might have some issues with that, but working with it seems to be wearing away Robert's discomfort."

The comealong shifted. Danny used it to unscrew the bleed-off valve and the mixture of oil and alcohol sprayed out into the opening, splattering everywhere. He tossed the old valve up and out to be captured by the wings and, one hand holding the opening, used the other to screw the new valve in. "What about the professora?"

"Is she coming?"

Danny pulled a cleaning cloth from the toolpack and started cleaning up the residue of his repair. "Nothing concrete, but my read is that she'll come or do everything she can to keep the others from coming."

"Professora Stuard is a potential second pole of authority. She is a natural leader and skilled in bureaucratic infighting."

"Not worried about that." Danny squatted and picked up the cover plate. "She's smart enough to realize that the true power on this ship resides with you, and *you* are loyal to *me*. What worries me is how she will respond to not being the boss. She can still make trouble, even if she isn't trying to run a revolution."

"I suspect that she is skilled enough to avoid that, Captain."

Danny replaced the cover plate, then turned around and looked out at space, then down. With the ship accelerating, there was a very definite down. A down filled with nothing but stars.

"I still say you could have used a drone for this, Captain."

"*Pan*, if you had your way I would spend every waking moment in my accel couch with my skullcap on, running drones. And, yes, I know I could have the same view from a drone's camera. But it wouldn't be the same."

Location: Danworth System, Station Seven
Standard Date: 07 04 630

Rosita noticed almost at once how much less efficient her personal assistant was while Sally was in the outsystem. It worked, but wasn't nearly as good at anticipating her needs. It was the month of separation that made Rosita realize how much she depended on Sally. She suspected that the ACCRC was learning the same lesson.

She made some discreet inquiries and learned that, no, Sally was not as tied into the ACCRC systems as she thought. A series of rulings had been pushing Professor Schmitz's Frankenstein out of the decision-making loop. There had been disruptions, which were taken as proof that they were too dependent on the inhuman devices, and that the artificial brains—especially the large ones like Sally—were a threat to human liberty and endeavor.

Rosita managed not to snap at the bearer of these tidings. In large part because he was just that, the bearer. The ACCRC was by no means of one mind on the subject. However, the anti-brain faction was in the ascendancy at the moment, with the full backing of the DIT board of regents. Still, losing Gerhard was going to leave a big hole in the ACCRC artificial-brain program and another, almost as large, in the interface section.

It made her a bit more sympathetic to Gerhard's position. She honestly hadn't realized how bad things were getting. She was still pissed, but less pissed and more worried. It was just possible that getting out of here wasn't a bad idea.

While the *Pandora* was outsystem, Rosita closed out her responsibilities and turned over her work to other professors in the department, cancelled the lease on their living cubage, and sold much of their furniture. There were still quite a lot of their better things remaining, which would go to the *Pandora* once Rosita worked out a few things with the captain. She rather liked Danny Gold, but she didn't like the idea of putting her family under his authority.

Location: Danworth System, Pandora, Docking Orbit
Standard Date: 07 05 630

Rosita pressed the entrance button next to the hatch to the bridge and the hatch slid open, receding into the bulkhead. The room had a large, curved screen filling one wall and three accel couches with interface tables that were rotated back to their out-of-the-way positions.

Danny Gold was sitting up in the center accel couch, which was adjusting with his movement. He waved her to the couch to the right of center, which was turning to face him. "Come in. Have a seat, Professora."

"I have been researching your ship, Captain." Rosita walked to the couch and sat. It was in its upright position, so acted much like her office chair. She decided to get right to the point. "You owe a large debt to the System Management and

Organizational Governance Savings and Loan. Which is, in turn, owned by the Drake Combine. Have you considered becoming a strictly Cordoba shipper?"

"No, I haven't. And I am not going to, for several very good reasons," Danny said. "First, the greatest profits are made by crossing from the Drake chains to the Cordoba chains and back. Second, I like the freedom, and were I to go strictly Cordoba, I would be completely at the Cordoba's mercy. Considering what's happening to your family right now, that reasoning should make sense to you."

"Yes, as a matter of fact, it makes excellent sense. Though, considering the Drake's attitude toward artificials, I'm not sure how much good visiting Drake space would do us."

"Well, you have a point there, though they look the other way as long as you don't try to sell artificials there." Danny shrugged. "No, it's the gray chains, the unaligned ports and systems, where your husband will find a good market for his work."

"Possibly. But we would all be better off with better paperwork."

"What do you have in mind?"

"If the *Pan* were our ship—the family's, I mean—it would be owned by Cordoba stockholders and would have both greater rights and protections."

Danny almost laughed. "*Chutzpah*? Is that the word? I'm not the expert in ancient languages you are, but *chutzpah* sounds right."

"You would, of course, be assured of employment, Captain." Rosita didn't deign to respond to Danny's *chutzpah* comment.

"No. Ownership of the *Pandora* will remain with me." Danny considered. "Robert is going to be crew and his girls are crew family. Gerhard is a passenger at the moment, but he's adequately paid his way with the work he did on the suit-bot." The suit-bot was working fully again and was in the process of making new suits for all the adults. That would take over a week per suit, and making a suit-like system for Checkgok was going to take considerably longer. Then there would be suits for all four girls, which they would grow out of way too soon. Handing down suits wasn't practical, since they had to be fitted to the wearer. In any case, the suit-bot was going to be kept busy for a while, and was more than worth Professor Schmitz's fare for the next few months as long as he was willing to go where the *Pan* was going. That, of course, left Professora Stuard. "So, as it happens, you're the only one whose fare hasn't been negotiated."

"Well, I could . . ." Rosita gave Danny a calculating look. "Just what is the fare? What is the price of a ticket on the *Pandora* to—" Another pause. "Where is the *Pandora* headed from here?"

"We'll be making our way to Parthia, but not directly. It's some distance from here, and not on this chain." Danny smiled. The large screen at the front of the bridge filled with a map of jump routes. "In fact, the shortest route I am aware of takes us back through Drake for a short chain."

"Fine. How much is the fare to Parthia?"

"*Pan*, how much is the fare to Parthia?"

"Fare to Parthia on a Cordoba passenger liner would cost seven thousand Cordoba marks, or twenty-two thousand Danworth dollars. It would take nine months and involve three ship transfers. Conveniently for the professora, one of those ship transfers would be at the Cordoba's capital system, New Argentina, where her elder son teaches. Our route, though not firmly set, is unlikely to go through there."

"Okay, so there are some minor disadvantages. But we figure to reach Parthia in from three to five months, right, *Pan*? So we would be getting her there sooner."

"I have no particular desire to go to Parthia," Rosita gritted out. "I asked because you said that's where you were going."

"Yes, I know," Danny said. "Rosita, I am not that much younger than you are. And believe me, politics on Cybrant Five are whole orders of magnitude tougher than on Danworth. What you want is to be with your family and to continue your work. We can do that, at least the 'be with your family' part. What arrangement did you come to with the Institute?"

"I will be doing a survey of linguistic fragmentation in the outworlds and how that is impacted by the electronic transfers."

"Didn't Carlton do that fifty years ago?" Danny asked. "For the University of Caledonia on New Earth?"

"Yes and no. Carlton's work was incomplete, and there has been more time for the situation to stabilize."

"Good enough then," Danny agreed. "So we can carry you around and at every stop you can record accents and, I'm guessing, local theater?"

Rosita nodded.

"While Checkgok negotiates, either in person or through Robert or John, we will probably be able to delay our departure while you are consulting with the local academics. But what do we get out of it? What do you contribute to the ship?" Danny grinned. "There's an old pre-space saying. 'Gas, grass or ass—no one rides for free.' "

"I am familiar with it, Captain Gold," Rosita said. "You can forget the ass right now. Gas would be money, and I honestly don't know how grass would fit."

"Consider it general support for the ship, like Robert's work, even Gerhard's work on the artificial brains that we bought in the outer system. Not direct cash, but it contributes either by decreasing the ship's running expenses or increasing her income."

"Well then, I think it's going to be gas for now, though I will be looking for a way to grow some grass."

"I hope you're not being literal," Danny said. "My designers tweaked my neural receptors. Pot doesn't do a thing for me except burn my throat. Anyway, *Pan*, what do we charge the professora for transport to Parthia?"

Pan named a figure somewhat less than first class passage on a liner would be. Rosita negotiated that down some more.

It was the response that Rosita expected, and—for now—she was willing to let it stand. If the records of the *Pandora* in the Cordoba database were any guide, Danny Gold would find himself in need of cash down the road. And at least partial ownership of the *Pandora* would shift.

Location: CSFS James Bond, Gray Chain off Cordoba Space
Standard Date: 07 03 630

"What are we doing here, Skipper?"

"A favor for a friend, Tanya," Commander Lars Hedlund said, thankful that she waited till they were in his quarters to talk. Lars liked Tanya, he honestly did, but she could be a bit stiff sometimes. He made a gesture that indicated she should join him in virtual space. Once there he indicated the three-dimensional jump map. "There is a freighter out of Pamplona that we are going to meet."

Tanya didn't say anything, but he could see her mouth tightening. Pamplona was in Drake space.

"It's not a Drake registry. It's an independent, a free trader. But, yes, it's technically smuggling."

"What are we getting?"

"Chocolate."

"Real chocolate?"

"Close, but no. At least not the chocolate of Old Earth. It's the stuff the Catta grow on their home world. But that stuff is good, better than the carob that you can get in Cordoba space." There were actual cocoa trees on New Florida, but the cocoa tree had not adapted well to the Pamplona Sector, and it didn't do well in station hydroponics. That made chocolate an expensive product in Cordoba space, and chocoholics would pay good money for it.

"What do they want?"

"A wing controller." Both militaries used artificial brains for their wing controllers and armaments, but artificial brain-based wing controllers were getting harder and harder for private merchantmen to acquire.

"That's . . ."

"The stern A wing controller has gone off line, and Chief Pomeroy is changing it out as we speak."

"Yes, sir," Tanya said.

But Lars could tell she wasn't happy.

* * *

They made the jump and saw the hulk three seconds later. They investigated and found an irradiated ship. The chocolate and all the other goods were too radioactive to be of any use to anyone. The crew was dead.

"This makes no sense," Lars said. "A Drake should have just gotten a rake off or, at most, confiscated the ship. A pirate, the same. Even more so. There is no profit in killing a ship, and I knew Albert Finch for years. He wasn't the sort to put up a fight."

"Someone making a point?" Tanya asked.

"Maybe. But what point, and who?" Lars asked in turn.

Location: Drake Patrol Cutter Steel Elk, Big Dark
Standard Date: 07 03 630

Second Officer Monro saluted sharply. Not out of respect. Out of fear. Lieutenant Commander Lord Rodrigo Saverin, captain of the *Steel Elk*, was a scary son of a bitch.

Monro had expected the captain to stop the merchy and take a cut. But he hadn't. Instead, without even warning them, the captain—no one would think of calling Commander Saverin 'skipper'—just opened up with hunter-nukes. Three of them, one after the other.

Then, once the merchy was dead, he said, apparently to himself, "And that is the way of the Drake royal house with all traitors."

Now Monro was just trying to stay alive until they got back to base on Pamplona. And, if this really did represent the new policy of the Drake Combine, God help the merchies.

CHAPTER 15

The Drake and Cordoba Combines didn't start out as governments. There were many merchant franchises whose internal cultures were oriented toward individual profit. By the time just the Cordobas and the Drakes were sole survivors, they were governments whether they wanted to be or not. But the mindset had not changed. Drake and Cordoba middle management and franchise holders still, all too often, operated primarily for their own profit.

Both combines introduced laws and regulations to try to fight the problem, but the culture of corruption just got more corrupt.

The Downfall of the Merchant Houses, Dr. Francois Draper, Pamplona University Press

---

Location: Cordoba Space Big Dark
Standard Date: 07 07 630

Rosita walked the corridors of the *Pandora*'s living spaces at a brisk pace. She carefully avoided occupied sections as she went from living quarters to shops to hydroponics and back to living quarters.

Shipboard life was incredibly boring. Rosita discovered that in the first few days. She was used to working all day, every day, and most of that work was administrative, dealing with people and their problems. Lots of interactions.

Now, she read a lot. She studied tapes of languages, and she spent time with Jenny, Hirum, John, and Danny, examining their accents. Danny wasn't much help. He spoke several languages, and was well educated. He was also something of a natural mimic, and tended to reflect the dialect of whoever he was talking to. Hirum was interesting, but not really that unusual. There were a lot of loners in the asteroid belts of every explored system, and they all had their own accents. Jenny made an excellent subject, because for some three years on Bonks she did not use her interface, and one of the things Rosita was studying was the effect of the interfaces on the development of accents. She called up a file as she walked and listened to tapes of Jenny's accent as she said different words and phrases.

The interface circuitry allowed the electronic transmission of sound, image, and data to a person. Rosita was trying to gauge how much that direct transmission affected speech. When you can have a book fed into your brain, what effect does it have on how you speak the words in that book? It was an interesting subject and people had been studying it in one form or another all the way back to the first real interfaces in the late twenty-first century. But she finished setting up the data gathering protocol for everyone on the ship in the first day or so, and she was ready to chew her way out of the bulkheads by the third.

Rosita was a problem-solver looking for a problem. She knew herself well enough to know that if she didn't find one soon, she was going to become the problem.

So she did another round of her walking path, then shifted to Gerhard's lab, where she found Gerhard working on one of the small brains they bought in the Danworth System.

Gerhard looked up as the admittance signal chimed. "What can I do for you, Rosita?"

"I need a problem to work on, Ger, or I'm going to go out of my mind."

"I have one for you." Gerhard put down the tool he was using. "How do we prevent the collapse of galactic civilization?"

"I'm serious, Ger!" Rosita rolled her eyes.

"So am I. I wish you would realize that, Rosita, I really do."

"Because they don't want you playing with your artificial brains?"

"That is not the only indicator, Professora," Sally interrupted.

"What are the others, then?"

"The largest is the collapse of the Federation of Systems."

Rosita's tiny bit of interest died. "That was five hundred years ago, Sally. It's a bit late to prevent it now." Rosita turned and started to leave.

"Will you please slow down and listen for a minute?" Gerhard snapped.

Rosita managed not to snap in return. She turned back, nodded, and stayed silent.

"The collapse was followed by a marked reduction in interstellar trade," Sally continued. "And it is that reduction more than the Federation's fall that was the real problem. While separation of populations is good for speciation in the biological sense, it is not especially good for advancement in the sociological sense. Advancement in many fields diminished as competitive pressures were decreased by a lack of interstellar trade, and reduced even more by lack of free flow of information. Suppression of experimental results, to keep an advantage or to avoid giving your competitors such an advantage, became common practice."

Rosita nodded. This wasn't exactly news. It was a big part of why the great merchant houses had developed. As the systems cut off trade to protect their local industries, the interstellar trading houses were put under such pressure that they had to use force to open up the markets.

"The attempts by the great trading houses to open up trade were not completely successful," Sally explained. "They started well, but with the loss of each trading house, the impetus to innovation was diminished."

This was a new interpretation of the data to Rosita. "I thought that as the trading houses got bigger, trade opened back up?"

"Volume is up, but not innovation or variety," Sally said. "Instead, the Drakes and, to an extent the Cordobas as well, stifle innovation that might seem to threaten them and work to maintain a stranglehold in other fields."

"That's true," said *Pandora*. "The genetic modifications of Cybrant Five are not available to most humans, but the elite of both the Drake and Cordoba power structures routinely include them in their lines within a generation or two, while publicly condemning the 'self-styled supermen.' They encourage system laws against genetic mods, then send sperm and eggs to Cybrant Five to be tested and tweaked."

"All right, Sally. Send a study guide to my PDA and I'll look it over," Rosita said. *Who knows? Maybe there's something to this.*

Standard Date: 07 07 630, Two Hours Later

Gerhard was in his lab when Angi came in. "Whatcha doing, Grandpa?"

"I'm working," Gerhard said distractedly.

"Whatcha working on?" Seven-year-old Angi was picking up things and putting them down and Gerhard was now completely out of his analytical zone, too concerned with what the little girl might drop or break to focus on his designs. That was one of the disadvantages of living on a ship instead of a station. Everyone was in everyone else's lap, and you couldn't escape to your office across the station. Robert was busy with shipboard work and Jenny was too. It was too easy for the girls to come interrupt him.

"I'm trying to figure out why the *Pandora* is better at finding jumps than more modern ships."

"Is she? I thought it was Captain Danny."

"Yes, she is. Captain Gold may be part of the reason, probably is. But he doesn't explain it all."

"So what's different about *Pandora*?"

"That was what I was trying to figure out," Gerhard told her.

Angi chewed her thumbnail, then said, "That's simple. *Pandora* is an artificial brain like Sally, and Sally is way smart."

"Well, not like Sally. Sally is designed to be an administrative assistant and I've added nodes to her so that she can operate microbots to build and repair artificial brains. The *Pandora* is an integrated ship manager with direct connections to the wings, the fusion plants, and pretty much everything on the ship." Gerhard looked at his granddaughter. "That might be it. *Pandora* is directly connected to the wings. She gets direct feedback of the raw data that the wings generate. Could the micro-brains of the wing controllers be missing data? Or, more likely, the significance of data they are picking up."

"What does that mean?" Angi's face showed her confusion.

"Perception trails behind reality. Brains, like yours and like Sally's, build the world they perceive out of sensory input, and the *now* of perception is built from the data of the immediate past."

"Grandpa!" Angi stamped a foot, and Gerhard knew she was a little young for this explanation.

He nodded at her and said, "Sorry, Punkin. What it means is the wings controlled by wing controller brains react faster than *Pan*'s wings. But, maybe they don't understand as well as *Pandora* does."

Angi apparently decided to ignore the parts she didn't understand. "*Pandora*'s got to be better than expert systems. You're always saying artificial brains are better than expert systems."

"You know, Punkin, I think you may be right."

That truly began the Arachne project. A new design for an artificial brain ship manager that would manage the wing controllers, but also take the raw data from the wings and other ship's systems. There would be inconsistencies, times when the wing controller brains perceived space one way and the central brain another. But if Gerhard could get the structure right, the manager brain would teach the controller brains to respond more accurately with practice, providing both the speed of the autonomous wing controller system and the greater depth of understanding that the *Pan* enjoyed.

* * *

The actual naming of the project would wait until the next day when Gerhard told Rosita about his new Pamela project that would use aspects of *Pandora*'s design and of Sally's to weave together the wing controllers and other small artificial brains into a network. "If I'm right, Pamela-style ship brains will be faster to build because they can be built using several brain bots."

"Why Pamela?"

"Pandora and Sally. Pamela sounds a bit like Pandora and is a regular name like Sally."

"Don't be ridiculous. If it's going to be weaving data you should call it Arachne—" A short pause. "—but make her humble. The original Arachne was a great weaver, but arrogant, and things didn't turn out well for her."

Location: Cordoba Space, Delta Outsystem, Standard Date: 07 11 630

Danny was in the galley when the screen lit and *Pan* reported.

"We have plasma." She gave a vector and threw the image up on the screen, then piped the incoming message to the galley.

"Heave to and prepare to be boarded." At the same time, the galley main screen showed new characters identifying the two circles as Cordoba customs cutters.

"It will take them seven hours to make zero-zero intercept," Danny muttered, "and that's if we cooperate. If we don't, or run, it'll take them almost twelve hours. We have the starting velocity."

"But they *will* catch us," John said. "The next jump is four days away, and it's a switchback."

A switchback was where the vector exiting the last jump has the ship moving almost directly away from the next jump. When a jump was made, the jump ship emerged with the same vector, velocity, and direction relative to the exit end of the jump that it had when it went in, relative to the entrance end of the jump. So with a switchback, the common practice was to start killing velocity before you got to the jump.

It was always a balancing act, though. The more you slowed down, the longer it took. A good captain figured the angle he wanted for the next several jumps. In this case, they left the jump with plenty of velocity, but in the wrong direction.

"I know, John. They have us good and proper." Danny agreed. "Start us heaving to, *Pan*. And let everyone know we have company."

Location: CSFS Tortuga, Bridge

"You figure they're smugglers, Captain?" asked Ensign Hubbard from the engineering station.

"They're all smugglers, Hubbard, even the ones flying Cordoba colors." Pavel Stein scratched his stubbly chin. He was a seventy-five-year-old lieutenant commander. His stubble had a bit of gray in it, but his hair was still light brown. If he was lucky, he would retire a full commander in another twenty years. "In all my years, I've never met a trader who wasn't smuggling something. The trick is separating the dedicated smuggler from the casual smuggler."

Chief Petty Officer Garnjag, the cruiser's bosun, looked up from his screens. "Which do you think this one is, Skipper?"

Stein turned his head to his bosun. He was a casual commander, at least among his bridge crew and senior staff. "I don't give a crap at this point, Bosun. I just want to find enough contraband to force them to cough up a bribe."

The captain and the bosun shared a grin at the shocked expression on the ensign's face. Hubbard would learn, and here was a nice object lesson for the kid.

The *Tahiti* signaled and Pavel turned to the screen. "Our turn, Jacki!"

"Sure, but it's such a big juicy one," Jacolin Tie, commander of the *Tahiti*, said. The agreement to take turns was long-standing but often modified. It all depended on what they found. If it was a big haul, they would share and the turn wouldn't switch. That happened with the last ship, through, and Pavel was just reminding her that they were still the primary. Jacki was trying to horn in as she usually did, and if they got a big haul, he'd probably let her.

Location: Pandora

It took a few minutes to confirm everything, giving Rosita time to get to the galley. The other ships were indeed the Cordoba patrol cruisers, *Tortuga* and *Tahiti.* They were stationed here looking for smugglers, and they were going to examine *Pandora* in detail.

"Did you think they were pirates, Captain?" Rosita asked as she walked up to Danny. "Not a real customs patrol?"

"Do you think there is a difference, Professora? My, you *have* led a sheltered life." Danny grinned.

Rosita rolled her eyes. "*Pandora*, would you mind opening a channel from us to the *Tortuga*, please."

"Go ahead, *Pan*," Danny said, clearly wanting to see what she had in mind.

Well, I'll show him. "Good afternoon, Captain Stein. Would you mind putting me in touch with your Stockholder Relations Officer? I am Professora Rosita Stuard, a tenured professor of linguistics at the Danworth Institute of Technology, and a Cordoba stockholder. My husband, son, and others on board are also stockholders." *At least the girls will be, while these cretins are aboard. And if we can come to an agreement, perhaps Danny Gold will become a stockholder, covering the entire* Pandora.

The time code on the screen indicated twenty-eight seconds and started counting down. That was the amount of time it would take Rosita's words to get to the *Tortuga* and the reply back.

Now is the opportunity to get some ownership in the Pandora, Rosita thought as the clock counted down. At twenty-two she said, "Sally, please confirm the immediate transfer of one share each from Gerhard to Angi and Geri, and one from me to little Rosita."

She turned her attention back to Danny. "Captain, the laws protecting stockholders from unreasonable search and seizure of their property are quite strong. However, for non-stockholder residents of Cordoba space, the bar is set quite a bit lower. If the owners of this ship are stockholders, it will be much—"

"I get it," Danny said. "*Pan*, how severe are those legal differences?"

"She is quite correct," said *Pan*, "both in terms of what they can search and in terms of what we have a legal right to have on board. For instance, if the lab is ours, it might well be subject to seizure. On the other hand, as Robert's property, legally acquired, it's protected."

Just then the *Tortuga* responded. "Of course, Stockholder. Our SRO is Mr. Davis, who is in engineering at the moment, but we'll have him up here before we've matched course. It would be helpful if you could send us the proof of stockholder status now."

"Is there really any hurry, Captain?" Rosita asked. "After all, it will be hours before we get close enough for you to send a boat across." Then, to Danny, "That bought us another thirty seconds or so. But the captain is probably getting a little suspicious. It would be better if we settled this quickly. It's not that what we're doing is really illegal, but it could be seen as attempting to hide contraband behind stockholder status. Which doesn't come up to probable cause, but brings us a lot closer."

"What do you have in mind?" Danny asked.

"We give you a share of stock and you give us ten percent ownership in the *Pan* each." *That would give the family control of the* Pandora. *We won't get it, but it's a very good starting point.*

"Better yet, I give you one percent ownership each and you give me a share of Cordoba each. Doesn't that seem more equitable?"

"Come now, Captain. A share of Cordoba stock is worth . . . well, perhaps not as much as this ship, but much more than one percent. And I would remind you, the clock is running." Rosita pointed at the numbers on the screen counting down to the *Tortuga*'s next response.

"Ten percent total. Five to you and Gerhard, five to Robert and the girls. That gives you all a safe base on the *Pan*, anyway," Danny said quickly, without looking at the clock.

"Done," said a new voice. Gerhard walked into the galley, followed by Checkgok.

"Gerhard!" Rosita started, but Checkgok interrupted.

"Most of the cargo that is still aboard is the property of Clan Zheck. Is not that property still subject to examination?"

"Yes, it is—"

That was when the comm came back up. Captain Stine smiled pleasantly and said, "Oh, there is no particular hurry, but stockholders are expected to have that sort of documentation ready on request. Is there a problem?"

Danny looked at Rosita, then waved a hand, as though passing responsibility for dealing with the *Tortuga* to her.

Rosita nodded and turned to the screen. "More an opportunity than a problem, Captain. Your fortuitous presence acted to remind Captain Gold of the value of stockholder status. Nothing underhanded, just business. As of about ten seconds ago, Captain Gold became the proud owner of a share of Cordoba Combine Limited, and my husband bought ten percent of the *Pandora*. We do have a little more negotiating to do, Captain, but be sure we will have all the documentation to you in electronic form before we dock and will hand you the papers on your arrival. Even if the ink is still drying."

Rosita turned to Checkgok and Danny signaled *Pan* to stop transmitting. "The problem is, Checkgok, that Cordoba Limited may not be sold to institutions. Or, rather, that when it is, it doesn't carry all the stockholder rights. I could sell you a share, but the property in the holds would still belong to the clan, not you. I can't sell your clan *a* share. I would have to sell them enough shares to cover every clan member and I don't have that many. The law is designed to keep people from splitting their stock by selling to corporate bodies that they own. I don't think they ever considered your sort of people when they wrote the laws. On the other hand, if they had, it's likely that they would have outlawed sales to aliens, period."

"So selling me a share wouldn't protect the clan's cargo?"

"I didn't say that. It wouldn't give the cargo *full* protection. But it might give it some, and it would certainly give you standing in Cordoba courts. It might not protect the cargo, but it would give you the right to complain if the cargo was seized. And in this case, that might be enough."

Location: CSFS Tortuga, Bridge

"Well, Ensign, if you were a virgin, you aren't any more," said Captain Stein, disgustedly. "We just got screwed right through our suits. Bosun, get Davis up here. And when they send us that documentation, I want the both of you to go through it with a fine-tooth comb. We might get lucky."

Then Pavel Stein called the *Tahiti* and told Jacki what had happened. "You still want a share of this one, Jacki?"

"Oh no, Pavie," Jacolin said, smiling sweetly. "Enjoy your stockholders." Then she signed off.

* * *

It took Warner Davis a few minutes to get up to the bridge from the engine room, and he was still wearing a fairly worn flexsuit. It was one of the older models with the internal musculature, even though the regs specified the newer models. "What the hell is going on, Skipper? I was working on the stern C. You know how it's been sticking."

"We have customers, Warner. And guess what? They're stockholders."

"So let them go, Skipper. We don't need the hassles, and we sure as hell don't need the Department of Stockholder Relations going over the ship's books."

"I'd agree, but they are apparently sharing out the stock just for our benefit. And I don't like the idea of them getting away with it."

"Skipper, even if you're right, hell, even if they are hiding a hold full of hunter-seekers to deliver to the Drakes or the frigging Skull System pirates, it doesn't matter. Once an investigation gets started, we're cooked."

Captain Stein sneered. "Maybe. But you're going to go over their paperwork and if you find something, we're going to run a little bluff. We can always back down out of deference to stockholder rights if they look like they're going to fight."

Warner shrugged. He hated it when the skipper got a wild hair up his ass. But he knew better than to complain.

* * *

It was almost an hour later that *Pandora* finally sent the documentation. And wonder of wonders, it did have a bug in the works. Well, at least a Parthian. It was obvious, and the people on *Pandora* made no effort to hide the fact that the transfers were made after they were seen by the *Tortuga*. Unfortunately, that didn't do much good. The same investigation that might find it reasonable grounds for searching

Pandora would put the captain and every member of the crew either in prison or up against a wall.

The best point for running a bluff was the sale of the share to the Parthian Checkgok as agent for his clan, in exchange for twenty-four damaged artificial brains. Four for ship's boats, five for ship's drones, three for mining drones, and the rest for everything from personal assistants to translators. The interesting thing was that in exchange, the bug got not only the one share but also other valuable considerations not specified in the contract. Warner was pretty sure what those other valuable considerations were. What the whole deal was about was putting the questionable cargo in the hands of a stockholder.

* * *

By the time the three ships matched course, Captain Stein was almost resigned to the loss of any significant bribes.

Almost.

He was less resigned to the fact that Jacki would be getting the next merchant through and would be crowing about this for months. He sent Davis, Ensign Hubbard, and the bosun over to have a chat with the captain and crew of the *Pandora*.

"We're closing to wing distance. *Pandora*, please cut your wings," Davis commed. *Pan* cut her wings so that the flapping of the magnetic wings wouldn't interfere with the docking shuttle. The shuttle continued its flight and docked. The moment it was docked, *Pandora* resumed her one standard gravity acceleration.

They were met at the lock by Captain Gold and Doctors Rosita Stuard and Gerhard Schmitz, who handed over the actual documents to examine. All the proper codes were in place. In fact, the codes were more up to date than *Tortuga*'s.

"We are less than two weeks out of Danworth, Lieutenant Davis," explained the professora.

"And we're running light since we sold most of our cargo in Danworth and didn't buy nearly as much equipment as we expected to. Prices were ridiculous," added Captain Gold.

"I noticed that you sold quite a few of the artificials to the professor." Warner Davis paused for effect, then continued, "Quite recently."

"Right, Checkgok did. But the professor is an expert cyberneticist, and what use were the busted brains to Checkgok?"

"It kept holding out for a better price," added Professor Gerhard Schmitz. "Until you showed up, that is. Never believe it when they say you fellows are never around when needed."

"I did notice the 'other valuable considerations' mentioned in the contract," Davis said as they walked down the corridor to the lounge. With the ships accelerating, they had gravity. "Would you mind hinting at what those are?"

"Now, Lieutenant, none of that," said Professora Stuard. Twenty-four hadn't been all the brains they bought. Checkgok decided that the brains would be a major seller on Parthia because the Jackson-Cordoba Trading Company, which controlled most of the trade with Parthia, had almost an embargo on the sale of artificial brains to the Parthians. There were over a hundred brains onboard. Fortunately, they didn't take up much space and could easily be hidden.

"It's perfectly all right, dear," Gerhard interrupted. "It's not a secret, Lieutenant. It's just a bit vague. You see, Checkgok is very impressed with *Pandora*, Sally, and the other artificials, and it wants me to try to teach his clan's scientists about how artificials and interfaces are made, in the hopes that the Parthians—or at least his clan—can have the advantages that such devices give us. Things like your flexsuit. We have our own suit-bot, you know. That's how we met. They had a damaged one. The poor thing had a broken matrix and, well, I repaired it. It's happily making flexsuits for the crew now. In fact, it's almost finished a new flexsuit for Robert. It's booked solid for the next few months, just on crew and family, of course."

Warner Davis was in a flexsuit. However, Ensign Hubbard and the bosun were in the newer, externally-muscled work suits. "How did you manage to get your own suit-bot?" Davis asked the captain.

"It came with Spacer Outis. He was running a tailor shop on a little rock in the Morland system until the bot got damaged."

"Morland's a good distance from Danworth," offered Ensign Hubbard cautiously.

"True enough. But once we had Hirum and the suit-bot . . ." Captain Gold stopped as they reached the lounge.

Pandora's lounge was a large room designed to act as a family room, school room, game room and, as now, a convenient and comfortable place to entertain. There were plush chairs and a variety of finger foods set out. John was there, wearing the traditional chef's hat.

"This is Able Spacer John Gabriel, our enviro tech and chef. He's fixed up a few snacks. Everyone have a seat, or do you want to get right to your inspection?" He looked at Ensign Hubbard, not Lieutenant Davis. At least in theory, Hubbard and the bosun were there to inspect while Lieutenant Davis was there to protect them against any overreaching by the ensign.

The ensign looked to Davis, and Davis, with a grimace, said, "We might as well sit down and chat a bit. From the files you sent there are, suddenly, whole sections of the ship that are off limits absent probable cause. About the only part of the ship we could search would be those cargo holds leased to the bu—ah, Parthians."

"And here is their representative. Checkgok, these are Lieutenant Davis, Ensign Hubbard, and I don't believe I caught your name, Chief," Captain Gold said.

"Garnjag, sir."

"Checkgok has two roles on the ship. It is the trade representative of the Zheck Clan and, at the same time, the trader for the *Pandora*. Some of the cargo belongs to the ship and through the ship to me, and of course, the professors and their family. As to which is which, you'll have to ask Checkgok. I couldn't possibly keep track of it all."

"It is all quite clearly delineated, Captain," Checkgok said rather stiffly. "In fact, the record of what cargo is owned by the ship and what is owned by the Zheck clan has already been sent to the *Tortuga*."

"Yes, we received them," said Lieutenant Davis. "Your clan seems to have done rather poorly?"

"Not at all. We have letters of credit from the System Bank of Danworth and from the Danworth branch of the Cordoba Bank. While such documents might not be all that useful in Drake space, in Cordoba space they will allow us to refill our holds soon enough."

"Not that we're pleased to be running light at the moment," Captain Gold added. "It's never profitable to run empty."

"We are not running empty, Captain," the Parthian said. "We have a good stock of equipment that is in need of repair." It turned its eyestalks to the crew of the *Tortuga*. "About the only bargains we could find in Danworth were in the junk yards out in the belts. Our hope is to do some repairs on the equipment as we travel and sell it in outsystems."

They chatted and after a few minutes, Davis said, "The problem, of course, is that the Zheck Clan goods are not, in fact, *Checkgok's* goods. They belong to a clan, and as such are subject to inspection. And in the case of even the slightest discrepancy . . . for instance, the Conda rose sap. That is from a Drake world, and it's hardly likely that you have the proper seals to prove it was transferred legally. Now, old spacer that I am, I understand how these things happen. But—" A quite histrionic sigh. "—young Hubbard, here, is right out of the academy. All book learning and academy discipline."

Hubbard tried to look stiff and offended, but mostly only managed confused.

"Hubbard is liable to insist on a thorough search and there's not much I can do about it. He's technically within his rights."

"And what do you think it would take to convince Ensign Hubbard to get off his high horse and stroll around with the mortals?" asked Professor Schmitz.

Ensign Hubbard's look of outrage would have been much more convincing if he wasn't grinning.

"Ship's safety is of course paramount," Davis said, and there wasn't even a hint of humor in his voice. "We've been having trouble with the stern C wing for months and it's getting worse. I was working on it when you folks showed up, as it happens. And I am fairly sure that it's the control circuitry."

Hubbard blurted, "I thought it was the lining, sir."

"So did I," Davis told him. "And I still think that's a part of the problem. But the control circuitry isn't compensating the way it should."

"Are you authorized to buy a new controller?" asked Professora Stuard.

"No, I'm afraid not, except in case of an emergency. And while it's an increasingly severe problem, it's nowhere near emergency status yet."

"Well, I don't see how we can help you then," she said. "After all, I wouldn't want you to get in trouble for having unauthorized parts."

"Oh well, as to that, minor repairs we can do. It's expected."

"You just can't pay for it," Professora Stuard said.

Lieutenant Davis shrugged meaningfully. "I did notice that two of the artificial brains that Checkgok sold to Professor Schmitz this morning were wing controllers. It would be helpful if we could replace the stern A and C together."

"I don't think that is necessary," said Professor Schmitz. "With a proper tie-in, the artificial for the C should be able to fit itself to the A's output."

The discussion got technical then, but when the customs patrol left, Lieutenant Davis was carrying a case with an artificial brain the size of a grain of rice and connecting circuitry in it. And the inspection never got past the lounge.

* * *

"You lucky bastard," Jacolin Tie groused. "You got a wing controller brain. Your Davis is bragging about it. You could have tried for two and shared."

"I did try for two. Well, Warner did." Commander Pavel Stein decided not to mention that even if they had gotten two, they would have kept them both. "Besides, what are you complaining about? You're lead on the next one."

CHAPTER 16

The shield missile represents a major leap in weapons development. Its effect on the political stability of the Pamplona Sector is harder to judge. Certainly it had an influence, but how much and in which direction is harder to say.
From the debate between Doctor Gregory Forbush and Doctor Ellen Drake, University of Danworth History Department, Standard Year 674

Location: Delta System, Cordoba Space, Pandora
Standard Date: 07 12 630

Delta System had no habitable planets. It started out as a military system and, to an extent, it still was. There were five Cordoba jump chains that came together in Delta system. That made it an excellent place to put a naval base to control all five chains. It also made it an excellent place to tranship cargo. However, the borders of Cordoba space moved away from Delta system decades ago, so while there was a naval base, it was an older one with not a lot of ships.

On the other hand, there were thousands of warehouse stations holding billions of tons of goods. There were banks and factors and merchants of all sorts. It was an excellent place to buy cargoes from all over Cordoba space.

Standard Date: 07 16 630

"I'm a space viking," caroled Angi Schmitz.

"Space vikings are bad," insisted little Geri.

"Space vikings are courageous, and I am courageous."

"Space vikings don't exist," Jenny told the arguing girls. "What you run into are pirates. And you don't want to run into pirates. They send hunter-nukes after you."

That got the girls' attention, and Jenny ended up telling them the story of their encounter with the *Brass Hind.*

* * *

Angi sat at the table with Rosi and Geri, and listened to the story. It was exciting and she liked it, but she thought Jenny must be fibbing. She didn't say that out loud. She liked Jenny and didn't want the older girl mad at her.

She knew that sometimes people lied, but she just wasn't sure this time. What she found most unbelievable was that another kid would be able to come up with the suggestion that would save the day. She looked over at Rosi and Geri. They were all ears, and she could tell that they believed every word.

Angi had no notion of the validity of the suggestion itself. She was seven and she was still studying the history of the Cordobas, not the really old stuff before the first jump ship. So she decided to ask her dad.

* * *

Robert sat Angi on his lap and asked, "So what's the problem, Angel?"

She told him Jenny's story. He found the story unlikely, partly because of the notion that in the middle of a battle the adults would be consulting a ten-year-old, but mostly because he wasn't at all sure that a ship's boat could do that. None of the ship's boats he had ever flown could even fly without a person on board.

A thought stopped him.

That wasn't entirely true. The ship's boat on the *Pan* could be sent out on its own. It generally wasn't, but it could be. And there was a very different feel to flying it than there was to the other ship's boats he had flown. He still doubted that Jenny Starchild came up with the notion, but maybe the idea itself was real.

"It could be, Angi. It could be. Let me talk it over with your granddad and maybe Captain Gold."

* * *

Gerhard looked up from his scope when Robert came in. "What can I do for you?" He was just a little irritated by yet another interruption of his work.

"It's not urgent, Dad, but if you have a minute I'd like to get your take on a story Jenny Starchild told the girls. I think it's probably made up, but it did get me curious."

Gerhard looked back at the scope and realized that it was past time to take a break anyway. Besides, in his experience, Jenny was an honest kid. "I've got time, son. I'm just grumpy when I'm working. What's the story?"

"Well, the way I got it from Angi, Jenny told the grownups how to stop a hunter-nuke. Using a shuttle."

Gerhard laughed out loud. "Oh? How? Seriously, I didn't think Jenny had the imagination to make up something like that. I mean, you know hitting the nuke with a shuttle would be like hitting one bullet with another. The stuff of fantasy."

Robert grinned back at him. "Yep, I know. But according to Angi, they ran a superconducting cable out of the shuttle and used it to produce a mag wing to fool the hunter and make it go off ahead of time."

Gerhard felt the blood drain from his face as the import of those words reached him.

Gerhard's specialty was cybernetic brains and control circuitry, and he realized that a very strong, rapidly fluctuating, magnetic field would fry the brain of any hunter-nuke. It would fry any artificial and almost any circuit up to the size that involved visible wire and larger. It was the equivalent of the EMP of pre-space nukes. Except it was stronger and, being contained and controlled, lasted much longer. Even if the hunter-nuke had not been fooled into going off, it would have been rendered so much junk by passing through the wing. That, after all, was the major reason that hunter-nukes were designed to go off when they got in range of an active wing.

His first impulse was to report the new discovery to the Cordoba Combine. He was a Cordoba Stockholder and had the same loyalty to the Combine that would be expected of any citizen of any country throughout history. Even more, because he was a fairly privileged person in the Combine's structure.

But that impulse was quickly contained. Contained by his recent experiences on Danworth and the willingness of the Cordoba Stockholder Relations Officer for the Danworth system to side with the cretins.

He knew, or thought he did, what the Combine would do. It would suppress the whole thing and him with it. *Them* with it, for the suppression would include Danny Gold, *Pandora*, and her entire crew. Include his granddaughters, his wife, his son.

No. In spite of his loyalty to the Cordoba Combine, he would not be sharing this tidbit. Not with the Cordoba Combine, anyway.

On the other hand, if Jenny Starchild's story was true, there really were pirates in space and some of them came equipped with hunter-nukes. And that meant this ship needed weapons to fight them.

"What is it, Dad?" Robert asked, sounding concerned. "You've gone white."

Gerhard took a breath, stood up, walked over to the pedestal that held Sally's cybernetic brain, then walked back to his chair while he tried to figure out what to do. "Robert, don't talk about this, not to anyone. Sit the girls down and make it clear that this is a secret."

"Come on, Dad!" Robert said. "Even if it's true, it's just a trick and it uses up a ship's boat every time you pull it, even if it works."

Gerhard started to explain, then stopped himself. "Trust me on this, son. At least for now."

Once Robert left, Gerhard called the *Pandora*. "*Pan*, Jenny told the girls about your encounter with the pirate."

"What did she say?"

"She said you used a shuttle with a superconducting cable to mimic a ships wing."

"Excuse me for a moment, Doctor. I need to discuss this with Captain Gold."

It was only a few moments, then Danny Gold came on the comm. "That's essentially what happened. I wish Jenny hadn't shared it, but . . ." He laughed. "It was her idea. I would prefer you not mention it. It's a useful trick and one I'd like to keep to ourselves."

Gerhard felt a momentary relief as Danny spoke, but it was only momentary. Just what they already did gave the basics. As soon as their 'little trick' reached the ears of a halfway competent engineer, the secret would be out. "Captain, this is a strategic game changer."

"I don't see the great advantage," Danny told Gerhard. "We were lucky it fooled the hunter-nuke as it was, and it was a pretty expensive defense."

"No. Actually, you were unlucky that it fooled the hunter-nuke. If it had tried to go through the wing to get to you, its circuitry would have been fried. Though I sus— I'm honestly not sure if it would have been set off by the field. I know if I were designing one, it would be. But if they got fancy, put in a safety circuit to keep it from taking out friends' wings, it would have gone through the wing and become an inert piece of nuclear space junk. Its brain would be fried and it never would have gone off.

"Nor do you need a ship's boat to put up the wing. Something not much larger than . . ." Gerhard stopped again. ". . . *Pandora*, how are hunter-nukes launched?"

"The same way as other missiles," *Pan* said, "by using the wings."

"See, if they were going to be fried by the wing, they would be fried on launch," Danny Gold said.

"Captain Gold, I know what an electronic pulse like that is going to do to a circuit."

"Pan?" Captain Gold asked.

"I'm not sure, but I think I know where we can find out. Hirum served in the system defense force for his home system for several years, and according to his records he was a missile tech for part of that time."

"It would be Hirum," Danny Gold muttered. "Call him, *Pan*. Ask him about how they launch hunter nukes without frying their brains."

Almost, Gerhard objected. But they needed to know.

Moments later, Hirum said over the comm, "They're hardened for the launch, but they can't operate in that state. Hunter-nukes are launched in a Faraday sheath. It's popped by a simple timer after the nuke is out away from the wings. Mostly the timers are set for long enough for the nukes to get well away from the launching ship."

"That would explain it," Gerhard agreed.

"So you're saying we have a brand new weapons system?" asked *Pandora*.

"No," Gerhard said, wondering if Hirum was still in on the discussion. "I'm saying we have the nubbin of the beginnings of the concept of a brand new weapons system. We will have to come up with ways of launching the wing without frying them. Probably the same sabot-style Faraday sheath that the hunter-nukes use to survive being launched by the wing."

"Couldn't they put a second sheath on the nuke in case it ran into . . ." Captain Gold stopped speaking, and Gerhard knew where his mind was going.

Yes, of course they could, Gerhard thought, *once they realized the danger.* But it would add materially to the size, weight and expense of the hunter. And, for that matter, figuring out when to activate it would add to the complexity of the artificial brain that ran the nuke.

* * *

Danny Gold used his implants and *Pan*'s cameras to locate and observe everyone on the ship. It was automatic for Danny, trained reaction and instinct working together. Dangerous situation, locate all threats and targets.

He didn't know these people, not well anyway. What he did know was that this was dangerous knowledge, the sort of thing that would potentially upset the balance of power in the Pamplona Sector.

What Danny wasn't at all sure of was whether that would be a good thing.

Well, he knew one other thing.

You couldn't get the genie back in the bottle.

Danny stopped. Actually, he might be able to recork that bottle. It would be messy and involve the deaths of four little girls and six adults. But it could be done.

No. *Pan* would not approve, especially since several of those people were her owners now, and the rest were her crew.

Danny liked to think that he wouldn't have done it, anyway. And maybe he wouldn't . . . but only maybe. Danny really didn't want to be involved in politics and he was afraid that this was going to put him there, right up to his eyeballs. He thought it through, but he thought fast. *Pan*, he sent on a dedicated channel, *include Hirum. Fill him in on what we know so far. We are going to need him for this. Include Jenny too. She already knows, and it was her idea.* Then, on a wide link, he said, "All right. I wish we could all suffer specific amnesia, but we can't. So our only real choice is to go the other way. Doctor Schmitz, I need you to start working with Hirum and come up with a design for anti-hunter-nuke missiles. One that works. In the meantime, we need to keep this absolutely secret. Doc, what effect would a wing like that have on ordinary grapeshot? Or sand, for that matter."

"Depends on the wing," Gerhard said. "And the angle. But there is a good chance that it would deflect it."

"That's good news, because if anyone finds out we have something like this, we are going to have to fight off frigging *fleets* who will be throwing everything they can think of at us." Danny looked at them all again. "So let's not tell anyone, shall we. Not even your wife," he added, looking at Gerhard.

It was Robert who answered. "That won't work, I'm afraid. Dad did a much better job of hiding his side projects from Mom than I would have expected, but that was because she wasn't paying attention."

"She was busy with departmental affairs," Gerhard said, defending his wife.

"Which she very much isn't now," Robert said. "She'll have it out of him inside a week, and besides . . . if we are going to figure out the political consequences of this, she is the one we want to talk to."

Danny considered. Robert was probably right. "What about John and Checkgok? They're the only ones left on the *Pan* who don't know." He looked over at Jenny. "What do you think?"

Jenny looked a lot like a deer caught in a bright light. But after a minute she said, "John's not good at keeping secrets when he drinks."

Hirum said belligerently, "I don't think we should tell the bug." It wasn't the first comment he had made about Checkgok and he knew that Danny disagreed. When Danny looked at him, Hirum's mouth took on a hard line. "It's not because he's a bug. Well, it is, but not the way you think. You're going to turn him over to his clan when we get to Parthia, right? Well, when you do, he's going to be obligated to tell them about any tricks he's picked up, and this is the sort of trick that might let Parthia hold off the whole Cordoba Spaceforce for years. Not that I would mind that all that much, but you don't tell secrets like this to someone who is going to have divided loyalties."

Danny nodded. "Then we need a cover story for both of them to explain what you're doing, Doc."

Gerhard shrugged. "In spite of all appearances, duplicity doesn't come naturally to me."

Danny considered. "Something moderately innocuous, but potentially profitable enough so that you want to keep the details secret. . . . Hm . . . Doc, you're working on a new sort of construction drone. One that can be tossed at a rock in space and put to work finding and processing ores. The idea is we find an asteroid and drop off your drone, then come back in a year or so and pick up a cargo of processed metals or rare earths or whatever. Sort of a manager for mining drones. It's got to have maneuvering capability to make a soft landing on the rock. Hirum is helping you with the mining part of it, because of his experience in Morland. Oh, and Doc, if you actually can come up with such a manager, we would all appreciate it."

"That's actually a very interesting project," said Gerhard.

"Glad you like it. But we need brains that can run our anti-missile missiles. So how are your other projects going?" Danny was asking how much time Gerhard could dedicate to the new stuff. Because if the professor was busy, some of the projects he was working on would have to be put on hold.

"The repairs on the brains we bought in the Danworth outsystem are going fine and the new ship brain design is coming along quite well." Danny knew that Gerhard wanted to make a ship's brain that would be able to use the wing controllers and still have *Pan*'s ability to read the shape of space by using some of Sally's structure to administer the smaller brain subsystems. But the new weapon took precedence.

"You know that the mine manager bot will have some of the same issues, and the same architecture might work well for it," Gerhard continued after a few moments of thought. "Not the shield missiles, of course. They will be more reactive, more instinctive, in their response pattern . . ."

He trailed off and Danny sighed. It was a good thing they had Sally, otherwise Professor Gerhard Schmitz would never actually *do* anything. He'd keep reworking the designs forever.

"Sally, please coordinate with Robert and Hirum. And keep me informed of your progress." He gestured to the others and they left the professor to his musings.

Gerhard didn't notice.

* * *

Checkgok proved profoundly interested in Doctor Schmitz's new project. One of the most difficult things for the Parthians was asteroid mining. Sending Parthians out to work on rocks far away from clan and kin was slow torture and that had limited their exploitation of even their home system. But that project wouldn't show results for weeks, or even months.

For now, Checkgok was deeply involved trading goods using John, Robert and, sometimes, Danny or the professora, as its front. It was buying and selling, moving the *Pandora* around in the Delta System, loading and unloading cargoes, until their bank account was noticeably lower, but their holds were bulging with goods.

Location: Cordoba Space, Delta System
Standard Date: 08 08 630

"When will we be leaving, Captain?" Checkgok asked.

"Whenever you tell us to." Danny looked away from the game of Planets he and John were playing on the lounge's main screen. "You're the master trader, and most of the cargo on the *Pan* belongs to your clan. So, you tell me when and where."

"In that case, Captain, can you find me a route to the Smoking Badger system in Drake space?"

The Smoking Badger system was named after a comet that no longer existed. It was a chunk of rock and ice, and when the jump into the system had first been made, the ice and rock looked like a badger sitting on a log and having a smoke.

The smoking badger, fifty years later, crashed into the second largest planet in the system, a Jupiter-sized behemoth that was only ten light minutes from the small yellow sun. Badger's Grave had four moons of a size to have atmospheres, and one of them even had considerable oxygen and an ecosystem of sorts. Unfortunately, it was inimical to humanoid life. Gravestone was mined for a set of complex chemical compounds that were common on its surface, but the population of Smoking Badger lived in stations that dotted the system.

"Why on Earth do you want to go to Smoking Badger?"

"Because we have almost a million tons of Coskga oil, which is much better for processing the fungus from Gravestone than the Drake's Trom oil. If we can get it to the Smoking Badger system without running into a Drake patrol ship, we should be able to sell it at a considerable profit."

Danny was already scanning the rutter, looking for a route to Smoking Badger. He needed to make a loan payment anyway, and the only place he could do that was in Drake space. "Who owns the oil? Clan Zheck or the *Pan*?"

"Clan Zheck owns most of it. However, you, in the person of Danny Gold, own twenty-two thousand tons. Which should bring you up to date on your note to SMOG Savings and Loan."

Location: Averseian System, Border Space
Standard Date: 09 24 630

Everyone was at stations as they went through the jump into the Averseian system. Rosita was at the comm station since *Pan* didn't have a comm officer, and Rosita liked being on the bridge when they made jump.

"Welcome to Averseian, *Pandora*," came over the comm. The screen split to show the space around them with inserts for the oncoming comm messages. This insert showed a man in the uniform of a Cordoba Spaceforce captain.

There was a short pause, then, "*Pandora*, we show the Drakes as having a want out on you. A complaint was filed by Casa Verde Station. Improper departure procedure. And there's a counterclaim that you were falsely accusing them of financial manipulation. Would you care to comment?"

"Not without the particulars of the complaint and the advice of counsel, I wouldn't," Danny said. The locals at Casa Verde station had tried a scam to get the *Pan*, and Danny escaped with empty holds and half-empty tanks. Apparently, they wanted to get their counterclaims in before he got back to Drake space and filed a complaint.

The rest of the screen showed not just the empty space that was really there, but the borders between Cordoba and Drake space, and each asteroid or station was colored in Drake blue or Cordoba purple. The Averseian System was border space. The system was owned by the Drakes, but out here there were two forts, a Cordoba Spaceforce fort next to the jump into Cordoba space and a Drake fort next to the jump into Averseian insystem. The two jump points were less than a light second apart.

"That's probably wise. But you're still in Cordoba space until you get half a light second from the jump, and it occurs to me that you might want to stay in Cordoba space until you get these little technical difficulties worked out."

Another voice, and another insert came over the comm. This one showed a man in a Drake Spaceforce uniform. "As much as it pains me to question the motives of my *esteemed* colleague, Captain *Junior Grade* Alvarez is probably just looking for a tip."

"Oh, come now, Commander Bronson. You know we have to keep track of such things," Alverez replied, though he didn't look all that put out by the suggestion.

"Have to protect the rights of residents of Cordoba space, don't we? Captain Gold, I have another note here, stating that you're behind on your payments to SMOG. So that's another thing you might want to clear up before you cross into Drake space."

"Thanks, Captain Alvarez. I appreciate it."

"Meanwhile, if you just stay in Cordoba space for a few hours while we're working it out, you will give Captain Alvarez plenty of time to have a cutter come alongside and inspect your cargo for a little rake off," Bronson said.

"I am *shocked*, but not really surprised, that you would attribute such venial motives to me," Alvarez said, then, sighing theatrically, continued. "Isn't it always our own motive that we see in others?"

"That's excellent news, Captain, since several of us are Cordoba stockholders," said Rosita.

Danny told *Pan* not to transmit, then said to Rosita, "That's the sort of thing that we probably don't want to broadcast to the Drakes."

"Why ever not, Captain? You know that there are reciprocal agreements in place between the Drakes and the Cordobas. The Drakes recognize Cordoba stockholders as citizens and there are Cordoba embassies in Drake space."

"Officially, Professora, officially. But what's official and what happens aren't always the same thing."

"You have Cordoba stockholders aboard?" Commander Bronson's voice was considerably cooler now.

"Hey," Danny offered, trying to lighten the suddenly tense mood. "I had to make enough for the loan payments somehow. Besides, it's just a couple of professor types doing scholarly research, and their family." He had *Pan* send the names and backgrounds for everyone to both the Drakes and Cordobas. The cat was out of the bag, anyway.

"I'm afraid that we're going to have to investigate," Commander Bronson said. "There have been reports of espionage by—"

"There are always reports of espionage. Your public information bureau produces them weekly to justify—" Captain Alverez started.

"And your VP of System Relations puts out threats of—"

"Gentlemen," Danny interrupted, "if you are going to start the next consolidation war right here, would you mind greatly if we got out of the way first?"

There was a pause of several seconds. *Pan* reported responding to several queries from the expert systems on the Drake and Cordoba forts. Then Captain Alvarez came back on. "Captain Gold, you're a citizen of Cybrant Five?"

Danny sighed quite audibly. "Technically, yes, Captain, though I am not on speaking terms with my family, and haven't been for decades. But, yes. Between the Cybrant Five citizenship and ownership of the *Pan*, I have the equivalent of Drake space citizenship."

"In that case, I suggest that you escrow your share of Cordoba stock for the duration of your stay in Drake space, and not mention that you own it."

"That was our plan, Captain."

"In that case, Captain, don't be too hard on Doctor Stuard. It was probably for the best. Cordoba stockholder status is not the best set of credentials to have in Drake space, but it's better than being a non-citizen resident. And, as to the Parthian, I would keep him on ship as much as you can."

"It, Captain. Checkgok is a neuter female, referred to as 'it.' "

"It, then," Captain Alvarez said. "But keep it on ship, because some of the worlds in Drake space are going to see it as an 'it' in the pejorative sense. As an animal or a monster.

"Now, as to the rest, let me negotiate with Commander Bronson, but don't expect to get out of this without a bribe. I respect your stockholder status. Bronson doesn't, not at all."

* * *

Rosita sat in the comm chair with her lips buttoned. She was furious at herself and at the situation. The bribe was a large one, and Danny made it clear that at least a good portion of it was because of her blurting out that they were stockholders. Still, it wasn't payment for nothing. It did get their papers confirmed and the Coskga oil registered as legitimately transferred.

But a large part of her anger was based on fear. The tension between the Drake and Cordoba Spaceforce officers was real, in spite of the fact that they had known each other for what was clearly a long time. What was happening with the military? Both militaries?

CHAPTER 17

"Everything is very simple in war, but the simplest thing is difficult. These difficulties accumulate and produce a friction, which no man can imagine exactly who has not seen war."
On War, Clausewitz, Pre-space Treatise

Location: Cordoba Space, CSFS Indiana Jones, off Parise Fleet Headquarters Station, Parise System
Standard Date: 09 25 630

The chief petty officer saluted as Tanya swung into the loading dock from the shuttle, and the ship got back underway. Absent acceleration, they would have been in microgravity, and apparently the ship's policy was to maintain motion whenever possible. "Ready for inspection, Grand Stockholder."

Commander Tanya Cordoba-Davis of the Cordoba Spaceforce didn't flinch at the use of her civilian rather than her military title. Instead, she returned the salute in the proper military manner. She still resented it but had learned not to complain. What was more of a problem was the inspection itself. She should have simply been escorted to the bridge so she could read herself aboard. Read aloud the orders that gave her command.

"Very well, Chief." The exspatios were in dress blacks, not the whites of a Spaceforce sideparty. Exspatios were tasked with inspection of shipping and boarding actions against other ships or stations, even drops onto planets. Basically the same role that in pre-space days had been performed for navies by marines. But they weren't marines any more than a spacer was a swabbie. Suggesting they were tended to leave the one suggesting it in the hospital.

Tanya approved of the sentiment. The loading dock was white enamel and spotless. A little too spotless. Every piece of equipment was in place and looked unused. That bothered Tanya as she stepped up to a first spacer. He presented his flechette gun. She held out her hands.

For a moment nothing happened. Another bad sign. Then he passed it over. By now, Tanya was seriously worried. She took the gun down. She disassembled it and passed the parts to Jimmy as she finished with them.

Gunny Dugan didn't say a word as he took the parts. Neither did anyone else.

Shit. This capacitor hasn't been used. If someone tried to fire this at full charge, it could blow up. The SC24 flechette gun fired a magnetic needle at anything from a slow, mostly harmless, 10 MPS to 3,000 MPS—at which speed it would cut right through the armor on a tank or ship's boat. To do the latter safely, the capacitor had to be worked in, used at lower charges, which left a minor but noticeable discoloration. The gun also kicked like an enraged mule and took both skill and strength to use properly. For a moment, Tanya just stared at the oh-so-clean and useless capacitor. Then she looked at the spacer. He was a bit red in the face, which was the first really hopeful sign she had seen since coming aboard.

She took back the rest of the weapon and reassembled it, minus the capacitor. Then she returned the weapon to the spacer. She handed the capacitor to Jimmy Dugan. This was roughly the equivalent of giving someone an old pre-space rifle after carefully—and publicly—removing the firing pin.

Tanya went down the line, repeating the process. Three more unused caps. Finally, discoloration. The weapon was clean and well maintained, but had clearly seen use. Tanya smiled at the short, stocky private in front of her.

In the squad of ten spacers, there was one functioning SC24 at the end of the inspection.

"Would you like to explain this, Chief Weber?" Commander Cordoba-Davis pointed at the capacitors that Jimmy was still carrying.

"It's an honor guard, Grand Stockholder." The chief was gritting his teeth.

"I know it's an honor guard, Chief. That's fairly obvious. But this is supposed to be a Hero-class warship of Cordoba Trading, isn't it? Tasked with the interdiction of pirates in the Parise Quadrant, where we can expect to be running up against Drake Combine privateers. It is not a glori . . ." Tanya paused. A horrible thought just occurred to her. It was possible that Mom had been playing tricks again. "What are your orders in regard to me, Chief?"

"Orders, ma'am?" The chief was clearly confused. "Why, to show you every courtesy."

Tanya closed her eyes and counted to ten. After all the work she had done to make her rank real, rather than a perk of her privileged birth. *Every courtesy.* Code for "give the pampered aristocratic brat whatever they want so the Spaceforce's budget doesn't get cut." She should have expected it. But she hadn't. She'd done too much work, tried too hard.

Many major stockholders' children attended the Academy. But it was a separate academy within the Academy. One that focused less on astrogation than on Cordoba politics. One where the graduating rank was a function of the power of one's family. By that ranking system, she would have graduated the academy as a captain and would have been an admiral for the last five years.

That wasn't the Academy Tanya attended.

At least, not the only one. She took astrogation as well as business law. Jump charting math as well as economics. And she graduated with a compromise rank. Higher than the ensign that her middle of the class ranking in space ship tactics would have provided, but lower than her family's position within the stockholder ranks would have entitled her to.

She lobbied for ensign. Her parents lobbied for captain. She was made a lieutenant, which was actually quite a victory. She was assigned to a real ship, given real duties, and Command Gunnery Sergeant Jimmy Dugan to teach her how to do them. In the last fifteen years she had served on five ships. Always, in spite of her best efforts, promoted a bit before she was ready. Always . . . until now. She used Jimmy as her guide. Got him to write a fitness report for every fitness report received through channels and finally, according to Jimmy and her last captain, managed to catch up with her meteoric rise.

Now this.

She was being treated as a grand stockholder. Not as a captain. Because these people were told she was a grand stockholder, not a captain. Their future captain. Tanya gritted her teeth. "Is the captain on board?" The chief petty officer should be aware of the orders placing her in command.

"Yes, Grand Stockholder." Chief Weber hesitated. "Captain Iminate is very busy with matters of ship's business. I'm sure I can provide you with whatever you need."

Tanya doubted it. She really did. By tradition, the outgoing captain should have been here to meet her. It was fairly clear now that this little inspection was meant to delay her, which it had done admirably. She wasn't officially in command until she read her orders aloud to the present commander of the ship and relieved her of command. It was always easier to get decisions reversed before they became official.

This was beginning to look less like Mother's interference and more like Spaceforce politics. Tanya pursed her lips, thinking. At a guess, Commander Iminate was on the comm right now, calling in every favor she could find to get the orders changed.

Tanya looked at Jimmy. He nodded about a half a millimeter. It was time for the gloves to come off.

"Chief Weber, you can stay right here while I go to the bridge. That is what you can do for me." Tanya started for the lifts.

Weber stepped in her way. "I'm sorry, Stockholder. But Captain Iminate orders no civilians on the bridge."

Tanya was in dress whites. Hardly civilian clothes. She narrowed her eyes, looked directly at Weber. "Chief Petty Officer, my orders from Admiral Cartwright are to take command of this vessel. Now, you can move aside, or *be* moved aside." Admiral Cartwright was the head of the Cordoba Spaceforce personnel section, and her father's second cousin.

It was clear from the confused expression on Weber's face that he had no idea what was going on. Jimmy caught his eye and he moved aside.

Tanya and Jimmy took the lift. Jimmy was still carrying nine out of ten of the capacitors from the honor guard.

* * *

As Tanya reached the bridge, Commander Iminate was busy explaining to Admiral Frankin why putting a spoiled stockholder who wanted to play spacer in command was not a good idea. "Admiral, we run anti-piracy patrols. Real pirates, who fire real weapons."

"Then you might want to have weapons that work." Commander Tanya Cordoba-Davis held out her hand and Gunny Dugan placed one of the capacitors in it. "The SC24s of the honor guard you sent were shiny and new. The capacitors without a trace of discoloration."

Commander Iminate's face turned even redder than her anger had made it. She was a tall, thin, red-headed woman. But most of Tanya's attention was on Admiral Frankin's image on the bridge's main screen. There was a bitter twist to his lips that said he knew he couldn't stop her from taking command, but he wasn't happy about it. Tanya was pretty good at reading expressions, and Frankin was making no effort at all to hide his displeasure, or who it was directed at.

Only about half-conscious that she was doing so, Tanya stopped and came to something close to parade rest. She kept her eyes on the screen, not on Commander Iminate.

"Who gave you permission to enter my bridge?" Iminate demanded.

"Admiral Cartwright." Tanya handed the cap back to Jimmy and pulled out her orders from the admiralty. As tradition dictated, they were printed orders. An electronic version was already in the computers, both here and on the Spaceforce station. But it didn't become official until she read the orders. Tanya decided to take

Iminate's demand for who had given her permission to be here as a request to read her orders. "By order of . . ."

By the time Tanya read the brief note, Iminate's face had gone from red to white, making her freckles both more prominent and less attractive. Tanya was stretching the rules a bit by reading the orders like that, and Admiral Frankin's expression—as well as Iminate's—suggested that they weren't going to let her forget it. But by now Tanya was pretty sure that there was nothing she could have said that would have gotten things off on the right foot.

"Very well, Commander Cordoba-Davis." Admiral Frankin pointedly didn't give her the courtesy "captain" that was due an officer in command of a spaceship. "Meet Commander Iminate, my new S4. You can check with her for all your supply needs."

Location: Cordoba Space, CSFS Indiana Jones, off Parise Fleet Headquarters Station, Parise System
Standard Date: 09 28 630

Tanya used her interface to sink into the augmented reality of the shipnet. The familiar mechanical feel of the ship's computer was comforting. As she moved through the hatches and past the panels, the net informed her of the last recorded maintenance check. And, at least according to the computer, it was all in order. The *Jonesy* was a new ship, just five years from the yards at New Argentina. Which didn't make her much different from the fifteen-year-old *James Bond* where Tanya served as the exec for the last two years.

Her exec, Lieutenant Commander Eric Chin, was a plodder. That much was obvious. A member of the extended Chin family and almost five years ahead of her in the academy, Chin was just starting his ten year stint as a lieutenant commander. Not incompetent by any means, but not inspired either. Chin did his job conscientiously. He was a fan of Commander Iminate and not a fan of grand stockholders who used their status to get rank, then presumed to command real spacers. That attitude was shared by most of the crew. Tanya passed through another hatch and again the computer reported maintenance on the mechanism within the last six months.

Conversation died as she entered the bridge. She examined the readouts both visually and through the net. It was a habit she developed on her first tour out of the academy and acted as a check on the instruments and the main computer. "What's the word on our request for a shakedown flight, Mr. Givens?"

Lieutenant Charles Givens, the officer of the watch, was another Iminate adherent. "Fleet Command says they will get back to us. But the ship is just back from a patrol of the Carson chain."

Carson was fifteen days from Parise along the fastest route, and they spent a month and a half patrolling the route in both directions, in company with the *Harriet Tubman*. The fleet practice was to keep a big chunk of the fleet in Parise to respond in force to any major incursion.

It seemed to Tanya to be a somewhat wasteful policy. It limited the patrol ships available. It wasn't like the Drakes wanted a war, but pirates were a real threat, not to mention the smuggling that was growing ever more endemic.

It seemed that both governments' control over commerce in the Pamplona Sector was slipping away and there was nothing anyone could do about it. She considered the reports of the battle off the Morland outsystem jump. That was some clever tactics on the part of the free trader. What was it? The *Pandora*. She wondered what had happened to it.

Location: Pandora, Drake Space, Smoking Badger Standard Date: 10 15 630

Checkgok went over the reports as *Pandora* made her way insystem. The suit bot was finished with Robert's flexsuit and working on a new one for Hirum. There were four more artificial brains repaired by Doctor Schmitz, two for ship's boats, one for a drone and one for a chemical separation unit.

All the brains, repaired or not, were hidden away in a safe that was, in turn, hidden in a corner of the ship that looked like a waste disposal unit. They would bring even higher prices in Drake space than in Cordoba space, but they were illegal to sell here. Possession of them was not a crime, but possession of a bunch of them not in use was considered evidence of intent to sell, and that was illegal.

Checkgok killed the display and locked the file.

* * *

The SMOG offices at Smoking Badger were plush in an understated way. Natural fiber deep carpets covered the floors, the walls were coated in woods from planets light years away. Everything was tasteful. And Danny was convinced that if they stole the *Pan* from him, they would do it in the most elegant manner possible.

He was ushered into the presence of a loan officer who apologized for the unfortunate confusion back on Casa Verde Station. Very quickly, the money was transferred to the bank and confirmation of the transfer and the right codes were provided. Danny was clear of added interest and late fees for the next six standard months.

* * *

When Danny got back to *Pandora*, he went to the bridge to find Rosita Stuard sitting in her preferred seat, the comm station. She turned toward him as he stepped through the hatch. "At some point, we're going to need to hire a soldier, preferably someone Spaceforce," she told him. "Sooner would be better than later, because it's going to take some time to work out an effective usage doctrine. None of us have the skills."

Danny paused for a moment, then continued toward his seat. "I agree. But even before that, we need a political strategy. I'm frankly a little shocked at how well Gerhard is doing on the design for the shield missile brain. And even more surprised by the body Hirum and Robert came up with for the thing."

The body was an array of micro fusion plants for energy, and hydrogen tankage both for thrust and for plasma to fill the sails. There was a robot to spin out the superconducting cable. And the whole thing was wrapped in a Faraday cage with a set of magnetic grapples to give the ship's wings greater purchase to fling the missile faster.

"Captain, I don't like the Drakes. They have been rude and offensive ever since we hit Drake space. And they don't respect the rights of—" She stopped. "I know that the Cordoba stockholders can be arrogant, but there is a difference."

"Perhaps." Danny let his lips twitch into a smile. "But it's not nearly enough to make me want to turn such a destabilizing weapon system over to them. No. If the Cordobas win, they will stamp out the small traders just as quick as the Drakes. And they will clamp down on artificials just as fast as the Drakes. Not to mention what will happen to Checkgok and his people. 'Bug-eyed monsters' will be the threat *de jure*, once the Drakes are gone."

"So you want to give it to the Drakes?"

"By preference, Professora, I wish no one had ever thought of it. Now that we have, we need to introduce it in a way that won't mean victory for either side."

"Give it to the gray lanes?" she asked.

"Which gray lanes?" Danny threw a map of the Pamplona sector on the screen and highlighted the various gray lanes as he spoke. "Concordia Station is out for Concordia Station and doesn't care about Donnybrook, who doesn't care about . . .

you get the idea." He shook his head and cleared the screen. "If I could, I'd give it to the old Solar Federation."

Rosita snorted. "You think they were any better? They alternated between totalitarianism and revolution until they were trashed by their own colonies."

"I agree. But, putting aside giving them to the Cordoba Combine, what do you recommend?"

"I don't know . . . yet."

Location: Drake Space, Smoking Badger
Standard Date: 10 21 630

Danny walked into the galley, grabbed a chair and set it by Checkgok's nest. "Where to next, Checkgok?"

"I think it is time to return to Parthia." Checkgok's left eyestalk focused on Danny while its right continued to scan the reports it was reading on the small screen next to its nest. Danny didn't take offense. He knew by now that was just how Parthians were put together. Natural born multi-taskers.

"I have several routes ready. There's no direct way to Parthia, but there are three chains that could put us there. The shortest has very few systems on it, the longest has almost a dozen systems."

After some discussion and consultation of his own database of goods, Checkgok went with the middle one. They would stop in one more Drake system, then take a gray route to a Cordoba chain, then from there to Ferguson, and pick up the Canova chain, which would take them to Parthia.

Location: Cordoba Space, Parise Fleet Headquarters
Standard Date: 10 25 630

Tanya took her seat in the briefing room, wondering what was going on. There was a weedy little man with Admiral Frankin. His suit was one of the older model flexsuits and it had seen better days.

Frankin looked around the room through steely blue eyes in a sculpted face, and everyone settled. He waved at the weedy little man. "This is Pierre Fabrice Duprey. Pierre is the merchant on a Jackson-Cordoba trade ship, the *Bonaventura*. There is a gray route from Drake space to the Parise-Ferguson route."

No one even pretended surprise. Tanya could have given him the real space area where the gray route intersected the Parise-Ferguson route, though she didn't know the location of the gray jump.

Admiral Frankin met the silence with a tight little smile. "Fortunately, Monsieur Duprey is also a patriot."

Tanya wondered how much Monsieur Duprey's patriotism cost the Cordoba Combine, but the admiral was still talking.

"When he learned that the Drakes had the jumps of the gray route, he came to us."

All thought of levity left Tanya at that point. Frankin waved at the briefing room screen and used his interface to bring up a jump map, with coordinate dumps to the augmented reality system of all the officers. It was a five-jump string, and Tanya could already see where to set the blocking force. Just beyond the first jump out from Cordoba space there was a longish jump, eight light months with a gap of almost two light minutes to the next jump in the string. Tanya ran their optimal course back and did some quick calculations.

The Drakes would come out in range of their sensors and a little over twenty hours travel away. It would be a tough fight. The Drake admiral was a man called Huffington, a sparkplug of a man, known as an advocate of a more aggressive stance. He was political and didn't have a lot of combat experience, but from Tanya's reading of the reports on the man that was likely to make him more aggressive, not less. He had an augmented squadron in his area. Three Dragons and six Falcons, plus a half dozen of the Deer class custom cutters. Equivalent to the Nobles of the Cordoba Combine, the Deer class were the workhorse of the respective space forces. The cop on the beat, backed up by the heavier main battle ships. The Deer had three ranks of four wings, like a freighter, but the wings were larger and the ships smaller.

On the other hand, the Deer were not all that likely to be involved in the upcoming fight. Their presence just meant that Huffington could bring his whole main battle force. So, three Dragons and six Falcons to face two Demigods and four Heros. *Those aren't good odds.* Tanya was trying to come up with the support ships needed when Admiral Frankin announced his brainchild.

"Our intelligence is firm that Huffington will need some weeks to gather his forces, but he will be coming as quickly as he can. That limits our window. When I first heard of this I held the reserve back from deployment, so our forces will be concentrated soon. We can get in place before he gets here, but we don't have time to bring up reinforcements. Not even from Carson. I've sent dispatches to New Argentina, but it will be months before they can get back to us. Huffington will expect us here." The place Tanya decided was their best defensive position lit up. "But we will be here." The other end of that section lit up. The exit of the preceding jump as the Drakes would be travelling.

It was insane. "Sir, standard doctrine is to avoid fighting at a jump exit. It gives the enemy the first shot, and that can be decisive."

"I am aware of standard doctrine, Commander Cordoba-Davis," Frankin said coldly. "But in the *real* fleet, we sometimes have to improvise." He then went on to describe his strategy, which was innovative and so crazy that it might even work . . . if Huffington did exactly what Frankin wanted him to do. But if Huffington had any inkling of what the plan was, they were going to get slaughtered.

Tanya tried twice more to point out the dangers in the plan, and each time Frankin pointed out her status as a grand stockholder as proof of her lack of understanding. Meanwhile, Senior Captain Rodriguez and most of the staff were acting like a Greek chorus endorsing Frankin's view. Rodriguez was made the field commander of the operation.

Tanya was afraid that the plan would leak. Free traders like Monsieur Duprey were loyal to their pocketbook. First, last, and always.

Location: Big Dark, Drake Space
Standard Date: 10 29 630

"It's alive!" Gerhard Schmitz cackled, leaping up from his work chair and raising his arms to the ceiling of his lab.

Danny winced. "Really, Doc? You're doing Frankenstein jokes?"

The lab was a comfortable room. The walls were set to an eggshell white, and the floor to a textured dark brown. There was a console and the pillar stand that held Sally and a work table where a small brain the size of a pea was wired into the sim trainer case. It was that brain that Gerhard was cackling about.

"Well, yep." Gerhard grinned. "The thing about artificials that's hard to manage is that they have to operate a long time in varying circumstances. They need to be able to learn and adapt, but that opens the way to them adapting in ways the builders don't want. That's the core of truth in all the fears about artificials." Gerhard made a gesture with his right hand and the lab's main screen lit up with graphics and a virtual world—the shield missile's eye view of the space that the brain thought it was flying through.

Danny nodded, and Gerhard continued. "With something like a hunter-nuke, that's less of a problem because they have a really short life expectancy. Launch the thing and in a few hours it blows itself up. It has no concept of death and its only fear is failure. But what happens if one of them gets lost and wanders around for days or years? So even hunter-nukes are potentially dangerous, though the danger is grossly overstated.

"But these are, in essence, defensive devices. Their job is to protect their ship from the evil hunter-nukes. It means that they are much safer. If they get lost, they aren't likely to go hunting up a new target if they don't find the one they were sent after. They can even be picked up after the battle by sending out the right signal."

"And that means?" Danny asked absently. He was watching as the virtual superconducting wire spread out from the shield missile body and powered up.

"It means that they don't need nearly the amount of restraints that a hunter-nuke would. They need some intelligence, but their character, if you will, can be more straightforward."

Danny watched as the speck of the virtual hunter-nuke approached the shield missile.

Gerhard continued, "It has to figure out how to suck in the hunter-nuke, how to deflect the grapeshot, or sand, or wheat. That sort of thing. And that, in turn, means we can make smaller brains, and that we can set up training sims to train the master brain much faster. I'm pretty confident I can come up with a good anti-nuke shield missile in a few months, and I've already put together a workable one with a very simple brain."

The hunter reached the shield missile's wing, and Danny could see a massive jerk. A dead hunter-nuke sailed out the other end.

"Okay, Doc. Make up a couple of the idiot sort and let me and *Pan* find places to hide the missile bodies that Hirum and Robert designed. I want to have something other than a ship's boat to do this with if we run into trouble while you're working up the real one."

Location: Gray Route, Two Jumps from the Cordoba Chain
Standard Date: 11 16 630

They came through the jump, and *Pandora* reported, "A fleet is approaching the next jump, Captain." She sent a visual to the bridge screen and a data dump to Danny's brain. The next jump was short, less than two light hours.

Without thinking, Danny reacted. "Kill the wings, now!" Then they were in freefall as *Pandora* stopped the flow of plasma to the wings and killed their power. *Pandora* was now a rock in space, emitting very little energy as the aurora of magnetized plasma dissipated.

It took Danny only a few moments to realize why he'd reacted.

* * *

In the galley, John was frying sliced kulava root, and suddenly there was no gravity. The kulava and the hot grease went up and kept right on going.

John reacted out of years of experience. Using one hand to hold himself in place until he could hook his feet into the holds, he used the other to hit the emergency blowers that would suck the grease and the dinner into a filter and keep him from third degree burns. He got his feet placed and the emergency procedures going, then called the skipper. "What the hell happened?"

* * *

Angi was chasing Geri through the corridors, trying vainly to get a pair of ship pants on her brat of a little sister. Geri was having a ball playing keep away from her. Suddenly she was floating. Her last footfall pushed her up off the deck.

Geri wasn't completely unfamiliar with zero g. She had played in the zero g park at the center of the university station since she was a baby, and there had been drills since her daddy had signed on to the *Pandora*. She braced for a quick return of gravity, but it didn't happen. Instead, she sailed on till she hit the ceiling. By then she had tucked, and she bounced feet first back toward the floor. Then her big sister grabbed her, which was cheating.

* * *

Robert was locked into his station, running a drone on the hull with his implants, so he saw the wings go down. The drone was locked down on the outer hull, but in the middle of a weld on a back-up support for the Mid D wing. He left the drone on auto while he used his interface to find out what was going on. First with his daughters, then with the ship.

* * *

By the time Robert, John, and the others were calling and asking what was going on, Danny knew. "It's the vector."

Rosita and Gerhard were still asking questions, but Hirum, John, and Robert were all watching the arching vector of the fleet.

Danny might not have decided to explain to the professors, except Jenny and Checkgok were also looking confused. "If you come through this jump and release enough plasma to maintain a standard gravity, this is your course to the next jump."

An arc appeared on the screen and presumably in their virtual space as well. "But if you come through cold with just enough wing flap to make jump and go ballistic, you end up missing the next jump." Another line appeared. This one much straighter, but still slightly curved. "These are both approximations based on assumptions about your vector coming into this jump."

Danny highlighted the jump point they just came through. "The ships up ahead are dumping a lot of plasma and seem to be running two point eight standard gravities of acceleration. That's pushing harder than you ought to for anything but a very short time. Say, no more than ten minutes. But to get to the gate we know about, they are going to have to be at it for at least another hour."

Danny added a track based on the position and acceleration of the squadron of ships ahead of them. That arc, when traced back, didn't intercept either the first standard transit route or the ballistic vector Danny put up, but it came a lot closer to the ballistic track than the power track. "When we add in the current vector and acceleration of the bogies, this is *Pan*'s best guess as to their track." A new track appeared and all the old ones dimmed. "The intriguing thing about this track is how long the bogies stayed ballistic and dark before going active and bright." A point on the track blinked.

"I'm intrigued, Captain," Professora Stuard said. "But I don't understand. By my read they went active fifty-eight minutes and forty-three seconds ago. But I don't see the significance."

"That's right, but add in the rest of their transit time to the next jump and you get one hour and fifty-three minutes."

"And?"

"And, the light from the moment they lit off their drives will arrive at the far side of the next jump one hour and fifty-four minutes after they lit them, or one minute, to the second, after they arrive at the far side of the next jump."

Danny checked with *Pan*. "*Pan* is watching the far end of the jump, but she hasn't seen anything yet. At this range, we won't, unless whoever is over there lights off their drives." Danny meant "fed plasma to their wings." If they just flapped their wings, it was unlikely that the dim light of the aurora would be enough for *Pan*'s sensors to pick up.

"Are we sure that anyone is over there?"

"No, but it seems— "

There was suddenly a point of light. At this distance it was very dim light, but *Pandora* had excellent sensors. It lasted for five seconds, then it was gone.

When a ship—be it merchantman or warship—accelerated, it did so by flapping magnetic wings. Those wings imparted energy to the lonely bits of sand and stray atoms of space. Most of the energy changed the vector of that space detritus, but some was absorbed as heat, then given off as light. A wing ship flapping its wings through space glowed with a nimbus of fairy light which varied in intensity with the thickness of the space dust it was traveling through. But even traveling through the dust cloud of a not-quite-born sun, a wing ship didn't glow like this.

This was a ship venting plasma into its wings to produce the maximum possible acceleration. From the pattern and flow of the hot plasma, it was a warship. And by combining the acceleration and the amount of plasma glowing like a flickering torch in its wake, it was a small- to mid-range warship. Four ranks of wings, but it probably weighed less than half what *Pan* did when she was fully loaded, and *Pan* was a small freighter.

"Just one ship?" asked Checkgok

"So far," Danny said, "My guess is it's a scout on the jump and there's a squadron further back. *Pan*, you see anything over near Jump 37,472,324?" That was the next jump in the gray route into Cordoba space. If there was a blocking force, that was where it ought to be.

"No, Captain, but I wouldn't unless they lit off their drives."

Location: Off Jump 37,472,325 One Hour and Fifty-four Minutes Earlier

Commander Tanya Cordoba-Davis grimaced as her ship went through the preplanned maneuver. They hadn't seen anyone since they arrived on station a week ago. The reports that the Drakes were planning an incursion were looking less and less likely. For the last week, they spent ninety percent of their time in freefall and the rest in these violent maneuvers that demonstrated that they were warships.

Each ship adjusted its vector to stay near the jump, but doing it individually so as not to demonstrate to anyone that there was a fleet here, but spoiling the effect by accelerating at speeds only a warship or a pirate might use. It was, in Tanya's opinion, an idiotic combination of ignoring the rules and slavishly obeying them. And it seemed likely to buy them the worst of both worlds.

Tanya checked the ship's systems and crew status through her interface. Exspatio Jorgenson was caught by the accel, as was Spacer First Binger. Someone had failed to lock down a stanchion in Leading A.

"Ms. Allen," Tanya sent over the ship net, "report to the flagship." Then she traced the action as Ensign Petra Allen slipped the laser through the gaps in the flaming wings of their acceleration. Petra was doing quite well.

The flag's response wasn't so careful. Their laser went through the plasma fields of both ships, and when a laser passes through gas and dust it is not only weakened, it leaves a visible trace. It was unlikely that the enemy could read the response but certain that they saw it happen. It was a curt acknowledgment of receipt of the *Indi*'s message, plus a note that Senior Captain Rodriguez was busy. Which was pretty much what Tanya was expecting. Senior Captain Rodriguez was very much of one mind with Admiral Frankin, and looked at this as his path to rear admiral.

Tanya hadn't been in favor of this deployment. They were at the wrong jump, and—worse—on the wrong side of it. Standard doctrine for centuries had been that you defended a jump point from the entry side, not the exit side. It gave you all the advantages of forcing the enemy to come to you and you could see them coming, rather than giving them the first look and therefore the first shot. You looked for a jump with a good distance between it and the next jump and you set a scout out near the exit of the jump, or jumps, into local space. But those were only as trip wires to get good reads on anyone coming in, then run like hell. You didn't try to guard the exit of a jump.

Location: Pandora, Off Jump 37,472,326

"Do you think they saw us?" Checkgok asked.

"Who?" Hirum asked.

Checkgok used his mouth-hand to throw up a circle around the squadron that was approaching Jump 37,472,325.

Hirum checked the clock. "The light from our arrival should be reaching them just about—" He paused for a moment or so. "—now."

Location: DSFS Mnementh, Approaching 37,472,325, Code Charley 5

The Dragon-class warship *Mnementh* sailed through space, flapping five ranks of wings and dumping plasma like a drunken spacer dumping cash. It had twenty-seven telescopes of varying sorts that could be pointed in any conceivable direction. Twenty-six of them were pointing at the exit of jump Charley 5, just as they had been for the twenty-seven hours since they exited jump Charley 6. One of them was pointed back at jump Charley 6. It recorded the arrival of a burst of light from Charley 6, but the tech who was supposed to be watching was helping his fellow tech with the plotting of the movements of the Cordoba ship on the other side of jump Charley 5. "The admiral's right. It can't be a single ship," he said. "First of all, there are at least two classes. My guess is Hero and Demigod class. Two Demis and four Heros. This last one was a Hero. See the swirl pattern here?"

The *Mnementh* was the only ship in the squadron that even had a telescope pointing at Charley 6. They were sure there couldn't be anything back there, and even if there was, it would just be a Drake ship. The important thing was the Cordoba plan. A plan that Admiral Huffington knew about.

The eight ships of his squadron were spending all their time and energy watching the space around the exit of jump Charley 6 and comparing notes to get the most accurate possible read of the enemy ships' location relative to the jump. It would be two hours old when Huffington's squadron came out of the jump, but by now they had good tracks on what they estimated to be six ships. They knew where to point their sensors as they exited the jump.

Now they were just waiting.

Location: Pandora
Time: 54 minutes later

As soon as the Drake squadron made jump, *Pandora* powered up her wings and dumped plasma. There was a window—not exactly of blindness, but of delayed sight—and Danny wanted to use it to his best advantage. For the next hour and fifty minutes they would accelerate massively, then go dark again and watch whatever was happening over there right now.

CHAPTER 18

I make up my opinions from facts and reasoning, and not to suit anybody but myself. If people don't like my opinions, it makes little difference as I don't solicit their opinions or votes.
William Tecumseh Sherman

Location: Gray route, two jumps from the Cordoba Chain
Standard Date: 11 16 630

Tanya Cordoba-Davis jerked up as the alarms sounded. She grabbed her headset and pulled it on, sending out queries from her internal link even as she was pulling on the stronger headset. What she got back almost froze her. Almost, but not quite. *"Flush plasma to the wings! Emergency override! Get me a flap pattern on bogie four and adjust our flap to counter sand."* Then she started pulling on her flexsuit.

The Dragons and Falcons of Huffington's squadron came out of the gate as a complete surprise. And the lasers that followed only microseconds later blinded the main C-D sensor array. The backups came online automatically when the primaries went down, but the *Jonesy*'s ability to see was degraded.

Worse, they came through in a group instead of singly, as Admiral Frankin and Senior Captain Rodriguez had done everything in their power to arrange. That was why they were set up here at the exit of a short jump rather than at the entrance of a long one. So short that the Drakes could see their ships if they were under power. They wanted the Drakes confident. They wanted them to come through one at a time, fat and happy, each perhaps getting off the first shot . . . but each and every one of them facing six to one odds.

One at a time.

Going through a jump singly was standard practice. It was easier and quite a bit safer.

The whole of the plan had been based on that fact. The standard interval was two minutes, though that varied a lot depending on gate size and fleet velocity.

This was a smallish gate and to get all the attacking ships into it at once took coordination. A safe interval at the standard velocity for this gate would be five minutes, each ship exiting the gate five minutes after the last, getting off one shot, then being swamped by the massed fire of six Cordoba warships.

As that flashed through Tanya's mind, the first sand hit the *Jonesy*.

Damage reports poured in. That sand, like the lasers, scored half the C and half the D quadrants of the *Jonesy*. The wings were operational, though there was a fault in C forward, but the C-D laser array was gone. Just gone. So was the backup sensor array.

"Spin us," she flashed to the bridge. *"Clockwise rotation, 180 degrees."* More damage and injuries, this time from the spin as the rotational acceleration of the ship produced sideways gravity. Then, a few seconds later, the completion of the maneuver reversed it. People at duty stations and in their bunks were tossed one way, then the other.

Inevitably, not everyone was properly tied down for free fall. There were fourteen injuries reported, three of them serious and one spacer had been outside working on a power conduit. It might have been the plasma dump or the enemy's sand or the rotation, but Spacer Dickens was gone. And a spike in the stresses on the wings shortly after the rotation suggested that what was left of Spacer Dickens was now going thataway at a noticeable fraction of the speed of light.

The wings picked up plasma and dust, anything, and imparted velocity to it. But the more dispersed the mass, the greater the effect. Plasma left at ninety to ninety-five percent of the speed of light. As the particle got bigger, the percentage of lightspeed got smaller. Sand got up to a bit under fifty percent of the speed of light if everything went well. Chunks of not particularly magnetic matter were even slower. Spacer Dickens was probably not traveling more than one or two percent of the speed of light, if that, but he was accelerated to that speed in around a hundredth of a second. The hoary old chestnut about being caught in a wing ship's wings being a *fast* way to die flashed through Tanya's mind.

Tanya kept one eye in the augmented reality of the shipnet as she made her way from her cabin to the bridge. They must have known. Admiral Huffington must have gotten word of Admiral Frankin's plans. It was the only way they could have arranged this. The Drakes must have come through jump 37,472,326 dark, and stayed dark all the way across to 37,472,325.

Tanya checked the vectors of Huffington's squadron. No, most of the way. She grabbed the side of the hatch to the bridge as she read the pattern of the *Jonesy*'s wings. Givens did the right thing, concentrating on keeping a plasma screen between them and any sand and keeping the flap pattern random enough to be hard to predict.

"Good job, Chuck," she said as she slid into the captain's chair. She took another heartbeat to confirm the pattern and motion of both her squadron and the enemy. There were no orders yet from the flag. She used her interface and her hands on the controls to map out a route that would put them behind the *Hercules* and let them build velocity. "Put us on the track."

The A-B laser array fired and one of them caught an incoming hunter-nuke. The nuke wasn't dead but it was blind, deaf, and dumb, and the *Jonesy* was slipping behind the *Herc*, so the nuke wouldn't be able to find their ship.

It was twenty-seven seconds since the Drake fleet exited the jump.

Time: Ten Minutes Later

Tanya flashed orders through her link into ship's systems and felt the responses. The *Hercules* was gone. So were the *Batman* and the *Audie Murphy*. Now it was just the *Shiva*, the *Harriet Tubman*, and her *Jonesy*. But *Hurk*, *Murph*, and *Bat* hadn't died alone. One of the Falcons was gone and a Dragon was badly damaged. Not that it was a survivable rate of exchange. The Drake ships were a bit better than Cordoba ships close in.

Their squadron, what was left of it, needed to get space room. That was clear to Tanya. So clear that she sent a request on the fleetnet suggesting that they pull back. The response—aside from blistering the decks—made it clear that Senior Captain Rodriguez wasn't letting the plan go. He had too much invested in the plan to step back from it. Retreating now would be the end of his career.

People were going to die.

Tanya was going to die.

Even Rodriguez was going to die, all because he couldn't face being wrong.

The logical thing to do was to get her people out of here. But she didn't. She couldn't. She was an officer in the Cordoba Spaceforce, under orders. So maybe Rodriguez wasn't the only idiot on the fleetnet. Tanya fought her ship.

Fortunately, her bridge crew didn't receive his response. They weren't tied into fleetnet, but shipnet. She could feel them through the shipnet, complete with side bands of emotional reaction to the events surrounding them.

The wings were controlled and coordinated by sixteen ratings backed up by computers. The ratings were supervised by four petty officers, commanded by SPO

Carpenter. Senior Petty Officer Carpenter hated the drills, and Tanya had almost demoted the woman. But she was doing well now. They all were. The laser clusters were manned by four specialists under SPO Gunderson. The fusion plants—two of them, one forward and one sternward—were under her chief engineer, Lieutenant Boatright and Warrant Officer Second Boyes.

Tanya was tied into it all through the shipnet. She was aware, in the back of her mind, of every injury, every damaged conduit. And the crew could feel her too, feel her confidence in her orders. They were in tremendous danger; they could die at any moment. A bit of sand or round shot could get through and take out their lasers, open up a route for a hunter-nuke to get in.

Lasers weren't effective ship-to-ship weapons. Between the spreading of the beam over ship-to-ship distances, and the protection that the plasma of the wings provided, the energy a laser delivered to the target simply didn't compare to the energy of a kinetic strike. On the other hand, hunter-nukes had to get close and at a range of a couple of hundred or even a thousand kilometers, a laser was plenty powerful enough to blind a nuke or even slag it, with enough time on target.

Once the lasers were gone, it was duck or die—and at these ranges ducking was out of the question. That was what killed the *Murph*. That first sand the Drakes threw just after they emerged got through and killed most of its lasers. It had just been starting its rotation when the hunter got in range of its wings.

It was more luck than skill that saved the *Jonesy* in those first seconds of the battle. But then the drills Tanya insisted on came into play. They killed four hunter-nukes with lasers and their fluctuating flap patterns stopped most of the round shot that was thrown at them. Her crew was doing well. Better, honestly, than she expected. The drills lacked the level of intensity of a real battle, and the crew's resentment of being placed under the command of a "Stockholder Captain" had been a cancer in the shipnet. That cancer was gone now, cut away by the terror of real battle.

"Shift us, Chuck," she sent, along with a schematic of the adjustment in the flap cycle. The Drake ships just launched another load of grapeshot and she wanted her wings in position to scatter what was left after Rodriguez deflected them. Senior Captain Rodriguez put his wings where they would do the *Shiva* the most good, and he wasn't much concerned with where the shot went after he deflected it. Tanya learned that in the first few salvos of the battle.

She sent an order to guns to launch another load of grapeshot. She would have liked to coordinate, but Rodriguez didn't care for "puffed-up grand stockholders who thought their stock was brains." His instructions were to stay out of his way "since she didn't have the stomach for a fight."

Salvo after salvo were exchanged, and the two fleets slowly got closer and closer together.

Tanya concentrated her fire against the smaller Drake ships. The Falcons were about the same size as the *Jonesy*, but they had twelve laser arrays rather than the eight the Hero-class ships sported. But their wings were a bit smaller and less powerful, and lasers weren't very effective against sand or round shot.

Tanya kept an eye on the entire battle, not just the fight the *Jonesy* was in.

Throughout the battle, she and the other smaller ships focused their fire on the Falcons and left the *Shiva* and the *Hercules* to fight the Dragon-class ships. *Mnementh* and *Faranth* traded blows with the *Shiva* and *Hercules* until the *Herc* was lost. Now it was two dragons against the *Shiva*. The *Faranth* was spilling air and its C5 wing was down, but the *Mnementh,* Huffington's flagship was undamaged.

There! Tanya was expecting it, hoping for it. One of the Falcons shifted wrong and she got a good hit. Its center D wing went down, and it turned to avoid attack through weakened defenses. But wait . . . it was pushing. . . .

Tanya, using her interface, ran calculations, graphed vectors and positions, timed flaps and projected flap patterns. The Falcon was shifting and rotating to hide its damaged wing and was pushing up against the wings of another Falcon. Not a big problem, but that other Falcon was commanded by a nervous sort. Tanya had already seen that, and the Nervous Nellie was showing it again. She was moving out of Falcon One's way, farther than was truly needful. In just a couple of minutes, that would force the dreadnought to shift out of her way. The whole maneuver was available to Tanya. The computer calculated, and Tanya decided. She sent flashing orders to her gunner and the wingmen under Carpenter. Confusion and consternation came back at her, and she repeated the order with emphasis.

A double shot of canister went out, was caught by the wings, then thrown. Not at one of the smaller ships, but at the *Mnementh*. Specifically, at a gap that was going to open up in the *Mnementh*'s wings in thirty-three seconds.

Tanya then turned her thoughts back to the Falcons and was so engrossed in the battle that she didn't even notice—thirty-three seconds later—when over fifty magnetized BBs, traveling at a considerable fraction of the speed of light, ripped a hole in the Drake flagship *Mnementh*'s bow big enough to fly a ship's boat through.

* * *

"What the fuck was that?" Rear Admiral of the Gold John Huffington jerked up out of his thoughts. He was overseeing the battle and contemplating the political advantage that this victory was going to bring him. Until just a second ago, everything was going swimmingly. He was given a *cause bellum* by the Cordoba swine, and given it before his fleet ever entered Cordoba space at all. Now anything he did was clearly in response to their attack on his peaceful exploration. And who could prove who shot first? That glorious imagery had made the interruption all the worse. "How the hell did the Cordoba's get through your wings, Captain?"

Quickly, he scanned the data and couldn't tell. Couldn't even tell with certainty which of the Cordoba ships scored the hit. But it had to be the *Shiva*. The Cordoba Heroes had been concentrating on his Falcons.

A cold finger of terror swept through the admiral. He knew that people died in war, but not him. Not Admiral John Huffington! And to fight that icy fear, came boiling hot rage. "Kill that ship, Captain." He indicated the *Shiva* through the link. "Use the hunter-nukes. A full salvo."

* * *

"They're launching hunter-nukes," shouted Ensign Gallagher from the gunnery station.

"Get us the hell out of here!" shouted Senior Captain Rodriguez. "Order the Heros to shield our retreat."

* * *

"New orders, Captain," came flashing into Tanya's mind from her communications officer, and then came the orders themselves, with all the proper codes attached.

They were ordered to shield the retreat of *Shiva* and block the nukes.

In a way, it wasn't a bad tactic. Hunter-nukes were set to attack a specific ship. They might not go off if they encountered her wings instead of the *Shiva*'s wings.

Might.

Maybe.

If they were *incredibly* lucky.

But orders were orders, and she started shifting *Jonesy*.

It wasn't in time, not entirely. Two of the nukes got past her and went on after *Shiva*. The other four impacted her wings, and three were thrown away, so much scrap. The fourth blew, and took out her forward A wing. The feedback blew out the control runs to the whole forward section B, C, and D wings, and melted a fair chunk of the nose of her ship.

Tanya tried to shift her ship to get away, but it was way too late. Two more hunter-nukes came after her, taking out her center row of wings and crashing the fusion drive that powered them all.

When a hunter-nuke goes off against a wing, it's almost a hundred miles away from the ship that is projecting that wing. The power transfer does the damage, and there's very little additional radiation. But the last hunter-nuke didn't go off against a wing. It closed to within half a mile of *Jonesy* before deciding it was close enough and blowing up.

Even half a mile is a long way, and a hunter-nuke mostly doesn't have much in the way of a warhead, only a megaton or two. Besides, space doesn't transmit concussive force at all well. But it was close enough to fry any electronics that were still operating on *Jonesy*, not that there were many. The circuit breakers held, for the most part. The EMP was stopped before it fried the brains of most of the crew. But they were a live crew in a dead ship, destined to die from lack of air in a few days. Less, really. The nukes that took out the wings caused lots of secondary explosions, and much of their atmosphere vented into space, as well as Chief Weber and a dozen others.

* * *

Shiva kept running but Admiral John Huffington was having none of that. He didn't want any witnesses, and besides, he was pissed. For now, he left the light cruiser alone and concentrated his force on the heavy. *Shiva* ran for three hours before he took them out with a salvo of hunter-nukes. The electromagnetic energy of those nukes fed back into *Shiva* and her fusion plant blew.

There was not the least possibility of survivors.

* * *

Tanya pulled the sheet of shieldgold loose. It wasn't a lot harder than natural gold, but it was almost as heavy and in quarter-inch-thick sheets. She didn't have a lot of time . . . or a lot of hope. But she was a Cordoba-Davis. She kept at it.

She was in a non-regulation flexsuit, which helped. The musculature built into the suit was mostly there to keep her skin from stretching from internal pressure, but it also gave her a little extra strength. The micro-gravity of the slowly rotating hulk helped with the work, but the shieldgold still had mass, so she was careful of how much force she imparted as she passed it to Private Fairbanks. Fairbanks was part of *Jonesy*'s exspatio force, the space-going equivalent of marines. When they were organizing the force, someone looked back into history and found the Latin for "from space," and it caught on for the spaceborne combat forces.

Fairbanks caught the two-meter-long strip of shieldgold with difficulty. He was in exspatio space armor, but its external muscles didn't quite compensate for its extra mass, and doing this sort of work in it was exhausting.

Tanya turned back to the Mid C wing generator and started tearing a new strip of shieldgold off the ruined piece of equipment. Meanwhile, Fairbanks would take the strip she had passed him to the midsection of the hulk that had once been *Jonesy*, where Master Chief Gunnery Sergeant Jimmy Dugan would be busy lining the walls with the shielding material.

The med section was the safest place on the ship. It was inboard from their water storage and next to life support. By the time she had the next sheet loose, Spacer Markum was there to take it. She had been at this for three hours now and she was surprised that she hadn't already run out of time.

Tanya knew that the Drakes fired the first shot, and she knew enough politics to be fully aware that the Drake commander would not want witnesses. They were in the gray lanes, not in Drake space. Firing without warning, as the Drakes had, was an act of war. So they were probably going to get nuked again, and this one would be set to go off a lot closer.

She was pulling shieldgold off the stern C wing generator when the blast came, and it was just chance that she was shielded by it. Fairbanks wasn't so lucky. His armor had some radiation-shielding properties, but it was nothing like as good as being in the shadow of shieldgold.

His armor froze, and Tanya knew what happened. She grabbed Fairbanks by the arm and started dragging him back to the med section. She wondered, as she bounced from corridor wall to corner to ceiling to floor, if the Drakes would send another nuke. And, if they did, whether she would be in shelter when it arrived. And whether that shelter would survive the blast.

As it happened, the Drakes were apparently satisfied by the nuke they sent. There were no more blasts.

Location: Pandora

"Multiple nuclear explosions at the next jump, Captain," *Pandora* reported almost two hours later as the light of the battle reached them.

Danny didn't need the report. He was plugged in and saw the events through his link with *Pan*.

They watched the battle. Even a couple of light hours is a very long way, and details like who was throwing round shot were effectively invisible. Still, this was the closest Danny ever came to a full-scale battle. Mostly—in fact, almost always—the jump was too long to see what was happening on the other side. But this jump was only a little under two light hours. Close enough so that with their present velocity and acceleration of one standard gravity, *Pan*'s standard running speed, they could skip the jump and reach the other end of it through normal space in only nine days. This end of the jump was only about another four hours at their current vector and acceleration.

They watched the battle and it was quickly obvious that someone had screwed the pooch. It was six to nine, and the nine had gotten off the first shot in a coordinated volley. Put together with what they had seen of the Drake fleet before it jumped, it was not going to be a good day for the Cordobas. Most battles in the ongoing conflict between the Cordobas and the Drakes were two to four ships against two to four ships. Six to nine wasn't the biggest disparity Danny ever heard of, but it was bigger than usual.

"What are two fleets doing in the gray?"

"It's apparently not as gray as we thought."

"*Pan*, adjust our accel. Buy us some time before we have to decide whether to take the jump. It's possible it might all be over before we get there."

Location: CSFS Indiana Jones

"How long has it been?" a crewwoman asked.

Tanya consulted her internal clock. "Two hours and fifteen minutes. If they were going to hit us again, they would have already done it."

"Why don't I take a look around?" Master Chief Dugan offered.

"Make it quick, Master Chief," Tanya said. "I'd guess the walls are glowing."

Jimmy grinned and waved. "I'll be careful, Skipper."

A few minutes later, he was back. "It's hot out there all right, Skipper. And the ship's boat is melted."

"So we wait," Tanya said, though she wasn't at all sure for what. Of the thirty members of her crew who survived the battle, eighteen were either in the shieldgold shelter or, like Tanya, shielded by chance. The rest suffered severe to fatal doses of radiation poisoning. Fairbanks was on the border. Any naval personnel who hadn't been shielded were dead, even if they were still walking around.

Pandora, Approaching Jump 37,472,325

The nukes worried Danny, and he didn't want to take *Pan* into a fight if he didn't have to, but he knew that there might be people over there in need of aid. Besides, the trip between jump points took several hours, and by now hours had passed since the last nuke went off. Also, they had been able to watch the survivors get back into formation and head for the next jump.

A couple of light hours is a long way.

Pan had good sensors, but something as small and dim as a ship, even a big one like a Dragon or Demigod, is hard to spot. They saw the nukes blow, and they had what they thought were good reads on the surviving fleet. It was enough for *Pan* to get what she thought was a decent read on the battle, but not enough for a high level of confidence.

By that read, the Cordoba fleet was destroyed. The Drakes lost one of their Dragon-class ships and four of their smaller Falcon-class ships. What hadn't been trashed was moving away from the jump at a standard gravity.

But they weren't sure, and based on that uncertainty and the fact that there were kids on the *Pandora*, Danny had the *Pan* make a loop around the jump. At the end of the loop, Danny entered the jump at an angle, with a vector that would give him a shot at running if it proved necessary.

* * *

Pandora and her crew came through the jump and found the hulk. There was only one. The space where the other ships should be were expanding clouds of radioactive junk.

At first glance, it looked like the hulk was just as dead. But as the *Pan* bounced radio waves off the hulk, she saw that the shieldgold had been concentrated around the med section and made a guess.

"I see it, *Pan*," Danny agreed. "I'll take the new boat over." They'd put together a new ship's boat out of parts picked up in Danworth and other ports and were back up to their complement of two. Doc Schmitz fixed one of the busted ship's boat brains that they bought in Danworth. The new boat was actually a bit brighter than the old one. More talkative, anyway, sharing a constant report of the electromagnetic environment like a happy German shepherd, reporting on all the interesting smells he was smelling.

"Ooh, that's hot!" Boat Two sent over Danny's link as they made their way to the hulk. They managed to identify the jerry-rigged shack of shieldgold, and Danny found a hole in a bulkhead that let him get to it. He wasn't wearing any sort of suit, because there are two ways of avoiding radiation. One is to stop it, the other is to be as transparent as you can to it. Oddly enough, the human body is fairly transparent, as long as the exposure is not too much or too long.

Using a glove, Danny knocked on the lock door and waited. It wasn't a long wait.

* * *

It took a couple of hours to get the former crew of the *Jonesy* aboard *Pandora*.

"So what happened?" Danny asked after they had everyone stacked in the *Pan*. They were going to be stretching life support, but that mostly meant they were going to harvest and freeze some vat meats early. That would leave the environmentals producing more O2 and less CO2. They were also going to freeze some of the CO2 out of the atmosphere for a while. It would still get a bit stuffy and they couldn't do it forever, but it would work for a few weeks. There was a lot of redundancy built into *Pan*'s systems, and John had been using the gardens as an extra source of income, growing plants and meats for sale.

The crew quarters of the *Pan* were full to bursting, though, and people were bunking four to a room.

"We got word that the Drakes found, or learned about, a gray route into Cordoba space and that Admiral Huffington was going to use it to invade. Admiral Frankin felt that it was a probe, and the best option was . . ." Tanya Cordoba-Davis' voice trailed off.

"Was it bad intelligence or is Frankin an idiot?"

"Admiral Frankin believed that there would be damage to the Cordoba Combine's reputation if we retreated before the Drakes."

"Frankin's an idiot. Go on," Danny said.

"Captain . . ."

"Leave it, Commander. Frankin is a paragon of military virtue. So goes the party line. I get it. Go on with your story."

Tanya kept silent for a moment as she worked out how to respond. She had been thinking exactly the same thing. To an extent, she still was. But Captain Gold's comments made her look again. The plan might have worked if word of it hadn't leaked to Huffington. She hadn't favored the plan, but it wasn't so much stupid as it was risky. What killed so many of their people wasn't the plan, but Rodriguez's inability to abandon it after it dropped in the crapper. She tried to explain the reasoning behind Frankin's position as best she could, but clearly Captain Gold wasn't buying.

"Whatever," Captain Gold said. "The upshot is we have a Drake fleet in Cordoba space and we don't know where they're going."

"They'll head to Parise. It's a major linkage and a vital connection between New Argentina and a fair chunk of Combine space. And right now it's not defended worth a damn. At this point, all Admiral Frankin has are the forts at Parise and a bunch of Noble-class patrol boats that are all out patrolling. We need to get there and warn them, tell them what happened."

"What difference would that make, Commander? You just got through saying there is nothing there to defend the place with, and your Admiral Frankin knows they're coming. Otherwise, why send you?"

"If the Drakes take Parise and can hold it long enough to get reinforcements, it's going to take a major force to push them out."

* * *

"Not my problem, Commander," Danny said.

The woman was near to shock and he could see she was falling back on her training. She was also a Cordoba patriot, loyal to the Cordoba Combine.

But Danny wasn't a Cordoba anything. He was a stockholder by convenience. He was a Drake expatriate with little loyalty to the Drakes and none at all to the Cordobas. He told the commander, "In case you haven't noticed, this is a civilian ship with children on board. We'll drop you and your crew at Ferguson, and you can report in from there."

Tanya argued, but Danny wouldn't budge.

CHAPTER 19

"People should either be caressed or crushed. If you do them minor damage they will get their revenge; but if you cripple them there is nothing they can do. If you need to injure someone, do it in such a way that you do not have to fear their vengeance."
Niccolò Machiavelli

Location: Pandora, Ferguson System Naval Station, Cordoba Space Standard Date: 11 20 630

"What happened?" Commander Kevin Evans, skipper of the *Enola*, the larger of the two Ferguson System Defense boats asked as *Pandora* made the jump into Ferguson space. Danny was on the bridge, and so was the Cordoba commander, Tanya Cordoba-Davis.

There was no Cordoba naval presence in Ferguson space. There was the Ferguson System Defense Force, consisting of two jump-capable patrol boats and fifteen non-jump-capable insystem boats.

Danny told him, and the *Pan* was escorted to the Ferguson insystem by the *Enola*. They lost two more of the *Indiana Jones*' crew on their way insystem. Radiation poisoning.

* * *

The Ferguson CEO, John Zeek, got on the comm within minutes of their exiting the final jump to near Ferguson orbit.

Danny called Tanya to the bridge, then listened as Tanya asked John Zeek to send one of their cutters to Parise to warn them.

Zeek added Commander Evans to the call and the commander appeared in another box on the bridge screen, saying "We don't have a fast courier. We have a couple of outmoded patrollers. The Cordoba Combine has not allowed us any more."

"Do you think the Drakes are going to be any better? If you do, you're in for one hell of a shock." Tanya's hands were shaking.

"No, we don't, Commander Cordoba-Davis," CEO Zeek said. "But between you and the Drakes, what we think doesn't make a hell of a lot of difference, does it? My system is probably going to get smashed, either when the Drakes come in or when you folks come to take the system back, and there's not much we can do about it. Do you expect me to thank you for that?

"I'm sorry, Commander. I really am. We will do all we can to take care of your people here on the station, but we literally can't do anything more than that."

Tanya didn't say anything, and Danny could see the effort that silence cost her. Evans was right, and Tanya had to know it, but knowing something was true and accepting it were two very different things. He activated his mike through the interface and said, "I have a lot of very sick people here, sir. How soon can we get medical care to them?"

Arrangements were made and in just a couple of days, *Pan*, no longer crowded with Cordoba spacers, was back on her way to Parthia.

Location: Pandora, Canova System, Cordoba Space
Standard Date: 11 27 630

The moment they exited the jump, they were awash in radio signals. Danny called up the scans of the space around Canova. There were two Parthian traders at Canova, both human crewed, one owned by the Jackson-Cordobas and one owned by a consortium of the Jackson-Cordobas and the Gkok clan. And both were sending queries to the *Pandora*. They were surprised to see *Pandora* because they heard about her from *Fly Catcher*, which came back to Parthia and was gone again.

Danny took the call from Captain Andri Jackson of the *Fortune Find*. "They figured you'd be long gone with the cargo, Captain," explained Andri. "Opinion was mixed as to whether you had dumped the Zheck bug on a port or just out the lock."

Danny grinned and looked over at Checkgok. "Now why didn't I think of that?" he asked.

"Because, unlike Captain Kesskox, you are not a *cheskek*, Captain," Checkgok said.

Captain Jackson laughed. She was a heavyset woman in her early sixties, young for her position, with a deep bellowing laugh for a woman. "I take it your bug didn't get along with Kesskox. Well, I never noticed her as being any worse than the rest of them."

Danny didn't point out that calling them bugs wasn't necessarily the best way of gaining their respect, which was easy enough because Captain Jackson was off on another subject. "Did you really drink a Parthian Banger? I'm as broad-minded as the next woman, broader-minded than most—" She winked at him. "—but that's a bit weird even for me."

"It was an accident, Skipper. I was messing with the auto-tender, making up names of drinks."

"Done that," Jackson agreed.

"And I even had to pay for the drink." Danny grinned. "*And* the milk chaser! Those things are *spicy*." He didn't tell her about the effect of the banger on Parthians that he, *Pan*, and Checkgok all figured out. That was valuable information.

"Well, good luck to you, Captain." Jackson ended the call.

Pandora didn't stop in Canova. They had their cargo for Parthia and saw no reason to pay the docking fees.

Location: Pandora, Parthia Outsystem, Cordoba Space
Standard Date: 11 30 630

After coming out of the next to last jump to Parthia near space, Danny went to the lounge and called up the main screen to show a graphic of the system. The lounge wasn't crowded, even with everyone there.

Checkgok, using his mouth-hand on the keyboard, explained, "Parthia has seven planets, only one of which is habitable. There are three large artificial worldlets in orbit around our homeworld. They are owned by the Gkok who own one, and the Fkis, who own two." As it spoke, it highlighted the stations on the screen. "All three stations guest representatives from groundside clans, and between them they guest several of the important clans of the planet."

Checkgok continued his explanation, then they reached the next jump and were in easy radio range of the stations and the planet.

Pandora sent their bonafides to Gkok Station.

"*Pandora?*" The surprise in the voice of the Parthian astro-controller was evident. "While what you did was indeed legal, I don't think you're going to find very many clans willing to deal with you after absconding with Clan Zheck's goods that way."

"And I wouldn't blame you folks for that attitude at all . . . if that was what I did," Danny said kindly while Checkgok sputtered indignantly. But Danny had already sent *Pan* instructions not to open Checkgok's link until he signaled. "In fact, I wouldn't have come here at all, except I had some cargo to deliver. To Clan Zheck."

Then he opened Checkgok's channel.

Location: Gkok Station, Parthia System
Standard Date: 12 01 630

Fourteen hours later, *Pan* having made orbit around Parthia and the ship's boat having docked with Gkok Station, Danny, with Checkgok at his side, made his way to the Zheck section of the station.

It was different than a human-built station in many ways. First the halls were wider and a little higher. Parthians scuttled and rarely rose to full height unless they were upset. It was crowded, more crowded than any but the oldest stations in human space. Danny noticed that the Parthians were giving him and Checkgok as wide a berth as the wide hallways allowed, though among themselves they seemed comfortable with virtually no personal space. They rubbed one against the next with little concern.

The station was also almost entirely without augmented reality projectors. Instead, the walls, and even the decks, were covered with fabric coverings. There were actual fountains dotting the corridors and Parthians would dip a mouth-hand into them as they passed for a quick drink.

Gkok Station rotated for gravity the way most stations did, and the bottom outer level was run at five percent over Parthian planetary gravity, which was a bit over a standard G. They reached an elevator and went inward five levels to the Zheck quarters. The room was well lit by Parthian standards, which meant the light was a little bluer than was comfortable for humans.

A Parthian about a third of Checkgok's size but whose pattern of spines was a match to Checkgok's waved a mouth-hand, and the other Parthians in the room moved away. It then indicated a passage with its left eyestalk and left mid arm. All without saying anything.

Danny and Checkgok took the direction and preceded it into another room. This one was empty, with two Parthian nests and a human style chair. The older neuter male went to the smaller nest and, using its eyestalks, gestured for them to take the other nest and the chair. It waved Checkgok to silence.

"I am Zheckdsank, the senior trade representative of the Zheck clan on this station. Just to confirm, Captain Gold, you accepted *kothkoke* from Goldgok?"

Danny blinked. The combination of the last part of Checkgok's name with his last name—especially combined with the accent of the speaker—took him a second to parse. Over the months since Checkgok had joined his crew, Danny had come to realize that Parthian thought processes and language were very much *not* human. He had even realized that while Checkgok was in one sense a single word, in another it was a phrase. Sort of, but not quite, like someone named Running Bear or Cartwright. Now it seemed that the name of his crewman was a bit more flexible than he thought.

He glanced at Checkgok and saw that the Parthian was in shock. He looked back at Zheckdsank, the older neuter male Parthian and said, "Yes. But, honestly, we thought of it as more a temporary matter. It needed a ship and *Pan* and I needed a cargo."

Zheckdsank's mouth-hand manipulated a control and a screen filled with the flowing Parthian script. "There was blood spilled. Your blood, Captain?"

"Yes, but not much, and it was clearly an accident."

"That's rather beside the point," Zheckdsank said. "If we take the position that it was a matter of convenience, then it wasn't a valid oath and Goldgok was guilty of defrauding the ship of Clan Kox. Now, based on the testimony of the crew of Clan Kox, fines and penalties have already been assessed to Clan Zheck and there will be considerable trouble in recovering those funds. If this was a matter of convenience, it will become the next best thing to impossible. Given all that, I think that we must consider—" One of the eyestalks twisted to point at Checkgok. "—it is, in fact, Goldgok." Then its eyestalks came back to Danny, and it added, "At least for now."

Danny looked over at Checkgok, and the Parthian's eyestalks and mouth-hand expressed resignation. Then the mouth-hand moved up and down in its version of a human nod.

"Very well," Danny agreed. "We'll come back to that later. In the meantime, about our cargo . . . most of which belongs to Clan Zheck?"

Zheckdsank's eyestalks lifted, indicating pleasure. "There, things are excellent. Even if the clan had not been under the impression that our goods were lost, we would be impressed with the quantity and quality of the goods you are returning to us. You must understand, Captain, that the rental of *Fly Catcher* was an expensive undertaking for the clan, and the purchase of the goods to fill it was an even greater one. We may never get back the cost of the rental. That is a matter for the interclan adjudicators, if not one that will lead to a clan war. However, your holds . . . that portion of the goods in your holds that you describe as the property of Clan Zheck, will more than pay back our investment if sold wisely."

Location: Pandora Ship's Boat

"So, tell me about the names," Danny said, as they were riding the ship's boat back to the *Pandora.*

"The name of an individual Parthian includes the name of the clan. Where it is placed is up to the clan. Clan Zheck places it at the front. A temporary adoption, renting of the worker, doesn't involve the changing of the clan name, but a permanent adoption, selling the worker, does."

"So you were figuring it as temporary. Well, so was I. I don't know how it's going to work out. Worse, I don't know enough about your culture to know what we should do. Do we keep calling you Checkgok or do we change it over to Goldgok or just Kgok? Say, that might be the best thing . . . leave it open?" Danny could tell by the scrunched-up mouth-hand and scrunched down eyestalks that this idea didn't appeal to the Parthian.

"No, Captain. To call me Kgok would be to name me clanless. Along the lines of calling a human a bastard, but much farther along those lines."

"So, Goldgok or . . . ?"

"Goldgok. It has to be Goldgok. It's a crime to claim a clan name that the clan does not grant."

"Goldgok it is, then. And know this . . . you are welcome to the Gold, for whatever that's worth. Then what about visiting your clan? Can you still do that?"

"As the representative of the Gold clan, certainly."

"Well, we do need a cargo." Danny grinned.

"And there are the negotiations about the running expenses. And the negotiations I undertook with Dr. Schmitz to provide Clan Zheck with his skills and services. There is much to discuss with Clan Zheck."

Location: Pandora, off Gkok Station, Parthia System

Danny went directly to the galley and drank a Banger as soon as they got back to the *Pan.* It was only a couple of days since he'd drunk the last one, but he knew that Ck— Goldgok had to be feeling like shit right now. And Danny wanted the bug to know it had a place with the *Pan.* He poured the horrible glop down his throat in one long swallow, then had the traditional milk chaser, practically gargling the milk.

Professora Stuard watched Danny and lifted an eyebrow, then she looked at Checkgok— No— Goldgok, Danny corrected himself mentally. He followed her gaze. The Banger was working, or at least seemed to be.

"Goldgok here," Danny said, pointing, "is a permanent member of the Gold Clan. So sayeth the Zheck clan. They are taking the position that the adoption wasn't just valid, but permanent. It all has to do with Parthian clan politics."

For a moment there was silence in the galley, then Professora Stuard said, "In that case, you probably need to clarify that you're not part of the Gold Line from Cybrant Five anymore."

"Why bother? The Cybrant system is in Drake space. Besides, I'm not all that impressed with the way Clan Zheck treats its people."

"Just in case, Captain. And it's about your reputation among the *clans*. Among the Parthians. Since Clan Zheck is playing it this way, they almost have to cozy up to us to defend their own reputation. Well, to you. But the Parthian news feeds that I have been able to translate using Sally, and what we have learned from Checkgok—excuse me—Goldgok of Parthian languages, are all over the place about us. Trade to this system is very limited. You have to be a licensed trader or a Parthian-allied clan. That's the *Fly Catcher* and three others that are owned in part by Parthian clans, but crewed by humans. The rest are all owned by a couple of companies that have special licenses."

"Are we breaking the law, Professora?" Danny asked. "We're here publicly, after all."

"No. The licensing board is breaking—or at least bending the heck out of—the Cordoba regulations. Besides, we had a Parthian clan member on board. That made us legal." She grinned suddenly, as a thought apparently struck her. Then she looked over at Goldgok. "For your sake, I'm sorry your former clan decided to play it this way, Goldgok. But, honestly, from our point of view, it works quite well. Clan Zheck is going to have to legally recognize the ship as a clan by Parthian law. That means we are automatically licensed to trade here, and the licensing board can't do a thing about it. It makes Parthia our legal homeworld."

"Yes, that will benefit the clan," Goldgok said with lifted eyestalks. Under the influence of the Parthian Banger, it was—for the moment—quite reconciled to its new clan. How much of that reconciliation would remain after it sobered up was another question.

Location: Zheck Clan House on Parthia
Standard Date: 12 05 630

"What came over you?" asked Zheckfiss, Goldgok's mentor in the Clan hierarchy, when Goldgok showed up at its room. The room was as it had always been, somewhat cluttered with records and files. It had a prized human-built computer system and screen with a Parthian keyknob.

"A Parthian Banger," Goldgok said ruefully, going to its accustomed nest, then waving an eyestalk at Zheckfiss in inquiry.

Zheckfiss waved for Goldgok to squat and said, "So Kesskox informed the council of clans. Whatever were you doing consuming such a thing?"

"I didn't *consume* anything. Captain Gold did, not knowing what it was."

"That seems unlikely. I suspected that this Captain Gold ambushed you with the concoction, but according to Kesskox, you were a willing participant. In fact, it describes your behavior almost from the moment you left the system as that of a spoiled tadpole with little regard for clan, or even Parthia as a whole."

"Actually, I was trying to avoid the scent and guessed wrong. I assumed that if someone drank a Banger, it would be either Captain Kesskox or the first mate."

"Could this Danny Gold have been in league with Kesskox? A plan to get you to abandon the clan's goods? And then Gold betrayed Kesskox, in turn?"

"No." Goldgok was certain. "But in the first weeks after Concordia Station, I was beginning to think so. It seemed the whole universe was out to get me. And that is an important thing. I must—"

Goldgok stopped and looked at its mentor. "I have just remembered I am Goldgok, and the knowledge gained by the Clan Gold is the property of Clan Gold, not Clan Zheck. This much I can say on the matter and no more. Clan Gold is in possession of knowledge that Clan Zheck is in need of, if it is to send more of its members into space."

That put a damper on the discussion and soon enough they turned back to matters of business. Goldgok could see Clan Zheck's point of view, but the casual way that the clan sacrificed its members bothered Goldgok in a way it had never bothered Checkgok.

* * *

Zheckfiss watched the young Parthian who had been its student and friend. *It had such promise,* Zheckfiss thought sadly. *It could have been a clan member of distinction and worth.* In spite of the fact that Zheckfiss was in favor of the project, it regretted the loss of Checkgok almost as much as the loss of goods when the *Fly Catcher* reported. Now it looked like the loss of goods was going to be made good, at least in part, but the loss of clan reputation was another matter. It turned back to the console and began to write up its report.

"Well," came the voice of Zhecktitick, a neuter male and a member of the governing council of clan Zheck, "Goldgok is certainly changed. Do you think it was telling the truth?"

"Yes, Councilor, I do. Not that it makes a great deal of difference. The Kox will maintain their claim that we defrauded them."

"No. They will maintain that we owed them no less than we paid when the council found against us for the running expenses of *Fly Catcher*, and without Checkgok to dispute their charges, they padded the accounts, just as we suspected. But they will not push the matter more. And we have too many enemies in the council of clans to dispute the matter." Zhecktitick waved an eyestalk vaguely in what Zheckfiss realized was the wrong direction to indicate the planetary capital city. "What interests me is the notion that the Gold Clan might have information that is valuable to us."

"It's still possible that the human was aware of the effects of the drink and did it intentionally in order to gain a cargo, from what Goldgok said. It . . . no . . . *he* was in fairly desperate straits."

Zhecktitick's mouth-hand wiggled in the Parthian equivalent of a shrug. "I almost don't care about that. To me, the important issue is that with the cargo in hand and a legal justification for keeping it all, he still returned our goods to us."

"Yes . . . if the records their ship sent are to be believed." Zheckfiss waved his mouth-hand to indicate it didn't really doubt the records. "We should check and be cautious. But, assuming that everything does check out, what are you proposing?"

"Either way, Kgok is out of Clan Zheck now. It is Goldgok or clanless. But assume for the moment that it really is Goldgok, given in return for accidental injury and as a test, just as it claimed. Further, assume that the Gold Clan has passed the test, as it seems now. In that case, we may have a way to recover not just most of the wealth from this fiasco but at least some of the clan's reputation."

"How?"

"We treat it as a clan test and the Gold Clan as a newly-trusted allied clan. That will put the dishonesty of this matter right in Clan Kox's mouth-hand, even if we don't actively challenge their overcharges in the council of clans. At the same time, we may gain a human ally, if this Gold can be trusted. You know we have been being systematically cheated by the humans and the spacer clans. Also, the Cordobas have prevented us from producing the wing ships necessary for interstellar travel. It was just luck that the Kox got *Fly Catcher* in settlement of that debt. And you know as well as I that the Cordoba representative never expected Kox to be able to get the wreck working."

"Yes, of course. Wait. . . . You think that the Gold Clan would defy the Cordoba Clan for us?"

"Why not? We know that the other human clans object to Cordoba's domination."

"Perhaps."

Location: Gkok Station, Parthia system
Standard Date: 12 06 630

Jenny walked along the station corridor, trailing three little girls on tethers. Angi resented the tether, feeling that at eight years old, she was too old to need such restraints. But Jenny wasn't buying. This was a strange station in an alien system. There were humans who lived in the system, but not many. Most of them lived in the asteroid belt, mining the asteroids for ores and water. Parthians didn't like deep space mining, or any sort of solitary profession.

That did mean that Gkok Station had a human section in it with a restaurant that served safe human food. John wanted to see if he could get some recipes and maybe some human-edible Parthian foods. Jenny asked to go along because she wanted to get out of the ship. Then the brats all insisted that they wanted to go too.

Most of the time Jenny was okay with the younger girls, but this wasn't one of those times. This time Jenny didn't get her way, so she was walking behind John with Angi, Rosita, and Geri trailing along.

They came to a lock with a sign over it. **Rick's Old Earth Bar and Grill**.

An old fat man came out as they passed through the lock and said, "You the folks off *Pandora*?"

"That's right," John said. "I'm enviro tech and ship's cook John Gabriel and this is my apprentice, Jenny Starchild. These are daughters of Able Spacer Robert Schmitz." He pointed. "Angi, Rosita, and Geri. We're hoping to get a better read on foods that the Parthians and humans can both eat."

The fat man was gossipy and interested in the latest news. He set them up with tok-flavored ice cream, explaining that while the Parthians were fond of tok, for them you had to use non-dairy ice creams because they were allergic to something in mammalian milks. The girls played games at the table while John and Rick—whose real name was Norman—talked about foods and the political situation.

Location: Pandora
Standard Date: 12 06 630

Jenny climbed onto the chair next to the galley counter. "Mr. Norman isn't the easygoing fellow he makes out to be."

John blinked at Jenny, and Rosita Stuard lifted an eyebrow in question.

"He wasn't as happy to see us as he tried to seem," Jenny continued, trying to explain. "He spent a lot of time asking John questions, and they weren't about foods or recipes. He wanted to know what the *Pan* was doing here."

"Well, that's natural enough." John went back to placing the food and drink into the cold box. "We're strangers here. Of course he wants to know our plans."

"What did he want to know?" Rosita asked, after taking a sip of coffee.

"He kept asking about jump points and jump surveys," Jenny said.

"Yes," John agreed. "He did seem to wonder about that a lot."

"You think he works for the Jackson-Cordoba Trading Company?" Rosita asked.

Jenny shrugged and looked to John, who shrugged as well. They both looked back at Rosita.

Rosita considered. The JCTC was one of the great families of the Cordoba Combine. They had acquired most of the territory in the Canova System a few years ago and had an effective, if probably illegal, monopoly on trade with the Parthians. That monopoly probably accounted for over half the family's income and Rosita wondered how they were going to react to the presence of the *Pandora*.

Location: Canova System, Station One Standard Date: 03 09 631

Conrad Jackson-Cordoba returned the side party's salute with the precision that should be expected of an admiral. He was a tall, handsome man with black hair and an olive complexion, with a hint of an epicanthic fold to his eyes. He was sixty and looked twenty-five. Forty years before, he went through the "academy within the academy" and came out a captain. He was now an admiral, but it was a political rank and only came into play when he was dealing with the Cordoba Spaceforce. He was the commissioner for Parthian Affairs for the Canova government, and of course, Vice President in charge of Political Relations for the Jackson-Cordoba Trading Company.

But all of those jobs were just a part of his real job. He was the fixer for the Jackson-Cordoba family, the guy Uncle Tobin Jackson-Cordoba called in when he needed something done. There were half a dozen people in the Jackson-Cordoba family who outranked him, but none in the field. As it happened, he was on Canova when the *Pandora* passed through, but it had been on another matter.

He was in Canova overseeing the construction of a new deep space warehouse station when Danny Gold showed up, and he sent emergency messages to their allies telling of the attack. Word arrived by way of a gray route from his uncle Tobin just days before the relieving fleet from Morland.

After the inspection, he went directly to his meeting with Commodore Rodriguez.

"Welcome aboard, Grand Stockholder," Rodriguez said. "But as much as I would like to stay and chat, there has been an attack on the Cordoba Combine and I have to respond."

"I know, Commodore, and I'm only here to help. Have you read Commander Cordoba-Davis' report on the battle?"

There was a tightening around Miguel Rodriguez's eyes. "Yes, I have, and it seems altogether out of character for the officers involved. No disrespect, Admiral, but Commander Cordoba-Davis isn't from a real Spaceforce family."

"As it happens, Commodore, I think I can help you with that. But I'm going to need a favor."

Commodore Rodriguez waved him to a chair. "The Spaceforce is always happy to help the great families, Admiral. What can I do for you?"

"With the Drake incursion so close, the Canova government feels the need to defend itself and would like to add some forts to the approaches to Canova."

"And you want me to stop . . ."

Conrad shook his head. "Not at all. I want you to authorize it."

"That's against policy, Admiral. You know that."

"Yes, of course. But under the circumstances, with the Drakes so close and the possibility of military reverses caused by the clearly overwhelming force that the Drakes have brought to bear, I'm sure you will agree that it's necessary."

They worked it out. Canova would get its forts, and Tanya Cordoba-Davis would be told to sit down and shut up. Even more, Senior Captain Rodriguez was a cousin of Commodore Rodriguez. After Tanya's report on the senior captain, she was going to have to resign her commission. The Rodriguez family insisted.

The truth was that Conrad would be stretching things to force her out of the spaceforce, but he had the authorizations from Great Aunt Angela Cordoba-Davis. He would apologize later, if it proved necessary.

But Conrad wanted those forts.

CHAPTER 20

The Parthian anatomy involves the exterior spines as a system of echolocation as well as hearing. Hundreds of spines are involved and the time difference between sounds arriving at individual spines can locate both the direction of the original sound and the echos quite effectively. In this the eyestalks act as specific amplifiers to the Parthian sense of location and environment. Though the echolocation is located in a different part of the brain than sight, the two senses support each other quite well.
This had unexpected advantages in the introduction of the Parthian neural interface.
Doctor Gerhard Schmitz, lecture on the Parthian interface system, standard date 03 15 645

Location: Pandora, Parthia System
Standard Date: 12 08 630

Rosita sat at the comm station on the bridge and scanned the network with Sally translating. After three days they were finished unloading cargo, and Clan Zheck was apparently done deliberating. The text running down the left side of the screen said "Clan Zeck announces that they recognize Clan Danny Gold as a legitimate clan and an ally to Clan Zheck."

There was more about Danny Gold being separate from the Gold Line of Cybrant, but still a related clan.

Rosita pursed her lips. It appeared important to Clan Zheck that the clan relationship be explicitly stated.

On the screen there were two neuter males squatting on nests and talking. A Parthian interview.

"It's purely for show and a disappointing show at that," said the representative from Clan Kox, a distinguished-looking neuter male. "We are deeply disappointed that Clan Zheck is going to such ridiculous extremes to avoid embarrassment. It is not only sad, but in a way dangerous to Parthia as a whole. You don't know humans like our clan does. They have no sense of honor at all. They are all *cheskek* to one degree or another. It's their nature and they can't help it."

"From all reports, this *Pandora* brought a hold full of goods for Clan Zheck," said the representative from Clan Jkap. Clan Jkap was deeply involved in the production of news and entertainment programming.

"Then be sure he felt that it would bring him some profit. They are not all short-sighted, just utterly self-obsessed."

The interview continued, and there were more questions from other reporters, as well as commentary.

Rosita flipped the channel and got another news show, with other clans arguing about what the presence of the *Pandora* meant to Parthia. Both Kox and Zheck were looking less than spotless but, surprisingly, everyone was quite impressed with Danny Gold and *Pandora*. Sort of like the human response would be, if a lion actually did lie down with a lamb, and the lamb was allowed to get up again.

Location: Zheck Clan House, Parthia
Standard Date: 12 12 630

"What does Clan Gold want for the information that Goldgok says is vital to the welfare of Clan Zheck if we are to continue in space?" Zheckfiss asked once Rosita was seated with a cup of mint tea. They were in Zheckfiss' office again, since it was the clan's master trader, and Clan Danny Gold was now an important trade partner to Clan Zheck.

Professora Rosita Stuard, representing Clan Gold along with Goldgok and with the assistance of the artificial brain Sally, said, "We have been thinking about that since Goldgok pointed out that your people didn't already know it. What we've decided is based on our desire for an ongoing relationship between Clan Gold and Clan Zheck. We feel that such a relationship would be of great interest to both your clan and ours. Can you tell me if *Fly Catcher* or any of the other ships which trade with Parthia have surveyed the system for additional jumps, aside from the one route that leads back to Canova?"

"No, they have not. None of those ships are equipped with the sort of testing equipment needed for such a survey," Zheckfiss said. "Goldgok knows this."

"That's what we were expecting to hear. However, it's not entirely true. Any winged ship has some ability to scan for jumps and older ships like the *Pandora*, that use a combination of intelligent artificial brains and a tied-in crew, are better at it. *Fly Catcher*'s crew was not equipped with internal interfaces. Was that for some religious or cultural reason?"

Zheckfess' eyestalks twisted to focus on Goldgok. "Partly. But it is also because our nervous system is more distributed than a human's. Our brains are in a sheet that sits under our upper shell. It's concentrated in the front quarter of the shell, near the sensory organs, but it's not nearly so localized as a human brain."

Rosita nodded. The answer was what she was expecting. "Yes, we have all of this from Goldgok," she confirmed, "and we didn't doubt it, but we wanted you to be aware of how our thoughts were flowing. As it happens, our elder male breeder is an expert in human cybernetic interfaces and has been examining Goldgok since we joined the ship. One Parthian doesn't make an adequate sample, and there's less data on your people's physiology than we would like. But he thinks that he probably can work up an interface that will work on your people. This would be useful for your people and profitable for us. What we would like in exchange for information about your people is information about your people. We want Doctor Gerhard Schmitz of the Gold Clan to be able to examine living Parthians and perform autopsies on deceased Parthians, in consultation with your doctors, to learn if we can safely provide your people with interfaces."

Rosita hid a smile as the eyestalks and mouth-parts of the Parthians scrunched up. Even Goldgok, though he knew what was coming and had time to get used to the idea, wasn't comfortable with it.

"There are political ramifications to your request that you may not be fully aware of. Did Goldgok explain the reasons Clan Zheck was trying to get into the outsystem trade?"

"Not really. At least, not that I am aware of. But it joined Clan Danny Gold before my family did, so I may have missed that part." She turned to look at Goldgok.

"Not in any detail. It was internal Clan Zheck business, and Captain Gold didn't push the matter. I believe that the ship *Pandora* may have deduced some of it, though we haven't discussed the matter."

Zheckfiss wobbled his eyestalks in acknowledgment. "There was a divide between the planet-based clans and the clans that had operations in space even before the humans found our system. For the first several years, we—the non-space-going clans—were kept almost ignorant of what was going on in the rest of our system. It divided the clans into two groups. The much larger group was the clans that didn't have any presence in space, and only a dozen or so clans had any real presence here at all. Those clans were charging the rest of us a premium—including the Kox clan. However, the Kox clan found itself in difficulty and our council found an opportunity. We, with the backing of several other clans, rented

Fly Catcher, and we had hoped that the cargo from that ship would force the prices down. Make the other space-going clans lower their prices to compete.

"We also expected to make a great deal of profit. However, when *Fly Catcher* returned with records that Goldgok had left it on—what was it?—Concordia Station, taking all of our goods and leaving the crew of *Fly Catcher* only their own property and without the funds needed to make the trip back, Clan Zheck was left with both a financial and a political nightmare. We had to sell much of our clan property to make good the financial losses of our backers. Those properties have already been sold, and not at the best prices. We can't get them back. Our backers were upset by the story Captain Kesskox told, and even though you have brought back goods, they aren't much more satisfied. We bought them out at their insistence, but now they want back in."

"It seems to me that your backers, having already eaten their cake, want you to bake them a new one." Seeing the confused looks on the Parthians, Rosita added, "Never mind. I simply meant they wanted it both ways."

"I couldn't agree more. But there are political reasons why we can't afford to push that point. If we do push, it will embarrass the clan councils of the clans that backed us and destroy alliances that have lasted for generations."

Rosita shook her head, feeling uncomfortable in the higher gravity. The *Pan* usually ran at a standard gravity, ten meters per second acceleration, slightly more than an Old Earth gravity, but Parthia had a gravity of 12.3 meters per second. "I'm sure that this has a bearing on our request, but so far I am not seeing it."

"Were we to grant your request and word got out, it would embarrass the clan at the worst possible time. Right now, things that would normally cause no more than a casual wave of the eyestalks could lead to public breaches of relations between Clan Zheck and our allies."

It made excellent sense to Rosita—more, in a way, than she was expecting. She was used to the political infighting of a university, and while this was more group-oriented than what she was used to, the outline of the thing was not all that different. "Let me think about it," she offered. "There is no great hurry unless you're planning to send your clan members to space in the near future."

"At this point, we aren't planning to send our clan members to space at all."

"Well, I think you will change your mind about that. In the meantime, however, let's talk about your proposal for the figuring of the running expenses of the *Pandora* and the percentage of the cargo that belongs to Clan Zheck."

Location: Pandora, Parthian Parking Orbit
Standard Date: 12 15 630

"We are going to be here for a while," Rosita Stuard reported a few days later, sitting in the lounge with Danny. The lounge didn't echo quite as much as it used to. The new Parthian wall hangings Danny purchased and installed saw to that.

"We have a solid agreement about how much of the cargo of the *Pandora* is ours and how much is Clan Zheck's." She gestured at the lounge's big screen and a set of graphs appeared, the functional content of the agreement. "We have agreements for the exchange of neurobiological data with Clan Zheck, though we are waiting on the possibility of autopsies."

Another set of data came up on screen. "The important point, though, is that Goldgok believes that he can parlay the stake we have into a lot of money. He knows the local players and by now he's up on the recent events."

Danny looked at the graphs and data sets on the screen for a few moments, then nodded. "What am I going to do for the next several months? I didn't mind bringing Goldgok home, and since that didn't work out I'm fine with it staying on. But that doesn't mean I want to sit here twiddling my thumbs while you people play corporate raider."

"I think while we are here you should go out and survey the outsystem for jump points, Captain. We will want to stay on Gkok Station—at least Gerhard and myself and, of course, Goldgok—but the rest of the crew should go with you."

Location: Gkok Station, Trading Floor
Standard Date: 12 15 630

Goldgok's eyestalks roamed in a careful pattern, examining the commerce board that was against the far wall of the trading floor as well as the couches and plants that dotted the curved floor of the large open room. It looked at the couches and the Parthian traders of dozens of clans as they worked buying and selling goods. Prices changed on the main board as individual traders made bids, both electronically and through gestures of their eyestalks and mouth-hands. It saw a trader from the Fes Clan and moved in that direction.

* * *

Goldgok held its temper. Barely. This was the third such remark it encountered since it entered the trading floor of the station. None of them were out-and-out refusals to deal, but all of them were, in effect, insisting that he pay a surcharge to them for them having to deal with a pervert. Still, Goldgok didn't allow its mouth-hand to scrunch up or change its eyestalks' motion. Its center arms didn't assume a threatening posture. Goldgok simply assured the agent from Clan Goks that Goldgok wouldn't bother him further, nor would Clan Gold pay any surcharge to deal with anyone.

Goksfik made the Parthian equivalent of a smirk and turned away, confident that Goldgok would be forced to deal with him on his terms soon enough.

Goldgok left the floor. This would take study.

No. This would take no study at all. He'd already done it in Danworth, when he used Robert to front for him. All he needed was a new front.

* * *

Back in its room, Goldgok scanned the reports. He needed a trader, but not a prominent one. He went looking for clans that were in trouble. And he found one in an unusual place. Clan Kiig was invested in the equipment trade and lost quite a bit when *Pandora* showed up with her holds full of human-made equipment. Add to that the poor *guk* harvest, and Clan Kiig was in real trouble . . . and in need of funds. They were selling almost fifty of their members on the open market.

Goldgok had Rosita and Sally make the arrangements, as the human members of Clan Gold were well thought of, unlike itself. They rented the apprentice trader, Kiiggaak. They paid a large deposit, in essence paying the full purchase price with an agreement that the Kiig could buy Kiiggaak back at any time before *Pandora* left, at a set price. That had the advantage that it didn't change its name, so no one would need to know that they were dealing with Goldgok at all.

Location: Parthia orbit, Gkok Station
Standard Date: 12 18 630

Kiiggaak was less than thrilled to be here, but the clan needed the money. It was all Clan Zheck's fault, really. First seeming to lose its investment, then showing up with so much more human equipment than was expected. That trashed the market in human machinery at just the wrong time. Kiiggaak reached the lock and used its mouth-hand to push the admittance key. There was a pause, then the lock opened and he was looking at the infamous Kgok. It almost said it out loud, but caught itself and said, "Goldgok," instead.

"Come in," gestured the neuter female and, unwillingly, Kiiggaak complied.

They walked into the chamber. "I'm sure you've heard the rumors," Kgok said. "They are almost entirely false, with just that half-*guk* kernel of truth that makes them hard to refute. Would you like to hear our side of the story?"

Kiiggaak would rather not have anything to do with these perverts, but it gestured assent. What else could it do? For the next few hours, Kiiggaak heard a story that was both like and unlike the rumors. And at the same time, bit by bit, learned what was wanted of it.

The ears of a Parthian are not single organs. Instead, a number of the spines on their backs near the front of their bodies are wired into their nervous system, and vibrations along those spines give them both hearing and a spatial sense. That had the effect of making any sort of ear mic difficult to produce. But Doctor Gerhard Schmitz had managed it and it wasn't even all that visible. It did take tuning, and the sort of electronic devices that Doctor Schmitz worked up were primarily neural-net systems, so they had to be trained.

It took a few weeks, during which Goldgok and Kiiggaak got to know each other. Kiiggaak slowly realized that the big neuter female wasn't going to get drunk on Bangers and make inappropriate advances on it.

Location: Parthia orbit, Gkok Station
Standard Date: 12 23 630

Kiiggaak walked out onto the floor and made a gesture with its right eyestalk, a tentative offer on dak fur. It got a response and made more offers, then it offered other items for sale. It was just one of many traders on the floor and was mostly unknown here. Kiiggaak represented a company that was owned by Clan Gold, but that ownership was not obvious. Kiiggaak listened politely and at the same time listened to the spine mic that it wore.

Kiiggaak was getting surprisingly good deals. The prices were better than any of them expected, even Goldgok. Gradually, through the day, Kiiggaak realized that the traders on the floor were cutting their eyestalks to spite their mouth-hands as they attempted to punish both Goldgok and Clan Zheck for not being exactly the perverts they were painted as.

This was all turning out to be an excellent learning experience. Kiiggaak was in quite a good mood by the time it got back to the rooms of the Gold Clan on station. Those rooms were located in the small human section of the station. It felt even better as it walked through the rooms, not noticing the aroma. The aroma was a subtle thing, not consciously noticed by most Parthians, but it felt like home.

Location: Parthia outsystem, between TjisKee and Sikikee
Standard Date: 01 01 631

Danny sat in the command chair of *Pan*'s bridge with his control cap on and his mind linked with *Pandora*. He felt the wings and the space, and he felt Jenny and little Angi in the background. John was in the garden. Hirum, in his new flexsuit, was working on the hull. All that data was flowing through Danny's mind, but in the background—an almost meaningless hum of information compared to the feel of space around him. Two weeks into the outsystem search and no jumps so far, but that wasn't bad. They had plenty of time.

He felt the space and thought at *Pan* to shift the beat pattern a little, and shift them up a bit from their previous course. Yes, there was something. It might be a jump, or it might not, but it was the closest thing so far.

Ten hours later he knew that it wasn't a jump and the *Pan* shifted back to the survey. At the very least, they were getting a feel for the space junk in the system.

Location: Parthia orbit, Gkok Station
Standard Date: 01 01 631

"You drank a Banger?" Goldgok asked Professora Rosita Stuard. "It wasn't necessary here. There are several breeders on station."

"Perhaps. But this is the human section and I want you and Kiiggaak, as well as any guests we have, to feel comfortable."

Goldgok nodded its mouth-hand. "Any word from Captain Gold?"

"They are still surveying. So far three not-quite jump points have been found, but no real ones. That was as of . . ." She paused, consulting her internal clock. ". . . seven hours ago. They are four light hours out, and the last message was three hours ago."

Rooms in Gkok Station, near Rick's
Standard Date: 01 03 631

"Mr. Norman of Rick's Cafe," Rosita told Gerhard as they lay in bed, "is at least as shifty as Jenny thinks he is. He pumps me for information every time I enter his restaurant, and you know Sally is catching cyberattacks on almost a daily basis."

"Luckily," Gerhard said, "the system computers are expert systems with very little in the way of neural net support. It gives Sally a major advantage in dealing with them.

"I had Sally set up a 'honey box.'"

That was a virtual system that was designed to let probes in and make them think that they were successfully invading the main system.

Gerhard grinned. "Sally is filling the honey box with what we want the spies to know, basically that *Pandora* is doing a mining survey of the outsystem, between the planets TjisKee and Sikikee, and we have hopes of selling mining bots to the Zheck and possibly other clans."

It wasn't exactly information that would endear them to the Gkok, the Fkis, or the other space clans, but it prevented them from realizing that *Pan* was actually looking for jump routes.

"I know. Sally told me. I'm also working with Sally to find out what the Jackson-Cordoba Trading Company is up to."

"I'm more concerned about the tech level of the Parthians. They don't have anything," Gerhard complained, changing the subject.

"Of course they do. Their tech is different, that's all."

"I'm not blaming the Parthians, Rose," Gerhard said, still grumpily. "They were barely into solid state when they were discovered. It's us. The Cordobas and that Jackson-Cordoba cartel that are the problem. They've got the whole system convinced that artificial brains are dangerous."

"Had," Rosita corrected. "Having the *Pandora* show up has gone a long way . . ."

"I'm not talking about the politics. I'm talking about the scientists. And, yes, they are trying since we got here. But they are so far behind . . . and their life expectancy doesn't help."

The life expectancy for a non-breeder male was fifty-two standard years, fifty for a non-breeder female. Breeders lived a bit longer, but were highly focused on breeding new Parthians. When you considered the roughly ten years they spent as what amounted to tadpoles, that didn't leave time for most Parthians to acquire more than one professional skill. Gerhard had three: cyberneticist, interface designer, and biologist as part of the interface designer.

"It wouldn't be so bad if their shorter lives made them more fractious, but the hive nature means that they are less willing to question professional wisdom."

"I thought you liked Zheckpak."

"I do." Zheckpak was a Parthian electrical engineer the Zheck clan rented to Gerhard to help with integrating his electronics with native Parthian systems. "And I like Togkok and Siskiik. They're bright, capable, and hardworking. But if something is written in a textbook, it might as well be written in stone to them."

"How did we end up on the subject of Parthian scientific conservatism yet again?" Rosita asked the ceiling. Not getting an answer, she turned back to her husband. "What exactly don't they have?"

"Huh? What are you talking about?"

"You started this diatribe by insisting that the Parthians don't have anything?"

"Oh, yes. They don't have molecular printers," Gerhard said.

"They don't have . . ." Rosita stopped herself. Every asteroid miner, every station job shop, every everyone, had molecular printers. Little Angie had one in her toy box on the *Pandora*.

"The Jackson-Cordobas are working really hard to keep the Parthians out of the modern universe."

"I'll see what I can do," Rosita promised. "The Costas are coming into the station for resupply at the end of the week, and I'll see if I can beg one from them." The Costas were one of the small families of deep space miners who were making a living extracting materials from the asteroid belts to provide to the Parthian orbital industries, and they were on good terms with Rosita. "What about the Arachne?"

"It's coming along. We can't do the weights transfer until the *Pandora* gets back, but the structure seems good."

Location: Pandora, Parthian Outsystem
Standard Date: 02 11 631

It was almost a surprise. Danny felt the wings shifting, the pressure smoothing. The jump was small, twenty thousand miles across, and they were moving fairly fast. *Pan* was running through the space, and Danny was expecting another false alarm, but just as they got to the possible jump point, it settled into place and they slid through.

Six light days. Not a long jump, but it put them well past the Parthian Kuiper belt into the inner Oort cloud, a good place to put stuff you didn't want noticed. It would be fairly valuable information, even if it was a one jump cul de sac, but Danny was hoping for better. "We're going to stay out here for a while, *Pan*, and see if we can find a few more links."

"Skipper," said John over the shipnet, "we ought to report back to give our people contact directions."

"Right. *Pan*, work up some mail drops that we can shoot back to Goldgok and the professora."

It took them a day to jump back and send the new itinerary to the professora on Gkok Station.

Location: Rick's Cafe, Gkok Station, Parthian System
Standard Date: 02 11 631

Rosita walked into the restaurant and saw the big, beefy man in the captain's cap and a worn flex suit. She walked over and offered her hand, saying "What can I do for you, Captain?" After all, he asked for this meeting.

"You can tell me where the *Pandora* is and what you people are still doing here after three months."

"Well, I suppose I could, Captain," Rosita said, taking a seat. "Not that I will, but I could. What makes you think it's any of your concern?" She didn't look up at Captain Farris, a Cordoba stockholder with two shares.

Still standing, Farris said, "The *Pandora* doesn't have a license to operate in the Parthian system. We have to respect the native rights, you know."

"In that case, let me put your mind at ease," Rosita said, examining the menu and pointedly ignoring the looming captain of the recently arrived Cordoba trade ship *Bonaventure*. "The Council of Clans has accepted Clan Gold as an official Parthian clan."

That was true. It took some fairly significant bribes and was a close vote. By virtue of the fact that Goldgok was a member of Clan Danny Gold, and that clan had a working alliance with Clan Zheck, the council in its wisdom recognized Clan Danny Gold, with Danny Gold as the primary breeder, and the clan having several secondary breeders and one not-breeder.

"There were a few . . . well, more than a few . . . jokes about our clan being rather breeder heavy, but that's an internal clan matter, and the council felt that it was no one's business but ours. I like Parthians, Captain. They don't butt into other clans' business."

Finally, Captain Farris took a seat across from her. "And where is your ship?"

Now Rosita looked at him. "Again, what concern of yours is that?"

Farris' red face got a little redder, then he took a deep breath and leaned back. "I'm a stockholder."

Rosita nodded. "Yes, Captain Farris, I know. So am I. What's your point?"

"There is a long standing informal agreement not to get involved in internal Parthian politics. And as part of that, none of the wing ships—not even the ones owned by Parthian clans, not even *Fly Catcher*—does jump surveys of Parthian space."

"Really? Why ever not?" Rosita asked politely.

Deep breath, then another deep breath. "As long as the Parthians are limited to their system, with only occasional exceptions, the rest of the universe is happy enough to leave them to their own devices. But the Cordoba Combine has laws about slavery."

Rosita snorted. "Yes, I am familiar with the laws, Captain. You can't keep a stockholder as a slave, and aside from that, you're supposed to call it something else."

Rosita saw the captain's face getting red again and backed off a little. "Look, Captain, we are just learning the ways of these people, but their clans are in fact closer to hives and you know that. You must. We aren't trying to rock your boat. We just want to be left alone to do our business."

The talk was fairly unproductive. Rosita didn't give the captain what he wanted, and the captain managed, barely, to keep his threats veiled. But he threatened both legal and extralegal action if the *Pandora* were to share any information on jumps with the locals . . . or fail to share that information with the Jackson-Cordoba Trading Company.

The *Bonaventure* stayed in Parthian space for two weeks, then headed out again with full holds.

Location: Pandora, Parthian Outsystem
Standard Date: 05 26 631

Three months later, Danny sat on his preferred seat in the galley and called up the latest message from Gok Station.

Pan now had several new insystem jumps. One of them was to a point just two AU from the primary and well off the elliptic. Two of the jumps had chains that went out into the big dark. The first was five links ending just a touch over two light years toward galactic north spinward. The second long one was a single jump that ended up two and a half light years toward galactic south spinward. None of those jump routes was yet a way to reach another star system, either explored or unexplored—but they were a good start.

The message was a report and Danny laughed as Rosita's voice rolled over him. "With you out of the way, Goldgok and Kiiggaak have acquired a warehouse full of goods that we can sell in any number of systems. A lot of those goods will sell better in Drake space than in Cordoba space. But it will all sell quite well, Goldgok assures me. And I have no reason to doubt it.

"Only around fifteen percent of those goods actually belong to Clan Gold. The rest are owned by a selection of planet-based clans that, if they don't care for Goldgok personally, do trust Clan Gold with their money and goods. After all, Clan Gold brought back Clan Zheck's goods when it didn't have to.

"Gerhard is convinced, even without access to bodies, that he can build an interface for a Parthian brain and insert it with the same sort of nanobots that were used to install human interfaces.

"It's almost time for us to go, Captain."

Danny looked over at John Gabriel and lifted an eyebrow. "What do you think, John? Can you find us an excuse to stay out here for a few more months?"

"Sorry, Skipper. We could, but we're getting low on ice cream and a few other vital stores."

Geri, who was playing with a Parthian doll, looked up at the mention of ice cream, then said, "We have to go back, Captain."

Danny sighed, then instructed *Pan* to turn them back toward the jump route to Gok Station.

CHAPTER 21

> The only thing that'll cost you more
> The choice you'll come to rue
> Is to refuse that costly lore
> Which comes with postage due."

From the Song "Postage Paid" in the movie Bimbos In Space

Location: Pan's Galley and Virtual Space, Parthia Orbit
Standard Date: 06 05 631

Jenny slipped into virtual space in time to hear and see the meeting through *Pan*'s sensors. It felt a little like she was sneaking in, but she knew perfectly well that if she wasn't allowed, *Pan* wouldn't let her in.

"Why back to Ferguson?" Goldgok asked. "Even though the Drakes have been pushed back, things are going to be unsettled. Besides, we have tentative contracts based on taking the other route. We can take this gray route back to Drake space and sell our filters at Canda." Goldgok highlighted a route on the jump map *Pan* was displaying on the large galley monitor.

"Because I want to play rutter tag." Captain Gold called up a map of the Parthian system. The sun was a G1 and a bit brighter than Sol. It had seven planets. Kkiitiik, the innermost planet, was twice the mass of Old Earth, but so close to the sun as to be useless. Parthia, Kikiskis in Parthian, was the second planet. Out beyond Parthia was a gas giant, Kjiksis, about the size of Saturn at about the distance of the asteroid belt. It had half a dozen moons, one of them big enough to be terraformed and, between the heat put out by the gas giant and the sun, warm enough too. However, life, for whatever reason, never developed on it.

Beyond Kjiksis was KjeeKtee, about the size of Neptune, orbiting at six AU. TjisKee was next out, again about the size of Neptune, but with much less atmosphere. It was mostly water ice and in an orbit at about fifteen AU.

Finally, there were a pair of twin planets, Sikikee and Sukket, close enough to the same size so that it was hard to say which orbited the other. The twins were out at twenty-two AU and beyond them was a Kuiper belt.

"You know that survey I did while you were ripping off your fellow Parthians to fill our holds?"

"It was all quite legitimate, Breeder," Goldgok said snootily. "As you are a breeder, it's not expected that you should understand the workings of finance."

Jenny giggled, which *Pan* didn't send to the lounge.

Captain Gold laughed. "Fine. While you were engaging in legitimate trade using a proxy, I was surveying your outsystem. I got pretty lucky. There is a jump into your outsystem, far enough out to have a secret base if we can get someone to put it in." He highlighted a jump. "But even more importantly, there were jumps to chains in the big dark." Now Captain Gold shrank the system map and highlighted several jump points. "The short one goes just a touch over two light years toward galactic north spinward. The long one goes two and a half light years toward galactic south spinward. Ferguson is seven light years galactic south spinward of Parthia in real space. If anyone is going to know a jump that hooks up to that chain, it's probably going to be someone in the Ferguson system."

"Is that likely?" Goldgok asked examining the display with one eyestalk while the other looked at Captain Gold.

"Honestly . . . no," Captain Gold said. "But there's a fair chance that we can find some jumps that get us closer. I want to find a route to Parthia that doesn't go through the Canova system if we can. The Cordobas may not be as nuts as the Drakes, but they are more corrupt. I want a back door."

That made sense to Jenny, sort of, but she didn't get why it was so important. That was why she was listening to the meeting. It seemed the grownups were more and more nervous lately.

"Very well, Captain," Goldgok said, consideringly. "In that case, we need another ship."

"We need two or three more ships," said Doctor Stuard, interrupting their conversation. "We need a scout ship in the Parthian system to provide our allies on the clan council with more economic muscle."

Jenny knew she was referring to clans Zheck and Kiig for the most part, though at least a dozen others had nominally friendly relations with the new Gold Clan.

"We need a space station that is not under the eyes of the Jackson-Cordoba Trading Company. That means out in the Oort cloud around the Parthian system, far enough away so that they won't see anything unless they know precisely where to look. For that, the Parthians need their own jump-capable ship. We need another trade ship and we need an explorer to scout for routes."

"I'd rather play scout than merchant," Captain Gold offered. "But I suspect that we are going to need to be all three for now."

"Why do we need all these things?" asked Jenny. She didn't mean to interrupt, but it just popped out.

"Because the Parthians are going to get crushed soon if they don't get their industrial base upgraded," Captain Gold said.

"Why?" Jenny asked. Through virtual reality, she saw the looks exchanged by Captain Gold, the professora and Goldgok. The adults trying to decide how much to tell the kids. Since John wasn't here she figured they would brush off the question, but they didn't. The professora gave a minimal shrug, leaving it to Captain Gold.

"Because the Parthians are both a threat and a tool, even a weapon, for whoever controls them. There are nine billion Parthians. That's not as many people as were in the Sol system when it got trashed, but it's a whole lot for the Pamplona Sector. They have spaceships and biotech that is in some ways actually superior to human biotech, even if they don't like altering their own physiology. It's like there is this big cache of gold sitting out in the open. There's going to be a fight over it, and whoever wins the gold, the Parthians lose." Captain Gold looked over at Rosita.

The professora took over. "At the moment it looks like the Jackson-Cordobas have grabbed the sack of gold, but that's not going to last. Besides, we are going to need a base somewhere. Since Clan Gold is a Parthian clan, Parthia is likely our best option."

"Why?" Jenny asked again, though she didn't want to sound like little Geri. She was worried because the adults were starting to sound like her parents did before the asteroid.

Again, there was the look exchanged between the captain and the professora. This time it was Captain Gold who waved for the professora to explain.

"Because I am increasingly convinced that the present balance of power between the Drakes and the Cordobas is not going to last. In fact, I am now seriously concerned that neither polity will survive for very long. When it all comes apart, we will need a place to hide.

"Speaking of which, have you managed to adjust the contracts?" Rosita asked Goldgok. "Are you going to want to keep Kiiggaak?"

"No. I think we want to keep it as an in-system agent. And that can be done best if we return it to its clan and deepen our relationship with Kiig. Besides, even though it has learned a great deal, it would not be happy among humans. What I was thinking about was acquiring some engineers for the ship."

Rosita considered that. She knew perfectly well that as the trader for Clan Gold, Goldgok had the authority to hire crew. But this was a little more serious, even if Goldgok didn't realize it.

She looked over at Captain Danny Gold, and he gave a slight nod. "Well, look into it then. But if you can, find some who won't object to artificial enhancement."

Goldgok's mouth-hand scrunched up, but it agreed.

"We also need to finalize our agreements with Clan Zheck and possibly Clan Kiig about the printers and the manufacture of wing ships. They have much of the needed technology, but some of the vital bits are missing."

The molecular printers, if not absolutely necessary for the production of wing controllers, were the next best thing to it. And that was what the Parthians wanted more than just about anything else. They knew that without wing ships they were effectively trapped in their home system.

"Are you willing to give up your Wilson-Clark IIIs?" Danny asked Gerhard.

"I'm willing to give up one of them," Gerhard said. "And if Goldgok can make a good enough deal, two of the three."

"Between the mine manager brains, and the possibility of wing controllers and fusion plant controllers, I can make an excellent deal," Goldgok said.

"Then we will be leaving two of the Wilson-Clark IIIs and one of Pan's printers here?" Danny asked.

"On the planet," Goldgok said. "Clan Zheck wants to keep them away from the Jackson-Cordobas' notice, and the brains themselves are quite small and easy to hide. They will be able to disguise some of the other work as supplies for us."

"Fine. And we get controller brains and everything else to make shield missiles in large numbers?"

"Yes, but even with leaving them the two Wilson-Clark IIIs, the brains are going to be the bottleneck," Gerhard said.

Location: Girls' room on the Pan, Parthia Orbit
Same Day

"You've grown," Rosita said to her granddaughters, as she sat on a bottom bunk.

"We found a really big asteroid and Daddy made us these," Little Rosita said as she pulled a pendant from under her shirt. It was on a gold chain. Gold was no longer the monetary metal it was on Old Earth and was only moderately rare, but tradition made it more valuable than simple supply and demand would explain. Still, the real value for the six-and-a-half-year-old was that her daddy went on a spacewalk to get the gold to make it for her. Each of the girls had one, and most of the rest of the gold from the asteroid in the Parthian Oort cloud was now on the station and would be sold for use in making electronic components.

The months while Grandma and Grandpa were insystem made a change in the girls. They were more grown up and thought of *Pan* as home. Her little future academics had been transformed into little spacers, and Rosita wasn't at all sure she liked the change.

Location: Kiig Council Room, Parthia Standard Date: 06 06 631

"We need Kiiggaak back!" said Kiigssik. They were in a small, dingy room which was where the Kiig council had met for the last hundred years. The Kiig were a borderline clan with interests on the planet's surface and minor interests in space. They owned a small piece of one of the human-crewed jump ships that traded with the Parthian system and a manufactory in one of the Fkis stations. The clan had twelve active breeders and about eight hundred members, with seven hundred on the planet and about a hundred on the station.

"I'm not disagreeing, Kiigssik. But I don't see how we can possibly afford to return the deposit," Kiiggook said.

"I know, but you don't seem to understand how much it has learned while working with Goldgok. The clan needs that experience!"

"I'm a bit concerned about what *sort* of thing it learned from that pervert," said Kiigfesk, a breeder male and the representative of the breeders on the clan council.

"That was all Kox propaganda, Breeder," Kiigssik insisted.

"I don't doubt that there was a lot of self-serving blather in the Kox version of things, but where there's *that* much smoke there is probably a fire somewhere."

"Maybe," Kiigssik agreed doubtfully, "but it doesn't change the fact that working with Goldgok these last months has allowed Kiiggaak a great insight into the actual prices of production in the human systems. And we need that insight."

"We need our own space station and two new zero-g factories too. But I don't think we are going to get them any time soon," Kiiggook said. "What part of 'we can't afford it' didn't you understand?"

"I do understand that. But, honestly, we need Kiiggaak back even if we have to sell some more laborers to pay for it."

"Who to?" Kiigfesk asked. "We weren't the only clan to take a bath in the recent market upheavals. There is a glut on the market for workers."

"Maybe the *Pandora*," suggested Kiiggook. "If Kiigssik is really so convinced that we need Kiiggaak back that he is willing to sell more of the clan, I'll withdraw my objection. We are going to have to pull back some on our zero-g production for a while anyway."

"What about the devices?" asked Kiigfesk. He was talking about the bodies of some missiles that Clan Gold was contracting for.

"Clan Zheck will be making most of the parts that are made in gravity. We will be making the superconducting cable in our factory in Fkis Station Two. But while the project will help, it's not going to make up our losses, and it's also not going to occupy all our people on the station. We're still going to have to cut back. If we don't sell some of our engineers, we are going to have to bring them home and put them to work in the *guk* fields."

Location: Fkis Station, Parthian orbit
Standard Date: 06 07 631

Kiigdis squatted on the pad and used its mouth-hand to select a slice of dohkc meat. "Did you hear the clan is going to be shipping some of us down to the planet to work in the *guk* fields?"

"That's just a rumor," Kiigzak said from across the table. They were sharing a large bowl of tiskas.

"No, it's not. I got it from Kiigvok and it works in the personnel section." Kiigdis gestured emphatically with its right eyestalk. "It was going to be fifteen of us going back, but they got some new project, so it's only going to be five."

"I don't want to grow *guk*." Kiggzak's mouth-hand scrunched up, "I'm a qualified shuttle handler and I have experience living and working in zero-g. Putting me on a *guk* plantation, cutting stalks of weeds with a bronze chopper, is a waste of my skills."

"Don't be ridiculous," said Kiigdis, eyestalks drooping morosely. "It will be a steel chopper."

Location: Fkis Station, Parthian orbit
Standard Date: 06 08 631

The next day the Kiig station staff was called to a meeting area.

Kiigvok, a neuter male from the personnel section, gave them the news once everyone was in place. It waved its eyestalks in a sweeping gesture. "You know that things are really tight in the clan's finances. Well, in spite of some new projects, we just don't have enough work for all of the staff. We have an offer to buy two space-qualified engineers and there are going to be some people sent down to the planet. I have to tell you that the sales are to the Gold Clan, and that will mean traveling out of the system."

Surprisingly, they got seven volunteers. It wasn't that they *wanted* to be traded from the clan of their birth, but most of them didn't want to be sent back to the planet.

When Goldgok and a human showed up to talk about implants, four of the seven decided that they would rather go down to the planet after all, but the other three were willing. Two of them were actually intrigued. They saw humans using their interfaces to control machinery and envied them the ability.

For the return of Kiiggaak and a sum of money, Clan Gold acquired three new crewmembers, all of whom agreed to be fitted out with implant interfaces.

Location: Pandora, Parthian Orbit
Standard Date: 06 08 631

Goldgok, followed by Dr. Schmitz, strolled into the lounge. It saw Danny out of its left eyestalk, and with its mouth hand scrunched about halfway up and over to the left side said, "The new interfaces are ready for the new crew."

Danny looked at the Parthian and recognized the expression. It translated as "it's necessary." It was a bit like the expression that Goldgok still got over the Bangers. Disapproving, but willing because it was needful.

Danny had other concerns. "That's experimental surgery. No one has ever actually stuck a probe into a functioning Parthian brain before. We don't know if your brains have the plasticity needed to interface with the implants."

The brains of a Parthian were structured even more differently than the brains of an octopus or an insect.

"I'm fairly confident on that score, Captain," said Dr. Schmitz. "I've seen the functioning of the Parthian brains under scanner while they were thinking, looking, listening, touching, tasting, and pathing."

Pathing was a sense Parthians had that humans didn't. It was connected to hearing, but because of the way the bugs heard, it included something of echolocation and a sensitivity to winds and air currents. It was one of the reasons that Parthians didn't do well in suits, even big suits. There wasn't much chance of them using that sense in space. It wasn't a prime sense for Parthians like sight was for humans—and Parthians, for that matter. But it was a basic one. Along with scent, it affected the primitive parts of their brains.

"That's great, Doc. I'm glad you're confident and I hope you're right. But you know, and I know, that these guys are going out on a really long limb. So I am going to want to talk to them before you do any surgery."

Location: Pandora, Parthia Orbit Standard Date: 06 08 631

"Welcome to the crew of the *Pandora*," Danny said to the three Parthians when they walked into the lounge. They spoke some English and *Pan* was translating anyway, so there wasn't much difficulty in communicating.

"Thank you, Breeder," said the small one, a non-breeder male about half the size of the other two or Goldgok. Danny knew its name was Kiigvokx, now Goldvokx. It was an engineering tech that worked on the construction of rocket nozzles, which was rather more important for the Parthians than for *Pan*, which used the wings. Still, Danny was assured by *Pan* that Goldvokx had a clear understanding of engineering principles and could be taught what it didn't know.

Danny looked at the other two. They were neuter females about Goldgok's size, though their spines had different patterns and coloration. They were Goldfax, a ship operator, and Goldtak, a general spacer and one of the rare Parthians that was comfortable in vacuum. Goldtak had the bolts that held the vacuum mask in place.

"You people know what Doctor Schmitz wants to do?" They all nodded. "Well, you don't have to. I'm not going to *make* anyone go through experimental surgery."

"I thought it was vital to the clan?" asked Goldfax.

"Frankly, it is useful to the clan, and I suspect that in the long run, if it works, it will be vital to Parthians in general. But that doesn't mean you have to be the ones to take the risk." He looked at each of them, watching their eye stalks and mouth-hands for indications of nervousness or disgust. And there was some of that, but there was also curiosity and something else. Dedication, Danny thought it was. "All right then. We will do this one at a time. Who is going to go first?"

Both the females looked to the male and its eyestalks gestured assent. Apparently, even though female Parthians were larger, the males were more adventurous.

"All right. Once Goldvokx has gone through it, we will wait a bit to make sure that it's all working right for it. Then the other two of you will get your turns.

"But none of that's going to happen today, in part because this is politically sensitive here on Parthia. We want a chance to see clearly how it works before we go public with it."

Location: Parthian Outsystem
Standard Date: 06 12 631

Danny's mind flowed into the ship and felt with *Pan* as they flapped their way between jumps. The Parthia system, like most systems, had jumps all over the place. But less was known about the insystem jump routes here than in any system Danny Gold knew about. There was just the one standard route from the Parthian outsystem, actually a continuation of the jump route between Canova and the planet Parthia. That and the jumps Danny found on his survey were the only ones known in the Parthian system.

The jump they were headed for was out near TjisKee, three jumps from Parthia, and he was shifting the *Pan* in a curlicue pattern that would make it hard for any telescopes trained on them to follow them as they made their way to the jump. The location of the routes he discovered was proprietary clan knowledge with the Zheck clan.

It took them a day and a half to reach the hidden jump point and more time to find the asteroid once they'd entered it.

* * *

Danny strolled into lounge and saw the professor watching the asteroid they were approaching on the big screen. "Okay, Gerhard. It's time to drop your toys."

"Right," the professor said, then used his interface to signal Robert.

The shuttle launched and a few minutes later landed on a very large chunk of rock and rare earths.

* * *

Robert, in his new flex suit and tethered to the shuttle, reached into the cargo hatch and pulled the mining drones out. He tied each of them to the rock before fetching the next. They would use a set of tethers and pitons to make sure that they stayed attached to the asteroid, but Dad wanted the first attachment made before they were activated, because this chunk of rock floating in space had less than a fiftieth of a standard gravity.

Everything in place, he sent the signal and the manager bot woke up. It sent out several small bots to start a survey even before Robert got back to the shuttle and lifted off.

"Well, Dad," he sent, "if we get back to find that the robots have taken over the system, it's all your fault." He tried to sound like he was joking and mostly was. But he was a little uncomfortable leaving artificial brains to manage bots unattended by humans.

An hour later he was back on the *Pan*, heading for the jump point so they could continue their trip to Canova.

Location: Canova-Parthia Chain
Standard Date: 06 14 631

The surgery started with an injection, or rather a series of injections. Then Doc Schmitz interfaced with Sally and the two of them guided the nanites which would build the structure of the interface in Goldvokx. It took the nanites two days and during that time Goldvokx didn't feel a thing. That was the main reason that Gerhard Schmitz was so confident. He was quite sure that he could prevent any damage by simply turning off the devices.

Turning them off didn't turn out to be necessary. There were some bobbles in the initial activation as Goldvokx learned to distinguish its new sensory input from the much less organized natural input. "It's strange. I can hear the *Pandora* and she speaks with the accent of the Kiig clan. But why a breeder?"

"I am not a breeder, per se, but I was designed by humans who are much more comfortable with he or she than it. Also, I was inculturated into their way of thinking, both in my design and my training. I would guess that an artificial built by Parthians would think of itself as an it—not even as a male or female non-breeder. Just as a non-breeder of no gender at all."

Goldvokx's eyestalks crossed in a grin. "That makes sense, *Pandora*," it sent.

"You will now be able, through the network, to speak to other artificials, and even humans that have an interface," Sally told it. "Doctor Schmitz and I built a translation function into the interface, but be careful of it. There are things that will not translate in the best possible way until the system has learned how your mind interprets the signals better."

That turned out to be true. A lot of the overlying, or perhaps underlying, structures from which meaning were made were different in Parthians than in humans. And the fact that Parthian brains were more spread out caused their thoughts to be more duplicated—to appear in diverse parts of their brains at roughly the same time, but in differing detail. It was both like and unlike the way human brains worked, and the translations of thought between the two species taught Doctor Schmitz a great deal that he then used in designing artificial brains. But all that would take years to work out. For now, Goldvokx was enjoying its interface and the ease that the interface gave it in handling the drones and servos of the ship.

"But the best thing is that when I am linked into the ship, it feels like I am working with a team, only closer," Goldvokx told his shipmates.

"I can hardly wait," offered Goldfax.

"And it doesn't hurt?" Goldtak asked.

"No, but it tickled in some strange places at first. Sally says that's because there are several distinct neural nets that are all having to learn how the others work at the same time. She thinks that your interfaces will tickle less because they will have learned from mine, and yours can be installed with most of the weights preset to close to optimal balances."

"Is that why they are waiting before they do the rest of us?"

"That, and Captain Gold wishes to be sure there won't be any side effects."

CHAPTER 22

Susan Drake: *His rewards are small who will not put to chance to win or lose it all.*
John Franklin I: *Maybe so, but he's also less likely to end up in a shallow grave. We wait.*
From the play The First King of Franklin, published in standard year 524

Location: Canova Outsystem
Standard Date: 06 15 631

"*Pandora*, this is the *Bonaventure*. We need to inspect your cargo."

Danny felt himself stiffen even as *Pan* relayed the signal. There shouldn't be any ship out here, much less the *Bonaventure*. He stood quickly and ran for the bridge.

With a mental flip of an internal switch, Danny signaled *Pan* to send back to the *Bonaventure*, which was approaching from the port down bow about a half light-second away. "I thought the *Bonaventure* was a merchant."

The *Bonaventure* was feeding plasma to its sails, which were just starting to glow. At half a light second distance it would take a burst of grapeshot about fifteen seconds to reach the *Pan. Pan* would have a decent chance of dodging and a good chance of blocking the grapeshot, assuming the *Bonny* decided she wanted a fight. But *Pan* couldn't avoid the fight and it wouldn't be a short one. *Bonaventure* was on a matching course, not an intersecting course. From the vectors, it was clear that the *Bonaventure* coasted in, not under power. And that meant that they had to know that *Pan* was coming, and at least had a good idea of when.

Which was possible. The Canova system had a chain of seven short-hop jumps from the inner system to the outsystem, where the jump route that led to Parthia left the system. The chain of jumps made a zigzag loop halfway around the system in normal space. The start of that loop was thirty astronomical units and would take fifteen days to travel in normal space. It took five days and a lot less fuel to use the short jumps. On the other hand, from insystem you could see a ship entering the outsystem from the Parthian Chain just four hours after it happened. That meant there was time to send a ship from insystem to intercept them before they got all the way insystem. *Pan* was between jumps five and six on their way in. Time, but no reason. At least no good reason that Danny could think of. Still, *Pandora* was fifteen AUs from Canova II, the marginally habitable Venus-size rock where about half the population of the Canova system resided. So if the *Bonny* wanted to do something out where no one was looking, this would be the place to do it.

"There's official, and there's the way things are done, Gold," came back Captain Farris' voice a second later.

Danny reached the bridge and flung himself into his command couch. He strapped in as he signaled *Pan*. "Get us some distance and head for the jump insystem." After a short pause—Danny wasn't that used to crew—he commed, "All hands, action stations. Get the kids into safety suits. Have Robert and Goldvokx ready a couple of the shield missiles, just in case. *Pan*, run a backtrace on their vector. Assume they started at the insystem gate. When did they have to come through the gate to be where they are, moving on that vector?"

Pan was already shifting and the gravity was increasing as he dumped more plasma to the wings and shifted their course.

Then, strapped in, with captain's cap on, and ready, Danny signaled *Pan* to turn the comm back on and looked at Farris. "Captain Farris, I don't actually give a shit about the way things are done. And I especially don't give a shit about the way things *used* to be done. You don't have any legal authority to inspect my cargo, and you're not going to do it."

"I always knew you self-styled supermen were arrogant, but you take the fucking cake. You come in here, to our territory, and start messing in our business, and when we ask you for a bit of courtesy, you go and mouth off. Well, you aren't in Drake space now. If you don't heave to, I'm going to blow your old tramp to space dust. And no one's going to care, or even know about it."

"What? You don't have someone insystem with a telescope pointed at us? I'm surprised. I didn't figure you had the guts to take a piss without your bosses watching to make sure you did it right." Danny knew from *Pan*'s vector analysis that someone was watching the jump point into the Canova System.

Danny watched Captain Farris' face when that barb arrived very carefully, and he didn't much like what he saw. Farris wouldn't be that pissed off if Danny's comment wasn't pretty close to true. So there probably would be someone insystem watching. It wouldn't make any difference to this fight. They wouldn't even see what happened out here until a couple of hours after Danny got insystem, but they *would* see it. And that meant that Danny would have to be pretty darn careful of what he used, if he didn't want them figuring out what he had. And that meant that unless he was forced to it, he couldn't play with the new toys.

Besides, in spite of the fact that Danny knew how the universe worked, he was pissed off at people like Farris who figured that the fact that they could get away with something made it okay.

* * *

In a hidden tube off a refuse container, a cylinder sixty-seven feet long and eight feet wide waited and thought. Its intelligence was not great. More than a honeybee's, less than a parrot's. It did have a very small language center and an appreciation of music, part of its pattern recognition function. It knew what it knew and didn't have the wit or wisdom to question that. It would never gain that wisdom either, because once it was launched it had a life expectancy that would be measured in hours at most, and more likely minutes or seconds. All its memories were artificially created in virtual worlds. Its lack of intellect didn't translate into a lack of emotion.

No.

Shield Missile Able was as giddy as a schoolgirl on her first date. In just a few minutes, if it was lucky, it would be launched out into space. There it would run out some of its superconducting cable, and as it flew through space at a thousandth of the speed of light, that cable would pick up the magnetic fields it was flying through, which would tell it how the space was acting. In the meantime, it was loaded with the information on the enemy, the pattern of the enemy's wings and the flux of each of them, the position and probable course.

It knew its target, knew what it was looking for, and what it might face.

* * *

Goldvokx felt the spines on its back rustle with the flow of the *Pandora*'s wings as she flew through space on twelve wings flapping at thousands of flaps per second. It felt that flying in a way that was different than a human would, but one that allowed it the same level of interface. Its internal eyestalks were focused on the *Bonaventure* and watching for the variations in course and speed that would signal that the ship had launched grapeshot, or something else.

* * *

Jenny got the girls into their safety suits. Angi was watching the screens with avid interest. Little Rosita was clearly scared and Geri was blubbering, not knowing what was going on, but sure it was bad. "It's all right, Geri. I've been through this before and we weren't nearly so well prepared that time."

"I want Daddy!" Geri yelled.

"You know that your daddy is at work now," Grandmother Rosita told her. "Now, stop your fussing."

Jenny winced as Geri went from blubber to tantrum. She didn't understand how anyone who was supposed to be so smart and politically savvy could be that dumb when it came to their own family. She grabbed the other two girls and left the professora to the tender mercies of an enraged four-year-old, thinking, *At least it will keep them both occupied.*

"It's actually going to be pretty boring. Not as boring as the fight with the *Brass Hind*, but pretty boring."

"Why won't it be as boring as the fight with the pirates?" asked Angi.

"Because we're closer to this ship. A lot closer. When we were fighting the *Brass Hind*, it took the shots hours to cross between us."

* * *

Doctor Schmitz was plugged into the system, using Sally to analyze his new missile brains as they prepared for battle. With some difficulty, he didn't interfere as his son and Goldvokx fed them the information they would need. But he watched their reactions with the eye of a parent welcoming his children to the world.

* * *

The other Parthians were at their duty stations, with nothing much to do. All of them were wondering why Captain Gold didn't simply pay off the *Bonaventure*. This was, after all, his whole clan and there was no reason to take such a risk.

* * *

A bit under a light second away, the first mate of the *Bonaventure* was having the same concerns. Yep, everyone knew that the Cybrants were arrogant bastards but, to the best of his recollection, no one had ever called them stupid. "Captain, are you . . ."

"Shut your gob, Hardy. I'm sick of your gutless bellyaching. We're three times the size of that dinosaur, and two hundred years younger."

And it was true. The *Bonny* was bigger and newer than *Pandora*, and it had the newer interfaces that everyone said were better. But it didn't have much in the way of a ship's brain, and there were stories about what those old suckers could do. Besides, why was Gold so anxious for a fight? He could see the difference in size just as well as the skipper could.

"All right. If they want to play that way," said Captain Farris, "let's end this. Hardy, fire the hunter-nuke."

"Captain . . ." Hardy started. He knew that the bosses didn't want them to use the hunter-nuke unless they had to. Those suckers were expensive.

"Shut the fuck up, Hardy, and fire the damned thing."

Hardy fired the damned thing.

* * *

"Captain," came three voices over the net—Pan, Robert, and Goldvokx all reporting at the same time, that the *Bonny* fired a frigging hunter-nuke.

"What the hell is going on? In my entire life I've never run across a hunter-nuke until this year. And now two of the suckers?"

"That's an interesting question, Skipper," said Robert. "In the meantime, what are we going to do about it?"

"We're going to use Able and Baker both, that's what. Able to take out the nuke. Baker goes in five seconds later and I want it to go for that sucker's wings, if it can get there."

"Yes, sir."

Danny waited until both missiles were fired, then told Robert to send a salvo of grape.

* * *

"Captain!" Hardy shouted.

"I see it. Where did they get a hunter-nuk— Two hunters?"

"They're big for hunters, Captain. They don't fit the profile of anything in our records."

For vital seconds Captain Farris stared at the screen in shocked confusion. He didn't know what was coming at him and had no way of knowing what to do about it. Finally, he said, "Shift us, Hardy. North ecliptic, full power," ordering Hardy to move them up relative to the plane of the ecliptic of the Canova system.

It was too late. Not by a great deal, but too late nonetheless.

* * *

Able was cheerily feeling the space around it, seeing the hunter-nuke through several sensors, and sending its impressions back to Baker and the *Pan*. *"Here she comes, just a sailing through the void, singing do wa ditty, ditty dum dum nuke."* Able flung out its wire in plenty of time and it carefully waited to almost the last moment to power up the wing.

The nuke, with nothing to compare Able to—and totally shocked—didn't know how to react. That uncertainty wasn't quite enough to get it to go off. Instead, it went through the fully-charged wing and was reduced to slag. But Able was not unscathed. The hunter-nuke weighed fifty-three tons and was traveling at three hundred kilometers a second. Passing through the wing, it lost almost half of that velocity in a few microseconds. The strain of that vector change was more than enough to rip the superconducting wire right out of Able. It also made quite a flare, but five seconds later Baker sailed through that space, unaffected by the nuke or its leader.

It took Baker another seven and a half seconds to reach the *Bonaventure*. If the captain of the *Bonny* had even a clue what was going on, he might have saved his ship. All he had to do was kill his wings until Baker passed. The mass of the *Bonny* was such that it would be almost unaffected by the magnetic field that Baker could generate.

But Captain Farris didn't know that.

When Baker arrived, it encountered the *Bonny*'s wings, flapping just as hard as they could. Those wings managed to string the superconducting cable between the Forward B and the Mid C wings.

The superconducting cable did what superconductors do.

It conducted.

It conducted megajoules between the wings and the *Bonny*'s own wings were suddenly fighting each other. They lost two wings, generators blew almost simultaneously, and the feedback came within a hair's breadth of blowing the fusion drive. It did blow circuit breakers, taking down two more wings, and leaving a massive gap in the *Bonny*'s defenses.

Mr. Hardy jerked out of the system when the ship's damage reports made him feel like he had just had his right arm and left leg ripped out of their sockets. The feeling was gone almost as fast as it arrived, but as he looked at the screen, he almost wanted it back. If he could have just a few more seconds. . . . "You've killed us, you arrogant bastard," he shouted at the captain.

"Kiss my ass, Hardy," Captain Farris said, just before the grapeshot hit.

* * *

"Captain, why the hell did we do that?" asked Robert Schmitz.

"Because we didn't have any choice," Danny said, feeling every day of his eighty-four years and more. "Once the challenge is issued, there's nothing to do but play it out." Danny unstrapped from his command couch and stood now that *Pan* wasn't going to be making any more violent maneuvers.

"But . . . "

"Robert, once he fired the nuke, we had no choice."

"I know. I was talking about before," Robert said.

Danny heard him both through the interface and directly as Robert walked onto the bridge. He turned to face the young man. "Before, I didn't know he had a hunter-nuke. But, truthfully, even if I did know, it wouldn't have mattered. We can't afford to let them search us."

"Why the hell not?"

"Goldvokx, and the other new crew. Not to mention your dad's lab and a bunch of other stuff that we might or might not be able to hide. Even more importantly, we can't afford the precedent that they have the right to search us, shake us down, or in any way dictate our actions in regard to Parthia. 'Once you pay the danegeld, you never get rid of the Dane.' "

"I've heard the quote," Robert said. "It's one of Mom's favorites."

"So ask your mom about Cybrant society. The official tests and the unofficial ones." Danny paused, then decided to explain. "I killed a dozen people by the time I was twenty and I'd doubled that number by the time I left. There are lots of tests any child of the Cybrant System has to go through, academic tests, reflex tests, full medical examinations . . . those are all official types of tests and mostly nonfatal, even if you fail them. The danger comes if you pass them.

"There are only so many full breeder slots and a lot more candidates than there are slots. That led to the duels. The official duels were bad enough. We tried to force the other party to challenge because the challenged party had the advantage. The unofficial duels were, in a way, more restricted. They required some justification, but they were sudden, out of nowhere, fights. If it should be proven that the attack was unjustified, the winner could lose his breeding rights or even be executed. But it was a pretty high bar, so some of us carried personal recorder comms with us, so that if someone ambushed us, there was proof it wasn't a justified response.

"The idea was to engender politeness and a civil society, but the way it played out was politeness became a sign of weakness and invited attack. Arrogance and a sort of snarky pseudo-politeness was generally the best defense. Though I remember one girl who made a habit of being unfailingly polite to everyone, even the unlicensed. She killed fifty-three in 'self defense' before someone got her."

Danny looked over at Robert, who was looking both disgusted and confused. "What I'm saying is that growing up in the Cybrant System was a doctoral course in intimidation. How to do it and how to read it. Those guys were going to keep pushing, and their bosses were going to keep pushing, until something like what just happened, happened. And the longer it took, the more we backed off before we fought, the weaker we would seem and the more likely they would be to repeat the attack."

"Are you sure that . . ." Robert trailed off.

Knowing what he didn't want to ask, Danny answered. "Yes, I'm sure it's applicable in the larger universe. Cybrants aren't different in character than other humans. We just have faster reflexes and stuff like that."

"Fascinating," came Professora Rosita's voice. "If you don't need Robert on the bridge at the moment, I need him to deal with his daughter."

Robert went to see to his daughter and a few moments later Rosita arrived on the bridge. "I agree with your assessment, but we still need a story for the Canova government."

"We'll stick as close to the truth as we can, but I'm not sure we say anything unless we're asked."

"It's a safe bet someone had a telescope homed in on us. Once the light gets there, they are going to know."

"Yes, someone. But who?" Danny said. "We are going to get insystem two hours, maybe more, before the light from our battle gets there. So they aren't going to know what happened until then. We get someone asking what happened to our ship before that and we have evidence that they were sent out after us."

"Do you really think they'll do that?"

Danny twitched a shoulder. "No, but it's worth a shot. They know it was *Bonaventure* out here, else why have a scope on this chunk of space?"

"Because it's a jump point."

"No. We're halfway between jump points. Someone would have to be tracking the *Bonny* because of the time delay. Space is big, Doctor. A lot bigger than most people think. As far out as we are, it would be the next best thing to impossible to track us if we were trying to avoid it, because it would take them hours before they realized we changed our vector. But the *Bonny* was out here waiting for us, and Farris thought they had eyes on him. I'm sure of that. They start making accusations even after the news gets there, we can ask how they knew and what they were doing watching this area."

Location: Canova System Standard Date: 06 15 631

"Hello, *Pandora*," said a well-groomed figure on the screen. "This is Canova Control. Have you seen the *Bonaventure*?"

"Why do you ask?" Danny returned question for question.

"Well, they were headed for Parthia, so we thought they might have met you."

"Really? When did they leave?"

"Why do you ask?"

"Just trying to figure out where they might have passed us."

System Control gave a time, but not the right time. For the *Bonny* to have met them where it did, it would have to have left within a few hours of when they entered the outsystem, not the almost a day earlier that the Station Control officer mentioned.

"No, we didn't run across anyone between jump 518 and 515. What have you heard about the Drake incursion?"

"We sent off a report to Morland, but haven't heard from them yet. Last I heard, a force out of Hudson is moving up to push them back."

"I wondered about that," Danny said. "It seemed a bit risky from the Drake point of view."

"The Drakes are pirates in all but name."

"I don't disagree, sir, but I'm just a ship captain."

There wasn't much more to the conversation. *Pandora* wasn't stopping insystem, so there was no good excuse for Canova System to search the ship. Particularly since they were all stockholders, and Danny was a legally recognized clan on Parthia.

CHAPTER 23

The relations between the stockholders and the Cordoba Spaceforce have never been truly cordial. It is the Combine that buys their ships, pays their salaries, and gives them their missions. But the "bookkeepers and bureaucrats" of the Combine's civilian oversight have never understood the conditions or the traditions of the Spaceforce.
A History of the Cordoba Combine, *Admiral George Cordoba-Davis.*
Standard year: 625

Ferguson Station Three, Cordoba Space
Standard Date: 06 22 631

Danny called up the scans of the Ferguson insystem as they exited the jump. It was a crowded sky, but it was still three light hours and four jumps away. The chatter from insystem told him that the Cordoba Fleet ships were making final prep to leave the system. He had *Pandora* send their bonafides over lazer com, but aside from confirming that they were stockholders and warning them against using the chain to Parise, the fleet ignored them. By the time they reached the station, most of the fleet was gone.

"You have the best timing I've ever seen," Station Control told Danny on their way into parking orbit. "You came through just before the fuss and now you're coming back through just after it."

"You think it's over?" Danny asked the busty blonde.

"Probably. Tell you what, once you get on station, why not meet me at the Pagoda and I'll tell you all about it?"

"That sounds like fun," Danny agreed.

* * *

Rosita sat at the desk in her room, and used her interface to sink into the system net with the help of Sally. Virtual screens appeared before her, showing news articles, documents of the Ferguson system government, and even fleet records. She was searching for data on the Drake incursion.

What she found surprised her. The reports didn't jibe with her discussions with Tanya Cordoba-Davis, Chuck Givens, or any of the other survivors. The official report bore only the vaguest relationship to the reality.

Admiral Frankin, according to the official report, was the greatest strategist since Old Earth's wet navy Admiral Nimitz.

Captain Rodriguez was a paragon of naval virtues, brave and true, but faced with an impossible situation.

Tanya Cordoba-Davis was a competent but inexperienced officer who managed to save her crew more through luck than skill. And having done her duty, she resigned.

In leaked news reports, it became clear that Tanya was "allowed" to resign as an alternative to facing a courts martial for her failure to properly support the larger fleet units. The article in the Ferguson Cordoba blog suggested, without ever quite saying, that if Tanya were a better officer the Cordoba losses would have been much less.

All this seemed very strange to Rosita. She'd met Tanya Cordoba-Davis, who didn't seem to be the person portrayed in the reports.

It took Rosita and Sally almost an hour to find the pieces and put together what had happened. Frankin and Rodriguez were both of old line Spaceforce families. And, grand stockholder or not, Cordoba-Davis wasn't. The Spaceforce covered its own ass . . . and didn't consider Tanya one of its own.

That wasn't enough.

Tanya Cordoba-Davis was a grand stockholder and the Cordoba-Davises, while not directly connected to the Seventeen Families, were headed by Angela Cordoba-Davis, who was one of the Two Hundred. So why didn't the commander's family come to her rescue?

Sally highlighted an article. Rosita read. Conrad Jackson-Cordoba, Tanya's fourth cousin by marriage, arrived on the scene in the company of the relieving fleet. Then Sally used station records to find several contacts between Conrad and Tanya. Not what they talked about, but Rosita could guess. Apparently, Conrad told Tanya to sit down and shut up.

But why?

Further searching revealed that Angela Cordoba-Davis was Tanya's great aunt. She did not approve of Tanya's career choice, and had interests in the Jackson-Cordoba Trading Company.

Maybe . . . but it still didn't seem enough to justify Tanya's resignation. For some reason, Tanya was fed to the Fleet, chewed up, and spit out.

Rosita really wanted to know what that reason was.

The Stockholder's Club, Ferguson Station 3 Standard Date: 06 22 631

Tanya Cordoba-Davis played no games with the auto tender. Partly that was because there wasn't an auto tender. She wasn't in a spacer's bar. The club was a high class establishment with live waiters. Fine wood paneling shipped in from five systems away covered the walls. The floor was covered in Parthian silk rugs, the chairs were deeply padded, coated in Pang fur and the tables were carved Sing Ivory. The waiter brought her New Kentucky whisky in a crystal decanter and the snifter was a cut Torna egg.

Not that it was going to be any easier for Tanya to get drunk than it was for Danny Gold. She had similar genetic mods. It was the stock in trade of the Cybrants, after all, and her family could afford the best. But Tanya was hard-working and dedicated. So she shot the whisky back, poured herself another and shot it back with mechanical precision and no appreciation at all of the top quality hooch she was downing. With enough effort, she would get drunk, whatever impediments her genetics put in her path. She poured herself another whisky and thought about how she ended up here. . . .

Maybe her family was right and she wasn't cut out for the military. Being good at strategy games wasn't all there was to it. The military was just as political as the corporate jungle. Which she knew shouldn't have been a surprise, but it was. Her dad was military, but political military. He, at least, realized that if she insisted on going out in warships she needed to know how to operate in them. More out of concern for her physical safety than any interest in her military career, he found Jimmy Dugan for her.

Tanya took another drink.

Jimmy taught her. Starting with calling her a spoiled idiot on her first day at the academy. Tanya hadn't wanted to take any favors from her family. But Jimmy pointed out that it wasn't an undeserved promotion that he provided, but training in how to deserve the promotions she was going to get anyway because of her stockholder rank. She worked so hard to earn those promotions. To be worthy of the privilege she was born to.

Then, when she actually needed support, something for the good of the service, her family sold her out. To cover someone's ass. The Jackson-Cordobas had something on someone, or maybe just something Great Aunt Angela wanted. Conrad wasn't specific. He didn't have to be. He had the sealed message from her great aunt, saying that for reasons of family honor they couldn't support her.

Conrad explained that the Jackson-Cordobas didn't want an investigation of the situation on Parthia, and the Spaceforce didn't want its errors exposed. "If you fight it," Conrad Jackson-Cordoba informed her, "you will be courtmartialed for cowardice in the face of the enemy. Records will be produced to prove you ran."

Tanya agreed to resign . . . and now she really did feel like a coward.

Pandora, docked at Ferguson Station 3
Standard Date: 06 23 631

Danny showed Debby into the cabin, then nibbled on her neck. Debby was fifty, old enough to know how and young enough not to creak when she used that knowledge. Danny didn't creak either, even if he was close to twice her age. They'd had a good time at the bar and, unlike the college student, Debby wasn't into sharing. So they came back to the *Pan*, rather than to the apartment she shared with a friend.

"I was hoping to show you some of the Parthian woods we picked up," Danny said, "but they're still in the holds. Instead, look here. These sheets are from Bonks. Feel how slippery they are." Danny grinned, and Debby grinned back.

Some time later, they talked about local rutters. Debby sometimes played Rutter Tag with local captains. She had a good database. Danny didn't want to play Rutter Tag, because he very much didn't want to give up the jumps he discovered off Parthia, so he bought her rutters.

Debby's rutters were helpful, but wouldn't get the *Pan* where she needed to go. The nearest jump point listed in Debby's rutter was still over a light year away from the jump chain he had discovered out of Parthia System.

Pandora's Galley, Ferguson System
Standard Date: 06 24 631

"How was your evening?" Rosita asked, then sipped her juice.

"Entertaining," Danny smiled and fetched a cup of hot coffee, "but of limited value. I've uploaded the rutters I got from Debby to *Pan*. How was yours?"

"I think we should try to recruit Tanya Cordoba-Davis."

Danny stopped with the coffee halfway to his mouth. "What in space for? That naval robot has less originality than the suit bot."

"She's suffered a few shocks that may have loosened her up," Rosita said, and went on to explain her investigations.

"I'm not convinced." Danny sat across from her and sipped his coffee. "I don't think you realize how hard it is to put aside early childhood training. Besides, we're getting pretty Cordoba heavy in this crew."

"Not that heavy. Cybrant is in Drake space. So is Bonks."

Danny started to argue, but then shrugged. The truth was that Jenny and John had not been raised with any particular loyalty to the Drakes. The Schmitz family, however, were members of the Cordoba stockholder ranks, albeit minor members, of what amounted to the Cordoba aristocracy if by another name. Hirum had no loyalty to the Cordobas.

But it could be expected that Tanya Cordoba-Davis would still feel loyalty to the Cordobas, even if she was pissed at them at the moment. Danny knew how difficult it was for him to finally give over loyalty to the Cybrants. "Goldgok," Danny sent through the net to the Parthian's cabin, "would you mind coming to the galley?"

"I called Goldgok," Danny told Rosita. "Let's hear its view."

* * *

Goldgok came in and Danny listened again as Rosita filled it in on the recent history of Tanya Cordoba-Davis. Once the Parthian was brought up to speed, it suggested a compromise. "Hire her, but don't tell her about the new weapons. The point Hirum made about me applies to this member of Clan Cordoba."

"Assuming she'll take the job," Danny added. "Considering her wealth, she could buy her own ship. All right, Rosita, go ahead and approach her. But say nothing about the new weapons."

"We need some reason why we're trying to hire her."

"You said that she was dumped on by the Jackson-Cordobas," Danny offered. "Tell her we're looking for side routes."

"You mean a back door to the Parthia system?"

"Don't tell her that, but let her work it out." Danny had a thought and let a grin spread over his face. "*Pan*, come up with a game for the kids. In fact, come up with a couple of them, Sea Battles, or Angry Asteroids. Something, anything, except wingship combat sims. Have it use a weapon that is comparable to the new weapons.

Then we'll see if Jenny can get her to play the game. That way we might get some use out of the grand stockholder, without giving away anything vital."

Stockholder's Club, Ferguson Station Three Standard Date: 06 26 631

Master Chief Gunnery Sergeant Dugan showed his stock certificate at the entrance to the Stockholder's Club. The concierge sniffed and Jimmy grinned in sympathy.

"Yes, the club is technically open to any stockholder," the concierge explained gently, "but . . ."

Jimmy waved away the protest. "I'm just here to see to Grand Stockholder Cordoba-Davis. This isn't my sort of place."

"Well enough, then. Alex, take the gunnery sergeant to the Safari Room."

Jimmy followed the kid to the elevators and they went down two levels to a bubble on the skin of the station where they could look out at space through giant glass-plex windows. The commander was sitting at a table with a mostly empty decanter of New Kentucky whisky on the table beside her, and not noticeably inebriated.

"Skipper, you're an expensive drunk, that's for sure."

"Gee, thanks, Jimmy. Pull up a chair and I'll have the steward bring another egg." She held up the snifter. An accident of the structure of the Torna egg was that it refracted light in the visible spectrum. It was opaque to the high ultraviolet that the Torna saw in, but for humans the eggs were like holding a rainbow in your hands.

Jimmy just shook his head. "Skipper, you interested in a job?"

"What kind of job, Jimmy? Should I become an accounts manager at a station food market?"

"How about executive officer on a tramp freighter?"

"I think the accounts manager might be the better choice."

"Maybe, Skipper, but I don't think the foodmart is hiring. The *Pandora* is."

She looked at Jimmy. "This a real offer?"

"They seem to think so. But if you want a tramp, you could buy your own."

"No, I couldn't, Jimmy. I don't have the rutters. I have the military rutters, but not the civilian rutters to make a successful smuggler."

"You could buy those too."

"Maybe, but could I trust them? On the other hand, that's Danny Gold's ship. And if that ass is willing to hire a former fleet officer, something's going on, and I'm a bit curious about what."

Jimmy Dugan smiled as he followed his skipper out of the club.

Pandora's Galley, Ferguson System Standard Date: 06 27 631

Tanya gave the bug a half bow that was standard in Cordoba space when handshakes or salutes were not appropriate. She was almost sure that this was Checkgok, but not quite. It looked like Checkgok, but Checkgok was the only Parthian she had ever seen in person. "Hello, Checkgok."

"It's Goldgok now, Commander."

Tanya lifted an eyebrow and the Parthian explained. "The Zheck clan has confirmed my adoption by Clan Danny Gold. I am the chief trader for the Gold Clan. It is a new clan, based on Parthia, and the first established with human breeders."

Tanya felt her lips twitch. "Isn't that just a legal fiction?"

"No!" There was a short pause, then Goldgok continued. "I can see that it might seem that way to a human, but no. Danny Gold gained a great deal of respect by fulfilling the contract made with my previous clan. We do not draw the lines between family and business the same way that humans seem to. When he accepted my *kothkoke*, and then arranged for me to be able to fulfill my obligation to Clan Zheck, it established Captain Gold as an honorable breeder and, given the circumstances, he became the Clan leader of a new clan."

Tanya held up a hand. "I was just asking. I meant no offense."

"Of course." Goldgok waved one of its massive mid arms at a chair while it moved to its nest. "However, the assumption that it is a legal fiction, not a true clan, can lead to . . ." The bug paused again, apparently looking for the right words. ". . . errors in judgment."

Tanya sat. "Yes, we heard." A day and a half after *Pandora* arrived, another merchantman showed up from Canova system and rumors about the *Bonaventure* were all over the place. There was nothing official because the *Bonaventure* wasn't supposed to be between those two jump points at all, but there was a recording—not a good one, but a recording—that showed the *Bonaventure* there, then not there, and *Pandora* continuing its journey in system. "So, what did happen to the *Bonaventure*?"

"How would I know? The *Bonaventure* was nowhere near our course. The records make that clear."

Goldgok wasn't even trying to sound convincing.

Tanya grinned. "Fine, then. Jackson-Cordoba Trading aren't my favorite people at the moment. But you already knew that, didn't you?"

"Yes. Professora Rosita Stuard is quite skilled at informational analysis."

"She and her family own ten percent of the *Pandora*, is that correct?"

The bug nodded its eyestalks.

"And you are a stockholder with one share of Cordoba?"

Again the nod.

"What about the other Parthian crew?"

"Unfortunately, we don't have enough stock available to make all members of the crew stockholders."

So Stuard and Schmitz weren't willing to use all their stock to enfranchise the whole crew. "Is that what you want from me?"

The eyestalks moved in a different way. "No. Captain Gold sold some of the *Pandora* to acquire the stock. However, he is unwilling to sell more."

Tanya considered that, then nodded. She wouldn't be willing to sell off control of her ship either, if she had one. Meanwhile, she was on the beach and didn't have much of a clue what to do with the rest of her life. "Then why do you want me?"

"We need your ship handling skills and knowledge of Cordoba politics. Commander, we have been attacked by a Drake patrol ship that went rogue. We could use someone with military training."

"I hadn't heard about that," Tanya said. "Tell me about the Drake ship."

Goldgok did, though Tanya got the feeling it was leaving something out. It made her curious and that made her think that she might actually want this job, at least for awhile. "So you want me as first mate?"

"Yes, and chief engineer, shuttle pilot and common spacer."

"That's a lot of hats." Tanya grinned. "But I have some heads to wear them, I think."

"Really?" The bug didn't seem surprised.

"Yes. When the Spaceforce gave me my walking papers, some of the rest of the crew got dumped as well. Any of them who weren't willing to sell me out. That's Jimmy Dugan, my aide and an experienced exspatio gunnery sergeant. Spacer Fred Markum is a good kid and he can handle a repair drone. Lieutenant Givens was on the bridge and saw the whole thing. Givens doesn't like me much, but he's honest and never could keep his mouth shut. He's a qualified shuttle pilot. And Ensign Petra Allen, who was our assistant engineer."

"Do you want Givens?"

Tanya considered. "Yes. He's good at his job and I owe him."

"We, on the other hand, don't owe him a thing," Goldgok said. "If anything, the debt goes the other way."

"Good point." Tonya remembered sitting in the cramped shielded chamber waiting to die and hearing Danny Gold bang on the hatch. Whatever their later arguments, Danny Gold saved her life that day, and the lives of her surviving crew. "I guess we all owe you. All right. If we can work out the details, I'll provide some crew."

Spacer's Rest, Ferguson Station 2
Standard Date: 06 27 631

Jimmy walked into the Spacer's Rest to see Chuck Givens waving him over. "What's the word, Jimmy?"

Jimmy waved, but didn't answer until he was past the other tables to the large round table in the corner where the former crew of the *Jonesy* were gathered. Jimmy sketched a salute to Givens and Allen, then waved at Fred. He grabbed a chair and sat. Then he said quietly, "We have a job offer. And it's the *Pandora*."

"The *Pandora*?" Givens asked, not sounding all that pleased.

"Yep. The same ship that saved us," Jimmy said.

"But it's crewed by bugs," Petra Allen said. "At least, that's the rumor going around."

"And, as usual, rumor overstates the facts." Jimmy explained the makeup of the *Pandora*'s present crew as he punched in a drink order.

"Look, Jimmy," Fred Markum said, "I know we owe Gold, but I've never worked with one of the bugs. And the stories don't make it sound like something I want to try."

"Maybe not. But what else are you gonna do, Markum?" Chuck Givens said. "It's not like you can re-up in the Spaceforce. You gonna stay here and be a shuttle driver when the station can find you work?"

"You think I should take the job, Mr. Givens?" Fred asked.

Chuck Givens sat back in his chair, sipped his scotch, then set it on the table. "I think we owe Gold. Maybe more than we owe the skipper for getting us out of the battle alive. And however we feel about Parthians, we all need the work."

Jimmy didn't nod, but he knew it was decided. The crew would follow Mr. Givens.

Location: Townhouse of Angela Cordoba-Davis, New Argentina Standard Date: 06 27 631

Admiral and Grand Stockholder George Cordoba-Davis strode into the townhouse with his military cape swirling in the breeze of his passage. In spite of the weeks' long trip from home to New Argentina, he was still angry. However, it was important to be calm and logical when dealing with Great Aunt Angela. Though George still wore the admiral's uniform of his time in the Spaceforce, he was now a major political operative for his aunt as well as one of the family's best conduits to the Spaceforce.

He turned left and took the left hand curved staircase two steps at a time up toward the second floor landing that circled the main foyer. Approve of Tanya's life choices or not—and he didn't—that still didn't give Aunt Angela any right to leave her out in the cold this way. Family was supposed to mean— His thoughts cut off as his great aunt stepped out onto the second floor landing.

"Don't say it, George." Angela Cordoba-Davis was a hundred and sixty-two years old, and to a pre-space eye she would have looked a well preserved and fit fifty. She was wearing a silk gown that was hand-embroidered in a style reminiscent of the court of the first Ferdinand of Spain back on Old Earth. The townhouse also looked like a palace from Madrid in the fifteenth century old calendar, and the amount of gold and precious gems on the balustrade and woven into the wall hangings would have made the emperor of Spain have a fit of pure envy. "It has nothing to do with my views on your daughter's hobby."

And that says it all, George thought, cool calculation damping his anger even more. Because for Grand Stockholder Tanya Cordoba-Davis, a career in the military was, by its nature, a hobby. And George knew that just as well as his aunt did. Ending that career was, to Angela, no more than telling Tanya that her doll collection had to go into storage because it was time to go off to school. He also knew that Tanya didn't see it that way, and he wasn't at all sure that she would ever forgive them for what Aunt Angela had done. "Why?" he asked now.

"Downstairs," Aunt Angela said, then turned to the elevator on the landing.

George blinked at those words. Downstairs referred to the secure room in the basement of the townhouse. A room surrounded by several feet of shielding and security devices. He followed her onto the elevator, as he tried to put together what could be so secret. He didn't say a word as they rode down to the basement together.

* * *

The gold and jewels were conspicuous by their absence in the secure room. The walls were ceramicrete and if the chairs were comfortable, they were unadorned. This room was built for security and comfort, not for show. There was a constant scan for recording devices and every piece of electronic equipment on—and even in—his body was scanned and registered.

He went to one of the chairs and sat, not waiting for an invitation. The moment the door closed, he asked, "What?"

"New Kentucky and the Aegean Cluster." Aunt Angela placed her signet ring in the reader by her table and the holo screen on the wall opposite his chair lit up with a rotating three d jump map of the pamplona sector.

"Yes?" They had extensive interests in both systems. New Kentucky had a marginally habitable planet that was extensively terraformed. The high gravity made it uncomfortable, but the sugar content of New Kentucky corn was high and the New Kentucky oak barrels gave the whisky a unique flavor. The family owned a large property and distillery on New Kentucky and were in competition with several other great families. The Aegean Cluster was a set of three jump points that didn't share a star but did have extensive stations and industrial presence. Both were major sources of income and significant sources of conflict with the other great houses.

"Tobin Jackson-Cordoba can get us independent control of the whole quadrant."

"Bull. He's blowing smoke. The Spaceforce will never go along." George stopped. "Is that what this was really all about? Proving to the Spaceforce that we would sit on one of our own to keep their allegiance?"

There was a cynical twist to Aunt Angela's lips as she said, "Not as much as I would like. I think Tobin's boy Conrad is going to get most of the credit. But we need to keep the fleet out of it if we want to be in a position to freeze out Emanuel Cordoba. You know that he'll be trying to use the fleet to block any moves we make, and without Tobin's support there is a very good chance he will manage it."

"And what does Tobin get?"

"Parthia."

"The bugs?" George asked, then stopped. There was considerable interest in the Parthians because they were the only space-going aliens in Cordoba controlled space. The Cattans were in Drake space.

But little was known about the Parthians except that they had space travel when they were discovered and were an intelligent, hive-oriented creature that had breeders and non-breeders, were intensely clannish and conservative. And George suddenly realized that for him to know that little about them, there must have been a systematic suppression of information on them. "Just how many Parthians are there?"

"A planet full," Aunt Angela said dismissively, then stopped. "No. A system full, and not a colony system. A home world system."

"I think, Aunt Angela, that you may have been suckered by Tobin Jackson-Cordoba."

"It's possible. But it doesn't change the situation with your daughter. Her hobby is done. See if you can reconcile her to it, but—reconciled or not—it's over."

CHAPTER 24

It ain't what you don't know that gets you in trouble. It's what you do know that ain't so.
Will Rogers, Pre-space Entertainer

Pandora, Ferguson System, Cordoba Space
Standard Date: 06 29 631

Petra Allen was carrying her space bag into the *Pandora* when she saw the kids. There were four of them, all little girls.

Their leader, who looked to be getting close to a teenager, but wasn't there yet, said, "Hi. I'm Jenny Starchild, the ship's girl."

"We're ship's girls too," said the smallest of the little girls.

"These are Angi, Rosita, and Geri, Spacer Robert Schmitz's children," Jenny explained. "We're here to greet the new crew and show you to your quarters."

Petra looked over her shoulder at Spacer Fred Markum. He looked back at her and shrugged. Ships with kids on them weren't what either of them were used to, but he seemed to think it was all right.

"Very well," Petra said, looking back to the girls. "Lead the way." She knew the girls were here from their last trip on the *Pandora*, but she was so sick with radiation poisoning after the battle that she barely noticed anything.

The cabins were nicer than on the *Jonesy*. They were four by four meters. They had their own heads. And the heads had actual bathtubs. Like all ship's quarters, they were equipped with tie downs and covers for when the ship was not under power, but these were different. They had gimbels that let the bathtub rotate so that its "down" could be aft, or if the ship was rotating, outboard. The room. The room looked as though it was recently refurbished as well. The bulkheads and decks were newly painted in programmable coating, so crew could set the color and, to an extent, the pattern.

Once Petra stowed her gear, she tied into the system expecting to find automatics and an expert system. What she met was the *Pan*, a ship's brain, the first she had ever encountered. It creeped her out a little at first, having another personality connected to her brain through the interface, but she was surprised at how quickly she got used to it.

* * *

Pandora felt a bit overwhelmed. Fred Markum wanted to know where to stow the laser cutter bot when not in use. She explained to him that it went into container section three.

Pandora found having a lot of crew could be very annoying. She had a ship to run and Danny knew the ship. She was used to his knowing what needed to be done, where everything was stowed, and generally taking care of himself. The occasional trip labor they hired were only one or two at a time. Goldgok, John Gabriel, Jenny and Hirum arrived individually, or just a couple at a time. The professors weren't crew per se, and Robert was just one man. Jenny did most of the managing of the three little girls.

Now, she had three more Parthians and five humans, all of whom were crew and none of whom were familiar with the ship. No doubt the ship would benefit from the extra labor eventually, but right now she was spending more time orienting new crew than she was getting benefit from them.

Her design was for a crew of ten and supernumeraries up to another ten. But a ship's brain isn't a computer. It's a mind, one that works like a human mind. It gets used to doing things one way and can find it hard to change, even when it knows that change is for the better.

Then Tanya Cordoba-Davis used her interface. *"System data, rutter listings, download to console 17."* It wasn't actually in words. Just a set of interface commands. As though Cordoba-Davis thought *Pan* was a standard expert system.

Pan was explaining to Goldvokx. "The bots are partially programmable. I can set them tasks, but they are not bright and can get confused and stuck in repetitive cycles. They need to be watched so. . ." She didn't want to deal with Cordoba-Davis' prying.

So she dumped her out of the net.

* * *

The ship's brain threw her off the net. Tanya wasn't familiar with ship's brains. She didn't realize that they could get irritated. Her first unthinking reaction was that there was some sort of mechanical failure. That brought her out of her bunk. Even as she was jumping for the door, the possibility of a rogue brain occurred to her. That was a popular motif in fiction, the ship or station with an artificial brain that goes rogue and kills everyone, then goes on a rampage until the hero manages to take it out.

She bounded through the cabin door and down the hallway, in her robe and not much else. Entering the lounge, she shouted, "The ship's brain—" She stopped. Danny Gold was wearing his skull cap, and looking at her like she was crazy. Then he was looking at her in a different way.

Tanya closed her robe.

There was a short pause, then Captain Gold said, "*Pan* apologizes, but you're not authorized to look at the ship's rutters. Not yet. We need to get to know you a bit first."

"Well, she could have told me that."

"And should have," *Pan* said. "I do apologize. I'm out of practice dealing with a full crew, and I was trying to talk with several people."

"That's all right, *Pandora*," Tanya said. "I should probably have asked."

She turned quickly, and retreated to her room.

* * *

Pan started to apologize to Danny, but he interrupted.

"Actually, *Pan*, I think you handled that just about perfectly. In the future, just tell them 'access denied,' and don't dump them out until they try again. Frankly, I think Tanya of the pert posterior needed a wake-up call. This isn't a Cordoba starship.

"What I'm concerned about is the rutters. We didn't find any routes that lead back to Parthia or the cul de sac we found. Throw up a normal space map of the area around Parthia, would you?"

The holo lit up with a star map. "Okay, *Pan*. Start with the end of the cul de sac and zoom out gradually, adding known jumps as the volume increases to include them."

The first to appear were the jumps back to Parthia, then back out to Canova, and then the route to Ferguson, a jump out of Ferguson, then some more expansion, and suddenly a new point on the opposite side of the volume. "Wait, Pan. What's that?" It wasn't close. Danny checked the scale. It was nine light years and a bit to the galactic south anti-spinward, and showed as a blue light, indicating Drake space.

"It's a cul de sac off the Drakar system. It has been well scouted, as close as it is to Drakar, but no further jumps have been found."

"None that we know of. What's the source of that data, *Pan*?"

"The public Drake rutters."

"Damn. It *would* be Drakar. The capital of the Drakes, where they don't like artificial brains at all. All right, *Pan*, keep expanding the sphere."

The holo image shrank as its volume expanded and the links to other Drake systems and Cordoba systems showed up. But they were all a long way from Parthia. "So where do we go?"

"I think we must consult with Goldgok and, for now, base our route on the best trade advantage."

Pan got Goldgok on the comm.

"Well, oh master of trade, where should we go?" Danny asked, not caring where they went, so long as they went. It was the traveling that Danny loved, the feel of space through *Pan*'s interface. Planets and systems were just stops to get supplies. Where to go was Goldgok's problem, and Danny was happy to leave him to it.

"Hudson. We can get good prices on several of our products, and the lambfish is an item of request on several worlds."

"Hudson it is." Danny signaled Pan to cut the comm, and they went back to plotting their course.

Location: Cordoba space, Big Dark
Standard Date: 07 05 631

Tanya sat in her cabin and felt *Pandora* swimming through the void. The addition of *Pan*'s mind in the link made the shape of space much clearer. And, in a strange way, the Parthian Goldvokx's different sensory suite gave an additional perspective on how the data from the ship's wings was interpreted. Tanya realized that it was easier to spot jump points with the new perspectives. She wasn't sure which was more valuable, the *Pandora* or the Parthian.

* * *

Danny was feeling the same thing, at least so far as Goldvokx was concerned. He was used to *Pan*. But feeling the pressure of space rustling through "his" spines was a new sensation. "What do you think, *Pan* . . . ah, folks? Do you think that's a jump point?" He threw up an indicator in the location.

"I don't think so, Captain," came from Tanya. She indicated a ripple that he had felt, but not considered. Then, as the others considered it, they agreed, and so did Danny.

The more brains involved in the search, the better the searching, it seemed. But it was *Pan* that was the center of it all. By now they all agreed. Even Givens, who didn't like artificial brains any more than Hirum did.

Location: Cordoba space, Big Dark
Standard Date: 07 12 631

Danny lifted his cup to tell John Gabriel that he wanted a coffee, as he entered the galley. John waved back, pulled the coffee from the cold unit and placed it in the prep unit. He took Danny's cup as the captain reached the bar and had it back to Danny in a jif.

Danny took a sip and looked around the galley. Robert was there, so Danny spoke to *Pan* out loud. "We are going to need identification papers for the Cordoba Spaceforce."

"Former Spaceforce, Captain," Robert pointed out. "Fred is in no hurry to go back and Petra is happy enough with us. Jimmy's not causing any problems, either. Even if he is a friggin' exspatio."

"Okay, so some of them are fitting in," Danny conceded, a bit grudgingly. "Tanya and Chuck still have swagger sticks up their butts. I just came from a talk with Commander Cordoba-Davis on the proper maintenance of fusion panels."

Robert paused a moment to examine the data through his interface, then gave Danny a look.

"I know, but . . . Well, yes. Some of the helium guns are out of alignment and we are getting wear on the panels. We would have gotten to it. Remember, we've been short on crew."

"Yes, sir," Robert said, but it was clear from his tone that he didn't agree.

And the truth was, Danny didn't either. He just resented Tanya being right.

The helium guns that pulled the electromagnetic charge from the helium plasma were out of alignment, but not severely, not for a freighter. Unfortunately, some of the helium guns that sent the hot helium atoms down the tracks were slightly out of alignment and were gradually eating the far ends of the fusion panels. What made the discovery more galling was that Tanya was right. It was one of hundreds of minor repairs that had gotten put off while Danny was short on crew and had not been fixed yet. Also, military ships, which tended to be longer for their mass, needed greater precision to keep their systems in good repair. The various spaceforces made something of a fetish of that precision.

"Tanya's a grand stockholder. I think they're implanted at birth." Robert grinned. "Can't really explain Chuck, though."

"Spaceforce family. Probably implanted at that academy of theirs." Danny snorted. "Which, no doubt, explains Tanya. She's got two of the damn things. Anyway, the next stop is Jorgan in Drake space, and we are going to need papers proving that they aren't a grand stockholder and a bunch of Cordoba Spaceforce spacers, or the first Drake patrol ship we run into is going to lock us all up and throw away the key."

"Couldn't we just stay in Cordoba space?"

"I've got to make a payment to SMOG at Jorgan. It's overdue and the longer we wait, the higher the penalty. Besides, without the hidden route we found, Hudson's over a year from Jorgan. So we should get a good price for the lambfish and for a lot of the Parthian products." Danny didn't like showing Cordoba-Davis his hidden route from Drake to Cordoba space, but there wasn't really any option.

* * *

Sally, the Schmitz artificial, turned out to be very good at faking papers. Tanya Cordoba-Davis became Tanya Davis, graduate of the Pamplona Merchant Spacer Academy in Drake Space. Charles Givens became Chuck Givens, also a graduate of the PMSA. Petra Allen remained Petra Allen, but became a free-spacer off the Cogan family ship. Similar histories were developed for Jimmy Dugan and Fred Markum. Robert, the girls and the professors kept their identities because they were official in Drake space already, and the Parthians were not going to get away with any funny business with their papers. Parthia was in Cordoba space and there was nothing they could do about that.

Location Pandora, Big Dark between jumps

"Tanya, you want to play Nets and Rocks?"

Tanya let the resistance weight on the exercise machine return to the rest position, and turned to Jenny. They were in the exercise area off the lounge. "Nets and Rocks? I've never heard of it."

Jenny was standing in the center of the workout mat, wearing a virtual reality headset with the goggles up. "It's cool. *Pan* and the professora came up with it. You play a Parthian in an arena. You can throw stuff at the other Parthian with your mid-arms, and you have nets and rocks . . ." Jenny continued with an explanation of the game that actually sounded sort of fun.

Tanya wondered why Jenny would invite her to play, but this was her off shift and she wasn't tired or sleepy yet. "Okay, I'll give it a try."

Jenny offered her a head set. Tanya put it on and took a moment to take her stance and feel how her movements were reflected in her avatar's. She was in a virtual world, an arena of hard-packed earth with gates at either end. Her avatar was a Parthian neuter female with four legs and the two middle arms. Tanya stepped forward and her avatar moved, using four legs to Tanya's two. She moved her arms and the avatar's mid arms moved with them. In each arm was a net of force that she could wave back and forth. Tanya realized that the nets were a decent analogy for the wings of a wing ship, except that there were only two instead of the twelve that a freighter like the *Pan* had, or the sixteen, even twenty, that a warship might sport.

She enjoyed the game. As she played, she used the sims she ran at the academy and she took Jenny fairly easily in the first round and the second. She started explaining to Jenny why she was doing what she was doing. Jenny was doing fairly well.

Tanya reached into her pouch and pulled one of the big, heavy rocks to throw at Jenny's avatar. She watched the Parthian and the way she fluttered her nets, then threw.

Suddenly Jenny threw a net. Then, while Tanya stared in shock, Jenny threw another. The first net wrapped around Tanya's rock and pulled it to the ground. The second tangled her nets and dragged her arms down, so that the handful of arena sand Jenny threw wasn't blocked. Great letters of fire appeared before Tanya. GAME OVER.

And Jenny was crowing, "I got you! I got you!"

"Yes, but how? I didn't know you could throw the nets. Or the sand."

"Well, I might have forgotten to mention that part." Jenny grinned unrepentantly.

"Fine, then. How do you throw a net and how do you pick up sand and throw it?"

Jenny showed her and they played again. Tanya won one, then lost one, then lost a third. She kept slipping into thinking of it as Space Combat and forgetting that she could throw a wing—rather, a net—and then Jenny would catch her out. The sand was no problem. It was just grapeshot, translated.

All in all, it was a fun evening, and when Tanya got back to her room sweaty from the exercise, she checked with *Pan* to see if there was a non-aerobic version of the game. There was.

Location: Cordoba Space Big Dark between Jumps
Standard Date: 09 09 631

"I'd like to let Arachne run the Pandora captain," Gerhard Schmitz said as he walked onto the bridge.

The request pulled Danny from the half virtual world of the *Pan*'s flight and he turned to face Gerhard. "What?" Arachne was the name given the new administrative brain and series of separate artificial brains that Gerhard was working on. "Arachne is that far along?"

"It's been over a year," Gerhard said.

Danny waved Gerhard to a couch and went to his own. "A year is not a long time for the construction of an artificial brain capable of running a ship."

"We've managed to cut the time by using several brain bots and making the system as separate units." Gerhard took the indicated couch and waved at the screen. He brought up his work records and the outline of Arachne's structure.

"Isn't that going to increase the timing issues?"

"Yes, of course. That's what the Sally-based administrative portion of the brain is for, to take the somewhat independent actions of the individual units and put them together into a greater consciousness. We've talked about this, Captain, on several occasions."

"I know, Doc. It's just that I'm not really comfortable having another ship brain handling *Pan*. What do you think, *Pan*?"

"I think a partial test of Arachne's ability to weave reality out of data is worth looking at."

"What does that mean?"

"It means I am in favor of the experiment, but I want to be able to take back control if necessary."

"Okay. Gerhard, are you ready now?"

"Yes." As Danny watched, a series of instructions flowed back and forth between Gerhard and *Pandora*. Then, through his interface, Danny felt *Pan* recede and another presence flow into her place.

* * *

Arachne was awake. It was like her virtual practices but in subtle, indescribable ways, it was different. She felt her wings flap and the interface was different. She sent information back to her wing controllers, and over the course of several minutes she integrated herself from several parts into a whole. She was the ship.

She flapped her wings for hours, with *Pandora* there in the background, but letting her do it. Then they approached the jump and *Pandora* remained in the background as Arachne adjusted the electromagnetic stresses of her wings, feeling the shape of space. And with a twist she was through, in a whole different space.

Pandora let her glory in it for a few minutes, then gradually retook control. Then Arachne went back to sleep. She knew that this was not to be her ship and was grateful to *Pan* for the experience.

Gerhard had taken his wife's remarks about keeping this Arachne humble to heart.

Location: Drake Space, Jorgan Oort Cloud
Standard Date: 09 22 631

"Welcome back, *Pandora*. I'm guessing you found a jump route?" Elijah Sunderland grinned.

"Something like that," Danny confirmed, smiling at the old guy but declining to play rutter tag again. "We'll be shuttling over to your place in a few hours."

* * *

The planetoid habitat of the Sunderland family was much the same. Shelly Sunderland, the eldest daughter at twenty-two standard years, was running a bot that was melting rock to re-form the entryway as they came through. She waved but didn't look up.

Once inside, Agnes greeted Goldgok with all the joy you might expect for a returning sucker. And Goldgok made a show of checking his body pouch to see what was missing. But this time they had Robert's girls with them, and the younger three of the Sunderland children were introduced to Nets and Rocks while Danny and the professors talked politics with Elijah. Goldgok sold lambfish and bought atomic batteries.

"Can you give Shelly a ride?" Agnes asked Goldgok. "Just to the inner system. She needs to be out in the world where there are men folk who aren't her dads or brothers."

"I'm sure an arrangement can be made." Goldgok nodded its mouth-hand. "After the way you skinned me over the lambfish, you can certainly afford the fare."

Jorgan Insystem, Conrad's Station
Standard Date: 09 23 631

Shelly stepped through the lock at Conrad's Station followed by Danny Gold, Goldgok, and John Gabriel. She looked around at the massive plex windows that showed a sky full of stars, and at the carpeted concourse with eyes as wide as saucers. Shelly was a capable young woman and well educated, but it was all book learning. For the first time in her life she was setting foot on a station that didn't belong to her family.

Danny watched the girl with amusement tinged with a touch of envy. To see the universe all new and bright was a good thing. He signaled John and then left them to take care of his banking. Two hours later they were back at the docks and Shelly was situated in her dorm at Conrad Junior College.

Location: Pandora, Drake Space, Big Dark
Standard Date: 09 25 631

Tanya walked onto the bridge while Danny was going over routes with *Pan*. She watched the discussion for a few moments without interrupting until she had the gGAME

OVER cameist. Jorgan was on the same chain that included Bonks and Canda, and in the other direction went through Finch, Alenbie System, Cybrant—a place Danny preferred to bypass entirely—and eventually all the way to Pamplona. The Bonks route would take them to Drakar and another eight months before they could make the trip back to Cordoba space, which would be fine, except they would end up in Cordoba space almost a year from Parthia. They could survive that, but Danny thought, and Goldgok agreed, that the sooner they got back to Parthia with their holds full of trade goods, the better off they would be.

They were still looking for a backdoor into the Parthian system, but they were also trying to find other shortcuts and routes between Drake and Cordoba space.

Now that she understood the discussion, Tanya asked, "What do you know about Skull System?"

Danny looked at her and raised an eyebrow. "Just rumors, and the rumors don't paint an enticing picture."

"They shouldn't, but Skull System has routes into Drake space and Cordoba space.

"On at least three occasions, either we or the Drakes have sent fleets to put them down. It didn't work."

Danny stood up and waved Tanya to the captain's chair. It was her watch after all. "Why not?"

"Because the jump between Skull System and Cordoba space is thirty-two light years long and the jump to Drake space is thirty-seven." Tanya sat and pulled on the interface cap. "They have a set of fortified asteroids near the jumps with massive firepower. It's just not worth it to find another route."

"What about getting back?"

"There are arrangements that can be made," Tanya said, disgustedly. "So Jimmy tells me. The reason I mention it is because the Cordoba side comes out on a route that leads to Parise and then Ferguson."

"Gunny Dugan, would you mind joining us on the bridge?" Danny sent on the shipnet.

* * *

Jimmy arrived to see the skipper and Commander Cordoba-Davis, and a screen full of stars and jump graphics. "What can I do for you, Skipper?" Jimmy was always careful of protocol, and Captain Gold was the one who called him to the bridge.

"What can you tell me about the Skull System, Gunny?"

Jimmy blinked and looked at Tanya, then back at the captain. "Not as much as I would like. It's a gray system, but dark gray. They will deal with anyone. Not just smugglers, but out-and-out pirates. In fact, most of the independents avoid the place. Are you considering heading out that way?"

"I'm thinking about it. But the issue is getting back out of the system."

"That's not really a problem. There are pickets at the jump exits, but the arrangements are almost standardized by now."

"That didn't make sense to me, Chief Dugan," Danny said. "Sure, I can see corruption, but a picket at a single jump point? If a ship that's known to have gone to Skull System shows back up, the boss has to know just who let them through."

"They do." Jimmy let himself slip into parade rest. "From what I understand, there is someone fairly high up running interference for them."

"On both sides?"

"I don't know about the Drake side, Skipper, except to know that ships do go both ways through the Drake jump. So it stands to reason there's some sort of arrangement. I'd check with John Gabriel if I were you. He was a bit on the rowdy side before he picked up Jenny, if the stories he tells are anything to go by." Jimmy considered a moment, then asked, "Skipper, Skull doesn't have a good reputation. You think it's a good idea?"

"I'm not sure, Chief. But I need more rutters and they might have some of the sort I need." Danny Gold shrugged. "It's not something we have to decide right now, anyway. Goldgok wants to visit Finch for the feathers."

Finch, Jimmy knew, had a variety of large-feathered, cold-blooded animals that were more like dinosaurs than anything else. The four-legged bird-like animals all over the place were the reason for the name. Their feathers weren't actually that much like bird feathers on the molecular level, but they were colorful, sometimes iridescent, and in demand for hats and ornaments.

"From Finch, we'll likely go to Alenbie System. No habitable planets there, but there's a tar-like substance in the Oort cloud that is useful for making shieldgold."

"Cybrant, Skipper?"

"Not unless we have to. I'm not an outlaw, but once we set foot in the insystem, I am subject to challenge."

Jimmy wasn't sure of the specifics, but he knew that the licensed breeders were constantly killing each other on Cybrant.

Location: Pandora, Gardens

Danny stepped through the hatch and looked over the gardens. They were hydroponics in sealed shelves with grow lights. They were also quite lovely in a way, and they were full of plants from dozens of worlds, mostly Earth-descended and Parthia, but with sprinklings from all over. There were foods from Parthia that humans could eat and foods from Earth that Parthians could eat, as well as foods from other worlds that one or both could eat. The garden provided good food for both species, and all the ingredients needed to make a Parthian Banger.

John was seated at a table with an artificial bee in one hand. He looked up from a purple bell-shaped flower and said, "Hey, Skipper. The fruit of this sucker will make our salads tasty if I can get it to fruit."

"What is it?"

"Parthian *tokkissk*. Sort of a Parthian sweet onion, but with overlays of vanilla and oak."

"Oak?"

John grinned. "Just a touch, and the sort of oak flavor you get from aging whisky in oak barrels, not like eating the stuff."

"It sounds, ah, interesting, John."

John looked at him. "Well, since you're not here about the *tokkissk*, what brings you to hydroponics?"

Danny hesitated a second, then dove right in. "What do you know about how we can get into the Skull System?"

John sat back in his chair and looked at Danny for a long moment. "I don't know how to find the jump, Skipper, if that's what you're asking?"

"No. That's not the problem. Tanya has the location in her rutters, and the route to get there. It's a dogleg off the route between Cybrant and Forsythe. But there is supposed to be a Drake cutter stationed at the jump. How do we get by? Do you know?"

"Well, as to that, some of the Hudson lambfish ought to convince them that they need to make a short trip to scout the surrounding space, so they won't be right on the jump when we go through. On the other hand, once we get through, the pirates will have us under their guns."

"How do we deal with that?"

"We don't. Once we go through the jump, we deal with the Jolly Roger or we don't come back. Skipper, you sure this is something you want to do?"

"We're a trader, John. We trade."

"There's lots safer places to trade, Skipper."

"We need as many routes back and forth between Drake and Cordoba space as we can find."

"Maybe, Skipper, but there are better ways. What about Donnybrook?"

"That's a possibility." Donnybrook was another gray system. It had one star with three planets, none of them habitable, and had a bunch of stations and a population in the millions. It was about half-way between Cybrant and Congreve, and Danny had visited before.

Location: Drake Space, Finch Insystem
Standard Date: 10 06 631

Tanya flung a net, then reached under her Parthian body to the pouch that held the nets and grabbed another. Jenny quickly wrapped her nets around her arms and ducked under the flying net. But Tanya was ready for the move and had a rock on its way to catch Jenny.

GAME OVER came across both their headsets as Tanya's rock caught Jenny right between the eyestalks.

With their VR helmets off and breathing hard, Tanya complemented Jenny on avoiding the thrown net.

"Not that it did much good," Jenny muttered. "I have to jet. I'm due in the aft C wing assembly to help Goldtak with the drones."

* * *

Once Jenny was gone Tanya checked the ship net for who was doing what. Goldgok was on the comm with the merchants of Finch, who apparently didn't have any problem at all dealing with Parthians. The feathered cold-bloods of Finch were not, for the most part, good eating, and Parthian *ffikkesk* meat was a treat that was rare for the Finch hunters to get a chance at.

Her thoughts went back to the game. Over the weeks, Tanya's interest in Nets and Rocks had turned into suspicion. What if Danny Gold did have some way of throwing a wing at an enemy ship? She didn't see how he could, because the wing attachments were at least a hundred and fifty feet across, hundreds of tons of shieldgold, massive coils, and capacitors.

It would be like ripping out a chunk of an engine room and tossing it at the attacking ship. No missile could be big enough, though from what she had seen of the shuttles and the suit-bot, it was entirely possible that Professor Schmitz had come up with something that could manage the system if they could get around the size issue. She wasn't convinced that they had, but she was no longer quite convinced that it was impossible.

Tanya went looking for Jimmy Dugan.

* * *

"Gunny, you got a minute?"

Jimmy looked up, then turned to Hirum Outis. "You got this, Hirum?"

Hirum just snorted. Jimmy unhooked from the computer interface and got up, explaining as he walked, "There's a kink in the flow guide on the dorsal C and it's taking some adjusting."

"Coulda done it just as well without your butting in," Hirum muttered as they left the engineering control section.

"Could he have?" Tanya asked.

"Maybe, but it would take a long time. Outis isn't stupid, but he's not properly trained for that sort of work. What can I do for you, ma'am?"

Tanya hesitated for a moment, wondering about *Pan* and whether or not the ship would listen in. She knew that on a Spaceforce ship there were places where the ship's systems were not supposed to watch or listen—in your quarters, in the head, things like that. But she'd never been on a brain ship before and had no idea what it might do. She knew better, but she grew up with artificial brains as the villains in about half the holo-dramas. It didn't engender feelings of trust. "I want you to play a game with me."

There was just a momentary pause, like Jimmy was going to pull up short, then he continued. "A game?"

"Yes. It's called Nets and Rocks. Jenny showed it to me."

Jimmy glanced at the ceiling of the passageway. There were no visible sensors, but they both knew that meant nothing. Tanya nodded.

"It sounds interesting. What do you do with the nets and rocks?"

Tanya waited until they got to her cabin and led Jimmy in. She pulled a data cube and inserted it into the room reader. By long tradition, the private room reader of a person's quarters wasn't supposed to be hooked in to the ship's systems. On the other hand, it was Jimmy who showed her the hidden connections that did allow the private room readers on a warship to be monitored. It was only supposed to be done with a warrant, but things happened. She sat on the bunk and waved him to the chair and they both plugged in.

They were in the arena, both Parthian neuters, and Tanya started showing him the game. Jimmy picked it up quickly. He pulled up the menu of commands and realized on his own that you could throw the nets. Well, she knew that Jimmy was meticulous about checking the manual. He claimed you couldn't know what rules you could break until you knew what the rules were.

After they had played a few rounds, Jimmy stopped the game and said, "This is an interesting game, ma'am, but it surprises me a little. I mean, a gladiatorial fight is all about individual accomplishment, but Parthians are hive creatures. It doesn't seem their sort of thing. I could see them having fights in an arena, but not individual fighters."

"Well, I think you can have more than one on each side if you want to, Jimmy."

"That would make more sense. How do you think it would play out if only one side could throw the nets?"

"I think the side that couldn't would get slaughtered!" Tanya said, and it was her turn to glance at the ceiling.

"Even if they outnumbered the one that could. Who would win if you were playing with the ability to throw nets and say me, Mr. Givens and Miss Allen were all fighting against you?"

That was a very good question. Tanya considered it and thought back to the game with Jenny where she hadn't known it was going to happen. "It might depend on if they knew that I could throw the nets."

Jimmy nodded. "It would be a nice trick to have up your sleeve, wouldn't it, ma'am? On another subject, you know I talked to a friend of mine and he got hold of the after-action report on that little dust up with the pirate off Morland. And, of course, you've heard about what happened in the Canova outsystem."

Tanya looked at the ceiling again and nodded. "Well, perhaps we should play a game or two with the rules set up that way. But don't warn Chuck or Petra. I wouldn't want to spoil the surprise."

* * *

Danny stretched in his bed, then rolled out and headed for the head.

"Captain, I think Commander Cord—"

"*Pan*, while we're in Drake space, it's Miss Davis. Or First Mate Davis, or Tanya. But not Cordoba anything."

"Yes, Captain. I think First Mate Davis has figured out the nature of Nets and Rocks. She asked Chief Dugan to play with her."

"What did they say?" Danny asked while he was doing his business.

"I didn't listen once they got to First Mate Davis' quarters, but in the passageway there were significant glances at the ceiling."

"So how bad is it?" Danny washed his hands as he spoke. "And how much worse would it be if they knew?" Danny shook his head. "I'd almost like to just go ahead and tell them, but we don't know these people yet. And there is a world of difference between reporting that you '*think* we have a new super weapon' and you've '*seen* our new super weapon.' The first will just get you laughed at. The second will produce an investigation."

Location: Drake Space, Alenbie System
Standard Date: 10 23 631

They spent seven days in the Alenbie system, selling goods and buying Green Tar, and during that time there were congregations of the Cordoba Combine officers in Miss Davis' room almost every off shift. Miss Allen started playing Nets and Rocks with Jenny, and Mr. Givens was giving Danny and Professor Schmitz suspicious looks. Things were a little tense, but at the same time easing into something that looked a bit like familiarity. The crew was working together well, and the new hires were mostly in flexsuits. Miss Allen had lost out on the drawing for whose suits were built in what order, and the suit bot was working on hers as they left Alenbie. The holds were mostly full and the ship was in better shape than it had been in years.

Meanwhile, Tanya picked up on the financial situation of the *Pandora* and Danny's debt. That debt could well be an opportunity for her. It was true that she did have enough money to buy a freighter the size of the *Pandora*. What she didn't have was a good way of accessing those funds in Drake space. There were ways of doing that, but to try them under these circumstances would be to blow her cover. The best way to do it would be from Cordoba space. It occurred to Tanya that if there was some super weapon on the *Pan*, the *Pan* had to know about it. And artificial brains were supposed to be loyal to their legal owner. If she bought the debt and foreclosed—or even just converted it into partial ownership of the *Pandora*—that would give her access to the super weapon.

And that was where her planning stopped, because she knew that having dumped her, her family wouldn't welcome her back, even if she said all was forgiven. They would always suspect that she held a grudge . . . and they'd be right. The situation with the Spaceforce was even worse. She realized, now, that they had never accepted or trusted her, and after the reaming they gave her would trust her even less. She had the skills of a Spaceforce commander but the Cordoba Spaceforce wouldn't let her be one.

Location: Big Dark Between Alenbie and Franklin
Standard Date: 10 28 631

Pandora felt the return of a coded radar signal at the very edge of her range. She used a variety of sensors to observe the universe. Passive detection of light from long wave radio all the way to gamma rays, as well as coded radar and lidar pulses, readings of electromagnetic potential from her wings, and telescopic observation.

And with all of that, she almost missed it, even though it was right on the track between the two jumps. It was a light second off her course and although it was radioactive, the amount of radiation of any spectrum it was putting out was minimal.

It was a Drake flagged battleship, the *Kingfisher*. Or what was left of her, after what *Pandora* estimated as three high yield nuclear warheads went off within a kilometer of the ship.

* * *

Chuck Givens used a comealong to open the hatch to the personnel quarters on the Drake Spaceforce Ship *Kingfisher*. The stale air puffed out and in the room was a body. It was a woman in the uniform of a Drake Spaceforce Chief Petty Officer. She was seated, strapped into her couch, and looked to be asleep. She wasn't the first such body, nor the twenty-first. Mouth tight, he searched the room for any unfried electronics. He didn't find any.

It took a day and a half to search the *Kingfisher*, and while they found no survivors, they did find some standard memory cubes, most of them fried by the radiation. They found a lot of bodies, and some of those people lived for hours, or even days, after the attack, slowly dying as their air ran out and the radiation got them. The crew that repaired aboard the *Pandora* after the search was subdued.

* * *

"This is crazy." John Gabriel set the large bowl of klak bread on the table. "I spent thirty years in space before I went groundside, and only saw one wreck like this. Back in space a couple of years, and every time I turn around there's another battle or pirate attack or dead hulk in the space ways."

"I agree," Danny said, reaching for one of the small warm loaves, and Gunny Dugan nodded.

"I have been doing a survey since you mentioned that some months ago, Captain." Rosita Stuard sprinkled parmesan on the spaghetti in front of her. "It's not just actual attacks. The incident on Casa Verde is another data point. And there are others in the system databases. Over the last fifteen standard years, both the Drakes and the Cordobas have had a marked increase in criminal activity in general. It appears, from the data I have gathered, to be an exponential curve and we haven't hit the hard upswing yet." She looked over at her husband. "Gerhard was more correct than he knew, and the collapse of civilization in the Pamplona Sector is more imminent than any of us suspected.

"I think the best analogy between now and a point in the human past is probably the Dark Ages after the fall of the western Roman Empire," Professora Stuard continued. "Or perhaps the periods after the fall of one of the pre-columbian South American cultures. Maybe the old USA, after the fall of the republic in the mid-twenty-first century old calendar—"

"A bit less erudition and a bit more explanation," John Gabriel said with a smile. "I don't know about the children, but my ancient history is a bit rusty."

"Sorry. My point is that, for a variety of reasons, technological advancement seems to have slowed drastically, and in some areas even reversed. The suppression of artificial brains and of the search for jump points are two of the main factors where governments seem to be actively suppressing the technology involved."

That brought conversation to a halt for a few seconds. Then Tanya said, "That's very interesting and I'd love to read your paper on it. But what I am concerned about right now is who hit these people. It's not like there's a Cordoba route near here. And I haven't heard of any pirates that could take out a Falcon-class battleship."

"There are no routes we *know* about. But it's possible someone found one. *Pan*, what's the nearest Cordoba jump point to us here?" Danny was asking for the location in real space of the nearest jump point in the public Cordoba rutters. "And,

Tanya, would you mind checking your records and seeing if there is something closer to our location in the Cordoba military rutters?"

* * *

Tanya did examine her rutters, both the general military rutters and her private set. Then she assured Danny that she didn't have anything closer. Well, she didn't have anything *much* closer.

CHAPTER 25

When killing off a royal family, it's important to get them all. Don't leave survivors, not even little babies. Babies grow up.
Unknown political adviser, *2200 BCE, Old Calendar*

Franklin Outsystem, Nominally Drake Space
Standard Date: 10 30 631

Danny liked to be on the bridge when the *Pan* made jumps, so he was in his couch when *Pandora* came out of jump. The space near the jump contained a small ship, but the space around the next jump in contained three larger ships. All of the ships were squawking Cordoba Fleet IDs. Pan didn't wait. She sent her ID. Less than half a second after they emerged from jump, *Pan* got the challenge.

"Tanya to the bridge," Danny called. He then informed the communications officer on the CSF *Joseph Buckley* that the *Pandora* was an independent trading ship with Cordoba stockholders aboard. By the time he finished, Tanya was on the bridge but shaking her head and staying out of camera range. She mouthed "Rosita" and Danny continued. "Professora Rosita Stuard is aboard, doing a survey of linguistic changes for the University of Danworth. Her husband, son, and grandchildren are aboard as well, and I'm a stockholder too. I take it there has been a change in ownership of this chunk of space? I guess we'd better talk to the Stockholder Relations Officer."

The comm officer looked surprised at the request, but a few minutes later a young woman came on the comm, and explained. "Sorry, Captain. Things are a bit tense at the moment. Stockholder relations are barely even in the race in a situation like this."

"A situation like what?" Danny asked. "I don't want to screw up through ignorance and get my ship and several Cordoba stockholders blown out of space."

The young woman in the lieutenant commander's uniform got a considering look, then said, "The Franklin system has been liberated by units of the Cordoba Spaceforce under the command of Admiral Julio Chin. However, we are expecting a response from the Drakes at some point."

Danny nodded and glanced at Tanya, who looked worried and gestured that she wanted to talk to him.

Rosita arrived and Sanny waved her over. "Lieutenant Commander, this is Stockholder and Professor of Linguistics from Danworth University Rosita Stuard. I have a few shipboard matters to handle. Perhaps you can explain our circumstances to her?"

Rosita picked up Danny's cue without missing a beat. Danny let her keep the SRO busy while he stepped out of range of the camera and had a talk with Tanya.

* * *

"So what's up with Chin?"

Tanya grimaced and pulled Danny further from the camera. Then, in a low voice, she said, "He's political, but not grand stockholder. An old line Spaceforce family like Givens, but he's been involving himself in Cordoba management."

Danny lifted an eyebrow.

"You know that Spaceforce personnel receive a temporary grant of stock when they join up and more as they get promoted. They keep it until they muster out, and if they retire they keep it until they die."

"I've heard that," Danny said.

"If you own stock, you can give your proxy to someone or even sell it. But Spaceforce stock doesn't work like that. You can't give your proxy to anyone. You have to vote it or not vote it."

Danny nodded. "To keep officers from using coercion to get the proxies of lower ranking personnel."

Tanya shook her head. "Officially, yes. But the effect is to keep Spaceforce stock from being voted as a block. That limits the clout of Spaceforce, especially in regard to matters not directly related to it. That keeps the admiralty from, for instance, getting a retired admiral onto the board of directors."

"There are two ad—"

"Admiral Grand Stockholder Raul Allenby Denver-Cordoba and Admiral Grand Stockholder Paula Samantha Natasha Denver. Both members of the Two Hundred, and neither one ever commanded a ship in action."

"Okay, I get it," Danny acknowledged. "Chin wants to change that?"

"Among other things," Tanya said. "He wants Spaceforce to vote the Spaceforce reserve stock too. And, from some of the rumors I've heard, but until now not believed, he wouldn't be opposed to the military forming the basis for a new government."

"Are things that bad?" Danny asked.

"If he's invading Drake space without a Cordoba manager along, they just might be."

* * *

Rosita waved Danny back to the camera. "Captain Anderson would like to speak to you about Cybrant."

Danny spoke to the captain. "I can't tell you anything recent. I haven't been there in forty years."

"So I was informed. But if you aren't going to Cybrant, what are you doing here?"

"Looking for a route back to Cordoba space, Captain," said Danny. "We are also a registered Parthian clan, and we are trading as we go."

"What? Captain, you don't look Parthian. Wait a minute . . . aren't you the guy who rescued those Spaceforce personnel after they got mousetrapped near Parise?"

"Well, yes, I guess you could say that. We saw a bit of the battle from a short jump away and then found the survivors."

"Then, Captain, let me extend Spaceforce's thanks. I knew George Rodriguez at the academy. It's a great loss."

Danny just nodded, but he wondered what the reaction would be when these people found out that Tanya Cordoba-Davis was on the *Pan* with some of the survivors. Nor was it something he could keep secret. Danny thought fast. The longer it took for them to admit that Tanya was here, the worse it was going to be, because it would look like they were hiding things.

"Perhaps I should mention . . . After we finished our business in the Parthian system, we hired some of the survivors," Danny said.

"Really? That's the first I've heard about it. Who?"

Tanya was looking pissed. Well, she could just be pissed. The *Pan* couldn't afford to look like they were hiding things from the Cordoba Spaceforce.

"Tanya Cordoba-Davis, Charles Givens, Petra Allen, and two enlisted." Danny watched the captain's face as he named the officers. There was a touch of a grimace when he mentioned Tanya, but Chuck and Petra got fractional nods. "They needed berths and we needed crew. Besides, Cordoba Spaceforce training is the best."

"Perhaps we could have a chat with them."

"We're looking for a quick way back to Parthia, Captain. Could we perhaps go the way you came?"

"I don't think that's going to be possible, Captain Gold. The way we came is still a classified military route."

"In that case, we need to get to Congreve as quickly as we can. We have cargo our trader wants to sell here, but we weren't planning a long stop."

"I'm sure you can take the time, Captain." There was now not much warmth at all in Captain Anderson's tone.

Location: Pandora, Approaching Franklin
Standard Date: 11 01 631

"The royal station is gone, Captain," Pandora reported and sent Danny the visuals. There was still rubble where the royal space station used to be. Royal Station housed the royal family and their staff and the Franklin System Spaceforce headquarters. That was all part of a rather elaborate fiction.

Franklin was limited by the Drakes in what it could have for a spaceforce, but the royal family was related to the Drakes and were entitled to jump-capable ships for their personal use. "Can you tell how much of the fleet was at the station? Was the Franklin family yacht docked? What about the auxiliaries?"

The fiction meant the Franklin royal family could go trundling around the system sightseeing and in the process scout for jump points. But the royal family didn't want to spend all their time trundling around outsystem. Instead, they loaned their royal yacht to the Spaceforce. Spaceforce then ran a shakedown cruise, followed by a training cruise, followed by upgrades to the leather couches, followed by another shakedown cruise, then more training cruises, and so on. To facilitate all that, the Spaceforce was legally their yacht and its auxiliaries, and the Franklin System Spaceforce was legally nothing but the royal's personal retainers, paid directly from the royal purse. All of which meant that the Spaceforce headquarters for the Franklin system was located at the palace station.

Danny knew all that, and a part of him expected this. In a sense, it was two for the price of one for the Cordobas. They took out the royal family and the Spaceforce in one shot, and each acted as an excuse for taking out the other. Danny was never overly fond of the Franklin royal house. A stuffy lot if he ever met one. However, at least two thousand people lived on that station before its destruction, even if most of the ships were outsystem.

Location: Franklin Insystem, Station 1
Standard Date: 11 01 631

Petra saw the officer in Cordoba spaceforce whites waving, and pointed at him. Chuck Givens nodded, and they headed for the man. The Spacer's Rest was a standard spacer's bar, with entertainments of all sorts and spaces for enlisted and officers. Once they reached the bar where Captain Michael Ezarik stood with a group of other officers, he motioned a lieutenant to keep the others occupied and led Petra to a side room.

"Why me, sir? Commander Givens is senior."

"That's why you, Lieutenant. Besides, as the comm officer you were privy to the communications between Commander Cordoba-Davis and the fleet."

Petra told her story of the battle of the Parise/Ferguson chain again. And answered Captain Ezarik's questions. It wasn't the party line, but she told it, and the captain listened with care. By now, Petra was mostly disenchanted with the Cordoba Spaceforce and was almost belligerent about sticking to her story.

Then Captain Ezarik took Mr. Givens off to chat, and Petra went looking for Robert Schmitz. She liked Robert. She liked that he wanted to keep his kids with him, and she liked that he did his job and didn't make a fuss about it.

* * *

"So, Chuck, how did you get in this mess?" Mike Ezarik asked, looking at the bitter young man he didn't remember from the academy.

"I told the truth, sir," Chuck Givens said stiffly.

Captain Ezarik nodded. "Did George really screw the pooch that badly?"

"Yes, sir. They must have gotten word of our plans, just like the skipper said they might. They came through en masse and launched before we knew they were there."

"Do you think that Cordoba-Davis might have been the leak?"

"No, sir. I don't see any way or, for that matter, any reason for it. If the plan worked, it would have helped her career too. The news just leaked the way these things do." Chuck Givens shook his head. "It seemed like such a clever plan. If they'd come through one at . . ." Chuck trailed off.

"Do you think it would have worked?"

"Maybe, sir."

"Well, I don't. Not with the force ratios you were facing." Ezarik waved at the screen. "Cordoba-Davis was right, much as I hate to admit it."

"I don't like her either, sir. But she is good, and when we got beached she did take care of us. Got us the job on the tramp. And there is something funny about this tramp, sir."

"Really? I'll be talking about it with the grand stockholder later, but I'd like the take of a real Spaceforce officer."

"It's all just too convenient. There is this game they play called Nets and Rocks. You know every spacer plays Space Combat. Every tramp, every warship, anything with wings, plays Space Combat all the time. But they have this different game. And I wonder why."

"So what's different about it?"

"Well, it takes place in an arena and has two Parthians fighting with nets and rocks. Parthians have these really strong middle arms and they can throw pretty heavy stuff with them. Never mind. The point is, it's almost like they want a game that isn't Space Combat."

"Why don't you describe . . . Rocks and Nets, is it?"

"Nets and Rocks . . ." Chuck Givens went through a description of the game, including the fact that you could throw nets.

It wasn't much, and Mike Ezarik wasn't entirely convinced there was anything there. But the hairs on the back of his neck were telling him there just might be something. Besides, keeping someone like Givens as an informant might be useful, even if Gold was legitimate. He could probably sell the information to the Jackson-Cordobas, if nothing else.

* * *

Chuck Givens returned to *Pandora* in a more hopeful mood. Maybe Tanya was working undercover for Spaceforce and they would all return to the service as heros. In any case, it was nice to talk to real Spaceforce people again.

Location: Kindred Novelties, Station 1, Franklin System
Standard Date: 11 01 631

Danny perused the items in the Kindred shop. He'd last been here about twenty-two years ago. There were plates made of scales from the targ beast, ceramics of many types, and sets of crystal stemware in every color of the rainbow, plus loads more knickknacks of all sorts in the crowded little shop. The shop was owned by Albert Gold, a member of the Gold Line who hadn't passed the official tests. Albert was not legally entitled to breed in the Cybrant System, but here in Franklin he could. He—very publicly—resented the restrictions on his breeding in Cybrant, and was happily married to Margaret Silver, another Cybrant who had not passed the tests. He was also, Danny knew, a spy for the Cybrant System.

"Well, if it ain't Danny," Margaret said. "How's life as a free trader?"

"Well enough, Maggy," Danny said. "I get by and haven't had anyone try to shoot me in the back in years."

"You should have just thrown the math section. It would have saved you a lot of trouble."

"Like you did?"

"Of course not. Two plus two is five. Always has been, always will be," Margaret said.

But there was a tenseness in her manner. Danny spotted it, but he doubted anyone else would. "How do you like the new management?" Danny asked more quietly.

She looked around. "It's fine. Say, Danny, why don't you drop by our place for dinner? I'm sure Bert would love to see you, and little Sara is all grown up now." She tapped a finger on a blood red crystal tumbler that was on the shelf.

It was a signal for urgency. Danny shrugged. "Fine—" Then paused. "—and you need to come have dinner on the *Pan* before I leave. John Gabriel is a fine chef and we have lambfish all the way from Hudson."

Location: Bert and Maggy's Apartment, Station 1

Bert was putting away the sweeper as Danny entered the set of rooms. The door closed and Bert said, "We're clear, at least for now."

"How is it?"

"Prince Edward is still alive and in hiding, but he's the last of the royals," Bert said.

Franklin, in spite of its name, was a monarchy. The royal family were the next best thing to a Cybrant main line, and the two systems had enjoyed good, if unofficial, relations for centuries.

"The Cordobas made a clean sweep and have put in a stockholder board and new corporate-based government. Half the system nobles are dead and the rest are in hiding."

"How much support does the new government have?" Danny asked.

"More than I would have expected, but a lot of people are unhappy," Maggy said.

Danny looked at them. They were nervous, but that was all he could tell. "Do you guys need a way out of system?"

"Not us, Danny. Edward. As long as he's alive and free, the Cordoba hold on this system is going to be weak."

"Frankly, Maggy, I don't give a crap whether the Drakes or the Cordobas hold this system. And I think you know how I feel about rule by bloodlines."

"You made that quite clear when you left Cybrant," Bert said.

"Before he left, if I recall correctly," Maggy said sardonically. "That was why he had to leave."

"It's all ancient history. The issue here is a fifteen-year-old boy," Bert said. "Even if he is a prince."

Danny winced at the thought of a fifteen-year-old male who had been raised as a royal. On the other hand, he couldn't leave the kid. Even in the time it took them to get in system, Danny picked up that things were bad, and his chat with Margaret at the shop reinforced that. Franklin had been "liberated" from its royal oppressors, and the liberators didn't want any of those royal oppressors left for the population to rally around.

"Do you think you can find him?" Danny asked. "For that matter, how do you know he's alive?"

Bert's eyes shifted to the door to the bed chambers.

"Are you nuts? Here?"

"Where better?" Margaret said. "He was officially on the planet hunting when the attack came, so there is no reason for anyone to look for him on the stations."

"So what was he doing here if he was 'on the planet'?"

"He has your mod."

"I heard they were selling it," Danny agreed. For best results, the subcutaneous muscles that kept the skin of people with Danny's mod from blowing up like a balloon in vacuum needed exercise. Especially in childhood and the teenage years. It was a part of Danny's childhood training that he remembered hating with a passion. You ached everywhere after a space walk.

"So you were doing the training?"

"Yes. It was part of the deal." The deal was the ongoing agreement that allowed them to operate as spies for the Cybrant system and not be harassed by Franklin counterintelligence.

"Well, If I decide to agree to this, that will make it easier to get him to the *Pan*. Where did you want me to take him?"

"We were thinking Cybrant, but—" Bert hurried on before Danny could interrupt. "—that was before you showed up."

"Not a good idea anyway," Danny said. "There's a good chance that Cybrant is next on the list. Admiral Chin made it clear that I'm not to go to Cybrant. I told them that was fine with me and added some personal history they can easily check, so they would understand why I'm fine with it. But that still leaves the question of where . . ." Danny paused. "I assume you guys had hooks in the system spaceforce?"

"We try to be friendly."

"Fine. You're going to be my pals and give me a complete copy of the system spaceforce rutters."

"Danny, you know we can't do— "

"Sure you can. It's necessary to get the prince out safely. Who knows which of those jumps might connect with a jump route I have in *Pan*'s rutters, and I'm not going to play rutter tag with you while you're asking me to transport a fugitive. I'm also not doing this for free. You're going to have a talk with Goldgok, my bug of business.

"But we can talk about that later. In the meantime, trot the kid out and let's have a look at him."

* * *

Prince Edward Allen Golden Drake Franklin was listening to all this. He was, he thought, in a state of shock. His parents were dead, his older brother and sister, and his younger sister too. He was King Edward VI of Franklin, and it was his duty to lead the revolution that would restore the crown and throw the Cordoba invaders out.

But he didn't want to do that. He always did his best to avoid school work. It was sort of a game between him and his parents, them insisting that as a prince he needed to know politics, military tactics and strategy, plus a host of other boring stuff. Him insisting that as the spare, not the heir, all he needed to know was how to hunt, play cards, and dice. His parents won more than he did. He knew rather a lot of tactics and strategy, and he had a personal assistant. It was an expert system, not one of the artificial brains, so it could be trusted. It had no emotions to get in the way, and its calculations suggested the odds of a successful war of restoration were not good. Unless the Drakes came to the rescue, the chances of winning were less than one in twenty.

Meanwhile, he listened to Danny Gold—the next best thing to a cull—talking about his family like they were the culls . . . and he was royally annoyed.

He stepped into the main room with the full intent of telling the freighter captain just what he thought of him. And as he did, he accessed Danny Gold, captain of the *Pandora*, and got the captain's dueling history.

His mouth went dry. He felt like a rat in a maze, but every time he turned a corner, someone dropped another wall in front of him. Eddy knew his reaction times were fast, but he also knew the recorded reaction times of licensed breeders on Cybrant . . . and Danny Gold had killed a lot of them before sailing off in the *Pandora*. "Captain Gold," he got out.

The captain looked like a man of twenty-five. Golden blond hair, golden tanned skin. Even his green eyes had flecks of gold in them. He saw the captain look at him, saw his expression change.

The right side of the captain's mouth lifted just a touch, then Danny Gold spoke. "You should have accessed the files before you came in. I'm not all that impressed by your PA." Then the captain turned to Master Albert. "Don't tell me. You guys have gone back to expert systems." He shook his head. "Paranoia lives."

Master Albert flinched just a little. "The evidence seemed overwhelming . . ."

"Have you examined it?"

"Well, not exactly. But experts have."

"Whose experts?" Captain Gold asked. "I'm serious, Bert. There is something hinky going on. A whole lot of smoke, but every time I go looking for fire, there isn't one. Just more smoke, another unconfirmed report about a rogue artificial. And when one report is proved false, five more take its place."

Eddy checked his PA, and the PA, while unable to point to more than a few instances of rogue artificials, insisted that the many unconfirmed reports must be given some credence. Eddy looked at how much credence the PA gave other unconfirmed reports and compared them. It gave the unconfirmed reports of rogue artificials greater weight. And it didn't know why.

"You trust artificials?" Eddy asked. Danny looked at him and Eddy felt about five years old. "I don't mean wing controllers or even hunter-nukes. I mean true artificial brains, like the ones they used to use to manage ships and stations."

"As much or more than I trust people. An artificial can think of things on its own. Expert systems only tell you what they are programmed to tell you. So who programmed your expert system and what presumptions did they program into it?"

Eddy didn't believe this Gold Line defector. At least, he didn't want to. Eddy was designed to be smart. Smart people can generally figure out ways to keep believing exactly what they want to believe by explaining away the evidence before their eyes. Eddy, for now, explained that distrust of expert systems as the prejudice of a failed Gold Line breeder.

* * *

Danny watched the kid, wondering if anything he said would sink in. It didn't look like it. The kid was pretty skilled. He kept his face and body under control. Not surprising. Most golds and silvers, even the bronzes, had good conscious control of their faces.

Danny's progenitors and designers always had issues with empathy. It's harder to kill or enslave someone you empathize with, so the Cybrant System genetic engineers looked on empathy much as they looked on the appendix—something that had been useful once upon a time, but was now a potential problem.

However, empathy was closely connected, even interconnected, with a whole raft of analytical functions that were still very useful in dealing with other people. The ability to read and analyze facial expressions and postures, the ability to analyze and make predictions about the actions of others based on things like expression in the context of the overall situation: those things are needed. And they go with empathy. In fact, empathy is mostly those things, internalized to subconscious automatic reactions. The difference between knowing what someone is feeling and feeling what they are feeling is subtle and hard to separate.

Danny didn't want a Cybrant on his ship, not even a semi-Cybrant like this kid. It would be easy for Danny to leave him here. Too easy. That was the problem. He knew the kid was dead if he left him here, and he was still amazingly tempted to do just that . . . because he didn't want the bother of rescuing him.

Being a decent human being didn't come naturally to Danny Gold. It was something he'd had to learn, and something he had to actively work at, even now.

He turned back to Bert and Maggy. "Okay. We'll have to work out the details, but I'll take him. And once we get to some space that the Drakes have good control of, I'll—" Danny paused. "I guess he's a little young to just dump on the first Drake rep I meet. What do you want me to do with him, Bert?"

"I can take care of myself," Prince—no—King Edward said.

No one paid him the least attention.

Location: Pandora, in orbit near Station 1, Franklin
Standard Date: 11 03 631

Pan examined the rutters Albert Gold and Margaret Silver provided. They were extensive. There were thirty-two thousand jumps within an eight-light-month sphere, with bulges up to two light years from the system star. Most of them were insystem, and a wing ship with these rutters could get around the system in much less time than it took in most systems, even well-explored ones. That wasn't particularly useful in this situation, with the whole system under Cordoba—

Pan stopped. That wasn't right.

She mapped the Cordoba ships insystem, then the jumps, and she could see a dozen places where they could go through a series of jumps that the Cordoba military units probably didn't know about, skip around the system with impunity, and leave it in just about any direction without the fleet being able to stop them.

That would have consequences later, though. They would be declared pirates, and once the word got around they would be unable to deal in Cordoba space. The presence of Grand Stockholder Cordoba-Davis might ameliorate things, or it might not. There were fractures in the Cordoba power structure that *Pan* hadn't been aware of until Tanya came aboard. There were military units that would show them deference if they knew about the grand stockholder aboard . . . and there were some that might shoot even faster.

Pan turned her attention back to the conversation in the lounge.

"The Cordobas came out of the Alenbie jump route," Albert Gold was saying.

"What about the *Kingfisher*?" Danny asked.

"The what?"

"We ran across a Falcon-class battleship, well, its hulk, five jumps out from the outsystem jump into Franklin," Danny said.

"Why didn't you turn around and go back to Alenbie?"

"We didn't know what caused the wreck. It could have been pirates. And we couldn't be sure how long ago it happened. There are other routes out that way. For all we knew, they were behind us."

"Well, they got here two weeks ago and they had pretty good intelligence about our insystem jumps. They came straight in and took out the royal station before we knew they were here. They came out of here—" He used the interface to put a circle around a jump point close to the planet. "—and fired a series of nukes at Royal Station.

"That got most of the royal court and the Spaceforce command. Not to mention the royal yacht." The royal yacht was the closest thing Franklin had to an actual battleship.

"After that, everyone who could went to ground and they landed exspatios on the stations. The prime minister rolled over and showed his belly with no hesitation at all." The prime minister was just that, a king's minister who got his position from the king. There was an elected body, the House of Commons, but it wasn't very powerful. There were administrators and clerks and all the other government functionaries needed, but they all ultimately reported to the royal family and the nobility. At least, they had before the invasion.

"No reason for him not to," Danny said.

Pan noted an increase in Albert's heart rate.

The discussion continued.

CHAPTER 26

On the other hand, cul-de-sacs aren't always useless. Sometimes there's stuff in them, a frozen world where you can pick up liquid H, or asteroids of one sort or another. And there are times when knowing a place you can duck into to get out of sight can be pretty handy."
John Gabriel to Jenny Starchild, astrogation lesson

Location: Station 1, Franklin
Standard Date: 11 06 631

Eddy, sporting hair dyed black for the occasion, took the elevator to the station core, then floated out along the cargo corridors to a station lock. Once he reached the lock he glanced around, trying to look casual. The corridor security cams had been diverted in some way that Eddy didn't know, and no one was in sight. He keyed the code using his implant. His version of the upgrades didn't include the biocomm system.

The lock opened and Eddy floated in, pulling a pair of silicate gloves and a sack helmet from his pouch. The sack helmet was a clear plastic sack that went over his head and tied around his neck to make a good seal. It, like the gloves, could be folded into a small wad of plastic. Eddy filled his lungs, put on the sack helmet and gloves, then signaled the lock to depressurize.

There was plenty of time to prepare, so the lock wouldn't even report that it was opened.

Once the lock was open to space, he floated out, holding the guide rings. *Pandora* was in orbit three kilometers from the station, waiting for a chance to dock, unload cargo, and load up on local goods.

Eddy listened to the chatter, using his implants. There was a delay. The ship ahead of *Pandora* in the queue was having problems. Danny was complaining about the delay.

Eddy debated with himself. He wasn't supposed to jump for *Pandora*. He was supposed to wait. It wasn't that he might miss the ship. Eddy's spatial awareness was excellent for about the same reason that Danny Gold's was. Even at three kilometers distant, if he jumped, he would hit the *Pan*. No, the issue was the possibility that he might be seen. He would be floating through space, a human-shaped radar reflection, for ten minutes, showing up on scopes all over the place. But if he just sat here, he was eventually going to run out of stored air. Eddy was fully loaded up on chemically stored oxygen, but that only meant that it would be a full hour before he ran out of air.

Eddy fretted and waited. Then he jumped. Once he was in space, he curled up in a ball to make his shape different. If a normal were tossed out a lock or jumped, they would starfish as the arms and legs filled with fluids. Eddy figured that curling up would make him seem less like a dutchman and he wasn't wearing a suit, so had no locator beacon. He hoped that he would seem a glitch and that the filtering systems would filter him out of the data stream.

* * *

"Bow B lock opening," *Pan* reported while Danny was climbing into a ship's boat. Then she sent the vid feed from the lock's cameras.

Danny reversed his action. "*Pan*, see if you can find out if anyone spotted the little idiot. And hide the vid from that lock. I don't want our people to see it."

* * *

Eddy was still in the lock when Danny got there because *Pan* prevented him from opening it. "Okay. Let His Majesty out, *Pan*," Danny said, and the lock opened.

"Why was I held in the lock?" Eddy asked.

"Because you're an idiot who shouldn't be here yet," Danny said. "Now come on." Fortunately, most of the living quarters on the *Pan* were at or near the bow. He escorted the new king of Franklin fifty meters spinward, then turned him aft into hydroponics, then to a mostly empty pantry. He pointed. "Inside."

"What?"

"Inside. Now." Danny let his right hand fall to the hilt of his pistol. "I don't want, Tanya Cordoba-Davis or the other former Spaceforce personnel seeing you while we're still in range of the local authorities. For that matter, I don't want the professors or Robert seeing you, either."

Eddy went in, looking resentful.

Danny had Pan close and lock the hatch.

* * *

Eddy was most extraordinarily displeased. He knew about the Cordoba officers, but if anyone should be locked up it ought to be them. The truth was, Eddy knew that his suggestion was impractical. But it was wrong for the king of Franklin to be locked up in a cell.

The whole thing was offensive.

Location: Offices of the FSCG, Station 1

Tanya Cordoba-Davis sat in the outer office of the newly installed chairman of Franklin System's Corporate government. The office was carpeted, and an ensign was seated at a desk using a virtual keyboard to write something. Tanya could tell by the way the young man's fingers were flicking over empty space above the desk.

The newly installed chairman was Andre Chin, the nephew of Admiral Julio Chin. Andre was a minor stockholder with fifty-seven shares of Cordoba stock and recently resigned his commission as a commodore in Cordoba Spaceforce in order to accept the appointment.

As it happened, Andre and Tanya were at the academy together, and they had not been friends, though they might have been. While Tanya was trying to sneak into the military classes, Andre had been trying to get into the political classes. Each had considered the other a poser on some level. Which, Tanya was pretty sure, was a good part of the reason she was sitting in the outer office while Andre gloated and pretended to be busy with managing the new corporate government of the system. Tanya took a couple of deep breaths and firmly told her body to cut down on the production of adrenaline.

* * *

Just the other side of the door, Andre Chin was anything but gloating. Oh, he would have been gloating, but the truth was he didn't have time. He was using his implant and trained motions to call up file after file on possible administrative personnel.

The subjects of the Franklin crown didn't seem nearly as pleased as they should be with the new government. Just now, he was looking desperately for anyone who was both reasonably honest and willing to work for his administration.

It was not going well. When his aide told him there was a grand stockholder waiting to see him, he hadn't even waited for the name. He'd just told the aide to put the stockholder off for a couple of days. His secretary buzzed again. Andre used his implant to open the comm. "What now?"

"Grand Stockholder Cordoba-Davis decided to wait, Mr. Chairman."

"Cordoba-Davis? Send him in." He flicked his right hand and the screen blanked to an image of near space. The Cordoba-Davises were a powerful faction. Together they had real influence. And if this adventure of Uncle Julio's was going to get sanctioned, they were going to need that support.

The door opened and in walked Tanya.

"What the hell are you doing in Franklin?" Andre blurted.

He didn't realize it, but that was precisely the best thing he could have said. It completely diffused Tanya's simmering resentment.

"I'm sorry, Grand Stockholder. I heard about the battle, but . . ." He ran down, knowing better than to complain about his situation. "Anyway, I'm sorry about the board . . ." Again he ran down.

"It's all right, Andre," Tanya said. "None of it is your fault, and I would imagine you're pretty busy."

"Yes. Yes, I am, Tanya. But what can I do for you? Have a seat." He waved to a comfortable chair that was not in front of the desk, but off to the side and he turned his chair to face it as Tanya sat.

"It's the blockade. I'm working on a freighter, trading. We're trying to get back into Cordoba space and . . ."

"You're working on a freighter?" popped out of Andre's mouth. Then he shook his head. "I'm sorry again, Tanya. I'm operating on three hours sleep and, frankly, just seeing you here is quite a shock. Why don't you tell me about it? Start with the battle and tell me what really happened."

Tanya did. She sat back in the chair, relaxed, and began to speak. Over the next hour, she told him the story and found the commodore to be a very different person from the midshipman he used to be. Finally, she finished with, "So we have a full cargo for Parthia and no way of getting there unless we can get back to Cordoba space. We were told that the route you took to get here is still a military secret, but there must be something we can do."

"Well, there's no way I'm going to be able to get you that. It's not just military rutters Uncle Julio used. It's private family rutters, and a bit of good luck." Andre paused, and this time didn't let his mouth run away with him. "On the other hand, you're right that we aren't going to be able to keep this incursion a secret much longer. I'll talk to my uncle and see what I can arrange.

"Oh, you're not picking up any passengers, are you?"

"One possible, a friend of Captain Gold's. Rather, the daughter of a friend of Captain Gold. A fellow Cybrant expatriate. Captain Gold has no intention of returning to Cybrant."

"It's not just Cybrant. It's any place in Drake space," Andre said.

"Hence the problem. If we can't use the secret route you used to get here, the only way to get back to Cordoba space is through Drake space. You can't stop all trade, Andre. If you do, you'll have a revolution and the Cordoba Board won't be on your side."

"Believe me, I've mentioned that to my uncle."

"Is this incursion authorized?" It was Tanya's turn to blurt something out.

"Not exactly. The orders that Uncle Julio is basing this on are 'to harass the Drakes wherever possible to help draw their forces away from Parise.' And, yes, my uncle, the admiral, is aware that this is rather further than the orders probably intended. But the admiralty is frustrated with the board of directors, Tanya."

Tanya nodded. Her sympathies were mostly with the Spaceforce in this. As much as the Cordobas condemned the Drakes and the Drakes condemned the Cordobas, it increasingly seemed that they were mostly acting as scarecrows for each other. Strawmen to hold up to the mob to keep them quiet. "Can you do anything to help us get loose? It's not like your uncle's action will relieve Parise if the Drakes don't know about it."

"Fair point, Tanya, fair point. Give me a day or two, and I'll do what I can."

"I'll owe you one, Andre."

"If I pull this off for you, Tanya, you'll owe me several."

Location: Pandora, off Station 1
Standard Date: 11 08 631

The lock opened and a young woman with silver blond hair entered the cabin. Danny smiled. "All grown up, indeed. Yow!"

Sara Electrum looked Danny up and down, then said. "Yow right back at you, Uncle Danny. You know, I had a horrible crush on you the last time you were through here." Then she grinned a hungry grin.

"What were you, five?" Danny patted the air about three feet off the ground.

"Yes, but I was very mature for my age. Though I must admit it was more the notion of sailing around in the *Pan* than your person that attracted me."

"And another excellent match lost! I'm heartbroken." Danny patted his chest.

"Well, perhaps I'll bandage it up for you sometime, if I'm bored."

"*Pan*, we must arrange a load of boredom for Sara."

Sara grinned again. "Don't you dare, *Pan*."

"Oh, mush!" Little Rosita said disgustedly.

"That's right, darling, but we're just playing," Sara said. "I'm really a spy."

"Oh, that's okay then." Little Rosita giggled.

"Hide the super missiles and the magic sails, *Pandora*," Danny said, trying to sound worried.

* * *

"You really think she's a spy?" Hirum asked Robert after Sara went to her cabin.

"Pretty stupid way to go about it if she is, announcing it like that," Robert said.

"Actually, Danny is convinced that at least half the reason that her parents sent her with us is to spy for them," *Pandora* said. "And if her parents are any indication, she is probably a very good spy."

"What's the rest of the reason?" Petra asked.

"Partly simply to get her out of the war zone. But also, because the captain is a fully licensed breeder. Any children by him would have status in the Cybrant System, at least access to the tests."

"You mean, she's here to . . ." Petra's face turned red.

Location: Pandora
Standard Date: 11 09 631

Tanya was checking the alignment on the fusion plant when she got the call. She paused the bot and using her implants shifted the incoming image to her faceplate. Holding onto the wall of the exhaust tube with one hand, she said, "Hello, Andre."

"I talked to my uncle and you're cleared back to Alenbie. Sorry, but that's the best I could do."

Tanya watched his face and decided that there was something off. Not very, and Tanya wasn't entirely sure what it was, but she'd known Andre for a long time. Not well, but she'd played poker with him a time or two. He was holding a busted flush of some sort. "Thanks for what you managed, Andre. Like I said, I owe you one."

Andre Chin nodded and signed off. And now Tanya was sure. If he'd *really* gotten them clearance, he'd have insisted that she owed him several.

Location: Franklin outsystem, Alenbie route
Standard Date: 11 09 631

Tanya felt the wings through her interface and felt *Pan* and the Parthians as well. It was her watch, and they were approaching the getaway. About an hour away was the next standard jump and Tanya shifted the plasma feed to the C and D wings to shift their course a tad. Now they were approaching a different jump, one from the Franklin Spaceforce rutters. She waited, feeling the wings for almost an hour, then they were at the jump point and jumped.

The new space, about five light minutes to the stellar north and well out from where any telescope ought to be looking, had five jumps within fifteen light seconds. She shoved the *Pan* into a sharp turn and the Gs mounted. Tanya checked automatically. Everyone was belted in and safe.

More time. A hundred thousand klicks, even at the speed they were going, took time. The *Pandora* and her crew pushed through space with a constantly changing vector until they reached the next jump.

Again a jump, and they were out. It would take a special miracle for anyone not possessed of Franklin Spaceforce rutters to find them now.

Unfortunately, there were no more known jumps in this chain. It was a cul de sac. But at worst, it was a place for them to wait while whatever happened in Franklin worked itself out.

"Start looking for jumps, Tanya," Danny sent over the comm, "and take us back to standard running."

Tanya did, and the acceleration shifted back to the standard one G and gradual changes in direction. Tanya knew Danny was hoping for a jump route out of the Franklin system, but she didn't think they would find it. He thought that the addition of the Parthians to the crew added insight and improved their scouting ability. Tanya thought it *might*. But even if it did, finding a useful jump was a long shot, and Tanya knew Danny wouldn't have done this without her warning.

She just wished she knew what was up.

Location: Station 1, Chairman's Office
Standard Date: 11 10 631

Andre looked into the comm screen, at the face of Captain Burgin. "What do you mean 'they didn't show up'? We had telescopes on them, and they went through the jump."

"Send me the data," Burgin commanded, which made Andre want to slap him down. But he couldn't. The orders to mouse trap the *Pandora* in the big dark came from his uncle. He sent the scan data with a mental command.

"That's not the right jump!" Burgin said.

"It's not?" Andre spent more time at the academy on business and politics than on jump navigation. Since the academy, he had people to do it for him. He didn't calculate coordinates in his head. But once Burgin pointed it out, it was clear enough, if not obvious. If he hadn't had Burgin insisting they didn't come out, he wouldn't have realized they went through the wrong jump. It was less than a hundredth of a degree off where it should have been, probably much less than a light second.

"You're right, Captain. But at this point we can't even be sure it was intentional."

Burgin snorted.

"I didn't say it was an accident, but it might have been. In any case, I don't see what you expect me to do about it. You're the one with the ships."

"That Cordoba-Davis woman, did you warn . . ."

"No, Captain." Now Andre let frost cover his voice. "I didn't warn Grand Stockholder Cordoba-Davis. I had my orders and I followed them. I assume that Captain Gold didn't want to go back to Alenbie, or simply that the circumstances made him nervous enough to want to be elsewhere. And all I can recommend is that you send a ship after them. I will inform *Uncle Julio* that you missed them."

The look on Burgin's face was priceless and Andre cut the comm. *Good luck, Tanya. It looks like you might even be around to collect the one I owe you now.*

CHAPTER 27

The wing missile, or shield missile, changed the specifics of deep space combat, but not the broad outline. If the battle isn't next to a big rock like a planet, deep space combat is open field combat. Hiding is hard and rarely successful. As a tactician, I disapprove of that. It leads to pounding matches with outcomes less influenced by skill than by the size of the weapons. The wing missile was simply a better weapon.
A History of Deep Space Warfare, *Tanya Cordoba-Davis, Standard Year: 683*

Location: cul de sac off Franklin, Jump 46,026,361
Standard Date: 11 10 631

Danny sat up on his couch in the lounge where most of the crew were gathered and signaled *Pan* that she could open the pantry and let the king of Franklin out. The pantry was a food processing unit in hydroponics, and John Gabriel was the only crew member who knew about him.

A couple of minutes later, Danny said, "The mid C needs a new bearing pad on the rear coupler. I think that takes precedence."

"I am more . . ." Chuck Givens started, just as the king arrived in the lounge, complaining about the smell of the pantry.

"Nothing wrong with the smell of my pantry," John said. "That's just what processed foss oil smells like."

"More like what fossils smell like," said King Edward. "Captain Gold, now that the need for secrecy is past, I will expect better quarters."

"Life is full of disappointments, Eddy," Danny said, looking first at the king and then around the room to gauge the reactions. He knew the kid lost his family less than two weeks ago, and he understood that Eddy was scared and confused. On the other hand, Eddy was an arrogant little snot with a sense of entitlement that was truly monumental, and Danny had his own sociopathic tendencies that made it hard for him to empathize. Especially with people who annoyed him. "How are we fixed for cubage, *Pan*?"

"We can put him in eighteen, Captain."

"Him who?" asked Tanya with a sniff. "Who is this, Captain?"

Danny waved grandly at the kid. "His Majesty King Edward VI of Franklin." Danny looked at Eddy. "Assuming you're going to keep Edward as your reign name?"

"He's a fugitive," Givens said.

Danny nodded to Givens. "Or a refugee. Depends on who you ask, but, yes, according to Tanya's school chum, he is no doubt a fugitive."

"I am the rightful king of Franklin."

Danny happened to be looking at Tanya Cordoba-Davis when His Majesty made that pronouncement, and the rolling of her eyes made Danny like her better.

"You've put us all in danger by bringing him, Captain," Tanya said.

"Maybe, but I doubt it's much more danger than we would have been in anyway. Not if your guess about what Admiral Chin was up to is right."

"I suspect that Captain Gold is correct," said Professora Stuard. "And turning him over to the Drakes may gain us some credit with them."

Robert Schmitz laughed out loud. "Just where did this habit you have of picking up strays come from? I thought you Cybrants were supposed to be utterly lacking in empathy."

Danny looked at Robert, hooked a thumb at Goldgok, and said, "I fell in with evil companions and they are corrupting me."

* * *

Eddy knew they were laughing at him, and in that moment he hated them one and all. It was also all he could do to keep from crying. He forced dignity and said, "If you will direct me to my rooms, I will attempt to wash off the stink of that pantry."

He turned away and followed *Pandora*'s directions to the personnel quarters. And could hear snickering as he left.

Location: Cul de sac off Franklin, Jump 46,026,361
Standard Date: 11 13 631

Pan was scanning the area, with Danny, Tanya, Chuck, Petra, Goldvokx, Goldfax, and Goldtak all hooked into the net. Even King Edward, Sara, and Jenny were hooked in, for all the good it was doing. They weren't finding much of anything. As a rule, jumps were both larger and farther apart in the big dark than insystem.

"How much longer are we going to keep at this?" complained King Edward.

It seemed to be what he did best, Jenny noted. She'd been prepared to be in awe because he was a king. But the way he treated John, and the way Captain Danny, the professor, and Tanya responded to him washed away that notion.

After Tanya came about, Jenny switched her goal in life from master trader to warship captain. And Tanya was clearly unimpressed by King Edward. "Would you like to go back to Franklin?" Jenny sneered. "We could always turn you over to Chairman Chin."

"They would blow us out of space before you got the chance," Eddy said.

"We may end up having to try that," Danny said, and waited for the expression on Eddy's face to change before continuing. "Not the part about turning Eddy over to the chairman. But if we don't find another jump in a few days, we will need to seriously consider slipping back into Franklin and taking another route out."

"Is that wise?" asked Tanya. "They are likely to be watching that chunk of space. And while I'm sure you've worked up some grape, I don't think you want to trade shots with a warship." She looked directly at Danny and added, "Not unless you can *really* toss wings around."

* * *

Danny looked at Tanya, then around the full lounge. There were expressions of shock on most of the faces. "Well, if I could, I'm not sure I'd want to blurt it out."

Jimmy Dugan was in the power room, looking at the fusion rates, but Fred was standing at the coffee station, looking confused. Robert's little girls were looking up from the game they were playing. The professor was in his lab and the professora was in her room, correlating linguistic samples from Franklin. Goldgok was running an analysis of prices in Franklin System. Which left way too many people having heard Tanya's remark.

"Maybe not," Tanya said. "But we've been dancing around whatever it is for long enough. If you wanted to keep it secret, Rocks and Nets wasn't a great strategy."

Danny looked around again, and cursed himself for a fool. He hadn't figured on Tanya making a public announcement. Eddy would give the Drakes the information about the secret weapon in a heartbeat in exchange for regaining his kingdom. John Gabriel, who couldn't keep secrets when he drank, was having a snack. Givens was honorable, if irritable, but where would his honor take him? Petra was probably all right. She seemed to like Robert and the girls. Just telling her that mentioning the new weapon would put Robert in danger would probably be enough. And Fred was a good kid. He'd keep his mouth shut. "Even if that's true, this was probably not the best time to bring it up."

Tanya looked at Danny, her expression belligerent. Then she must have seen something in Danny's face, because she looked around the room again. While before she was watching for reaction, probably trying to guess who knew, now she was looking guilty. She looked Danny in the eye and said, "Perhaps you're right, Captain. My apologies." She looked at Eddy and her expression hardened for a moment. "And to you, Your Majesty." She bowed formally to Eddy. "For putting your life at risk."

Up to then Eddy's face had an expression of incomprehension that was just starting to edge into surmise. But at Tanya's comment, his face went blank and he turned to face Danny.

A part of Danny's mind was busy cursing himself for underestimating Tanya Cordoba-Davis yet again, while the rest of him was getting ready for Eddy to draw on him. Tanya was playing the situation. She knew Cybrant customs and, by now, how much of a Cybrant Eddy was. She was pointing out that if Danny was going to put the genie back in the bottle, he would have to spill even more blood, including Eddy's.

"This is not Cybrant," *Pan*'s voice rang out, "and the captain may not be challenged. Any attempt to draw on the captain will be considered mutiny. The mutineer will be executed, successful or not."

Eddy tensed even more for just an instant, then relaxed. Slowly, he turned to Tanya Cordoba-Davis and returned her bow with a shallower one of his own. "Your apology is accepted, Grand Stockholder. I realize that you had your own goals and couldn't concern yourself with whether or not I was endangered."

"Right out of the handbook," Danny said. "But in case anyone is wondering, let me reiterate. This is not Cybrant and dueling is not allowed on the *Pandora*."

"What?" asked Petra. "I don't understand."

Danny looked over at the incredibly young-looking ensign and in that moment she looked rather younger than Jenny Starchild.

Sara spoke up. "It's part of the quaint customs of Danny's homeworld . . . and my parents'. Its official designation is 'culling by combat,' though it's often called 'culling for manners.' I assume, Danny, that you're still working on whether you have to kill me and Eddy? But what about Tanya here? She's a grand stockholder, after all. And Mr. Givens . . . and, well, just who *can* you trust?"

"The Parthians," Danny said. "They are my clan, so I can trust them. The professor and professora were in on it, and so were Hirum, Robert and Jenny."

"I knew too," Angi said. "But I knew enough to keep *my* mouth shut," she added with a look at Tanya that was full of nine-year-old disapproval.

Danny looked at Angi and laughed. "How did you know, Angi?"

"I figured it out."

"Well, I haven't," Fred said. "Do you mean like in the game we've been playing? But that's impossible."

"What game and why do you assume it's impossible?" Sara asked. "Please recall, I just boarded at Franklin."

Danny looked around. "Go ahead, *Pan*. Fill everyone in. It's too late for any other course."

So *Pan* did, complete with vids of the battle with the *Bonaventure* and the earlier battle with the *Brass Hind*. After checking with Danny privately, *Pan* didn't give the specifications of the system. She finished with, "Now that it's out in the open, there are a number of sims I would like to see run by those of the crew with naval experience. This is still a new weapons system and the tactical doctrines for its use are, at best, poorly worked out."

Location: Cul de sac out of Franklin
Standard Date: 11 17 631

Chuck watched Gunny Dugan's cruiser blow into space junk as the shield missiles flew by. Jimmy had dropped his wings to protect his ship from wing interaction, but Tanya had a hunter-nuke right behind the shield missiles, and that blew Jimmy right out of space. Out of his force of ten ships, Chuck Givens had one left. He looked back to the battle and realized he wouldn't even have that for long. In desperation, he flung round shot at the shield missile.

Then everything blanked and up came **Simulation Over**. Along with numbers. The numbers meant that the virtual *Pandora* and the virtual patrol ship that was supporting it had just taken out his squadron while receiving only light damage.

He jerked off his headset and said, "This can't be right."

"My question," Sara said, "is whether Tanya is really that good, or is it the weapons."

"It's both," Eddy said. "Rather, it's the combination. Commander Cordoba-Davis is an innovative tactician, and the new weapons—aside from the advantage they give her directly—give her scope for those innovations."

Givens nodded, but not happily. He hadn't done as well when he did the sim with the shield missiles. He won, even when Tanya officially knew about the shield missiles, but he took a lot more damage.

On the other hand, now that he knew the trick with the shield missile trailed by a hunter-nuke, he could use it too. And unless Tanya kept yet another rabbit up her sleeve, he would take her out. In a way, that was what bothered him the most. He turned to Tanya, and she was just staring into space.

"I need to have a few words with Doctor Frankenstein," Tanya said.

"Grandpa's not Frankenstein," Angi insisted. She had been watching the sim avidly while waiting for her turn to play.

"Tell him that." Tanya grinned at the girl, got up, and left while Chuck Givens watched and worried.

* * *

Danny consulted with *Pan*, and reluctantly decided that they would have to chance going back through the cul de sac jump. "Four days of running sims and looking for more jumps and nothing useful. We won't be in the Franklin system all that long if we come in at the right vector. They probably won't even see us."

Location: Franklin Station 1, System Scan Room Standard Date: 11 17 631

The beep brought Kirsten Espinosa, the Cordoban scan tech, to the screen. A quick check of her interface pulled up the record. Three and a half hours ago, a ship entered this sector of space. The light reflected off that ship was just reaching Kirsten's sensors now. Kirsten watched the ship move even as she instructed the computers to analyze the wing flap and plasma flow. By the time it popped out again, forty-seven minutes after it arrived, Kirsten had confirmed that it was indeed the *Pandora*. She knew that it appeared out of a jump they didn't know about and disappeared into *another* jump they didn't know about.

Kirsten Espinosa was not a fan of the *Pandora*. It seemed insulting, the way the little free trader waltzed in and out of the Franklin system. Her boss liked it even less.

And the poor captain of the *Joseph Buckley*—who already got sent on one wild goose chase and was about to be sent on another—was coming to positively hate the *Pandora*.

Location: Pandora, Franklin Outsystem, side route to Alenbie
Standard Date: 11 18 631

It took six jumps and almost a day in Franklin space to get to an alternate route to Alenbie. But space is big, and by the time the Cordoba squadron knew where to look, *Pandora* was gone.

Location: Alenbie side route
Standard Date: 11 20 631

Chuck Givens had the watch as *Pandora* came out of jump three light hours from the third main route jump to Alenbie. They were in a chunk of empty space that—probably—the Cordoba fleet would not be looking at. He shifted the ship and aimed the telescopes. At only three light hours distance, *Pandora*'s telescopes were good enough to see a Cordoba ship, since they knew where to look. They were just over a light year away from Franklin, and just over six from Alenbie. Chuck checked the screens. They showed no one in the standard route.

Chuck carefully fed plasma to the wings and brought the *Pan* up to a full standard gravity of acceleration. The next five jumps were far enough off the standard route so that they wouldn't be seen no matter what they did. Then the two routes would converge. That would be the dangerous time, when they might run into a Cordoba warship.

Chuck didn't like thinking about being in danger from a Cordoba Spaceforce ship. He looked over at the captain. "You don't actually know that it was the Cordobas who trashed that Drake cruiser. What we got from it didn't include anything on the battle at all."

Captain Gold looked at Chuck and lifted an eyebrow. Chuck felt his face heat. "Well, you don't."

"From relative motion, it was likely traveling along the main Alenbie-Franklin jump route, and some time within a week or so of when we found it. If not, it would have passed out from between the two jumps on the main route. Given that, and the fact that we ran into a Cordoba squadron investing Franklin, how likely is it that it just happened to be someone else at the same time?"

"Still, we reported the ship. And when we talked to Captain Anderson, he said—well, implied—it wasn't them."

"He implied the same thing with me, Chuck, but that doesn't mean it's true. Probably, he just didn't trust us with the information. The fact that we found it and reported its destruction might be part of why Admiral Chin decided to arrange an accident for us."

"We don't know that he did, Captain. All we have is Tanya's guess and she has good reason to be bitter. We all do."

"Maybe. But, to my mind, it's more likely that the link into the chain is on the Alenbie side of where we found the *Kingfisher*. That means somewhere up ahead."

They made the jump and the next, then took another side route. This one came out in the Alenbie outsystem, near a mining facility. The green tar mined there was not essential to making shieldgold, but it did cut about five expensive steps out of a twenty-step process. On their last trip through, they picked up several tons of the stuff.

Location: Contested Space, Alenbie outsystem
Standard Date: 11 27 631

Danny looked at the object on the screen. It was a canister, ten meters long and four across, attached by a two hundred meter cable to a chunk of ice and rock. The whole mess, and mess was the right word, was spinning around. Danny ran a quick calculation. Whoever lived in the canister was living in about one-tenth standard gravity.

He shook his head and had *Pan* call the place. It took a few seconds for them to get synced then the screen lit with the image of an old miner. "I'm George Benson. Who the heck are you?"

A few minutes of introduction and conversation followed then Danny asked about the Cordobas and warning the rest of Drake space.

"Naw, the *Lucy Bug* got out with the news," George said, sitting in his cabin wearing a worn shipsuit and a headset. "So now I'm mining green tar with no buyers." George ran his mining bots by interface. That worked, but it was a lot of labor for George. He spent hours in the control helmet, hours that he really ought to spend in the gym to keep his bones from getting more fragile.

"What's the *Lucy Bug*?"

"Green tar freighter, comes in every quarter. Saw the Corgis coming in, dumped her whole load of green, and got out of here, dumping plasma like it was free. Must have been doing two and a half standard gravities when they hit the Finch route."

"Corgis?"

"Damn Cordoba dogs, come in here saying they are going to set up a corporate government. The Drakes may be assholes, but they mostly leave us be. The Corgis are attaching corporate fees to every damn thing."

"Well, I don't want them yapping after me," Danny told the miner. "I'd just as soon get out of here without them ever knowing I was here. Would you know how I might manage that?"

George looked at Danny with a crafty gleam in his eye. "I could probably help you with that, but why should I give you my secrets?"

"Because we're going to buy a bunch of your green tar and we'll pay good money."

"What use is money to me?" George asked. " 'Specially now, with the Corgis insystem likely to seize any money I show up with."

* * *

Tanya Cordoba-Davis wasn't pleased to be referred to as a Corgi. She didn't like dogs in general, and the Corgi was a breed of stumpy-looking, hideously yapping things. But more than that was the attitude toward the Cordoba Combine that the name represented. She realized that the Cordobas were not universally loved even in Cordoba space and put it down to the standard resentment of the have-nots for the haves. But this attitude wasn't just fear and resentment. It was contempt.

Tanya looked over at Chuck Givens and saw her own feelings reflected in his face, along with an answering disrespect for George Benson, and was glad they weren't cut into the transmission loop. Petra just looked embarrassed, and Jimmy seemed amused more than anything. She glanced over at Fred Markum; he was not paying any attention to the conversation. He was running some sim on the rear D sail.

Goldgok entered the discussion then, and Tanya went back to listening.

"What do you know about Skull System?" George was asking.

"Not that much, and what I do know isn't good," Danny said.

"It's not that bad," George said. "They've always dealt fairly enough with me. Good prices."

Tanya wasn't all that surprised. She knew that the pirates and smugglers of the Skull System had to have contact in civilized space, and even that they had connections into the Drake and Cordoba militaries.

"I take it you know a jump route to the Skull System."

"I might. I might. It'll cost you though," George said. "But it'll sure enough get you out of the Corgis' way."

"And find myself in a wolf's jaws instead?"

"I already said they ain't that bad," George said. "Besides, I haven't agreed to tell you how to get there yet. What have you got to trade?"

"We have a device that we can perhaps modify to help with your mining," Goldgok said.

Location: Benson Station
Standard Date: 12 05 631

George Benson stretched in his new flex suit as he watched the *Pandora* slip away at barely half a standard gravity. He was safe enough out here because the Corgis didn't know he was here. And even if they did, they didn't know the jumps to reach him.

George was feeling pretty good. He'd talked himself into a new flexsuit and the refurbishment of his old one as well as the fancy mining bot that feller came up with.

In exchange, all he had to give them was the route from the Alenbie outsystem to Skull System and a load of green tar. It was a route in his private rutters, one that neither the Drakes nor the Corgis knew about.

George did tell them about the security. That the Skull System pirates kept a picket force at the far end of one of the longer jumps in the route. And he gave them some recognition codes that he was pretty sure would get them safe passage.

CHAPTER 28

The Cybrant System main lines are designed to survive, first and last. They are born and bred to stay alive at any cost. They are not immoral, but amoral, and if they have any moral code at all, it's their own. Personally developed and generally not tied to the morality of their culture anymore than as necessary camouflage. They kill easily and without remorse. Combined with their improved reflexes and situational awareness, they are more effective killers than any group of humans in history.
However, this does not make them all monsters. Some of them are, indeed. And when a Cybrant main line goes bad they are the worst monsters you can imagine. But many are perfectly nice people and safe to be around. Safer than a deeply caring person who has self control issues. Just don't give them a reason to think of you as a threat and you'll be fine.
From a lecture on the Cybrant main lines, delivered by Doctor Rosita Schmitz-Davis, Standard year 700

Location: Gray Route, Big Dark
Standard Date: 12 10 631

Jenny was tied into the ship net from the lounge as the *Pandora* came out of jump. The image of the cutter ten light seconds out came into Jenny's mind and up on the main lounge screen at the same time. And the captain was sending a message the moment they came out of jump.

"Why don't we use lasers to attack ships?" Jenny asked Fred.

"Spread and power," Fred told her. "Lasers do spread some and over a few light seconds, even a powerful laser will spread so much that it will have little impact on a ship's hull. But a grain of sand is a grain of sand, and if it's traveling fast, well . . . force is mass times acceleration. A piece of sand hitting a hull at half the speed of light has a force at contact of close to its mass. Say half a gram at one-half light squared . . . figure about ten kilotons of explosive force when it hits. It's less than that, really, but still a whole lot of bang. And it doesn't spread until it hits the ship, or at least until it hits the ship's wings."

"We could have come through with attack lasers firing, but though we might have hurt them some, it probably wouldn't be enough to matter, at least not at this distance," Eddy said.

Jenny nodded. "Thanks, Fred." She ignored Eddy, as she usually did when he was acting all snooty.

Twenty light seconds later, the cutter's transmission arrived.

"Halt and ident— Okay, we have your recognition codes. You're the *Pandora*? What persuaded old George to give you the codes? Fuck! The Cordobas hit Alenbie and Franklin?" A short pause, maybe fifteen seconds. "Here's the skipper."

"*Pandora*, this is Commander Teage of the *Black Pearl*. Welcome to the end of nowhere."

Teage was a dark-haired man with a scar going from his right eye to the point of his chin. Considering the advanced state of plastic surgery, the presence of that scar was a statement. Captain Danny, for instance, didn't have anything like it, though he had been cut rather often in his youth. On the other hand, the man's smile was friendly enough, under the circumstances.

Captain Danny sent, "It's all in the data we gave you. So if you don't mind, let's let it wait until we're close enough for a reasonable conversation."

Eight hours later

Pandora got directions to the next jump on the route and exchanged data with the *Black Pearl*. The jump route would take ten more days, and they would be met by at least one more cutter along the way. There were apparently more routes in and out of Skull System than anyone suspected.

Location: Gray Space, Skull Station, Roger's World Orbit Standard Date: 12 20 631

"Yo ho ho! Welcome, *Pandora*," came over the comm. The woman on the screen was wearing a real tricorn hat, with a waving skull and crossbones flag behind her on the screen. "What booty have ye brought us?"

This is getting old fast, Danny thought. "No booty. Just trade goods."

The smile dropped a watt or two in intensity. "You don't find our motif amusing, Captain?"

"Frankly, it's a bit too studied, and way too over the top."

"Well, perhaps, but we enjoy it. What brings you to the domains of Jolly Roger Avery?"

"Roger Avery?"

"My great grandfather. He found this place some seventy years ago. He was an open, friendly sort, and had picked up the nickname Jolly Roger. He claimed he was descended from the famous pirate Henry 'Long Ben' Avery, and figured that meant his system should be the Skull and Crossbones system." She hooked a thumb at the virtual flag flying behind her on the screen. "The family has kept up the tradition. We're open, easy-going sorts around here, Captain Gold, but don't mistake our enjoyment of life as license. We can be as hard as a Cybrant main line when we need to be."

Danny suppressed an urge to smile at that, but he apparently didn't suppress it hard enough.

The pirate lass lifted an eyebrow, then gave him a hard look. "Are you one of those?"

"It's all right, lass," Danny said with his most piratical leer. "I'm mostly retired."

"I'll keep that in mind, Captain. My name is Sylvia Avery. We either inspect your hold or you pay a fee. Which will it be?"

"What's the fee?"

She named a figure in Cordoba credits and they got down to bargaining. Goldgok was brought in and they eventually settled on a high, but not unreasonable, fee. The new missiles were hidden, but even hidden things can be found. Pirates and smugglers are the folks most likely to know where to look. It was safer just to pay the fee and have the pirates think they had some especially valuable cargo.

* * *

For the next week they traded goods, and learned about the other ships in system. Which included the *Brass Hind*, now officially renamed the *Brass Ass*, and still commanded by Captain Rosalyn Victoria Flatt.

Location: Skull Station Trading Floor
Standard Date: 12 22 631

The only Parthian on the trading floor wasn't exactly mobbed, but he wasn't avoided. Goldgok could have sold the *Pan* empty in the first hour and at a good profit, but that wasn't its goal. Aside from the green tar, Goldgok wasn't interested in *selling*. Well, it did sell the filter cloth and a few odds and ends, but the equipment they bought in Franklin was for Parthia.

Here in Skull System, they had shieldgold production facilities. That was why there was always a market for green tar. Goldgok wanted as much of the precious material as it could get. He got it for a good price, too. Shieldgold wasn't just for wing controllers, though that was a good part of its use. It also worked as guides for any device where you needed to block or focus a magnetic field. Even molecular printers used small amounts of it to press molecules together while building up circuits.

They bought some heavy equipment, but mostly they would be carrying near their mass limit in shieldgold back to Parthia, to an economic effect not that different from the arrival of a Spanish treasure fleet in Madrid in the sixteenth century, old calendar.

Location: Pirate's Den Bar, Skull Station
Standard Date: 12 28 631

Fred Markum was a bit too bleary from the rum and thon juice. He didn't have Danny's constitution, so he was seeing pink Parthians, but he was enjoying the Skull System and feeling quite piratical.

"Back off, you pansies. I'm Loly Torgo off the *Brass Ass*," said a spacer loudly as she entered the bar.

Fred looked up and saw that she looked quite pirate like. She had dark coppery skin and just a hint of slant to her eyes, but she was next to two meters tall and bulky.

Gradually what she said worked through the haze of alcohol and thon juice, and Fred started laughing. "*Brass Arse* is right. The *Pan* suckered you pukes into flying into round shot."

"Who the fuck are you and what the fuck do you know about it?" If Fred was loaded, Loly was *over*loaded.

Fred, on the other hand, was shorter than average and slight . . . but he wasn't in any hurry to back down in front of anyone. Especially not with the amount of local rum and thon he had in him. "It was a jump out of Morland, and you were so busy chasing a fat grainer you didn't pay any attention to the *Pandora*."

Fred didn't know it, but Loly was on the *Brass Ass* at the time, and remembered the incident well. It led to the attempted mutiny against Captain Rosalyn, the one her lover died in. The *Pandora* caused the *Ass* to limp into Donnybrook for repairs.

Since then, they'd recovered quite a lot. The *Brass Ass* had a new set of wings and took a dozen prizes, and by now the captain had a reputation to give anyone pause. Captain Roz was a scary bitch and her crew took pride in that fact.

So rather than questioning Fred about it, Loly turned and punched him in the mouth.

Thon juice doesn't slow the reflexes. It speeds them. Unfortunately, Fred wasn't expecting an attack, and didn't quite manage to duck out of the way.

But he piled in, and by the time the bouncers got there, both he and Loly were battered and bloody.

* * *

Danny arrived at the cells at the same time as Rosalyn Flatt. He looked around and saw several people. There was a cute girl in a semi-flex, the sort that were becoming more and more common. It had a captain's four gold rings painted onto the suit sleeves. Pretty girl, Danny noticed with interest. She was small, with a heart-shaped face, and had a small mouth covered with bright red lipstick.

But there was the clerk at the desk that he had to deal with first. "I'm here for Fred—"

"I want Loly out of there, now," the little woman interrupted in a breathy voice.

Danny stopped and looked at her. He came in just ahead of her, but he shrugged and waved her to the desk.

She sniffed disdainfully and Danny felt the hairs on the back of his neck try to stand up straight. This woman was dangerous, and wasn't trying to hide it. And that meant she was either incredibly stupid . . . or far gone into delusion. Especially with the cultural norms of Skull System, being wantonly insulting to people you didn't know was risky.

The clerk was immediately deferential to the little woman, and her hulking subordinate was quickly brought out.

Then, while Danny was arranging for Fred's release, she proceeded to describe in a high and excited, breathy voice what she was going to do to Loly when she got her back to the ship. Danny didn't doubt that the little woman would carry out her threats, and it was clear that Loly was wishing she was still in the cells.

At that point, Fred was brought out and Loly blurted, "That's him!" She pointed at Fred. "The crewman off the *Pandora*."

"The what?"

"That damn little freighter off Morland."

Suddenly Danny was watching as the woman stared first at Fred, then at him.

"You like interfering, don't you, pretty boy?" the little woman with the captain's rings said in a voice that dripped ice chips, but still managed a winsome quality.

Danny bowed, never taking his eyes off the woman. "Danny Gold, captain of the *Pandora*. And you are?"

"Your death, Captain, your death." Then she giggled.

Danny looked at her for a moment, then quite deliberately turned his back on her. Fred was looking more than a little under the weather, and Danny kept one eye on the mirrored counter. It was a distorted image, but he could see Captain Crazy in it.

Location: Pandora, off Skull Station Standard Date: 12 28 631

"Everyone needs to be careful." Danny held up a bread stick like a baton. The crew, including Jenny and the younger girls, was assembled for dinner at his orders. "The captain of the *Brass Ass* is Rosalyn Flatt, and she is even crazier than she seems. *Pan* and Sally have been searching the records, and the artificial brain that runs the station here isn't happy with the crew of the *Brass Ass* in general and with the captain in particular."

Pan gave them a list of incidents.

"Fine, Captain. But what's that to us?" Chuck Givens poured spaghetti sauce over his noodles. "It's not like she's the only pirate on station here."

"No, but back a ways we ran into her, and she apparently holds a grudge. If I could, I'd order everyone to stay on the *Pan*. As it is, when anyone leaves the ship, I want . . ." Danny pointed as he finished. ". . . me, Sara, or Eddy going along."

Givens looked resentful and opened his mouth, but Tanya beat him to the punch. "I have the reflex mods, Captain."

"But do you have the *sociopath* mods?" Danny asked, holding up his bread stick again.

"Sociopath mods, Cap?" Hirum was always after more dirt on Cybrants. He was also looking better. He'd gained weight from John's cooking and was clean shaven now.

"That's what I call the mods that the Cybrant main lines get," Danny acknowledged, with a nod to the old grouch. "They're designed to make it easier for us to kill, to get rid of that working up to taking a human life. To eliminate, or at least limit, sympathy for our enemies." He gave Hirum a hard look. "They don't make me want to kill people, Hirum, but they do make it easier for me to do it and then sleep like a baby afterward."

"Actually, yes, I do, Captain," Tanya said. "They didn't call them that in the prospectus they sent my parents, but yes. The 'enhanced self-defense suite' is included in my mods."

Now everyone was staring at Tanya. She shrugged and said, "Hey, I didn't put it there any more than the captain did. Blame our parents."

Gunny Dugan grinned at her. "It's not blame. It's being next to a conscienceless killer."

"Do we scare you, Jimmy?" asked Sara, grinning.

"Just enough to be titillating." Jimmy grinned back.

"Well, in that case, come up and see me sometime." Sara half rose and leaned toward Jimmy, showing quite a bit of cleavage.

"What's that quote from?" Jenny asked, watching Sara . . . apparently for pointers.

Sara sat back down and Jimmy looked at Jenny with a grin. "I don't know, but it's very old. Maybe Roman."

"Well, if you guys can put your hormones on hold for a few minutes . . ." Danny turned to Givens. "Chuck, if there's a chance you're going to run into crazed killers, I'd rather you have a crazed killer on your side. It's not so much you, Petra, or Fred I'm worried about. It's the un-modded civilians. They lack both the genetics and the training. And yes, Sara, King Edward, and I have been trained in combat. It's part of growing up back home."

Givens just shook his head, and Danny couldn't blame him.

Location: Skull Station Food Mart
Standard Date: 12 30 631

Eddy looked around the market as John lectured Jenny on fruit. *Boring,* Eddy thought, wishing he hadn't been assigned as babysitter to the shoppers.

"See, Jenny," John Gabriel said. He touched an avocado to show her how ripe it was. "You don't want to squash it. You want to check and see if there's any give under the skin. But not too much g—"

There was a flicker in the corner of Eddy's eye. A movement that shouldn't be there, and combined with the warning, he reacted. He turned and saw a big woman. She had a flechette gun in one hand and a bloody cut across her face. That was the thing that sent Eddy into action. She moved like a wounded animal—a desperate, wounded animal.

All that was peripheral, fed into his mind as tactical data. What he reacted to was a type of motion, combined with the instructions he had in regard to Jenny and John. He was to look after them, protect them while they did the grocery shopping for the ship.

He spun and shoved. Jenny was closest, so he shoved her into John to get them down behind the fruit stand. He almost made it. The woman shot just as they were going down, but her gun followed them and that left Eddy a clear shot. He took it with no hesitation at all.

Center chest, five flechette burst.

Check for other threats. There. Little woman, aiming at him.

But slow. So slow.

He shifted the front of the barrel a few millimeters and fired again.

Check again. There. A man. Also armed. Staring in shock.

Not worth the chance. Shift, fire.

He was down.

Check.

Nothing.

Eddy gave the foodmart a good look while the patrons looked around in confusion, and some—the most alert—dove for the floor.

Nothing.

No more threats.

Then he checked on Jenny and John. John was fine. He'd ended up with Jenny on top of him. But Jenny was still falling when the woman fired. The flechettes stitched a line from her left hip to her right ear, ripping open her back and neck.

"*Pan*, we need a medic. Jenny's down," Eddy sent. He looked around. People were still scattering, most not even sure what was happening. He set the flechette gun on the floor in the aisle, well away from him. Station Security would be here soon, and with three dead and another injured, anyone armed was likely to get shot.

The thing that amazed Eddy even as he acted was how calm he felt. It was just like a sim. He didn't feel a thing. Not even concern for Jenny.

Station Security arrived and Eddy told them what happened. Well, mostly what happened. He told them the man was aiming at Jenny, but the truth was the man had his gun out, but was too busy staring at his dead companions to be aiming at anyone.

Jenny was taken to the med section.

Eddy was taken into custody.

He didn't resist.

Location: Station Security Office, Skull Station
Standard Date: 12 30 631

"What do you have for me, Al?" Sylvia Avery asked.

"I have a kid I never want to meet in a dark alley, Boss," Al said. "You know those crazy fucks off the *Brass Ass*? Three of them went after this bunch off the *Pandora*, and this kid took them all down in less than four seconds. And that was with them shooting first. Well, *one* of them shooting first. The other two didn't get a shot off."

"You sure they were involved?"

"The frigging vids show them with guns out, and all of a sudden, the kid . . ." Al described the incident from beginning to end, calling up the vids. Sylvia watched the vids and decided that she and Skull System would be very polite to the crew of the *Pandora*.

"Okay, Al. Patch me through to this kid. He's in the cells, right?"

"Interview room C, Boss. He came along quiet as a lamb. Said he'd already commed his ship. Oh, Boss . . . he says he's the king of Franklin."

"What?"

"He says he's Edward VI of Franklin, and he inherited the throne after the Cordobas killed the rest of his family."

"Oh, hell. You know, Al, he might be. The *Pandora* reported the Cordoba incursion to Drake Space when they came in. But they didn't mention having the last of the Franklin royals on board."

The screen shifted to the interview room. There in the seat on the suspect's side of the table sat a teenager. A good looking reddish-blond lad, well-built. Longish hair, a bit tousled. If she were looking for a single word, it would be "lithe." He seemed like he could take a nap or kill you with equal ease.

She opened the com so he could see her. "Good afternoon, Your Majesty?" Sylvia made it a question.

"Yes." He nodded regally. The kid did regal pretty well. "And you are?"

"Sylvia Avery. Princess Sylvia Avery, if we went in for that sort of title around here. You want to tell me what happened?"

"I would like to resume contact with my ship before making any comments for the record. I'm sure you've seen vids, so the timeline of events should be clear enough."

Silvia could tell that the kid wanted to add something, probably about how he hadn't shot first. But he didn't. The interview rooms didn't allow hook up to the station net, and the kid's ear bug would have been pulled when he was brought in.

"Well, this isn't Drake Space and we don't have diplomatic relations with your homeworld, so technically you don't have the right to avoid self-incrimination. But, as a courtesy, I'll get you a link to the *Pandora.*"

"Thank you," he said, then shut up again.

Sylvia wondered how well she was going to manage to stay polite to the *Pan*'s crew, after all. But she went ahead and called the *Pan.*

Location: Pandora, off Skull Station
Standard Date: 12 30 631

"I am starting to miss the days when you were the only one I had to bail out of jail," *Pandora* told Danny while she was talking to Sylvia Avery.

"It's tradition," Danny said distractedly. He was going over the vids of the encounter in the foodmart and checking on Jenny. Also, he didn't have anything like Pan's ability to multitask.

"*Pan*, get eyes on the *Brass Ass.*"

"I already have them under observation, Captain."

"Well, make it closer. If the skipper was that fucking nuts, who knows what the crew is going to do? Meanwhile, you'd better let me talk to the locals."

The screen lit up and Sylvia Avery was looking out at him, still in the open-necked pirate shirt and vest, but without the tricorn.

"Captain Gold, I don't know if you're aware of it, but we have a member of your crew in our interview room."

"I've just been reviewing the vid captures from the foodmart. I would say it's clear that our crew was attacked and Eddy was simply defending himself and his companions."

"I tend to agree, Captain. But there are some questions."

"Yes?"

"First, you didn't mention that you had the king of Franklin on your ship. Why is that?"

"Because, at least for the moment, it doesn't matter. At present, the government of Franklin is in the hands of Avery Chin, chairman of the board of the newly formed

Franklin Governance Corporation. Eddy is a refugee, and probably subject to arrest anywhere in Cordoba space."

"Fair enough. But why did they attack your crew? Are you saying they were out for the reward for King Edward VI?"

So Danny told her about the fight off Morland, an edited version. The one that didn't include how they dealt with the hunter-nuke. In fact, this version didn't include the nuke at all.

"Whatever caused you to interfere, Captain?" Sylvia sounded honestly curious. Not condemning, just as though she didn't understand.

Danny didn't say "I don't like pirates," though he was tempted to. Instead, he said, "It seemed like the thing to do at the time." He shrugged to indicate that he couldn't explain it either.

Sylvia's look said Danny was a nut job, but not the first she'd known.

"Jenny Starchild is owed compensation for the attack and her injuries," Danny said.

"Don't you think three dead bodies is enough compensation?"

"No!" Danny said. "I don't think three, or three million, dead bodies compensate her at all. Jenny didn't want them dead, and she didn't benefit from their deaths. The deaths simply stopped further injury to a twelve-year-old girl who was merely doing the grocery shopping."

"You aren't suggesting that my government owes compensation, are you?"

"Not necessarily. But I believe the *Brass Ass* certainly does. Surely the ship is liable for the actions of its captain and crew. Besides, from what I hear, they've taken quite a few prizes. There's someone else on that ship. Someone who can be held accountable. Whoever owns it." Danny knew full well that there were several people left aboard the *Brass Ass*, none of whom had the ability to fly the ship. Sally was researching the situation even before the attack and updated him with a full crew list as he and Sylvia were talking.

"That brings up a delicate question. Most of the ships that dock here are fairly short on papers and such. You're one of only four ships in Skull System where the owner—according to the Cordobas *and* the Drakes—is actually in command."

"So how do you normally handle such things?"

Sylvia laughed out loud. "We ask, Captain. Just like we asked you who you were." She made a gesture in the air that Danny interpreted as moving a virtual mouse, calling up a file. "In fact, the *Brass Ass* is listed as the personal property of Rosalyn Flatt. Now, since Rosalyn had no next of kin in the system, that would normally mean that the ship became the property of Skull System. But the crew could make a claim that would be judged by us. Are you making a claim?"

Danny looked at her for a heartbeat. "Yes. Two, in fact. First for Jenny Starchild as compensation for the injury done her, and second for King Edward VI of Franklin as the just spoils of a duel through attack."

"What's a duel through attack?"

"Cybrant law," Danny said, "which might or might not carry any weight here. If you're attacked on Cybrant and you come out the winner, you have a claim on the estate of the attacker. Depending on the circumstances of the attack and what a Cybrant court judges as how justified the attack was, you can receive the whole of the estate." Danny smiled a thin razor's edge of a smile, remembering what Sylvia said on that first comm call. He wondered if she still thought she could be that hard.

She didn't smile back. "Your claims have been registered, Captain."

Location: Skull Station, Interview Room C
Standard Date: 12 30 631

Eddy looked at the wall and didn't see it. He focused inward and adjusted his heartbeat to metronome precision. He stopped production of adrenaline and activated the scrubbers to pull it out. He was on an adrenaline jag more intense than any since he was ten.

He liked it.

That was the really dangerous part. He'd never been in a real fight before. Training bouts, but nothing real. The whole world was sharp as crystal and clear as glass, and he didn't feel any regret for the people he just killed. None at all.

He wanted to do it again. In spite of the fact that Jenny was injured, he wanted to do it again.

A small, still-rational, part of him was disgusted by that. Deeply disgusted.

Another small part of him was urging him, for the benefit of the people around him, to at least pretend that he was disturbed by what he'd had to do.

But he wasn't.

He felt great. Which mostly counteracted the effect that the government of the Skull System felt they might get from leaving him here in this not-quite-cell.

A smile twitched Eddy's lips, and he started to whistle a classic from before the first jump. "Bad to the Bone," with all the complexity of the rhythmic structure.

* * *

Watching the kid on the monitors, Al blanched. He knew the song, though he'd never heard anyone able to whistle it. And given the circumstances, it was altogether too appropriate.

* * *

Eddy's rendition was cut off when the screen lit and Sylvia appeared.

"Are you making any claims against the *Brass Ass*?" she asked.

Eddy was hard-pressed not to blink in surprise, but he had himself under control. By now, very firm control, so he didn't react, not visibly nor by even a slight jump in his heart rate. Instead, he considered.

Danny, Cybrant, duel through attack.

Then he thought of Jenny.

"Yes," he said. "But I will yield first claim to Jenny Starchild, who was injured by attackers in hiding through no fault of her own. I'll take the leftovers."

"This isn't Cybrant Five," Sylvia said.

"You asked if I were making a claim. I am. And in the Franklin System, attackers from ambush owe their victims. I can give you law and precedent if you're interested."

* * *

Sylvia wanted to curse. In fact, there was a law in Skull System that was fairly closely analogous to the Cybrant Five rule, and she'd hoped that Eddy would invalidate the claim Danny Gold made by declining to make one when asked.

But instead he reinforced it.

The girl, Jenny Starchild, was still in surgery. The flechettes ripped the kid up good.

In a way, Sylvia was in a situation similar to the one Stella Jones was in on Concordia Station. She needed to be seen to be fair. That was even more important among armed pirates than in more civilized locations. If the Avery family stopped being seen as fair, they would soon stop being, period. "Very well. Your claim against the *Brass Ass* and your yielding of primacy to Jenny Starchild have both been registered."

"Thank you, Princess Sylvia," the youngster said with such a friendly, innocent smile that Sylvia was tempted to laugh.

Until she remembered the video.

Location: Brass Ass, off Skull Station
Standard Date: 12 30 631

As she floated onto the bridge, Kia asked Jonathan, a dark, thin man with a knife blade of a nose, "Where's the skipper?" Jon had a scar on his right temple where a botched interface surgery left him marked, and he wore that side of his head shaved to show it off.

"How the fuck should I know?" Jon shrugged, then reached out a hand to stop his drift. "Last I saw, she had the first and Loly with her and was headed to the station."

"That was hours ago."

"Only a couple."

"Look, Jon. Call the station and see what's up."

"Come on, Kia. The longer she's gone, the better I like it."

Kia looked at him and he nodded. Mutiny was a constant consideration on the *Brass Ass*. Constantly considered because the captain was crazy and constantly rejected because the captain was a fucking homicidal maniac with eyes in the back of her head. That was why Quinton Williams, who was a scary bastard in his own right, got off in Donnybrook.

Jonathan turned back to the comm screen and, using his interface, called up the station. "What the fuck?"

"What?"

"The skipper's dead!" Jonathan said. "Killed along with the first and Loly. At the foodmart. By some kid off that free trader, the *Pandora*."

"The *Pandora*?" Kia remembered that ship. She was aboard at the time and sort of liked Pete Gannon. He was a fun guy, in love with the adventure of it all. But that was mostly beside the point. When they docked here, the skipper claimed the *Brass Ass* as her personal property, not owned by the crew. Kia knew for a fact that the skipper's family disowned her once the first mutiny happened.

"Let me at that comm." Kia kicked the bulkhead to launch herself to the comm section, and Jonathan looked at her in surprise. She shoved him away from the comm and called the station. Then she registered a claim on the *Brass Ass* as heir to the skipper. She didn't think she'd get it, but she figured making the claim might get her something.

Half an Hour Later

Jonathan looked at Kia's body, floating in the passage at the captain's door. He scratched the side of his head, then kicked off the deck, flipped, and kicked again, sending him back toward the bridge.

Once he got there, he made his own claim on the ship. Two, actually. As Kia's heir and as the skipper's heir.

Most of the rest of the present crew registered a claim on the ship, either as individuals or as a group. Mostly as both.

Location: Skull Station, Administrator's Office
Standard Date: 12 30 631

Sylvia looked at the list of claims. Then she got on the comm and called her dad. Sylvia was the station administrator, but her father was the System Administrator, and her family claimed ownership of the system. She reported the events.

Her dad listened and said, "It's your call, hon, but I'd stay out of it." Then he stopped. "No. Syl, find for the king of Franklin, but insist that he recognize Skull System."

"Oh, come on, Dad!"

"I know. It doesn't mean anything real, but the Franklin royal house are a Drake connection. If the kid ever gets his house back, it will be a real shot at legitimacy."

"Dad, I know you and Elizabeth care about that, but honestly, I don't. Screw the Drakes and the Cordobas they rode in on."

"We have over a million people living on the planet now, pumpkin. Those people can't run for it if the Drakes or Cordobas manage to get through the forts. Besides, what's it going to cost you? One dinky little patroller with a few hunter-nukes. I'll tell you what. You get us the Franklin kid's official recognition and we'll pay the station for the frigging ship."

"Now, that's a deal, Dad. That's a deal."

CHAPTER 29

Whether you're dealing in wars between star systems or dealing with back alley thugs, the rule is the same: "Don't bet what you can't afford to lose."
Carol Gold, Cybrant System

Location: Skull Station Docks
Standard Date: 12 30 631

Bobby sat in the ship's boat and watched the fight in the foodmart. It was all over the net. He pushed a button and watched the vid again. Snickering, with a certain amount of glee, as Loly got shot to hell. The bitch had never been willing to give it up. Not for Bobby, anyway.

His immediate reaction to the skipper getting it was relief. Dead, she couldn't kill him.

Then, concern.

What was going to happen?

The skipper and the first were the only ones with any real training in handling a wing ship. More importantly, the skipper was the one with the rutters. Bobby had no idea how to find a jump without rutters. The *Ass* was limited to local space without rutters.

It was this thought that brought Bobby up short. The skipper had rutters. She had rutters that no one else had. That was how she got them to Donnybrook and from Donnybrook to here. It was how she was able to catch prizes away from any support. And Bobby knew where the rutters were. They were in a necklace Captain Flatt wore all the time.

Bobby got up from the pilot's couch and headed onto Skull Station. To the morgue.

* * *

The morgue was five levels inboard from the rim, so the gravity was noticeably less. The room was white tile with hoses and drains, and the Tech was a middle-aged woman in green scrubs and a hair net. "Sorry, but everything on the *Brass Ass* is now in probate. What I heard is that it's going to end up going to the little girl who was shot."

"But I ain't talking about something on the *Ass*. I'm talking about Rosalyn's necklace. It has sentimental value, you see," Bobby whined.

The woman shook her head and turned away while she spoke. "Pretty sure that's covered too, but I'll check." She reached a desk and pressed a comm button.

* * *

Sylvia didn't get the call. She got a note in her inbox. She almost missed its significance, but why would the shuttle pilot off the *Brass Ass* go directly to the morgue to get a necklace? She called the morgue. "Send me the necklace and that shuttle pilot. I'll hear his claim."

A very few minutes later, a station security officer in the official tricorn hat arrived with the shuttle pilot, one Robert Jerome Li. "You can wait outside. Mr. Li and I are going to have a little chat," Sylvia said, with a smile that would cut diamonds.

Bobby Li swallowed.

It took Sylvia all of three minutes to get the story out of him. He whined it.

"The old skipper on the *Ass*, back when it was a Drake cutter, officially the *Hind*? He played rutter tag. All the time. Had this big ass collection, and he kept it in this watch fob, with a picture of his old lady on it. Fine little holo-pic engraved into the metal casing itself. After the mutiny, the skipper, ah, Rosalyn ended up with it. She scratched out the picture of old Captain Hickam's wife so it looked like she was cut in half, but she kept the pendant. I figure it's mine now."

"Not unless you're Captain Hickam's wife, it's not."

"Please, Miss. I'm owed something. All my gear is on the *Ass* and you gave that to the kid, or that's what I hear."

In fact, Sylvia got off the comm with her father only minutes before she got the call about Bobby Li wanting the necklace. Sylvia was amazed again at the speed of rumors in this station.

"Let me check something." Sylvia turned to her screen and set it on privacy, then replayed her chats with Danny Gold and Edward VI. They hadn't asked about personal gear on the person of their attackers, but had focused on the ship. She had no doubt at all that if they thought of it they would have included the clothing and personal belongings of each and every attacker, but they hadn't. So there was a nice legal case that this little doodad belonged to the station, not to Jenny Starchild.

And if Captain Hickam's wife wanted it, she could just come fetch it.

In the meantime, Sylvia knew the value of an extensive set of rutters.

She looked back to Bobby. "I'm sorry, Mr. Li, but you don't have any claim on the pendant. However, I will, out of my own pocket, pay you a finder's fee for pointing it out to me. And I'm going to see what I can do about getting your kit returned to you. But, if I were you, I wouldn't approach King Edward, or anyone from the *Pandora*, about it. They are quite upset about the little girl being hurt. Something bad might happen to you."

Sylvia smiled again, trying to put a bit of gentleness into it.

From Bobby's face, she wasn't successful.

"I have an idea. Why don't you wait at Mama Joany's while I deal with the crew of the *Pandora*?"

A much-chastened Bobby Li left to enjoy the favors of Mama Joany's boys and girls until his finder's fee ran out.

Sylvia turned back to the comm. "I've consulted with my father, the system administrator," Sylvia told King Edward. "We are inclined to see things your way, but there are some issues outstanding before things can be settled. We have to establish who we're dealing with. You're claiming to be the legitimate king of Franklin, and before we can deal with the later claims of reparation, we have to deal with that."

"I don't see why," said Eddy from the interview room, eyes narrowing. "What does it matter whether I'm the king of Franklin or not? I was shot at and Jenny was hit."

"Oh, it matters a great deal," Sylvia said. "The king of Franklin saying that he had given no cause we must believe. But some unknown spacer making that claim after killing three regular guests of the system? That would be another matter entirely."

Eddy looked at her for a long three count.

Sylvia knew that it was, at best, an iffy argument. There was no proof that Eddy—or Jenny, for that matter—didn't call up the *Brass Ass*, threatening murder. But there really wasn't any reason to believe they did, either.

On the other hand, it would be Sylvia who would be deciding the case, so she didn't need a great legal argument.

"Very well. How do we handle getting me recognized as the legitimate king of Franklin?"

"Simplest thing in the universe. We recognize you, you recognize us."

Eddy leaned back in his chair and looked at her. Then, after a short count, he smiled. "All right."

All of a sudden, Sylvia wasn't quite so sure who was over whose barrel. The kid didn't lack guts. He shouldn't have rolled over like that.

"I'll need to contact *Pandora* to get all the appropriate documentation. Oh, and your people have my flechette pistol. I'll need that as well."

"I'm not objecting, but why the pistol?"

"Two reasons. My seal is in the butt, and in recognizing me as King Edward VI of Franklin, you will—of course—have to grant diplomatic immunity to me and mine."

Now Sylvia was actually a little worried. Dad was so busy thinking about what they were getting in being recognized by this kid that he hadn't considered what they might be giving.

* * *

As soon as the comm call ended, Eddy leaned back in the chair, put his feet up on the table, and started whistling again. This time it was "Strange Bedfellows," the theme from *The Succession Wars,* a docudrama about the last Consolidation War.

This has worked out surprisingly well, Eddy thought. The pirate lords of Skull System weren't actually trained to play at the high stakes table. There were people in the Drake power structure who were going to be upset, but the smart ones, Aunt Izabella and Cousin Ferdinand, would realize that this was an in to Skull System. Potentially a way of bringing the Skull System into the Drake sphere of influence without firing a shot.

It was less than two minutes later, one minute forty-three seconds by his internal clock, when his pistol was returned. He was already talking with the *Pan* and Sally, working out the details of the mutual recognition and arranging for codes to provide free passage.

Location: Brass Ass, Skull Orbit
Standard Date: 12 30 631

Jonathan was camping on the bridge, along with most of the rest of the crew, when they finally got an answer from the station. He was belted into the captain's chair, but not wearing the captain's cap. The screen lit and a young man in one of those three-cornered hats they liked here came on. "The Station authorities have rejected your claims. You have twenty-four hours to collect your personal gear and . . ."

"You what?" Jonathan bellowed into the comm.

"It wasn't my decision," said the station comm officer. "The frigging king of Franklin put in a claim based on an unprovoked attack."

"So fucking what? I don't give a shit if it was the fucking emperor of never fucking land. This is our ship."

As pissed as he was, Jonathan wasn't about to forget the armed men and women behind him. He didn't trust any of them with a knife at his back, but in one way he trusted all of them. None of them were people to back down from a fight.

"We sailed on her, fought on her, and our friends died on her. We're the ones who brought in the freighter from Tongo."

"And you got paid. The ship was in Flatt's name. If you have issues with that, you should have taken them up with her."

Jonathan cut the comm and turned to the remaining crew. "We ain't leaving."

Not that they could.

The *Ass* had a single ship's boat. That boat was docked at the station, and there apparently wasn't anyone on it.

Where the fuck was Bobby?

Location: System Capital, Roger's World
Standard Date: 12 30 631

Roger Avery III read through the treaty of mutual recognition with a feeling that he had just been bitchslapped. Who was this kid? He called up the system brain. Pal had been the ship brain on the original Jolly Roger's ship.

"What do you think?"

"It fits my records and offers us quite a bit, but at the same time— See this clause?" A clause of the document lit up. "—and this one." Another lit up. "The first makes our recognition of him as Franklin's true and rightful king a fact, but the second lets him extend that recognition to other members of his family. His family includes Princess Izabella, Archduchess of Hellespont, and Ferdinand of Drakor. That means that he can extend that mutual recognition to Ferdinand without consulting us."

"So we should reject it?"

"No. Because if he does extend it, it means Ferdinand and Izabella recognize us. It's legitimacy. But up to them, not us."

Location: Station Security Chief's Office, Skull Station
Standard Date: 12 30 631

Sylvia saw Eddy sitting at the Station Security Chief's desk, chatting with the chief, who was sitting on the less comfortable chair across the desk. She was going to have to do something nice for Leo, because the man hated anyone sitting in his chair.

"Father confirms your treaty of recognition, King Edward. So now to the matter of the *Brass Ass*. Taking you at your royal word, the court finds that the *Brass Ass* and all the contents there that are not the personal property of members of the crew are forfeit to Jenny Starchild in recompense for the injury done her. Further, the personal goods on the *Brass Ass* belonging to Rosalyn Flatt, First Mate Jack Crandall, and Able Spacer Loly Torgo are also forfeit to Jenny Starchild. Sorry, Your Majesty, no leftovers." Sylvia smiled.

"What about the crew aboard?"

"With all due respect, that's Jenny Starchild's problem, not ours. You might want to contact them."

Location: Station Medical, Skull Station
Standard Date: 12 30 631

Doctor Chi Hughes stepped out of the operating room and stripped the sterile gloves from his hands. The monitors still showed his patient. Jenny Starchild was lying in a low-gee section of station medical, attached to wires and tubes. The damage done to muscle and bone were the least of it. Three flechettes had hit her spine and the back of her brain, shattering vertebrae and skull, which in turn sliced through nerve bundles and parts of her lower backbrain.

He turned to the spacer. "We did the best we could with what we had. We can do standard neural interfaces, but nothing this extensive."

* * *

"What does that mean?" John Gabriel wanted a drink more than he had in years. He never should have gotten Jenny involved in this. They should have stayed on Bonks, where it was safe. It was all his fault.

The doctor sighed, and said, "I'm sorry. She's going to live, but she's going to be somewhere between a paraplegic and a quadriplegic. She may have some use of the right arm, but the left arm, the legs, the internal organs . . . none of them are going to work the way they should. And though we can wire around some of it . . ." The doctor shook his head. "It would be different if we were on Drakar or Danworth and had an interface specialist, but . . ."

"What did you say?" John managed, barely, to keep from grabbing the doctor by the collar, but his question came out a shout.

"What?" The doctor took a step back, and John took a breath to get himself under control.

Very carefully, he said, "You said Danworth. We have a Danworth cyberneticist with us."

"Is he any good?"

"He designed the interfaces for the Parthians."

"Maybe." Doctor Hughes nodded cautiously. "She's your ward." The doctor indicated a station comm.

John moved to the comm and used his interface to set up the call to the *Pandora*.

* * *

Gerhard came on the screen. He was in his lab, as he usually was. "What's your prognosis, Doctor?"

"Not good. There was extensive nerve damage, and she lost some brain tissue to direct damage and more from swelling and oxygen deprivation."

John turned away as they talked, only understanding bits of the discussion.

It must have been ten minutes later when Gerhard called him back. "We can fix her, John. It's going to take some time to build the interfaces and the workarounds for the damaged nerve tissue, but she'll be able to walk again." Gerhard gave John an intense look. "The thing is, with this sort of extensive damage, it's actually hard to avoid building in a lot of networking interfaces. She's going to end up always—or at least almost always—plugged into *Pan* or Sally or her own artificial brain."

John felt a grin trying to emerge. The first time he even had the thought of a smile since he got the news. "Jenny isn't going to like that. She's still complaining some about the interface."

John noticed a sudden distracted look on Gerhard's face. He glanced over at Doctor Hughes, who looked like he was going to ask a question. John held a finger to his lips. He mouthed the words "let him think."

Doctor Hughes nodded, and they waited. But not for long.

"The repairs may not take all that long, after all," Gerhard said. "Arachne is ready."

John glanced at Doctor Hughes, who was looking both confused and interested. "Doctor, could you excuse us for a few minutes?"

"If it's in regard to my patient, no, I can't. Jenny is my medical responsibility, and I'm not going to allow some kind of unauthorized experimentation."

"Doc, we're nowhere near that yet, and we won't be doing anything that might hurt Jenny."

Grudgingly, Doctor Hughes left.

"You probably shouldn't have mentioned that in—" John started, but Gerhard interrupted him.

"It doesn't matter. He's going to have to know anyway. It's not like the interfaces for the Parthians. Actual nodes are going to have to be inserted, and connections and power supplies. We'll need a surgeon."

"Doctor Schmitz, I appreciate your willingness to help Jenny, but don't you think that we'd better clear it with Captain Gold?"

"No, I don't. The Arachne system is *my* development." The doc wasn't waiting on John. He was calling up screens of data even as he talked. "And if using it in Jenny means we don't have it for a new ship, then that's what it means." He stopped, went back a couple of screens, then said, "Though, as I think about it, using it in Jenny doesn't mean that at all. Though it will mean that Jenny will need to live on whatever ship in which we end up inserting the Arachne system."

"You mean she'll never be able to leave the ship?" John asked, on the edge of panic.

"Yes . . . It's complicated." The doc pulled up another screen. "Maybe she will be able to leave the ship. It will depend on how well the reality creator can integrate with Jenny's brain. She'll be able to leave Arachne after she gets used to the interface . . . I think. But when she leaves and then comes back, there will be a reintegration process. No . . . there *should* be a reintegration process. Nothing quite like this has ever been done before. She should end up remembering what happened on the Arachne when she was elsewhere, and the Arachne will remember being Jenny.

"John, the way this is going to work is Arachne is going to be part of Jenny and vice versa."

"I don't—" John started, then reconsidered. It seemed like the doc was crossing his fingers and hoping . . . but Jenny was going to be a cripple without this. "That's okay, Professor, as long as she's healthy and can get out on her own."

They called Doctor Hughes back in and got to work.

In only minutes, Doctor Hughes was shaking his head. "I'm not up to that sort of surgery, Doctor. For this, the surgeon is going to have to test the brain function as he moves the interface units around." He hesitated. "There is one guy in the system who might be able to do it. He's the Chief of Neurosurgery at Corgan Hospital. It's the best hospital in the system."

"So the Arachne system won't be on a ship?" John asked.

"The Arachne is designed to manage a wing ship. It won't be happy or fully healthy without one, but it'll be okay for a while, until we can put it in a ship," Gerhard said.

"Doc, Jenny doesn't own a ship."

"Well, she will when this stuff is installed," Gerhard said. "Danny can just give it to her if he wants the Arachne brain to run it."

John knew that the plan was to install the Arachne in the next ship that Clan Danny Gold acquired. There was even talk of buying the *Fly Catcher* from Clan Kox.

Doctor Hughes was smiling. "That's very generous of you, Doctor Schmitz. My understanding is that such brains are rather expensive."

"I don't know how I'll ever repay you, Doc," John added.

"Don't worry about it," Gerhard said, with pleased embarrassment.

* * *

When Danny was told about the plan, his comment was, "Well, it's a good thing she owns her own ship then, isn't it?"

"What?" John asked.

"The Skull System authorities have concluded that the *Brass Ass* is forfeit to Jenny as payment for the attack on her."

"Why did they do that?" In John's experience, the local system authorities weren't in any great hurry to go giving starships to little orphan girls.

Danny laughed over the comm. "Turns out Eddy's status as king of Franklin came in handy after all. The Skull system government wants legitimacy pretty badly.

"We'll have a place to put Arachne by the time Jenny is out of surgery. When are you going back in, by the way?"

"Not for several hours at the earliest. Probably not until day after tomorrow. Doctor Hughes, the doctor here who handled the emergency surgery, wants to bring up a neurosurgeon from the planet."

"That's fine then. Plenty of time to plan."

"Plan what?" John asked.

"Don't worry about it, John. You just stay there with Jenny."

CHAPTER 30

I'm not going to torture you, or exact revenge. I don't give a fuck about revenge. I'm just going to shoot you in the head and then go have dinner. Quinton Williams to Philip V. Dedalus in a bar on Donnybrook Station One, shortly before dinner

Location: Skull Station, Shuttle Port
Standard Date: 12 30 632

Eddy walked into the shuttle port to find Danny Gold, Tanya Cordoba-Davis, Sara Electrum, and Gunny Dugan waiting.

He was tired after the long day, but still felt his heart rate start to climb and called it to heel. The time for that was coming, but not yet. "What's the plan?"

"We've been chatting about that while you were dealing with your legal issues," said Jimmy Dugan. "Did you know that these flexsuits can turn off their beacons?"

"No, I didn't. I thought that was illegal."

"It is, but remember we have our own suit bot," Danny said. "It takes a special code and, as a safety precaution, the code has to be entered by the wearer."

Eddy grinned. "It's so nice to be working with criminals. What's the plan?"

Gunny Dugan grinned back, but it was a fleeting expression. Jimmy wasn't thrilled with Danny's plan, especially when it came to Tanya's part in it. "Danny wants me to sit in the shuttle and yak at the crew, while you, Tanya, Sara, and Danny go over there in flexsuits and sneak in."

"That's stupid," Eddy said, and Jimmy Dugan started to smile until Eddy continued. "Have the professora yak at them. She's better at it."

Jimmy lost his smile.

Eddy looked at Jimmy, then added, "And put Chuck Givens in the shuttle. He can keep their attention on the shuttle while the professora yaks at them. And that will let Jimmy here go along to babysit Tanya."

Eddy found the expression on Tanya Cordoba-Davis' face to be priceless. Eddy, it must be admitted, wasn't all that greatly enamored of the Cordobas. And Tanya wasn't just some soldier in the Cordoba forces. She was actually a Cordoba. Granted, she was a Cordoba-Davis . . . but that still meant that she was related, if distantly, to the chairman of the board of the Cordoba Combine. Jimmy and Fred were okay, and the other officers were at least people he could put up with. But any chance he got, he would stick it to Tanya. He couldn't help it.

Danny looked at Eddy, and Eddy looked back with defiance. But all Danny did was nod. "Your plan is better than mine. And you're right. Jimmy may not have our reflexes, but he's trained."

A quick comm call got Givins on the way to the shuttle and the professora onto the comm with the pirates, explaining that a boarding party was going to be coming aboard from the shuttle.

"Look, lady, I don't give a shit what sort of papers you may have gotten from that bitch Sylvia. You ain't boarding this ship without my say so and y—"

"That will be quite enough of that sort of language, young man. I am a full professor of linguistics . . ."

* * *

Danny shut the comm repeater with a flick of his mind and sent a message to Givens, telling him to start evacuating the air from the shuttle. Given's flipped down the faceplate on his helm and touched the panel, confirming the order. The pumps started pumping as the shuttle left the docks. The *Brass Ass* was five hundred kilometers behind the station, in parking orbit. The shuttle wasn't even pushing. It would accelerate for three and a half minutes, then turn around and start slowing. The whole trip was going to take less than eight minutes, and leave the shuttle a half a click from the *Brass Ass*. What the crew of the *Brass Ass* weren't going to realize—hopefully—was that as the shuttle was slowing, Danny and his merry band were going to climb out and jump off, then float over to the *Ass* and enter without knocking.

The *Ass* was tiny compared to the *Pandora*, but it was still a jump-capable ship. It had three sets of four sails and it was almost as long as the *Pandora*, if a lot more slender. The crew had quarters, but those quarters were dispersed throughout the ship. The command crew was forward with the front-wing crew, and the mid-wing crew and stern-wing crew might not see the command crew for days at a time. The armaments were stored near the wings, with most of them near the front wings. On a standard deployment, a good half the crew would be up front between command crew and armaments crew, with watches of four crew each at the center and stern sections.

What Danny didn't know was where the crew was now. And that was important information because it would tell him where to enter.

"Captain Gold, turn your comm back on," came Givens' voice over the override channel. "Those nut jobs just threatened to send a hunter-nuke at the station if I don't turn back."

Danny turned his comm on and heard the last of the exchange even as he checked location and vector with the shuttle's brain. They were two minutes into the trip, traveling at a bit over fifteen hundred meters per second.

"Mr. Bangcock, I've informed the station and system authorities of your threats," Rosita was saying in her "professor dressing down student" voice. "You're not making yourself any friends in the system with that sort of talk."

"Fuck off. They know I'll do it. I'm fucking crazy and you don't want to mess with me."

"Well, I don't actually care about your threats, Mr. Bangcock. However, I will defer to station protocols in this matter. Miss Avery, what is your judgment?"

Sylvia Avery came on and managed to sound almost as calm as Rosita. "We would prefer that this be settled peacefully, but if that ship fires a nuke at us, it will be destroyed, your property or not. I think the course of wisdom would be for you to have your shuttle stand away at a reasonable distance while you negotiate. You can always use more forceful means if negotiation fails."

"Very well. What would you consider a reasonable distance?"

"You turn that shuttle around and send it back to the station," Jonathan Bangcock shouted.

"That's not going to happen and you know it, sir," Rosita said frostily.

Danny listened to the argument and watched the clock. With every second they were going ten meters per second faster. At this point, even if they were to turn around, they would be most of the way to the *Ass* before they stopped, assuming that they kept the same accel.

The clock ticked down as they argued over whether the shuttle would stand off or go back, and they reached turn over. Givens flipped the shuttle in a smooth, flowing turn and they were decelerating toward a zero-zero intercept.

It was time. Danny opened the lock and climbed out onto the skin of the shuttle. With the shuttle decelerating, moving on the skin was like holding onto the side of a cliff or a skyscraper. But the shuttle was designed to allow it when needed, so there were hand and foot holds. Danny worked his way around on the hull of the shuttle as the others climbed out.

Suddenly the *Ass*' wings came up to full power. Any ship in space near a star or other radiation source always kept their wings up at low power as a way of deflecting radiation around the ship. Even stations had wings for that purpose. Now, though, the *Ass* was bringing its wings up to full power, the force needed to move a ship or to throw a missile or salvo of round shot.

Bangcock was threatening to throw a nuke again. And, under pressure from Silvia, Rosita was agreeing to have the shuttle return to the station. Danny gestured and headed for the lock, followed by the rest.

When Bangcock's threats convinced Rosita to call off the shuttle, Chuck increased the decel, and the weight on the boarding party increased. Danny got the figures on the new decel—fifteen meters per second, one point five standard gravities—and grabbed the handhold a little tighter. This would make the timing tighter, and it would mean they would spend more time in free fall.

Danny waited and ran calculations in his head. Then it was time. He let go and pushed off in one smooth motion and was floating free, with the ship decelerating off his new flight path. He looked around. The others did well. Jimmy was a bit behind, but jumped a little harder. Danny tossed him a weighted line and saw Tanya doing the same. There might not be gravity in space, but there was mass. Jimmy grabbed Tanya's line, and she reeled him in.

The extra distance was making this more difficult. They were spreading more than they should. Like the shot pattern of a shotgun, they were separating. More lines were tossed and reeled in until they were all clumped together. Danny located the ship and used his radio beacon's locational sensor to place them and their vector. They were going to miss. Not by much, maybe a hundred meters. They had small plastic canisters of compressed gas. Danny took careful aim and fired a controlled burst, then waited while the new course settled in.

* * *

Jimmy was embarrassed by the fact that his jump was off, and he was using his helmet comp to do the same calculations Gold was doing. He figured they would need another squirt, just a small one. But he waited. And waited. And Gold didn't act. Jimmy started to pull his own canister, but Gold signaled "no."

Jimmy ran his calculations again and realized that Gold was heading them toward the bow of the ship, not the midship. It was getting close now, and everyone started adjusting their position so they would land feet first. It was going to be a hard landing. They had a velocity of close to fifty meters per second when they jumped, and they were going to stop in considerably less than a second. Jimmy bent his knees and pointed his hand rocket. Then he waited. Closer . . . Closer . . . Now!

Jimmy fired, and for half a second he slowed. Then he hit the hull of the *Brass Ass* and felt the impact from the soles of his feet to the top of his head. But he took it, letting his knees bend to absorb the shock.

They were down, with the electromagnetic soles of their flexsuit feet holding them to the hull.

* * *

Tanya recovered from the landing and made sure Jimmy was attached before releasing the line. Then she headed for the access panel. The most common place for a wing ship to need maintenance was on the wing masts, so that was where the emergency hatches were located. Those hatches, by design—even on a warship—were set so that they couldn't be locked. You don't put locks on emergency doors. The hatches would have alarms, but there was little they could do about that.

There was a hatch at each wing. Tanya waited as the others all got to their hatches, then pulled hers open and rushed in, followed closely by Jimmy. In through the access lock, and they were in a service corridor. Twenty feet to the controls for the Forward C wing, and the crewman looked up as Tanya shot him. The same thing was happening at the A, B, and D forward. There were still the mid and stern sails, and they were probably manned if these were. But they didn't have enough people to do anything about that right now. Tanya, with Gunny Dugan at her back, headed for the bridge.

* * *

On the bridge, Jonathan Bangcock's interface sent him a warning just as Rosita Stuard was demanding that he allow the shuttle to return and pull him and his crew off the *Brass Ass*. There were too many things going on at once, and it took him vital seconds to respond to the warning. By the time Jonathan looked, none of the forward sails were responding.

Jonathan wasn't actually a stupid man, but neither was he a man to think things through. It took him too many seconds to realize what happened. The shuttle that had been moving right at him . . . that strange maneuver . . . just as it was getting ready to go back . . . that had it moving almost right at his ship . . . the bitch from the *Pan* picking just that moment to insist that he respond. . . .

"They're on the ship!" Jonathan shouted. He turned and manually pressed the button that would flush their last hunter-nuke. The forward sails were already down, but the ship's automatics tried to compensate by using the mid and stern D sails to fling the nuke. It wasn't thrown. It was barely even lobbed. But it was tossed from point blank range.

Five hundred kilometers is nothing. The wings on the *Brass Ass* extended a hundred kilometers. That distance would barely be enough room for the sheath on the nuke to blow, but when it hit Skull Station, there wouldn't be a Skull Station anymore.

Jonathan forgot that he didn't have the activation codes for the nuke, and no one else who mattered knew them. Not until much later.

* * *

Robert and Petra were both tied into the system. After Rosita talked with Sylvia and assured her that nothing would be allowed to threaten Skull Station, they loaded shield missile Charley into the tube. Charley was sitting there in its Faraday cage with a wired hookup to the ship's systems feeding it tactical data up to the microsecond, and it knew full well how fast it would have to react. There was a puff of gas from the *Brass Ass* and a nuke flung out to the wings. Only the mid and stern wings responded to the presence of the nuke, but they still managed to push it out at kilometers per second.

There was no time to consider. None. But there was also nothing *to* consider. All the considering was already done. There was a station over there with a quarter of a million people on it. Robert and Petra gave the signal and Charley was on its way.

Three quick wing flaps, each imparting velocity in a fraction of a second. Then Charley was there and spinning out his cable at a range dangerously close to the *Pandora*. But the *Pandora* cut its wings entirely as soon as Charley was out.

The cable was less than a quarter of the way uncoiled when Charley fed it power. Still, it was almost too late. Charley caught the nuke in its wing, but barely, and the slack in the cable changed what should have been an encounter of mutual destruction into something more like a calf roping at a rodeo. Or even a do-si-do at a square dance. The nuke was grabbed by the expanding magnetic field and flung around in a loop. But it massed almost as much as Charley and Charley was pulled as it pulled on the nuke. They spun in a circle and sailed away outsystem.

* * *

Sylvia knew for just a second that she and a quarter of a million people whose lives she was responsible for were dead. She knew that Rosita Stuard was wrong and made promises she couldn't keep.

Then the *Pandora* launched something, and Sylvia knew just a flicker of disappointed hope. Even another hunter-nuke was unlikely to be able to stop—

There wasn't time to finish that disappointed thought before the two missiles went off into a crazy orbit.

Sylvia never before experienced a space battle. She was born in the Skull System and raised here. But she'd seen vids and re-creations of hundreds of battles, everything from pirate attacks to full-fledged battles. And what she just saw was flatly impossible. Missiles blew up. They didn't grab other missiles and waltz them across space.

"What the fuck just happened?" Sylvia, in spite of her pirate image, wasn't prone to profanity. Still, no one in her control room was nearly as shocked by what she'd said as by what they just saw.

"I don't know, ma'am," said Peter Mullins. "But whatever you do, don't get in a pissing match with the *Pandora*."

* * *

Jonathan was watching the screen with a lost expression. He just remembered that the hunter he ordered flung wasn't armed. He was dead and—

"What the hell?" The *Pandora* just threw a missile of its own and—

"Impossible!"

* * *

That was when the hatch opened and a teenager in a flex suit with a gun in his hand came through. No one even noticed.

Eddy almost shot them anyway. He didn't know what happened, but he felt the slight jolt of the ship as it threw something.

Then Danny came in. By the time any of the pirates could look up from the screen, the bridge was full of armed people.

It was way too late to offer up any resistance.

* * *

"Mr. Givens," Rosita said over the comm. "Would you please go fetch Charley? According to Ms. Allen, it's still functioning fine."

Chuck Givens was almost as shocked by the do-si-do of Charley and the nuke as anyone else. He'd seen the sims and the recordings of the first battle between the *Pan* and the *Ass*, but none of that prepared him for this. Still, he was an officer, and if there was one group of people that he didn't want to have this technology, it was pirates. He turned the shuttle around again and tried for an intercept with Charley.

Missiles like the Charley and hunter-nukes didn't have much in the way of internal drives. They got most of their thrust from the wings of the launching ship. Their rockets were more in the way of guidance systems. So most of the matching of trajectory was going to be on him. Worse, the shuttle was headed in the wrong direction.

* * *

"Ma'am," Peter Mullins said, "that shuttle off the *Pandora* . . . it's just changed course again. Looks like it's going to go after that weird ass missile they fired."

"Call down to the shuttle bay and get a shuttle of our own launched."

"Are you . . ."

"Do it," Sylvia said. "We can apologize later, if it proves necessary."

* * *

Chuck Givens looked at the vectors. The way he was moving when he got Rosita's orders to go get Charley meant that he would have a lot of change of V to match with the missile. Much more than that shuttle from the station.

Besides, the shuttle from the station was a Craig cargo shuttle, which had more legs than his ship boat. There was no way he was going to get there before they did. Rosita Stuard was a professor, Danny Gold was a smuggler, the next best thing to a pirate himself. Rosita would talk until the pirates had the thing and Danny Gold would be too busy keeping his head down to do anything about it. Chuck couldn't let that tech fall into pirate hands.

He sent the self-destruct signal to the Charley.

There was a flash in the distance and Chuck turned the shuttle around.

CHAPTER 31

The question "what is self" has become more complex with the development of effective interface systems. Are we what we know when we can have whole terabytes of data shoved into our brains? I tell you we are what we know, and we risk our very selves in accepting this unnatural technology into our bodies.
Reverend Doctor Elizabeth Falwell, 2115 old calendar

Location: Skull Station
Standard Date: 01 01 632

Sylvia Avery called her father again, right from the control room, even before the residue of the explosion of the super weapon cooled to darkness. The techs were still trying to sort out what happened, and she was still hopped up from the terror she felt when the *Brass Ass* fired a nuke at the station.

She wasn't exactly terrified now. Her feelings weren't as immediate, but in a way they were even stronger. She wasn't going to die, not immediately, but her nation's whole navy just became obsolete and she didn't know what to do. She could still see those missiles dancing away from her home.

Those emotions must have shown, because the first thing her father said when he saw her face was, "What's wrong, Sylvia?" Dad was dressed in pajama bottoms and she could see he was in his bedroom. It was late night on the planet, but the station was on standard time and that made it even later on the station.

"This just happened, Dad." She sent him the recording of the attack and its consequences. "They blew up the super missile before our shuttle even got close."

"I would have done the same thing," Roger said with a considering look. "I wonder if we have enough . . ."

"Dad, I'm not sure I would have used it, whatever it was. If I'd been given time, yes. But something like this . . . I would have hesitated. And any hesitation would have been fatal for us on the station."

Roger nodded, then said, "Syl, I'm on my way up, and I'm calling a captain's council. In the meantime, that diplomatic immunity we agreed to for Edward VI of Franklin . . . it goes double now, and extend it to the whole ship's company of the *Pandora*. But don't let them leave."

"That won't be a problem. The little girl who got shot needs a surgeon from downside. It's going to be at least another day before— "

"Good enough," her father interrupted. "Please let His Majesty know that I would like to have a chat with him at his earliest convenience."

Location: Brass Ass, Skull Station Orbit
Standard Date: 01 01 632

Danny was in an access corridor floating toward stern D. "Grand Admiral of the Pirate Fleet, Roger Avery III, would like to have a chat with Eddy at Eddy's earliest convenience," *Pandora* reported to Danny and Eddy at the same time. Eddy was in mid C arresting a crewman.

In other words, they were both still in the process of cleaning the pirate crew out of Jenny Starchild's new ship.

"What's up, *Pan*?" Danny asked, even as Eddy asked, "What for?"

Pan filled them in.

"Good for Givens," Danny said. "*Pan*, tell Mr. Givens that I appreciate his quick thinking. Not that I think it's going to matter in the long run, but it was worth a try."

"Why won't it matter?" Eddy asked.

"Because he couldn't blow up their scan records. Skull Station saw it. They saw what it did. Even after he blew it, they will be able to find bits of superconducting cable. Even if they can't, the only thing . . ." Danny was floating down the passage, kicking from wall to wall in what amounted to a zero-g run, using each kick off to get him going down the passage a bit faster. He saw a flechette gun barrel peeking around a corner and changed his bounce pattern. "Don't try it. Even if you take me, you're still screwed!"

The gun came out again, this time in a hand, and Danny fired. "Stupid idiot!"

He got to the side corridor and looked at the man. He was an older man, and not clean. Danny knew Skull System law and knew what was in store for this character, assuming Danny was unwilling to take responsibility for him. He pointed and fired, then continued the conversation. "The only thing they really need to figure out what it was, is seeing how it grabbed the hunter-nuke."

"What was the interruption, Captain?" Tanya Cordoba-Davis asked.

"Idiot decided to fight," Danny said. It was true. After Danny saw the man, he didn't have much chance. At least not the way he went about it. Danny was in the open, true, but the distance wasn't great and the man didn't try to spray the corridor. He just stuck his gun out into it. It wasn't even a hard shot.

"Well, we have the rest, unless the bridge crew lied," Sara said.

"Good enough. *Pandora*, please have Fred bring over some drones. I'm going to want to have this ship gone over stem to stern. It's a pig sty, not to mention we don't know what kind of traps have been set up." Danny flipped a mental switch and spoke to Professora Stuard. "Professora, I need you to get yourself briefed on the politics of Skull System."

"I'm already doing so, Captain," Rosita said. "The system is governed by a captain's council of all the ships that have joined the Skull fleet, which is about half the ships in the system. You aren't required to join, but if you don't, you don't get a vote. It's fairly fortunate for us that Captain Flatt didn't choose to join. There is also a planetary government of landowners, but it yields to the captain's council on anything to do with space."

"Fine. Prepare a brief for me and Eddy, please. Tanya, you want to come?"

"I want to be there," said Sara from the *Brass Ass* bridge, before Tanya answered.

Location: Skull Station
Standard Date: 01 02 632

Danny followed Eddy into the chamber in Skull Station. It was circular and large enough so that you could see the curve of the floor. There were rows of seats around the edge, but there was also a large round table in the center of the room, with comfortable chairs around it. Behind most of the chairs stood men and women, some in space suits, some in the pseudo pirate garb that was the style in Skull System. A day after the taking of the *Brass Ass*, the vids of the dancing missiles were all over the system.

As they reached the chairs, Grand Admiral Avery asked more than said,

"You seem to have a large staff, Your Majesty?"

"I don't have any staff at all," Eddy told him. He stopped, turned, and pointed. "This is Danny Gold, First Breeder of the Gold Clan of Parthia, captain of the *Pandora*, and the owner of the missile you want to talk about. These are Grand Stockholder Tanya Cordoba-Davis, formerly of the Cordoba Spaceforce, Sara

Electrum, a spy from Cybrant and, of course, Professora Stuard of Danworth, Captain Gold's political advisor."

"Just how many governments am I dealing with here?"

"That's an interesting question, Grand Admiral," Professora Stuard said, walking up to the table and taking a chair. That led to everyone else sitting down as she finished. "And one that may have a bearing on our discussion. We are concerned about the possibility that civilization in the Pamplona Sector is in danger of collapse."

Danny didn't turn his head or widen his eyes, but he wanted to. This wasn't the plan. They understood that they couldn't prevent the captains of Skull System from realizing what the shield missile was. All they could do was help them—or not—in developing their own. So they agreed among themselves to negotiate with the notion of getting the best price they could for their help.

Mostly rutters. Pirates had to have rutters and know secret routes in and out of places to carry on their trade.

But Rosita seemed to be trying for something more.

Still, Danny was unwilling to spoil her play. He had developed considerable respect for Rosita over the past year and a half.

For the next couple of hours, Rosita—with the cold dispassion of an academic—described what she felt was the imminent demise of the Pamplona Sector in an orgy of war and lawlessness, with the invasion of Parise by the Drakes and Franklin by the Cordobas as the equivalent of the assassination of Archduke Ferdinand at the beginning of World War 1 on Old Earth. Or the attack on Donovan that led to the collapse of the Sol Federation.

The captain's council was impressed. They had their own datasets, and in many ways it was even more complete. Some of it was from the pirate side, and a lot was from the smuggler side.

What there wasn't was any sort of consensus that the coming collapse was a bad thing.

Several of the captains felt that the Cordobas and Drakes being busy killing each other would mean more and easier prizes. Others, taking a longer view, knew that the collapse would hamper trade and that they couldn't capture merchants if there weren't any merchants to capture.

A few, led by Roger Avery, even realized that civilization was a good thing.

"This is all very interesting, but what are you proposing?" Roger asked some hours later.

"We need cores of civilization to expand from as the present empires are collapsing, and alliances between those cores. That would be Eddy in Franklin, you here in the Skull System, Danny in Parthia, and others later. But those three governments as the start."

"Wait a minute. I'm not the government of Parthia. They have their own council of clans."

"Of course. But you're a clan and can act as agent for the council. They will have to confirm any treaties, but they will if we can come up with something workable. They aren't stupid and will be happy just to get a real seat at the table."

More talk ensued, and eventually a grudging agreement by the captain's council was reached.

* * *

Doctor Henry Cox's fingers moved in the Waldo-gloves as the micromanipulators followed the tracks of the wounds in Jenny Starchild's back, neck, and head. He used micro-staples that made a human hair look like a log in comparison to tie cells together, while Gerhard Schmitz backseat drove. "Place the DX5 unit there, Doctor. It will need to attach those two nerve bundles."

Doctor Cox pulled back a touch and the micromanipulators stopped their motion. Then he twisted a hand to select the grain-of-sand-sized unit to feed down the tube to a point in Jenny Starchild's medulla. He placed the unit and watched as Schmitz activated it. Micro-tendrils snaked out like the roots of a plant, and Doctor Cox went back to putting the little girl back together.

It took nearly as long as the council, and at times was almost as tense, but there was a collegial feel to it as Henry and Gerhard discussed where each microbrain would go and what it would do.

The surgery wasn't just work on the spine and directly damaged portions of the brain. The brain is an integrated system. To fix it properly, they needed new pathways of integration. They placed nodes in Jenny's visual and auditory centers. Others were placed around her body to keep track of her bodily functions—the working of her pancreas, lungs, liver, gallbladder and so on.

All the while, John Gabriel paced in the waiting room, wanting a drink.

And eventually had one.

Then another.

Then several more.

It was a somewhat inebriated and highly belligerent John Gabriel who met the two doctors when they finished. "How is she?" he demanded.

"We won't know that for some days, until the systems have had a chance to integrate," Gerhard said, fussily.

John grabbed him by the collar. "You said you could fix her!"

"Orderly!" shouted Doctor Cox, having more experience with overwrought family members of patients.

John got to sober up in the cells, diplomatic immunity or not.

Location: Arachne, formerly the Brass Ass
Standard Date: 01 04 632

Jenny woke slowly and felt her body. It was confusing. She had too many arms and legs. Way too many . . . and just the right number. She could feel space against her wings, but they were at low power and she could feel the fusion panels at her core. At the same time, she felt her body—her arms, her legs, her heart beating, her breathing.

She opened her eyes and saw the ceiling over her head *and* the space around her.

When Jenny first came aboard the *Pandora* and was able to use her interface, it felt unnatural, like a wooden leg that still felt, or a glass eye that still saw, with a hard-edged precision that seemed wrong. This had the same precision, but it didn't feel wrong. It felt like her.

What is going on? she wondered casually. The *Arachne* part of her brain told her. She got shot. She remembered that. She was in shock until she lost consciousness, so it didn't hurt, but she was sure that she was going to die.

Now *Arachne*, who was almost separate from her but not quite, was explaining that in order to fix her after she was shot, they had to cannibalize some of the subprocessor units that fit into *Arachne*'s web.

Jenny tried to move her own body, and there were twitches in the newly named *Arachne* as Jenny's will to move almost acted as orders to the ship.

But *Arachne* was learning very fast and so was Jenny. Now she actually willed her wings to move and they did—in a balanced choreographed pattern that didn't move the ship at all but was the ship equivalent of an early morning stretch.

Jenny was connected to the ship in a way that no one had been since the early—and unsuccessful—experiments into cybernetic ship systems. There was no wall. Jenny was *Arachne* and *Arachne* was Jenny. What made it work was Rosita's warning to Gerhard to make sure that this *Arachne* was humble. Even more than a ship's brain like *Pandora*, *Arachne* was focused on being of service, not being in charge.

And that left Jenny as the boss of the whole network. She was the ship. The wings were her wings. Even the units that Gerhard and the crew of the *Pandora* were still installing in her were part of her. And with every unit, the ship that used to be the *Brass Ass* was more the *Arachne*, more her.

Jenny wondered how long she spent asleep and her clock—the clock that was part of *Arachne*—gave her the date and time. Several days.

"Welcome back," *Pandora* told Jenny, and Jenny heard it in her ears and in the electromagnetic communication that *Pandora* and *Arachne* exchanged.

"Is John all right?" Jenny asked *Pan*, speaking aloud

"He went on a bender," said Petra, "but he'll be fine. He was really worried about you. We all were."

"I feel okay," Jenny said, and knew that it was both true and not true. She didn't feel any pain, not exactly, but she knew where each cut and bruise on her body was, and the level of healing. She knew where the artificial sub-brains were installed in her nervous system and in the ship. She also knew what they did, and she could call it all up in an instant. But it didn't hurt. She checked and decided that she wouldn't try to sit up just yet.

"So tell me about it?" Petra said. "The interface, I mean. Doc Gerhard said you are extensively tied into ship's systems."

"I am. I can feel the wings and, well, the whole ship. This isn't the *Pandora*. It's *Arachne*. Who is— Never mind. I know. This used to be the *Brass Ass*. Oh, they gave me the ship?"

"Sort of. You were awarded it for injuries done to you."

"It's strange. *Arachne* isn't like my interface with *Pandora*. She's part of me. I have this knowledge. I know all about the ship. It's part of me as though it's always been there, the same way I know what strawberry ice cream tastes like. *Arachne* should have a crew of forty officers and crew, including missile techs, engineering specialists, and boarding or inspection parties of exspatio. But that's based on a ship that doesn't use a brain. Do you think I should hire crew?"

"I don't know, Jenny. The *Arachne* isn't a cargo ship. She's a warship."

Jenny heard the worry in Petra's voice. "I know, but it's all right. We need an escort for the *Pandora* and once we get back to Parthia—" Suddenly Jenny smiled. "Once we get back to Parthia, they are going to need a warship to help guard the system.

"Petra, when I was seven, a rock hit the habitat my family lived on. It was sent there by a Drake warship because the system government was acting up. The Drakes figured that the planetary government would be more amenable to them . . . and they were.

"I spent two years in a refugee camp on Bonks, being taught that it was all my parents' fault for their sinful lives either while they were on the station or in previous incarnations. I can fight if I have to."

"Maybe so, but you're only eleven years old. You shouldn't have to fight."

"Almost twelve!"

"Fine, almost twelve. That's still pretty young to be a warship commander."

"I agree," said John Gabriel as he came in with a cup of coffee. "But I've talked about it with Captain Gold and Tanya Cordoba-Davis. Jenny will be owner aboard, but Danny thinks Tanya should be in command. At least until you're sixteen."

Jenny wasn't at all sure she agreed, but she figured it was the best deal she was going to get. Also, she knew that no matter who was officially in command, Jenny—through *Arachne*—could control the ship if she ever had to.

On the other hand, it might be wiser not to make an issue of that. Jenny wasn't sure whether that thought originated with the Jenny or the Arachne part of her brain. But maybe it didn't really matter.

"I guess I should talk to Tanya and see if she wants a job, but I don't know how I'm going to pay anyone. I don't want to be a pirate."

"Well, there is some loot locked away on board. The pirates fired off the last nuke and it got destroyed, but everything else on board belongs to you. Captain Gold and King Edward are in negotiations with Skull System over the shield missiles."

"Oh, no, not Eddy!" Jenny wailed.

"He's not so bad, Jenny," John said. "He saved us both, you know."

"He did?" Jenny remembered walking along in the foodmart, then nothing until she woke up in the *Arachne*. She found herself automatically contacting the station brain, Crossbones, and accessing the station records.

Crossbones wasn't a very smart station brain, about as intelligent as a monkey. It was good at filing and stuff, though, and added a level of intuitiveness to things like searching the records. She got to see the pictures of them walking along and Eddy reacting to something. She couldn't tell what, but he pushed her into John and was turning to face three people with guns. Then one of them fired a burst, and Eddy fired. And fired again, and a third time. . . . It was over just that fast.

"I guess he did, but he's still a boy. And he's still stuck up."

CHAPTER 32

Revolutions, Mr. Dickinson, come into this world like bastard children—half improvised and half compromised.
Attributed to pre-space statesman Benjamin Franklin

Location: Skull System Council Room, Skull Station
Standard Date: 01 04 632

The table was a large circle with robot servers embedded. Hanging above the center of the table was a large, translucent holo globe. In the globe was a star map showing the Pamplona Sector and the Skull System.

Captain Jack Allenby pointed, and a particular jump locus expanded to fill the globe, then expanded again to show a large rock with masts and other structures dotting it. "We use forts. We have to."

Tanya considered the point that Captain Allenby was making while she looked around the room. It was a big room and it needed to be. There were twenty-three captains, Tanya, Danny, Gerhard Schmitz, Rosita Stuard, Eddy, Sara Electrum, and—oddly enough—John Gabriel, as Jenny Starchild's official representative.

Allenby adjusted the view on the holo globe back to a view of the Pamplona Sector and the Skull System, highlighted in blue for the Drakes, purple for the Cordobas, and white for the Skull system. "Distance limits the ways the Drakes and Cordobas can get at us. That and the forts is all that keeps us safe." The massive forts arrayed next to the two publicly known jump points blinked red.

They were both very long jumps. It would take the Drakes or Cordobas *years* to go around them. The forts were big and heavy and armored with powerful launchers and heavy armaments; they would be horribly expensive to fight through.

Neither of the jumps were all that large in area, so it would be very hard to slip something in behind the forts.

"All that being said," Allenby continued, "if the Drakes or Cordobas were willing to commit enough force, they could take out the forts and take the jumps. And going to the aid of King Edward in Franklin or Clan Gold in Parthia might well be enough to persuade the Cordobas that expending the force is worth it."

Tanya, as the person on their side of the table with the most military experience, answered, "I understand, Captain, but what do you expect us to do about it?"

"A set of those anti-nuke missiles of yours would make the forts a hell of a lot harder to take out. Their best bet is to throw dozens of nukes at the forts, and even with our round shot we won't be able to get them all. But with your—"

"We call them shield missiles," Danny said. "We think they will work fairly well against round shot, and we know they will take down a ship's wing if they hit it right."

Tanya sent Danny a dirty look that he apparently didn't even notice.

"That just makes them more valuable to us," Allenby said.

Danny did something and in place of the star map, the holo globe now held an image of a shield missile. "Under the circumstances, we're willing enough to sell you the designs. But ours use artificial brains, and even for something as small as a missile brain, that takes time."

"What about expert systems?" Allenby asked. "That's just software."

"Sure. But you'll have to develop—" Gerhard was shaking his head, so Danny stopped. "What is it, Doctor?"

"An expert system missile will work. But it wouldn't have stopped the nuke that was aimed at Skull Station."

Tanya was surprised at that, and apparently so was everyone else. "Why not, Doctor Schmitz?"

"Because the brain of the missile felt the magnetic field *and* felt the impact of the hunter-nuke on it. It reacted on the basis of those feelings in a way that I would never have thought to put into an expert system, and in a way that I doubt I could replicate, even if I had the missile's brain to work from. I frankly don't understand how it did it, and *Pan* isn't entirely sure she does."

"That makes three of us, Doc," said Sylvia Avery. "I watched it happen, and I still don't believe it."

"Fine. But the expert systems will work," Captain Allenby insisted. "Look, Syl, I got nothing against the brains. I'm fond of Pal and Crossbones, and you know that. What bothers me is the time. You know that even simple brains take a long time to make."

"I know, Jack, and I want to have as many of these new missiles as we can get. But the Doc has a point. When it comes down to it, I want a brain guiding a—" She looked at Danny. "—shield missile, when my life is depending on it."

"How are you set up for manufacturing brains?" Tanya asked.

"Not as well as I would like," Sylvia said cautiously.

Jack Allenby laughed out loud. Sylvia shot Jack the same sort of glance that Tanya shot at Danny before, and Tanya was suddenly sure that Skull System didn't have any manufacturing facilities for artificial brains at all.

"I'll need something more precise than that," Gerhard said, apparently having missed Sylvia's look.

"Nothing," Roger Avery said. Then, with a look at his daughter, he continued. "I know it may hurt our bargaining position, but we have never had any facilities for the manufacture of artificial brains. They were never common and we, uh, acquired . . . what brains we needed." He took control of the globe and brought up an information listing. "We still have some tailor bots in the system, but real flexsuits have gotten rare. We have Pal for the system and Crossbones for the station, and some of our shuttles and twelve of our ships have brains, but that's about it."

Roger shrugged and continued softly, "I didn't realize just how scarce brains have become until I got to talking with Dr. Cox about the surgery on the Starchild girl." He looked around the room, mostly at the Skull System captains. "You do understand, if one of our people were to receive injuries of that nature, they would spend the rest of their days in a life-support chair. I am frankly amazed that what you did was even possible. So is Doctor Cox."

"No, I didn't realize that, Admiral," said Gerhard. "I can . . ." Then he stopped talking, and everyone waited because it was clear to see there was something more. "I was about to offer to fix that for you, but the truth is, I can't."

Now it was Gerhard's turn to take over the holo globe. He filled it with a model of Jenny, the brains, and pseudo-neurons installed in her. Then a schematic showing the production times on the brains and which printer made each. "Sally and several micro brain printers make up my factory and Sally is the crucial irreplaceable part. I could give or sell you one of the printers." He highlighted the printers in the schematic. "But without Sally it would do you only limited good." He wiped the holo of his images.

"I can sell you a few specialized brains, wing controllers, fusion plant managers, that sort of thing." Gerhard shrugged. "But I had to repurpose a set of brains that were to do everything from run a vacuum cleaner to control a watering system in order to have the parts to help Jenny. And I couldn't have done that without Sally. Also, they wouldn't work without *Arachne*'s manager unit managing them."

"How long did it take you to build *Arachne*?" Jack Allenby asked.

"A bit over a year. Mostly, Sally working on it with just guidance from me."

Jack Allenby shook his head. "That girl has the price of a ship—"

"And is worth every penny of it," John Gabriel said hotly.

"Not arguing that." Allenby waved a hand in a calming gesture. "If she was mine, I'd feel the same way. Just commenting was all."

"How much for Sally?" Roger Avery interrupted.

"Sally is a member of the family," said Rosita Stuard stiffly, "and not for sale at any price."

Roger Avery's eyes narrowed and took on a hardness that made the hairs on the back of Tanya's neck stand up.

Then Danny added, "Up to and including open war."

Roger looked back at Danny Gold and cold black eyes met frozen green ones. No one said anything for several moments.

Then Jack Allenby laughed again. "You're our sort of folks, Gold."

Avery looked at Allenby, then back at Danny, and nodded. He leaned back in his chair.

"Which still leaves the problem of introducing brain production into the Skull System," Sylvia said. "What will it take, Doctor? Assume for the moment that money is no object."

Now both Jack Allenby and Roger Avery were looking at Sylvia like she was nuts, and the rest of the captains didn't look thrilled either.

Sylvia stared them all down, moving her eyes back and forth like targeting lasers. "I came within half a second and one artificial brain of losing my life and a quarter of a million people. That's not going to happen again."

"And that's the problem in a nutshell, because what getting you that capability would entail is taking the facilities that make those missiles' brains off-line and tasking it with building a much larger brain—one that copies Sally's abilities. It would take five years." Gerhard paused. "Check me on this, Sally. To produce a brain with your functionality in regard to making brains, five years?"

Over the speakers in the conference room came the voice of Sally. "Two point seven, Doctor. It would need much less of my administrative abilities."

"That fast? I'm amazed," Gerhard said. "I've been tinkering with Sally for the last forty years, off and on."

"It's that tinkering that would allow me to make a much more efficient brain maker, Doctor, along with your knowledge of what would and wouldn't work and how processing groups can be alternately tasked to get the best results. The timing is based on the assumption that I would have you to consult with as the construction proceeded."

"Never mind Sally," said a woman's voice. It was one of the captains. "How much for the Doc?"

Rosita sniffed. "I'd have to think about it. There have been times in the last year or so when I would have gladly traded him for a half-empty box of tissues."

That brought general laughter and a decrease in the tension.

Gerhard called up the hologlobe again. "We brought three Wilson-Clark IIIs, but we left two of them on Parthia. The Wilson-Clark IIIs print and test brains in an integrated manner. A normal molecular printer doesn't. With the proper programming, a molecular printer can print a small brain, but it would take orders of magnitude more time to do it and the brain wouldn't be as effective."

"What about building a factory manager like *Arachne*?" Roger asked.

"That's what Sally was talking about, I think," Gerhard said, then apparently consulted with Sally. "Yes, at least in part. Though, as I think about it, we might be able to trim a little off Sally's estimate. What we're faced with here is reasonably flexible equipment that can be turned to a lot of uses, but not all at once. We only have so many brain printers, and if we use them to make a manager like Sally, we can't be using them to make shield missile brains or even the subsystem brains.

"If anyone is going to Danworth, you want to buy anything you can get that can be used to print neural nets. Especially if you find any Wilson-Clark III molecular printers."

"Congreve in Drake space used to have a production facility for artificial brains," added Jack Allenby. "There might be something floating around in their outsystem."

"Okay. If no one else is going to bring it up, I will," Roger Avery said. "The issue is that these people are planning to leave and take the only brain-making facility available to us with them."

Tanya glanced around and felt like a fat lambfish surrounded by hungry nearsharks.

"And you want us to do that," Danny said. "Because an allied clan to mine has been making shield missile brains and bodies, or at least the parts for them, since we left. That's roughly six standard months' worth of production. And they were already up and running. People, you want an alliance with the Council of Clans on Parthia."

"Franklin has a good, solid industrial base," Eddy added. "That industrial base could support and augment your own, once I regain my throne. We even have the technology to print neural nets, if on a very limited scale."

"Rather, the new Franklin Governance Corporation has that ability," Jack Allenby said.

Eddy's lips tightened a bit, but he held his expression in check. "Which circumstance does you no good at all. Nor is likely to in the future."

"Enough. We aren't going to settle this in one meeting," Roger Avery said. "Look, you aren't going to be leaving today, right?"

Danny nodded.

"Good enough. Let Jack and Sylvia represent the captain's council, and pick a couple of people to sit down with them and negotiate what you expect to get for this new innovation, and we'll leave any formal alliances until later. What about the *Brass* . . . no, you renamed it. What about the *Arachne*?"

"What about it?"

"You're going to need crew. I mean, the little girl who got shot isn't going to be able to handle it all by herself."

Tanya spoke up. "With Jenny's agreement, I'll be commanding the *Arachne*. I'll take Chuck Givens as my number one, and most of the Cordoba Spaceforce personnel, because they have military experience."

"That's not a good idea," Jack Allenby said. "We don't want a Cordoba-crewed warship wandering around loose with the knowledge of the shield missiles. It would be too easy for Miss Starchild to have an accident, leaving the ship in the hands of you people."

"Are you—"

"I'm not calling anyone anything, but we have to worry about it." Allenby faced John Gabriel. "And you should worry about it too, Gabriel, if you want that little girl of yours to grow up."

"We should instead crew it with pirates?"

"Not entirely. But, for everyone's sake, you need a mixed crew. Now, I have Petey Li. He's the third on the *Bontemps*. A good man, looking for a better berth. The lad's ready for first mate, and I dare say he has as much combat experience as your Givens."

At that point, several other of the captains insisted that they had people who were also qualified, even several options for captain.

Nothing was settled then, except that the ultimate decision would be Jenny Starchild's. Young as she was, it was her ship.

Location: Arachne, Skull System Orbit
Standard Date: 01 05 632

Jenny wasn't completely healed, but she sat, belted in, at the desk in the captain's cabin of the *Arachne*, with John sitting on her right. Then she opened the hatch as Danny Gold approached it. It was automatic, almost without thought. She was so integrated with *Arachne* that she saw the captain floating toward her hatch and used the automatics to open the hatch. She rotated the chair to face him and said, "Hi, Captain Gold."

"Hi, Jenny." Danny floated to the chair she indicated and belted himself in, giving John a nod. "Have you thought about crew at all?"

"Yes. *Arachne* told me about the meeting before it was over. I . . . we've been examining the records of the proposed new crew."

"That's good, but even with *Arachne* you're going to need an absolutely loyal core for your crew. I want you to take Goldvokx and Goldtak as additional security. That will make you a clan, with them as your first workers. They'll become part of your clan, but we have to get back to Parthia before we can get you official."

"Jennyvokx?" Jenny asked. "That would be hard to say."

"Starchildvokx?" Danny offered.

"That's silly."

"So make it Starvokx," John Gabriel said. "You made up your last name anyway."

"I didn't know you knew that."

"I guessed as soon as I heard it."

"Why'd you make up your name?" Danny asked.

"It doesn't matter," Jenny said.

In truth, she did it because she was terrified. At the time, the station had just been destroyed and she had no one. She heard a couple of older girls talking about people from important families being disappeared. Jenny didn't know if her family was important, but she wasn't taking chances. So when she was asked her name, she said Jenny Starchild.

Later, thinking about it, she realized that her parents were not the sort of important that the older girls were talking about. They weren't political, just working stiffs with decent jobs.

At this point, Jenny wasn't entirely sure what her name was back then. Johanson or Johenry or something that started with a "yo," anyway.

* * *

Danny was pleased with himself about offering the Parthians. They, at least, wouldn't be involved in any plots. "So it's Starvokx and Startak. They'll be happy with it. It's an honor to be chosen as cadre to a new clan."

This was, it turned out, a very old and hallowed tradition among the Parthians. When a new clan was started, the parent or allied clans gave of their members to cement alliances, as well as to keep the young breeders safe until they could breed and raise their own workers.

Location: Arachne, Skull System Orbit
Standard Date: 01 06 632

Jenny took the glass of green goo with black specks on top. The Parthian Banger was part of the duties of a human clan breeder. Danny drank them to keep the Parthians comfortable and Rosita had done it on the station. Goldgok told her about it.

Jenny was insistent that she was going to do her job. But just because she was insistent that she was going to do her job didn't mean that she was looking forward to it.

She grabbed the glass and chugged. Her mouth was on fire. She grabbed the milk and chugged that too. The fire wasn't out. There were still hot spots in her left cheek and under her tongue.

"More milk," she croaked, and John set another glass of milk before her. This time she didn't chug. She swished it around. She had to get the milk everywhere to put out the fires. John was looking amused, the meanie.

"You know, I could have done that for you," he said.

"No. It's my clan, so it's my job."

Tanya was watching Jenny and smiling a little, and Jenny felt herself smiling in response. Tanya understood. "You'll make a good captain of the *Arachne*," Jenny said.

"So will you, Jenny, once you're old enough," Tanya said.

"So now we bring over Starvokx and Startak and officially adopt them into the clan."

* * *

Starvokx and Startak found the new ship pleasant. They worked on the repairs and upgrades so they knew where things were, but now it smelled like home, and *Arachne* greeted them like clan members instead of guests.

Arachne also spoke as a neuter female, but there was something almost breeder-like in her tones. When asked, she explained, "I am always in contact with Jenny Starchild."

Startak nodded its eyestalks. "The pictures of Arachne show a half human, half spider. They are really quite attractive, for a human."

Jenny, now that she had the Parthians aboard, intended to introduce them to prospective crew members and watch the reactions. For the moment, though, Jenny still had questions. "How am I going to pay all of you?"

"What do you mean?" Tanya asked.

"Well, it's not like I'm gonna turn pirate. And I don't have any money. There was some loot in Rosalyn's quarters, but I can't run the ship on that forever. *Arachne* says we'll be broke after we buy reloads and restock, or close to it. The way they do it here is the crew gets a stake in the prizes, but there won't be any prizes."

"For myself," Tanya said, "I'm not worried about it. Remember, I'm rich, Jenny. But you're right. The military is generally supported by taxes, but who's going to pay you taxes? Danny?"

"Clan Gold is a recognized clan, but I don't know if it has that sort of resources," Starvokx said.

"What about the council of clans?" Tanya asked.

"It's possible," Starvokx said. "But I don't really know that much about clan politics. Never cared all that much, as long as I had a job to do."

"Well," said Startak. "It was a really big scandal when the *Fly Catcher* returned and told all those horrible lies about Goldgok and Danny Gold, but then . . . Well, never mind all that. Danny Gold has a good reputation, but I don't know what they are going to make of the Star Clan."

"I wonder what happened to the *Fly Catcher*. You think they just ran off like Goldgok says?" Jenny asked.

"I have no idea," Startak said. "But I never thought Captain Kesskox was as bad as Goldgok thought. I mean, you should read some of the things that the clans get up to . . ."

"Oh, don't get it started. Startak reads the Parthia gossip," Starvokx said.

"Well, it's fun," Startak insisted. "I don't believe the half of it, but it's entertaining."

Starvokx's eyestalks wobbled like drunken spacers leaving a bar, and Startak made as though to hit him with her left mid-arm.

"You were saying about the *Fly Catcher*," Jenny said oppressively.

"Well, Breeder, I don't think it was as bad as everyone thought. After all, you drank a Banger to make us comfortable. I bet that's what it was doing."

"Maybe you're right," Jenny acknowledged. She never met Captain Kesskox. "So you think the *Fly Catcher* will go back to Parthia, even after they find out Danny Gold went back?"

"Where else can they go?" asked Starvokx.

CHAPTER 33

The origins of the Parthian Banger are in a concoction developed even before the Parthians first went into space. It was developed in the hinterlands of Parthia, where they were used by the Parthian equivalent of fur trappers. Introduced into the space colonies after the loss of the first Gok station, they were used but had, at best, mixed results.

The introduction of trade with the wider universe offered several new products, and the modern Parthian Banger developed out of decades of experimentation. Fog bugs, for instance, have a spicy mint flavor to humans and an aroma that is mildly titillating to Parthians. The other ingredients all have other uses.

On the Parthian Banger, Zheckgoks, Standard Date 646

***Note:** On the Parthian Banger is still banned on parts of Parthia and Canova.*

Location: Ferguson Outsystem
Standard Date: 01 06 632

Captain Kesskox listened to the monkey in something close to shock. Danny Gold was a human, and had been in a position to take and keep a hold full of goods. There was no way that a human could resist that sort of temptation. Besides, without someone drinking the Bangers, Checkgok should have gone crazy months ago.

"What are we going to do?" asked Gokkox, *Fly Catcher*'s first mate. Gokkox was her partner when they drank the Bangers that were necessary to keep the crew from going insane.

No one in all the years since the first Parthian Banger was drunk had investigated how they worked.

For about the same reasons that Victorian sex manuals weren't the results of rigorous research.

Parthians found the whole matter embarrassing and more than a little disgusting. The Parthian biochemistry that normally produced the scent was the biochemistry of sexual arousal.

Breeders of both genders are pretty much always horny. That's their job, after all. The effect on a Parthian neuter who drinks a Banger is to make it not just drunk, but drunk and horny. That's frustrating as hell if just one Parthian drinks the Banger.

But if a male neuter and a female neuter drink it together, it can be a lot of fun.

Perverted fun, in Parthian terms.

But still fun.

Kesskox and Gokkox had fallen into the habit of drinking them together because having a drunk, horny Parthian with nothing to do with the horny can be dangerous. And, frankly, is cruel to the Parthian.

It wasn't something either of them was proud of, but they justified their actions because it was necessary for the welfare of the crew.

"I don't know, Gokkox."

"We have the ship. We could just leave." Gokkox didn't sound enthusiastic.

"And go where?" Kesskox asked. "Besides, you think the crew would go along with that? We're part of the Kox clan."

Gokkox's mouth-hand twisted sardonically. The truth was the Kox clan showed little regard for the crew of the *Fly Catcher*. It wasn't big enough to support a true subclan with breeders of its own like the stations, and even if no one talked about it, everyone knew what that meant. "Yes, Skipper. I think they would go with us."

"It doesn't matter, Gokkox. I've done a lot of things in my life, but I wouldn't do that to our crew. If I did, what would the rest of it be for?

"Things were going so well until we got here and heard about the *Pandora*'s return. Our holds are full and we were going to bring great profit to the clan. Maybe even get some respect." Kesskox let her eyestalks droop in defeat.

Gokkox looked at her and said, "You're not thinking of doing something stupid, are you, Skipper?"

The truth was that Kesskox was thinking it might be better for everyone if she got the *Fly Catcher* back to Parthia and expiated the sins of the crew by suicide. The Parthians, as a race, weren't any fonder of suicide than humans were. Sacrifice for the good of clan was one thing, but skipping out on your duty to clan by killing yourself . . . that was disgraceful.

She looked back at her long-time friend and occasional lover, and shrugged her eyestalks. "I guess not. But you do realize that it might not matter? Depending on what Gold and that little prig Checkgok said about us, the clan may decide to turn us over to the Zheck clan to use as fertilizer."

"So we go home. I'll call the crew together and let them know what's going on."

* * *

Gokkox's announcement was met first with silence, then with some of the crew proposing that they take the *Fly Catcher* and make a run for it. Others didn't like that idea and Gokkox was quick to point out that the Skipper was taking them home, no matter.

It was a grimly determined crew that passed through Canova and saw the fort under construction. It would guard the jump that was one jump out from Canova on the Ferguson route. They were stopped and questioned, but apparently everything wasn't in place yet.

"The Jackson-Cordoba Trading Company has acquired the Canova system," Senior Captain Herbert Jackson-Cordoba said, "and with the recent Drake incursions to consider, we are taking prudent and necessary measures to insure that Parthia is safe."

"Does the council of clans know about this?" Kesskox asked.

"The JCTC is not answerable to the council of clans," Herbert said. "Though I imagine they know about the fort we're building in the Parthian outsystem. I must say, your council of clans has been taking an increasingly belligerent attitude since that Cybrant hit the system. You would be wise to use whatever influence you have with them to get them to see reason, else you won't be leaving Parthia on a trading voyage any time soon."

This is just getting better and better, Kesskox thought as she signed off.

They got a decent look at the Parthia outsystem fort as they went by. It wasn't all that impressive, but it probably didn't need to be. *Fly Catcher* was the only Parthian ship. At least, the only ship that had a Parthian crew.

Location: Parthia Insystem
Standard Date: 01 17 632

The message was curt. Captain Kesskox was to report to the council of clans on the day after tomorrow to answer for its actions. The follow-up was even more curt.

"Get your perverted ass to Fkis Two to talk to our clan elders before you say anything to anyone else."

Kesskox pointed an eyestalk at Gokkox. "Well, that was to the point."

"You want me to come?"

"That would hardly help, would it?"

"No, but it would make me feel better. I hate seeing you face this alone."

* * *

The shuttle ride over was silent. Spacer Tokkox was unwilling even to bend an eyestalk in Kesskox's direction. Nor did anyone seem particularly anxious to see or acknowledge Kesskox on her way to the Kox section of the station. Once she got to the room, she was directed to a stand with a peremptory wave of a mouth-hand.

Kesskox looked around and saw Siskox in a corner. It was Siskox, many years ago, who explained the function of the Banger to a much younger Kesskox while they were both working on insystem ships.

The silence got long and Kesskox found that she wasn't in the mood to wait. "Well, what is it you wanted to see me about?" she asked in the tones of a breeder.

"You are not a breeder!" Breeder male Tetkox screeched.

"No, but I'm all my crew have had. For years now." Kesskox rose to her full height. "You're going to do what you're going to do, and I don't really care anymore. I guess that does make me a *cheskek*. So maybe Checkgok was right."

"Goldgok!" someone clicked.

"Goldgok?" Kesskox sank down on the stand in shock, then she started to laugh. "I bet that was a comedown for that prig. Smart move, though, on the part of Clan Zheck." Her eyestalks straightened in sudden surmise and she said. "Did they go all the way? Did they propose Gold as a clan?"

"Clan Gold is a member of the council of clans," Tetkox said haughtily. "Human or not, it's a true breeder, concerned for its clan, adopted as well as born."

Slowly, Kesskox turned both its eyestalks to focus on the little male, and the effect of the Bangers she had consumed over the years made her see the male as attractive. That just made her angrier. "That, Tetkox, puts him one up on you, for sure. Where was the concern for my crew when we were sent out without a breeder?"

The meeting went downhill from there. In fact, by the time it was over, Kesskox was convinced that the only reason she wasn't ordered to kill herself was that the clan was ordered by the council of clans not to let her.

Location: Zheck Clan House, Parthia

"We need that ship!" Zhecktiit lifted her mid-arms in emphasis. She was a breeder female and unusually large even for that largest of Parthian classes.

"We aren't going to get it," Zhecktitick pointed its eyes at the ceiling of the large chamber. Translucent cloths billowed out from the rounded ceiling, tacked in place at the apex and around the edges of the oblong chamber. The human-made lights showed through the cloths, bathing the room in shifting light and shadows. The birthing pools were just the other side of the left passage and the bubbling of the artificial streams provided a gentle background for this decidedly ungentle chat. It brought its eyes back to Zhecktiit. "Half the clans are blaming us for the belligerent stance that the Jackson-Cordobas are adopting." It pointed to a screen on the chamber wall with its mouth-hand. The screen showed a pattern of lights and symbols that would be utter gibberish to a human, but to Parthians was an elegant, even in its way beautiful, analysis of group dynamics.

"And just how are we to get to the materials Danny Gold found out in the Oort cloud without it?" Zhecktiit asked, her mouth-hand twisting in agitation.

Zhecktitick nodded its eyestalks. "I'm not disagreeing that we need the ship," the non-breeder male, who was the clan's senior political analyst, agreed sadly. "I just don't see any way of getting it. You know, and I know, that they are going to claim that the *Fly Catcher*'s return proves their argument."

"It won't stand up under examination before the council of clans. You know that we can force the crew of the *Fly Catcher* to tell the truth with what we know." Zhecktiit was referring to the knowledge of the effect of Bangers—rather, the effect of the *lack* of Bangers—on Parthian spacers. It was common knowledge that they were used among the spacers, but the absolute need for them was not understood.

"No one is going to thank us for bringing that out," Zhecktitick said. "And, frankly, I'm not sure how much it helps our case if the captain of the *Fly Catcher* was doing what it was doing out of concern for its crew and clan members. That goes a long way toward justifying its actions."

"Nothing can—" Zhecktiit started to say, but then stopped. After their talks with Professor Schmitz of the Gold Clan, they went through the records and examined reports. Extended lack of the aroma of breeders led to acute paranoia and murderous rages. There were several deaths in the early days of space exploration, to such an extent that the exploration of the Parthian system had been put back for at least a century. The problem wasn't as bad on Parthia itself, which was a populous planet, and on which there were many sources of the chemical cocktail. The loss of the first Gok station with all hands was just the most glaring example.

"Yes." Zheckfiss, their master trader, joined the conversation. "If you're going to send Parthians out into space, then someone has to drink Bangers. And if you don't have a human to do it, you need someone else." Then it added, a bit pointedly, "Or send a breeder."

"Your point is taken," Zhecktiit said. "But what can we do?"

Zheckfiss twisted its eyestalks. "I'm not altogether sure. But I am convinced that embarrassing the Kox clan just to score points is not our best strategy." It shifted its left eyestalk to point at Zhecktitick. "Partly because it won't work. Yes, we can make them look bad, but we won't make ourselves look good in the doing, and the Jkap will have their commentators asserting how vindictive we are all over the news nets."

"So we should just roll over?" Zhecktitick asked. "We are owed a great deal of money and can probably force the Kox to pay us."

"Yes, we can force them to, but what if we make a deal? You know that Danny Gold installed one of Doctor Schmitz's artificial-brain mining robot managers in the Oort cloud. And we can make a great deal if we can go pick up the refined metals."

"Yes, yes, so you have said," Zhecktiit said. "Assuming that the Jackson-Cordobas are wrong and the thing hasn't gone crazy."

"I think it's worth a try. If we can get the *Fly Catcher*," Zheckfiss said.

"And we might be able to. I have a source on the *Fly Catcher*'s crew. Nothing inimical to the crew or the Kox clan, but it told me that they doubt that the *Fly Catcher* will be allowed to leave until the JCTC gets the concessions it's demanding," Zhecktitick said. "That right there seriously diminishes the value of the *Fly Catcher*."

"How much?"

"Let me talk to them. I think that between that and their desire to avoid embarrassment we might be able to get it just for the unspecified amount they owe us," Zhecktitick said.

"What? The *Fly Catcher* is a jump-capable ship. It's worth twice what they owe us, at least!" Zheckfiss' eyestalks crossed.

"It would be . . . if the passage out of the system wasn't guarded by a fortress. And I said *might*. We might also have to cut them in on the product of the Oort cloud mining."

"That's mostly Clan Gold's. We can't go . . ." Zhecktiit started.

"I know that. But we do have authority to manage it in their absence, and if we can work a deal, there will be good profit for all the clans involved."

Location: Fly Catcher, Parthian orbit

"What? You're *selling* the *Fly Catcher*?" Captain Kesskox said, looking into the screen. She was floating just above her command pad, attached loosely by a belt. But it wasn't the lack of gravity that was causing her discomfort.

Siskox gestured assent.

"What happens to us?"

"That's why I called." The older Parthian spacer made a tired gesture with its mid arms. "I know why you did what you did." Even now it was clear that Siskox was uncomfortable talking about it. "But most of the clan council simply can't understand. They've never been out, not even to the inner asteroid belt, much less out alone in other star systems. But I got a chance to talk to Zhecktitick and I think it understands about the Bangers. The Zheck will need a crew and the council isn't happy with you or any of your spacers."

"So we will be sold with the ship." All Captain Kesskox felt was relief. Partly that was because she was a Parthian and the idea of being sold wasn't something that bothered her the way it might a human. But mostly the relief was because this sale meant she would probably be able to keep her ship and the sub-clan that she had formed with the crew.

"Yes." Siskox signed off.

Location: Council of Clans, Parthia

"If the council will give me a moment?" said Zhecktitick, waving both its mid-arms at the ceiling in the traditional gesture before it was fully into the chamber.

"We've agreed to take up the issue of the debt that you claim is owed you by Clan—" Gokwak started.

Zhecktitick waved his mid-arms again in a polite gesture of interruption. "I am simply attempting to prevent a waste of the council's time." It shifted its eyestalks to scan the large, half-full chamber.

"If you insist," Gokwak agreed. "But you're not making any friends by interrupting."

That much was quite obvious from the postures of the delegates. "It is simply that mediation by the council of clans is no longer needed. Clan Zheck and Clan Kox have come to an agreement and all debts between the two clans are now paid."

That brought silence for about two breaths, then a murmur of discussion that grew in volume and apparent consternation. It took one of the council porters pounding on a gong with its powerful mid-arms to quiet the hubbub enough for Gokwak to ask rather testily, "What agreement has been reached?"

"Some of the details are private, of course, but in general the *Fly Catcher* is now owned by Clan Zheck and there is an agreement between Clan Zheck—as representatives of our allied Clan Danny Gold—and Clan Kox to exploit certain goods in the Oort cloud of the Parthia system."

More hubbub and more pounding on the gong followed.

* * *

The camera zoomed out and displayed the news anchor with the council chamber showing on the screen behind it. "That was the scene in the council of clans this morning, Gekjkap," said Sikjkap. "What do you think this means to the balance of power in the council of clans?"

"That depends on whether this is a single deal or represents the beginnings of a true alliance between Clan Zheck and her allies and Clan Kox and her allies. If it's the beginning of a true alliance, the only word for the change is titanic. Zheck and Kox have been the leaders, or at least high in the councils, of the two largest factions of the ground-based clans. With the addition of the Danny Gold clan . . ."

"But the Danny Gold clan isn't here. It's outsystem to the last worker."

"Sure. But its alliances aren't. With the Gold Clan involved in this, the Kiik are almost certain to join in as well, and they have been doing quite well in space manufacturing."

"That's not the half of it, Gokjkap," added Fiffdak, an expert on business and a regular on the show. "That trader of theirs is rapidly turning into a master of business. Almost single-handedly, it has turned the fortunes of Kiik around, and with Kiik will come the Fiff and the Siki."

"How are the Fkis and the Gok going to respond?"

"That's the question, all right. They were already in trouble because they are too closely tied to the JCTC for most Parthians' comfort. Word that the JCTC is building a fort to keep us locked into our system has been a great embarrassment to them. With this new coalition, they have to be hurting."

* * *

Zheckfiss turned off the viewer on the *Fly Catcher* and gestured to Captain Zheckess. "You understand that 'off-the-books' cargo will not be acceptable this time?"

Zheckess, formerly Kesskox, nodded its—possibly, her—mouth-hand in an oddly human gesture that made Zheckfiss uncomfortable. "We . . . the crew, I mean . . . do have needs. Foods, equipment."

It was clear to Zheckfiss that Zheckess was trying to sound polite, but the intonations of a female breeder slipped out of its secondary voicebox. That made Zheckfiss more uncomfortable. "Yes, I understand. And the Zheck clan will make sure those needs are met. Including the Bangers."

* * *

Zheckess tried not to wince at the tone of that last.

Zheckfiss continued. "What do you need to get your ship ready to travel?"

"Travel where, exactly? A trip to the Oort cloud would take years."

"To a jump route discovered by the *Pandora*. A jump route that is a closely held secret of the Gold and Zheck clans."

"How?" Zheckess started, then tried to explain. "It takes a special ship to find jumps. And I'm not just going by what the humans told us. I've been trying to find jumps for years, and you just can't."

"It is apparently the feedback from the wings that makes the jumps more obvious, and that is much easier to understand with an interface."

"So we are to be forever denied—" Something in Zheckfiss' expression stopped her. "What?"

"We don't know how it worked, but we do know that Doctor Schmitz thought he had a workable interface for Parthians."

"Which isn't going to do us a lot of good."

"What do you mean?"

"I mean there are forts out there now," Zheckess said. "With the best will in the world, Danny Gold won't be able to get through them to come back. We're stuck in here and they are stuck out there."

CHAPTER 34

The technique of folding wings wasn't possible in the early days of jump travel. A wing must be at least a certain size relative to the mass of the ship making the jump. The level of overpowering that modern warships maintain simply didn't exist. Even now a ship like the Pandora, fully loaded, cannot "fold" its wings to any great degree and still make jump. Unloaded, the Pandora could decrease her wing reach by as much as twenty-five percent and still make jump.
The Arachne, on the other hand, can fold her wings to as little as twenty-five kilometers in length and still make jump. That represents a tremendous advantage if you know the small jumps of the system.
Tanya Cordoba-Davis to the Council of Clans, Canova, Standard Year 633

Location: Arachne, Skull System Station
Standard Date: 01 22 632

For the next couple of weeks, Jenny found herself interviewing potential crew, with the guidance of Tanya, *Arachne*, and John. The captain's council was fairly insistent that the chain of command not be all Cordoba spacers. John agreed with them. So they interviewed six candidates from the Skull System and selected Petey Li, Captain Allenby's suggested candidate from the *Bontemps*.

Petey was easy-going and didn't have a problem with Startak or Starvokx. Jenny was always rather good at reading people, even when she was a kid. With the addition of the *Arachne* and her sensors, Jenny was almost like a walking lie detector. This was something that she decided not to mention to anyone.

Petey was willing to forgo shares if he didn't have to attack merchant ships anymore. "A pirate's life seemed glamorous when I started out, lass, but it's a hard life that requires hard acts. I don't mind a fight, but there's something about going after a fat freighter that's too scared to fight and too slow to run that . . ." He shrugged. "I just don't like it."

"Well, that's good. We have an agreement with Captain Gold. We will be escorting the *Pandora*, and in exchange we will get a bonus based on the sale of goods once we get back to Parthia. But as a part of that, we will be getting flexsuits for the crew. Real flexsuits, made by Hirum's suit bot." Jenny sniffed disdainfully. "Not these stupid modern suits. So you will need to go over to the *Pandora* and get fitted. We don't have room for the tailor shop here. Besides, Hirum doesn't want to be on a warship."

With Petey's help they were able to find the necessary crew. Petra, by her own choice, was staying on the *Pan*, and Jenny was giggly certain that she was going to marry Robert Schmitz. Fred Markum wanted to go back to being a fighting spacer, and this was the ship to do that on. Jimmy Dugan was coming with Tanya and would train the *Arachne*'s exspatio force. But Jenny wanted everyone cross-trained. She wasn't any more interested in stealing merchant ships than Petey was, but she had a hunch that there would be prizes. Military prizes.

* * *

Jenny sank into the simulation and felt the crew. It was a new experience for her. During simulations on *Pandora* there was almost a wall between her and the crew, but *Arachne* was different. Warships have to have fast reactions. Warship crews need the tight interface for rapid transfer of orders and information. That was part of what Jenny felt, but there was something else as well. *Arachne*, from the beginning, never tried to be an independent entity, not since they installed bits of it in Jenny. *Arachne* worked actively at being part of Jenny. So Jenny felt Tanya, Petey, and the rest. She could tell what they were doing, and it was clear and natural.

Carla Creger was looking for targets for the C-D laser array and running sims. This was a warship. It had lasers for close-in defense against nukes, something that merchantmen weren't allowed. Carla was anticipating the incoming nukes with something like glee, while Edgar Rush was praying that there would be no nukes close enough to shoot, even in a sim. But Jenny knew from the records that Edgar's hit percentage was better than Carla's. It was as though everyone in the crew was part of her.

Tanya sent a quiet thought, *"This is different,"* with sidebars defining the difference from what she was used to. This lacked the hard-edged artificiality that made Jenny so uncomfortable when she first started interfacing with the *Pan*. *"I'm uncomfortable that I'm so comfortable,"* Tanya added. *"There is supposed to be a clear distinction between my thought and what I am getting from the shipnet."*

Jenny made an adjustment and *Arachne*'s net added a marker to Tanya's interface that simulated that sense of artificiality.

Other crew members liked the intimacy of the net. Some of them liked it a bit too well. When Jenny caught someone's fleeting thought, a thought that made her blush, she tweaked the net again to keep that sort of thought outside her head. It wasn't that she wasn't interested, but she didn't want to invade the crew's privacy.

The sim went on, using the ship's systems and virtual enemies. They were introducing the crew to the new shield missiles, and Edgar immediately saw the danger that didn't occur to Jenny, Tanya, or anyone. The shield missiles were vulnerable to laser fire.

Tanya thought at Edgar, *"What about spread?"*

"Some," Edgar conceded, *"but a lot of the spread when you shoot them at other ships is that last hundred klicks or so, when they are encountering the plasma field."*

Suddenly there were numbers and simulations flashing back and forth. Edgar, Carla, Tanya, and Jimmy, all tweaking the sims, and Jenny was following it all. It was Carla who thought of adding an umbrella, a small, reflective sheet on a short pole, that would stick out in front of the missile.

"It would block the sensors and a side shot would go right by it."

More simulations, more math, contacting *Pandora*, and getting Hirum in on the conversation, and Doctor Schmitz, and Danny.

Jenny was pleased, and so was Tanya. The crew was integrating surprisingly well.

Location: Skull Station
Standard Date: 01 25 632

Danny smiled at Captain Janis Tecumseh and lifted the champagne flute to his lips.

Janis smiled back, and showed him the bottle.

Things proceeded in a mostly predictable manner after that, and later they talked about routes. Janis and her ship, the *Warchief*, mostly operated in Cordoba space and knew a number of hidden routes. Janis was a straightforward, openly amoral woman, and made no bones at all about the fact that she was using Danny.

"I figure that with you as a Parthian clan, I can sell loot in the Parthia System. What I need is a route to Parthia that doesn't go through Canova."

"So do I," Danny admitted ruefully. "I spent the better part of a year in the Parthian outsystem looking for another route."

"Find anything?"

"Cul de sacs. A couple of fairly long ones. One of them is a five-jump chain that goes through a fairly dense section of the Parthian Oort cloud. There are some decent resources off jump three in the chain."

"Bet the bugs were happy about that."

"Less than you might think." Danny didn't correct her use of "bug." Nor did he mention the automated miner bots. "Parthians aren't big on operating on their own and, besides, they don't have any jump ships. It's all the Jackson-Cordobas."

"Want to play some rutter tag, Danny?"

"I'd rather just buy anything you have within a lightyear of Parthia's sun."

Janis' eyes glazed for a minute. "I don't have anything within a year, but I have two that are about two years. They are to galactic north spinward. Free hint!"

Danny considered. He liked Janis and enjoyed her in bed, but he didn't trust her as far as he could throw her. On the other hand, he really needed a new route into Parthia. "Where does it come out?"

"Are we playing rutter tag, Captain?"

Danny was still a bit ambivalent, but he said yes.

Janis gave a location and Danny sighed. It was close, very close. About a light week from the far jump. He gave her the coordinates for that jump.

"That leads into Parthia?"

"Five jumps to the belt between TjisKee and Sikikee."

"Mine is two jumps to the Canova outsystem, but it's a route that the Canovas don't know about and it's not all that far from the link to the Ferguson chain."

They played rutter tag until they each had both routes, and Danny gained a few back ways around the Ferguson area. Janis had locations for a number of cul de sacs in the area around Ferguson, good places to wait in hiding and go unseen by the Spaceforce ships.

"The Jackson-Cordoba Trading Company has twenty-seven ships. There are only a few that go to Parthia, but Parthia is key to their success. They have these big-ass warehouses in Canova where goods from Parthia are transhipped," Janis explained. "That's how I know what will sell on Parthia. I picked up a JCTC ship on my last trip. It was out of Parise, taking a back route to get around the Drakes, and sailed right into my hiding place." Janis grinned in pleased remembrance. "I loaded up my holds and let them go. No reason to cause bad blood."

Danny checked with *Pan*, then said, "Twenty-six ships. The *Bonaventure* had an accident."

Janis raised herself to look at him, causing the sheet to fall away. "What sort of accident?"

Danny looked into her eyes rather than at the breasts she had intentionally exposed. "It attempted an act of piracy against the *Pandora*."

She smiled and reached for him. "I knew there was a reason I liked you."

Location: Virtual Space, Pandora and Skull Station
Standard Date: 01 26 632

Silvia answered the comm to hear Captain Gold say, "It's time for us to leave."

"We'd like to send a ship with you," Sylvia said, "for security."

"You already have most of the crew on the *Arachne* and the new hires on the *Pan*," Captain Gold complained.

"Not that sort of security," Sylvia said. "But you folks are potentially useful to the Skull System and we're rather afraid of what the Cordobas would do to you if they realized that." They were more than useful, Sylvia thought. They might be the difference between survival and collapse.

"So tell us about the back doors." Danny was referring to the persistent rumors that there were other jumps between Skull System and the rest of Pamplona Sector. Those rumors were partially proved by the jump route out of Alenbie. But they were an important state secret of Skull System, because Skull System wasn't just one system. There were five stars and fourteen planets controlled by the captain's council. That was something that Silvia couldn't share with Gold.

"If there were more back doors," Sylvia said repressively, "they would almost certainly involve much longer routes, don't you think? After all, thirty-seven light-year-long jumps are rare. A more likely scenario would be a thirty- or forty-jump long route that would take months of travel time."

"It might be worth it, depending on what's along the route," Danny offered.

"So maybe it's a shame there isn't such a route, Captain," Sylvia said, not giving an inch, though if she had the choice, she would have. At the moment, however, the captain's council wasn't sure they trusted Danny Gold. And the best security, as well as the cheapest, for those back routes was to keep them secret. And that was another problem. Sylvia knew that Rosalyn had the rutters for the Cally route, a route that was supposed to be secret. That was worrying, and Sylvia wished now that she hadn't mentioned the fact that Rosalyn knew about it to the captain's council. It just scared everyone. The Cally route was another one with long jumps. Three of them, averaging ten light years each.

"Who did you have in mind to send with us?" Captain Gold asked.

Sylvia brought her mind back to the original topic. "You seem to get along with Janis fairly well."

Janis Tecumseh was an old friend of Sylvia's and her father's before her. Janis' ship was a converted merchantman but the conversion was major, and there was no way the *Warchief* was going to survive inspection by any Spaceforce ship, Drake or Cordoba. It had thirty-two lasers in eight banks, and it carried fifteen hunter-nukes and a heavy load of round shot. It also had a set of sweep wings at the bow and stern, not that useful for speed but helpful in aiming roundshot and hunter-nukes. All that cut into its cargo capacity rather drastically, so the *Warchief* carried less than half the cargo of the *Pandora*. As well, it was a less capable warship than the *Arachne* had been when it was the *Brass Ass*. Oh, it was fine for chasing down a fat freighter and taking their cargo. Or part of their cargo.

"Janis didn't seem in any hurry to give up her life of crime," Danny said, "and women get tired of me soon enough." He shrugged.

Sylvia lifted an eyebrow. "No good between the sheets, Captain?"

"You'd have to judge that for yourself."

"I think I'll pass."

Danny shrugged again, then got back to the subject. "What concerns me about the *Warchief* is that it's likely to invite the sort of scrutiny that we don't want."

"Janis is good at going quiet, and she knows all the back ways in the area around Ferguson."

"What about the formerly gray route between Drake and Cordoba space? Is there a way around it?"

"I don't know of one, but Janis might know a place to hide and watch until the guards are looking the other way."

"All right," Danny agreed. He would have a talk with Janis about the chain of command. The thing that would probably surprise Janis was that Danny wasn't angling for that command. He wanted Tanya—or at least the *Arachne*—running things. Tanya had real military training and he talked to *Pan* and Sally about the *Arachne* and how it was interfacing with Jenny. Danny trusted Jenny. He trusted the girl's judgment and he'd seen her come up with good ideas several times, if not always as obviously as when the thought of the whole concept of the shield missile came to her. With the built-in knowledge of *Arachne*, Jenny would give good orders.

Location: Arachne, Skull Outsystem
Standard Date: 01 27 632

Jenny/*Arachne* swam through space and the rest of her clan was with her, feeling the wings flex and the flow of the plasma. Startak and Starvokx were both sensing the input from the wings with the Parthian extra sense of "pathing." Pathing was different, more textured, than Jenny would feel on her own. It allowed more of the awareness of the shape of what was there in the *Arachne* to reach Jenny, and it was letting them all feel things that they couldn't have felt without it.

"It's like there are jumps everywhere. Hundreds of them, thousands of them. It's just that they're too little to use."

Fred's sense of wonder came back to Jenny, as did Jay's and Tiny's, and the rest. They were all tied into the shipnet and feeling it. Their emotions fed back to Jenny as a wonder-tinged appreciation, with overtones of cynicism, as several of her crew wondered what use the information might be. *"I don't know yet, but I bet between me and Professor Schmitz, we can think of something."*

Tanya's "Back to work, people," brought them back to their jobs. Even with *Arachne* and the drones it ran, there was a lot of work to running this ship, a lot more than there was on the *Pandora*. Jenny let Tanya hand out assignments and spent her time studying space.

Arachne's sensors weren't all she had. The wings gave feedback. The ship had radar and lidar, as well as passive receivers all across the electromagnetic spectrum. There were sensor techs manning those as well, and along with the raw data and *Arachne*'s interpretation, she was also getting the sensor techs' interpretations. It should have been utterly overwhelming. But that was what the artificial brain *Arachne* was ultimately designed for, to make available all that data without letting it overload Jenny.

It was comfortable. Jenny saw, as if she were physically looking at it, the *Warchief* paralleling their course. *Pan* was still loading shieldgold back at Skull Station. She sent out a laser comm to the *Warchief*. It was another artificial brain ship, but its brain was smaller and more focused than *Pandora*'s. Jenny and *Arachne* traded data on the shape of space with the *Warchief*'s brain, and suddenly the *Warchief* was complaining loudly that *Arachne* must be seeing things. *Chief* had been through this space before, and even if that chunk of space looked like a possible jump to Arachne, it couldn't be, because *Warchief* would have seen it.

"*Arachne*, this is Janis Tecumseh. What have you been saying to my ship?"

"It's the combination of data, Captain," Jenny shot back before Tanya could say anything. "Your *Chief* is very proud of her ability to find jumps, and justifiably so. But that can make it a bit hard for her to admit when someone else sees one that she missed."

"And just where is this jump located?"

Again Jenny didn't wait for Tanya's permission, though she sent Tanya an apology and explanation even as she was sending the coordinates to Captain Tecumseh.

"Sorry, kid, but there ain't a jump there," Janis reported. "We've been over that exact spot in the past and never a trace of a jump." That was not literally true, since the whole galaxy was moving along with everything in it, but it was still true for any reasonable notion of practicality. On the other hand, Jenny knew what she had seen.

"Tanya, take us through that jump," Jenny sent.

Then she looked across the bridge at the *Arachne*'s captain. Tanya looked first annoyed, then intrigued, as she examined the data. Then she started to smile. "It's a small jump."

"We'll decrease power to our wings," Jenny sent back with a set of values and a graphic of the effect on the space.

Suddenly the *Arachne* was shifting course, making a loop.

The *Warchief* followed along, Janis complaining that they were wasting time and adding comments about letting kids run the show. Tanya was sending back, saying basically that it was Jenny's ship. What Tanya wasn't doing, Jenny noted with a giggle, was sending the *Warchief* the data on how you had to operate to make the jump. Mostly, jumps were much bigger than the ships that passed through them, even including the area of wings. The average jump was several times the total wingspan in every direction. The jump they were looping back to was only one hundred eighty kilometers across. To use it, the *Arachne* would have to underpower its wings just as it entered the jump and jump through quickly.

Looping around to the jump took a bit over an hour. They hadn't been going that fast.

* * *

Tanya felt the *Arachne*'s wings flapping more clearly than on any other ship, and she watched the approaching jump with all the avid interest of a cat watching a mouse hole.

Closer. Closer.

Now.

They were through.

It was a short jump. They were two light seconds to system anti-spinward from where they were. Tanya put a targeting laser on the *Warchief* and sent, "Tag, you're it."

* * *

The *Arachne* disappeared and the *Chief*'s brain set up a howl. "They cheated."

"How'd they cheat, *Warchief*?" Janis asked.

"They folded their wings." On the *Warchief*'s main screen, a graphic of the *Arachne*'s wings was proceeding in slow motion. Flap, flap, no flap, then the wings—underpowered—flapping again, but reaching out only three-quarters of the distance they reached before.

Then, out of nowhere, there was an alarm. A targeting laser pinged them, followed immediately by the words, "Tag, you're it."

There, off their up port stern, was the *Arachne*.

Janis felt a cold rush of fear as her mind reached out to what something like that might mean in a combat situation, assuming that Cordoba-Davis knew about the jump and where it came out, and if they had been in a real fight. They were too far for a laser to damage them, but a load of sand or round shot . . . She wouldn't have the timing. She would have been hit. She could have died.

"*Warchief*, can you fold your wings?" There was almost no time. They were approaching the jump. "If you can, do it. People, give control of the wings to the *Chief*."

They hit the jump and Janis, even with her interface, couldn't follow what happened. But they were through the jump, and following the *Arachne* again. Janis was just getting ready to send a scathing reply, but they got tagged by another targeting laser, one that had to have been sent before they even hit this space.

"All sorts of opportunities, don't you think, Captain?" Tanya Cordoba-Davis' voice came over the speakers.

"All sorts," Janis agreed sourly.

CHAPTER 35

"Hit 'em where they ain't."
Nathan Bedford Forrest

Location: Skull Fort, Cordoba Space
Standard Date: 02 04 632

Commander Aksel Swenson of the Cordoba Spaceforce watched the three ships exit the Skull jump—in formation. He was surprised because the Skull System pirates weren't in the habit of showing off like that. It was the sort of crap that you would expect of a Spaceforce officer, and not most of those. Then the identifications came over. All three ships reported themselves as having stockholders aboard. In fact, all three ships reported themselves as being *owned* by stockholders. Even the frigging *Warchief*, which came through here three or four times a year, was suddenly claiming to be owned by a stockholder.

For just a moment, Aksel was tempted to drag them all in.

For just a moment.

Aksel didn't want to call attention to himself. He was here because he knew how to keep his mouth shut. And because he was already in so much trouble with the force that he couldn't afford to do anything else. So he sat out here, half a light second from the Skull jump, and watched who came and went. He then reported to the Cordoba fort that was just over thirty light seconds away, next to the main jump point into Cordoba space.

"Do you wish to speak to our Stockholder Rep?" Aksel asked.

"Yes, as a matter of fact, I do," said a voice with a slight upper-crust Yagan accent. "I am Grand Stockholder Tanya Cordoba-Davis, and I'm going to want to certify some stock transfers and arrange for some hand-carried documents to go to my family."

* * *

Tanya knew how she wanted to play this, and—after talking extensively with Professora Stuard, Goldgok, and the other Parthians, and sitting down with Jenny Starchild and the *Arachne*—she was convinced of the danger that the Cordoba Combine might collapse. She was less certain that the Drakes were in a similar situation, and that was what scared her. If the Cordobas collapsed and the Drakes didn't, the Pamplona Sector would slip into totalitarianism. The semi-independent little fiefdoms of people like the Cordoba-Jacksons and her own family were a part of the problem.

On the other hand, given the circumstances, she couldn't do much about that from within the Cordoba Combine. So she needed allies. There were, according to Goldgok, nine billion Parthians in the Parthia System, which was a bit startling to Tanya. Even the Cordoba capital world of New Argentina had a population of less than two hundred million, and most systems in the Pamplona sector had populations measured in the hundreds of thousands or millions. The whole human population of the Pamplona Sector probably wasn't more than twenty billion. So the Parthians were a potential counterbalance for both the Drakes and the Cordobas, and the Jackson-Cordoba efforts to contain them took on a much more sinister light.

She wrote up her conclusions and the message was ready to send in a tightly encrypted package to her great aunt. Her problem was . . . she wasn't at all sure how Great Aunt Angela would react.

"If it's hand-carried stuff, you probably want to handle it at the fort," said the Cordoba skipper of the *Ulysses*, an old ship Tanya suspected was in less than apple pie order. "We're going to be sitting out here sculling around for another month before we head back in where we can deliver any hand-carries."

"Good enough, Captain Swenson," Tanya said. "What can you tell us about the situation around Parise?"

"The system has changed hands three times since the initial attack. Right now we hold it, but the Drakes are only four jumps back, at the long jump." He sent the coordinates for a jump along the Parise/Ferguson route.

"You know a way around? We have cargo for Parthia."

"Not a short one. There is a route, but it goes through New Argentina and Delta."

"We know that one."

"Sorry I couldn't be more help. Maybe they can help you at the fort," Commander Swenson said, then added, "Not to be blunt, but Captain Tecumseh knows the drill. You either pay here or go through the jump at the fort and pay there. So if you're going to the fort, I'll be watching you all the way."

"We have been informed of the procedures."

Location: Cordoba Space, Fort at the Skull Jump
Standard date: 02 05 632

The fort was an asteroid that was brought in at considerable expense. It was heavily worked and two kilometers across. It rotated and maintained a set of wings that produced a shield for the background radiation of space, but also offered defense against attack.

It would easily take a force of a dozen ships to give this place a good workout.

The fort maintained a crew of three hundred and a civilian population of half again that number. There were two dispatch boats allocated to the fort, and Tanya used her status as a grand stockholder to commandeer one to send her messages to New Argentina, where the one to her family would catch the regular mails.

Tanya also sent a message to the stockholder's office of the Cordoba Combine, complaining about Admiral Chin's restraint of the legitimate movement of Cordoba flagged merchants.

Location: Cordoba Space, Parise Outsystem
Standard date: 03 02 632

It was a Cordoba picket ship that stopped them.

Well, not stopped them.

Asked politely.

Tanya recognized the face, but there was a wan look about it, and lines around the eyes that hadn't been there the last time she saw the woman. Now a captain, Katherine Allen Iminate had apparently gained her rank the hard way.

Tanya was actually tempted to let Danny, or perhaps Janis, handle Captain Iminate, but she didn't. "What's the situation, Captain?" she asked over the comm, bringing her image live with a thought to *Arachne*.

"You?" Iminate said. "I thought you were cashiered. I guess grand stockholders can buy their own navies."

"Not exactly cashiered. Thrown to the wolves, perhaps. But that's not important now. Is there a situation we need to know about, Captain? We'd like to get on with our trading."

"A *situation*? You arrogant— Good people have been dying out here."

Tanya was trying to be sympathetic, she really was. But it wasn't easy. "I am aware of that, Captain. Some of those people were in my command, ordered to sacrifice ourselves as a rearguard when Senior Captain Rodriguez finally decided to run, hours too late. The only reason any of my people are alive is because the Drakes thought we were dead. In any case, I am no longer in your chain of command and I *am* a grand stockholder. So I ask you again, what is the situation in and around Parise?"

Again, as Tanya saw before, Katherine's face went white and her freckles stood out like a star map. There was a pause, then apparently getting herself under control, Katherine explained. They had, with much fighting, retaken Parise, but the chain between Parise and Ferguson was still in dispute. Travel past Parise was at the merchant's own risk. The report was clear and concise. Katherine Iminate had always been a smart and capable woman . . . when she wasn't being ruled by her resentments.

"How is it that you are in a Drake cutter, Grand Stockholder?"

"The *Brass Hind* mutinied from the Drakes and was awarded as recompense when her captain attempted to kill Jenny Starchild. Jenny is underage and hired me to command the ship." Tanya didn't mention where they were when that happened. It wasn't Katherine's business.

Besides, the woman was a prig.

* * *

They sold some of their shieldgold in Parise, where the navy would have willingly bought it all.

In fact, the navy probably would have forced them to "sell" it all, if Tanya wasn't a grand stockholder.

Then they started on the route to Ferguson, but three jumps out from Parise, they switched to a side route Janis knew about. It wasn't that far out of the way, only a few light hours from the standard route, but no one not knowing where to look would see them. Plus, it was actually shorter than the standard route. It only took them ten days to reach Ferguson, rather than the fourteen that the standard route took.

Location: Cordoba Space, Ferguson Insystem
Standard Date: 03 12 632

Andri Jackson, captain of the human-owned *Fortune Find*, was in Ferguson for a short layover on her way to Layabout Station, a not-quite star system made up of a barely brown dwarf and its planets—or a not-quite brown dwarf and its moons, depending on how you looked at it. It was located on a side route to Hudson, and the main industry was the mining of green tar. Not like Alenbie, but they got some.

She was a bit surprised to see Danny Gold show back up, and even more surprised to see him in company with two clearly armed ships. "What did they think of you lot when you hit the picket?" she asked. There was a Cordoba picket one jump out from Ferguson now, blocking the main jump to the Ferguson outsystem.

Danny Gold grinned that grin of his at her. "Why, they were very polite, Skipper. In fact, as soon as they stopped messing their drawers and we told them we were all Cordoba stockholders, they told us the news and asked for the news of Parise. I think when we showed up they were hoping the route to Parise was clear again."

"It's not?"

"No. We took a side path."

"We're gonna have to play rutter tag real soon now, Captain Gold. Real soon."

"Funny thing. That's just what the commander of the picket wanted to do."

Andri looked at the handsome, young-looking Cybrant and considered. She knew the stories of what the *Pandora* did to the *Bonaventure*, though no one knew how she did it. For that matter, she knew that the *Bonny* had a hunter-nuke. Cousin Janet told her about it one time when she was drunk. Now here he was—with a real warship, even if it was a little one—and with the *Warchief*. Andri knew the *Warchief* by reputation and didn't want any closer acquaintance, so her first impulse was to keep quiet about the new fort on the way into Canova. But it wouldn't do any good. The news was all over Ferguson. "Captain, the JCTC has declared you persona non grata in the Canova system."

"I don't think they are allowed to do that, Captain. Especially not now that I'm a Cordoba stockholder."

"It may not be completely legal, Captain Gold, but they have a fort guarding the entrance."

"Not completely legal? It's not legal at all, Andri."

"The fort is legally owned by the government of Canova, Danny." Andri held up her hand as it looked like Danny was going to interrupt again. "They are using the Drake incursion as an excuse, and they are insisting that you, as a Cybrant, are a Drake sympathizer. It's enough to keep the Cordobas from doing anything about it, especially when they are busy fighting the Drakes up around Parise. I'm just telling you, Danny, you ain't getting through. I don't know what you did to the *Bonny* and, knowing Farris like I did, it was probably deserved. But between that and what the *Fly Catcher* has been doing in Parthia, you're not the favorite person of anyone in the front offices of the JCTC."

"What about the *Fly Catcher*?" Danny asked, distracted.

"Don't play with me, Danny. The frigging *Fly Catcher* has been going out to that mine you have somewhere in Parthia System, shipping in load after load of refined metals and liquid hydrogen.

"At least, it was. The JCTC has an armed merchantman sitting on the *Fly Catcher* until the council of clans tells them where the jump route is."

"What are those *cheskek* doing involved with our clan's mines?" Goldgok asked.

"Now, Goldgok, they have a ship. I bet Clan Zheck was getting pretty desperate for funds," Danny said. "What surprises me is that the mine bots worked so well. Shiploads?"

"Well, one shipload," Andri said. "We just assumed there were more."

"Honestly, I doubt it. Not that there couldn't be. The rock we dropped the sucker on was two hundred kilometers by three hundred kilometers, coated in hydrogen, but with a core of iron and rare earths. The mining factory we set up could only do so much, and we've only been gone nine months."

There was an urgent message on the shipnet from Professor Schmitz. *"We need to get to Parthia as quickly as possible."*

"What's up, Doc?"

"Sally wanted a self-replicating function in the mine bots. We put major governors on it, but if the miner found the right elements, it might have replicated itself."

"You're saying there could be an army of those mining bots out there?"

"Maybe. There shouldn't be, but the most likely situation for an artificial brain to go feral is if it's operating on its own."

"Later, Doc," Danny sent and went back to talking with Andri. "Okay, Andri. I know it's not your fault, but I *am* a Parthian clan and, comes down to it, so is Jenny."

"Jenny? You mean the ship's girl you had with you last time?"

"Yep, Skipper. She owns the *Arachne*. She has Tanya Cordoba-Davis, late of the Cordoba Spaceforce, as her captain, but Jenny is owner aboard. And I gave her a couple of Parthians to start her clan. The JCTC may not want me, but they have to let Jenny through."

"Not a chance."

"This isn't going anywhere, Andri," Danny said. "I'll give you a call next time I'm through Ferguson if you're here."

* * *

As *Pandora*, *Arachne*, and *Warchief* made their way back out from Ferguson, they discussed tactics and—hesitantly—Janis mentioned that there was a backdoor into the Canova System. The cul de sac that was one jump out from the main Canova jump wasn't actually a cul de sac. There was a jump at an acute angle from the exit, and it had a short chain that took it to another part of the Canova outsystem. "It's a good place to sit and watch the traffic to spot targets."

Lasers between the three ships sent packets of information as they moved from jump to jump. The ships together, flying in formation with *Arachne* in the lead and *Pan* and *Warchief* flanking her, gave them a combined coverage of almost two thousand kilometers and a mapping range of almost a light second. It was a trick they could only do with *Arachne* in the mix, and it picked up at least five potential new jumps on the trip from Ferguson to Canova.

Location: Cordoba Space, One Jump out from Canova Outsystem
Standard Date: 03 18 632

They came out of jump and could see the fort clearly. It was a big sucker. A rotating two-headed sledgehammer, big enough so that the heads had a standard gravity from spin.

It also had specialized wings. Most ship's wings were designed to produce thrust. They were optimized to move plasma and space dust, but it was possible to optimize wings for moving heavier loads by making the wings narrower and focusing the magnetic fields more tightly. These were nuclear-powered catapults and they could throw missiles like hunter-nukes at nearly twice the velocity of a ship's wings. Round shot also went faster, though not twice as fast. And because the forts could see a ship coming, they could blow it out of space mostly before it got into its own firing range.

The drawback was that these sorts of wings were expensive. They cost twice what a warship wing of similar size cost, and the forts were generally as large as the largest warships.

"It's amazing," Tanya said. "That must have taken their profit margin for a year."

"And, according to Andri, there's another one in Parthia System," Danny said.

"The Parthian trade must be worth even more than I thought," Tanya said.

"We shouldn't be surprised," Eddy said. "Franklin has a population of less than a hundred million, and controlling the import and export trade from Franklin would make a great house-sized fortune." He called up Tanya's image from the bridge of the *Arachne* and spoke directly to her. "If they were getting this sort of profit out of Parthia, they probably simply bought your great aunt."

Tanya's return look wasn't happy, but she nodded.

"Okay, folks," Danny said, "we've gawked at the locals long enough. Let's head for the side route."

They shifted their course and proceeded to the unguarded jump in plain sight of the fortress thirty light seconds away. At this range lasers were no good for anything but communications, and any shot—missile or round shot—would be immediately obvious and easy to avoid.

It took them seven hours to make the transit, with the fort yammering at them the whole time. But they never answered.

Location: Big Dark, Janis' route, approaching Canova Jump
Standard Date: 03 20 632

Jenny felt the wings and the delayed reports of *Pandora* and *Warchief*'s wings. She was getting a feel for space and finally understood why Danny loved hunting jumps so much. It felt much the same as a hawk must feel riding the air currents looking for game, or a surfer in the curl of a wave. You could leave yourself behind and just be in the moment.

Yet, as much as she enjoyed it, it didn't consume her the way it did Danny. She was too interested in other things. In the design of artificial brains, and the analysis of culture, in the workaday jobs of Startak or Fred. No one thing called to her the way they called to other people, and she wondered what she was going to do with her life.

Still, it was beautiful out here and there were those little jumps she kept spotting. Jenny turned her attention back to the upcoming jump. At Tanya's insistence, they were jumping in formation. They moved up, and with the help of *Arachne*, they were even flapping in sync. Then they were through, in the Canova outsystem, a quarter of the way around the orbital plane from the standard Ferguson route.

Location: Canova Outsystem
Standard Date: 03 20 632

Once they were through, they went dark and listened. The Canova government had a Gentry class courier boat at the fort. It was all wings and fusion plant, and it reported their trip across to the so-called cul de sac. The Canova sent a ship to follow them, and it wasn't back yet. At this point the whole system was wondering whether Danny Gold blew up another ship.

Tanya was feeling almost insulted that these idiots didn't realize that the *Arachne* was a real warship, and if anyone was going to be exploding spaceships, it would be her. Jenny grinned at that. She liked Tanya's attitude and liked that it was shared by most of the crew.

"Well, they don't seem to have noticed us," Tanya sent over the fleetnet.

"I didn't think they would," Janis sent in return. *"But we probably ought to keep emissions low. No plasma. We should make a slow sweep."* She sent a graphic that had them accelerating at a tenth of a standard gravity and slowly shifting their course to another jump. *"This will put us in the standard traffic lanes for the system, but I don't think we're going to be able to get out of Canova without being spotted."*

"As long as we're ahead of them, I don't really care," Tanya sent back.

"If the fort is where it's supposed to be and the shield missiles act as advertised, it's going to be like shooting fish in a barrel." Janis Tecumseh's thought carried overtones of satisfaction.

Location: Canova Insystem, System Control

"They got around us!" Debra Massingale reported. She was the duty scan tech on the scope that was directed at the Parthian jump chain. She had just seen a very dim fluctuation in her screen and called up the raw data. The fluctuation was way too small to make out details with the naked eye, but the augmentation programs showed it. Debra was a skilled tech, and to her eyes the fluctuations in the light indicated three ships. They were not venting plasma at all, so all their thrust was from the ambient system dust and zero-point energy. But even that produced a dim aurora that fit the profiles of the *Pandora*, *Arachne* and *Warchief*. They also fit the profiles of any number of other ships, but Debra was sure.

The word went out from System Control and general panic ensued. Just at the moment, Canova System had eight merchantmen and two construction ships. The two construction ships were owned by the Cordoba-Davis family, and had been leased at great expense to build the two forts they already had and one more on the third main route into Canova System. There hadn't been any rush on that last one, and it was still in the early stages of construction.

Suddenly the merchantmen captains were finding reasons to be elsewhere, and the government of Canova was having harsh words with the JCTC.

Location: Canova Outsystem
Standard Date: 03 21 632

The last normal space leg in the Canova outsystem took seventeen hours. Just as *Arachne* and the others were getting close to it, they got a series of orders from the Canova System Defense Force. Not that the CSDF was near enough to have any hope of enforcing the orders. The orders originated at Canova System Control, and had been traveling in the form of a pulsed laser for over four hours.

"Ships *Pandora*, *Arachne* and *Warchief* are ordered to stand to for inspection, and are hereby informed that a state of armed conflict does exist between Canova System and Parthia System. Further, until the discussions with the council of clans have reached a successful conclusion, Parthia System is under blockade. You are denied transit right, by order of the Canova System government."

Tanya looked around and sent over the ship and fleetnets, *"Are they nuts? They just gave us a cause bellum on a silver platter."*

There was a pause. Then the professora's voice came back over the net. *"Humanocentric thinking. That's got to be it. Danny is human. So are Jenny and Janis. All ships owned by humans, and while Danny may be legally a Parthian clan, he's still human. And Jenny hasn't been recognized by the council of clans."*

"I think it may be more basic than that," Danny sent. *"I think they just panicked. They had this carefully prepared legal argument for why what they were doing was justified. When they saw us over here, they realized that they couldn't physically stop us, so they just used the canned argument."*

"Frankly," Janis sent, *"I don't give a crap. We were going to trash the fort in Parthia the moment we came out of jump, anyway. This just makes it legal."*

"It was already legal," Tanya sent, and she sounded officious even to herself.

Location: Parthia Outsystem
Standard Date: 03 22 632

Three ships emerged from the jump in formation with their lasers already pointed in almost the right direction. The corrections and coordination took only microseconds, then they fired every laser they could bring to bear. The massed lasers of the *Arachne* and the *Warchief* blinded the fort almost before it got a glimpse of the attacking force.

Then they launched the birds, two from each ship, a total of six, in a staggered launch pattern. Three, then three more. After that, they kept up the lasers, as you might shine a flashlight at an opponent in a knife fight in a darkened room.

Anything to make the other guy blink.

* * *

On the fort, the crew was looking the other way . . . and not looking very hard. There were four ships in Parthia System, and the Jackson-Cordoba family owned—or at least controlled—three of them. The fourth ship was the *Fly Catcher*, and it was in orbit around the planet.

The first warning the fort crew had was an emergency signal, followed a few microseconds later by the lasers that burned out most of their sensors. After that was a short delay as backups came online. Then they were looking at three ships, and their computers were telling them that the ships threw something while they were blinded, but they didn't know what, or what vector it was on. It took them a second to respond and one of the crew managed to order the launch of a hunter-nuke.

Order it.

It took the fort three seconds to physically launch the ready hunter, and it took the Alert Fire Control Officer two seconds to decide. . . .

And it was too late.

The hunter exited the tube, but wasn't at the wing. The first of the wings was moving to reach it as three shield missiles with their superconducting cables half unfurled reached the location where the fort's wings were coming on line. As had happened before, the superconducting cable conducted, and the electromagnetic energy of two fusion-powered magnetic fields interacted in conflict.

The wings of a fort are very powerful and more focused than the wings on a ship. They are optimized for heavy masses and the energy density is higher. One of the wings blew.

And that was all it took. The rest of the shield missiles went through an expanding ball of plasma that moments before had been a five-billion-credit fort with a crew of one hundred fifty-seven people.

* * *

"Damn," Danny muttered. *"I was hoping to* capture *the fort."*

"We all were," Tanya sent back over the fleetnet. *"But someone over there was on the ball."*

Jenny was shocked and upset by the deaths. But she also remembered her family and the end of the space station she lived on until she was eight. At least these were soldiers, paid to take the risk. Her parents were civilians. There was a hardness in

Jenny that had grown up since that day. It wasn't that she didn't care, but she could weigh and balance things. *"What's the situation in the system?"* she asked.

There was light from the insystem, but they didn't know where to look for ships, so it took some minutes to find out what was going on. By that time, they were heading for the first of the jumps that would take them insystem.

Location: Parthia, Council of Clans
Standard Date: 03 22 632

Conrad Cordoba-Jackson was actually in the great hall of the Council of Clans when the news of the destruction of the fort reached Parthia. Zhecktoss was droning on about the importance of independent polities to the Cordoba Combine and trying to get the council to reject Conrad's latest offer. It wasn't going to work. Conrad had the votes on the council. They weren't exactly willing, but enough of the Parthian economy was dependent on foreign trade that he could destroy dozens of prominent clans if the council didn't take his deal.

There was a disturbance at one of the doors. A messenger.

Conrad accessed his data link and got word from the *Bonafortuna* in orbit. Someone blew the fort. It had happened just over eight hours ago, and the light just reached the planet. He tried for further information and got that there were three ships, a medium small freighter, no, two medium small freighters, and a patrol boat.

The messenger reached Zhecktoss, who listened for a moment, then turned to the dais where the council speaker was resting on a Parthian couch. "I have just received word that the fort the Canova government illegally placed in our space has blown up. I would call on the council to recess for a day while we determine what has happened."

Other messengers were entering the chamber and one of them was heading for the speaker's couch.

Conrad's interface called him back. It was the *Bonafortuna*, sending, *"It's the* Pandora *and two other ships. They sent a signal to someone here on the planet. Probably the Zheck or the Kiig. It's in the same code that Gold and his crew used while they were here."*

"Can you crack it?"

"No, sir. It's a book code and we don't have the book. But we can recognize it."

Shit, Conrad thought, not over the link, then sent, *"Three ships. Any word on the other two?"*

"Not yet, sir."

The Kiig seconded the Zheck motion, but Parthians required a third and a fourth. They got the third from the Gok, and that was a very bad sign. The fourth came from the Siik, another ally of the Zheck.

With very little ceremony, the meeting ended for the day and the hall emptied, but Conrad wasn't there to see it. He left the hall as soon as the Siik fourthed the motion.

CHAPTER 36

Family relationships are at the core of both Parthian and human politics, but those family relationships are different at their core. It makes things interesting.
Stareska, Second breeder, Starchild Clan

Location: Parthia Insystem
Standard Date: 03 23 632

The little fleet came out of the last jump into the Parthian insystem and pointed a comm laser at Gok Station. Right there, in orbit between Gok and Fisk Station One, were four wingships.

It made sense. There was a known route into the Parthian insystem, but not much in the way of side routes. Since few ships knew any other jumps, there was nowhere for them to run. Instead, the fleet was deluged with a storm of complaints and threats. They listened for a few minutes while Goldgok contacted the Zheck representative and they got the Parthian version of events.

* * *

"Okay, we have confirmation that the Canova government didn't have permission to build the fort," Professora Stuard said. "You're on, Tanya. We can always give them back later if we need to."

Tanya looked into the pickup and used her internals to bring it live. *"I am Grand Stockholder Tanya Cordoba-Davis, formerly of the Cordoba Spaceforce. The Jackson-Cordoba Trading Company and the government of Canova have entered into an illegal conspiracy to restrain the lawful trade of Cordoba-licensed trade ships. Your ships will stand down while the Parthian Council of Clans determines your status. Any attempt to leave the Parthian insystem will result in your disablement or destruction. Maintain your orbits and clear any movements with this fleet."*

That was the message that went to the four ships in orbit around Parthia.

What went out to the council of clans was official notice that Clan Danny Gold had returned, and that the fleet, under the command of Danny Gold and the new Clan Starchild, was placing itself under the authority of the council of clans.

* * *

The news feeds went nuts. Clan Jkap was all over the place. The JCTC placing of the fort at the junction was the center of the news for months, as well as discussions of the position in which it put the whole system and the entire Parthian race.

There was a very strong faction that wanted to accede to the JCTC. After all, Parthian workers expected to be put to work for the benefit of the clan. What was this but the same thing on a larger scale?

Parthians really don't think of liberty the same way humans do. They are focused on the welfare of the clan, not self-advancement.

But the Jackson-Cordobas didn't do a very good job of persuading the Parthians that they were concerned with the welfare of Parthian clans, or even other human clans. So there was also a large faction in the council of clans that wanted Parthia to have a greater say among the clans of the wider universe. And yet another faction that wanted to fort up the jump points and keep those disgusting humans out of Parthian space altogether.

The return of Danny Gold and the little fleet he brought with him was a brand-new earthquake in Parthian politics.

Location: Parthia, Council of Clans, Meeting Room
Standard Date: 03 25 632

"So, Conrad, what did you want to chat about?" Tanya asked.

Conrad looked at his cousin, and almost for the first time began to get really worried. This wasn't the inexperienced and traumatized kid he told to sit down and shut up back in Ferguson. On the fly, he changed his approach from bullying to reasoning. "The Cordoba Combine is coming apart. It's because of the distances and the jump routes. It's too easy for the Drakes to block our connections to the government in New Argentina. The whole Pamplona Sector is like some multidimensional swamp, full of nooks and crannies and places to hide. It's almost impossible to govern. With the Drakes cutting the main routes, all that are going to be left are the pirate routes."

"It's too easy for the Cordobas to cut up the Drakes as well. Admiral Chin has taken Franklin. Killed off the royal family to do it, too," Tanya told him.

"I heard. But that's just another point in the same argument. The great families are arming. That's why I'm in Parthia. The Jackson-Cordobas need the industrial base this place represents. It's close enough to the main lanes to be useful, but far enough out of line to be less than obvious. This is to be the base for the Jackson-Cordobas. Our bolt hole when it all comes apart. Your family is getting Yagan and points east."

"Not if Admiral Chin has any say in the matter," Tanya said. "He tried to have me killed." She paused. "Unless he had the family's permission?"

"Don't be ridiculous."

"Why are you here, Conrad?" Tanya asked. "You got me thrown out of the service. What now?"

"You have to get Gold to back off. Without your fleet, the Parthians will have to settle on whatever terms we give them."

"Why should I do that?"

"Because if you don't, your family's agreement with mine will cease to exist, and your family can't hold Yagan without our support in New Argentina."

"You said the Combine is going to collapse."

"It is, but it hasn't yet. With my family supporting the move, the fleet will take Yagan and your family will be destroyed."

* * *

Tanya sat back and a map of the Pamplona Sector floated to the surface of her mind. The shortest route from the main Cordoba Fleet base at New Argentina was by way of Parise-Ferguson-Canova-Morland to Yagan. Failing that, the Ferguson-Hudson-Morland route would get them there, assuming they pushed the Drakes out of the route between Parise and Ferguson. After that, it turned into a long route around, six months at least, to go around through New Kentucky. "First, you're assuming I care," Tanya mused. "Then you're assuming that the fleet will push Huffington out of the way and be able to come through Ferguson and through us here. I guess they could go around us, but after that it's still a long trip. And why bother when they have the Drakes breathing down their necks?"

"Your family has gotten a bit too big for its holdings," Conrad said. "They aren't part of the seventeen great families that control the Combine, but Great Aunt Angela and Great Uncle Tobin have an agreement." Angela was the head of the Cordoba-Davis family and Tobin Jackson-Cordoba was the head of the Jackson-Cordobas, who were one of the seventeen—if only barely. Between Angela and Tobin, they controlled—in their own persons—almost two percent of the stock in the Cordoba Combine. Since over three-quarters of the stock was never voted, that represented a powerful block. Big enough to move fleets.

"Angela won't consent to an attack on Yagan. I don't care how pissed she is with me."

"She won't be able to stop it, not with Uncle Tobin getting behind the attack and pushing."

Tanya considered. Conrad might be right. He might be wrong. He might even be feeding her a line of bull. But it didn't matter, because the thing that Conrad couldn't get his head around was that Tanya wasn't the boss. Danny Gold wasn't even the boss.

There wasn't a boss, unless it was the council of clans.

Tanya's personal boss was a twelve-year-old girl she'd grown surprisingly fond of. The council of clans was right now working out whether it was going to recognize that little girl and her artificial-brained spaceship as an official Parthian clan.

And Tanya realized—finally—what she should have seen years ago. Between the location of Canova and the size of the Parthian population, they were sitting in the system that was the key to control of the whole Pamplona Sector. She sat up and stared at Conrad. "You knew. Your Uncle Tobin and you knew about the importance of Parthia and Canova all along."

"Yes, of course." Conrad stopped and Tanya knew her expression had given her away. "Tanya, you don't have the muscle. The whole Cordoba-Davis family doesn't have the muscle to hold Parthia."

"You don't get it, Conrad. It's not about the Cordoba-Davis family or the Jackson-Cordoba family. It's about the Parthians. *They* have the muscle."

"Not to hold out against the whole human race, they don't."

Tanya heard the desperation and dawning realization in his voice. "No, you're right about that," Tanya said musingly. Then, slowly, she smiled. "They'll need human fronts, won't they?"

"You'd sell out the human race to the bugs?"

Tanya looked at her cousin. Her cousin who, she realized, intended to relegate a whole race of nine billion people to slavery. Parthians, not humans . . . but people nonetheless. Slowly Tanya began to smile. "Yes Conrad, I think I will."

EPILOGUE

Location: New Argentina
Standard Date: 07 03 632

Angela Cordoba-Davis watched the recording from her grand-niece and fumed. The alliance between her and the Jackson-Cordobas was intended to propel her house into the Seventeen . . . and now this.

Tobin was going to be livid. The arrogant bastard was likely to try to take Canova back from Tanya and her pirates. Angela's implant called up the files on the Jackson-Cordoba Trading Company to get a read on how many ships of what type they had. It was a lot. More than the Cordoba-Davis family owned by twenty ships.

Angela would be fine with Tobin taking out her niece, but too much of the stock was spread out among the family for her to go along with it. A breach in the Cordoba-Davis clan would destroy any hope for a seat on the Cordoba Combine board.

But she couldn't see how to avoid the fight.

The comm buzzed, and sure enough, it was Tobin.

Made in the USA
Columbia, SC
27 September 2023